The Magazine of
FANTASY and SCIENCE FICTION
A 30-YEAR RETROSPECTIVE

The Magazine of
FANTASY and SCIENCE FICTION
A 30-YEAR RETROSPECTIVE

Edited by Edward L. Ferman

DOUBLEDAY & COMPANY, INC.
Garden City, New York
1980

Contents

How F&SF Was Born
Edward L. Ferman

IN JANUARY 1946, two California writers and editors, Anthony Boucher and J. Francis McComas, came to New York City to discuss an idea for a new magazine with Lawrence Spivak, then publisher of The American Mercury, Inc. The magazine would contain new and old short stories in the fantasy, supernatural and ghost genres. Spivak was immediately enthusiastic about the idea and asked Boucher and McComas to assemble material for a test issue. In March, McComas wrote to Spivak:

> For the hitherto unpublished part of the magazine, we have lined up "off-the-trail" stories by Raymond Chandler, S. Guy Endore, Dorothy B. Hughes, Philip MacDonald, H. F. Heard and/or Stuart Palmer. I think you will agree that that is certainly a top-flight group of selling names! Both Chandler and Endore have a trunkful of our type of manuscripts, unpublished for lack of a proper market. We could certainly count on them to be regular contributors. For the reprint section we have such authors as M. R. James, H. R. Wakefield, John Dickson Carr, Fitz-James O'Brien, Robert Bloch and H. P. Lovecraft.

My father, Joseph W. Ferman, was Mercury's general manager (he would later succeed Spivak as publisher). In May 1946 he sent a memo to Spivak discussing details of the contract between the editors and the publishing company. It also notes that: "The new magazine will certainly have to be held up until there's a substantial recovery in newsstand sales." It concludes with a P.S.:

> I don't think the title is yet among those listed. *Supernatural Stories* and *Unbelievable Stories* sound a little too much like pulp. Here are a couple of additional suggested titles:

THE MAGAZINE OF TERROR & THE SUPERNATURAL

UNSUSPECTED WORLDS

FANTASY AND TERROR

But I don't think we have the right one yet.

Choosing the right title for a new magazine is an agonizing business. I suppose that in some high-level corporate offices, this type of decision is achieved through something approaching a scientific formula. But having been through it several times, I've begun to feel that one reasonably descriptive title is much the same as another in the long run.

However, in the early stages of a new magazine venture, the title decision seems a momentous one. The title that was finally settled on in late 1946 was *Fantasy and Horror,* and Boucher and McComas went ahead and purchased, at 1 cent to 2 cents per word, about 35,000 words of stories for the new publication. But Joe Ferman decided to postpone publication indefinitely, because of a substantial increase in printing costs and a shaky newsstand sale on Mercury's other magazines.*

Nothing further was accomplished until early in 1949, when Joe Ferman noticed the new *Avon Fantasy Reader* on the stands (with a sexy cover and titles like "The Villain and the Virgin") and wrote to Tony Boucher making two suggestions, one good, one bad:

> We have been discussing again the possibility of testing a one-shot of *Fantasy and Horror.*
>
> Do you feel that we would be diluting the spirit and quality of the magazine too much if a science-fiction story was used in each issue?
>
> Also, do you think we might add a story with a little more sex in it—or possibly a story with more sex in the title than in the story?

Boucher and McComas replied:

> We're very warm toward the idea of regularly including at least one science-fiction story. In fact, we'd been planning from the first to slip in borderline science fiction from time to time. The borderline between science fiction—look, let's save typing and call it stf—and fantasy (and even horror) is a difficult one to draw; the best of stf has or could have a very strong appeal to the fantasy reader. The

---

* These included *The American Mercury,* then a prestigious opinion journal, and several quality mystery magazines, most notably *Ellery Queen's Mystery Magazine.*

routine gadget-type of stf or the interplanetary horse opera we wouldn't be using; they're passé by now anyway among the stf mags which cater to the sort of audience we hope to attract. And intelligent stf would in no wise "dilute the spirit" of fantasy & horror.

Now we come to Sex. (McComas leers over my shoulder.—AB) We gather that your reason for bringing this up is the commercial success of the *Avon Fantasy Reader*. Their approach on this has been, as you've probably gathered, strictly a deceptive hocuspocus. An occasional story does have a sex slant (of the somewhat slavering and obvious pulp kind), but even that never remotely lives up to the cover.

We're afraid that deliberately trying to get sex in could be a very bad idea. If an editor starts looking for a sexy story or an author is asked to produce one, the result is apt to be either purely unprintable or simply in questionable taste. We're all for sex where it is a natural and well-integrated part of a fantasy story; we'd like to feel that our editorial standards in that respect would be far more liberal than those of, say, Street & Smith.† But we're doubtful about going out hunting for it.

The story in this first issue with the most marked sex element is the Stuart Palmer "Seek and Ye Shall Find"; retitling that, with a humorously sexy twist, might be a very wise idea indeed.

The editors later suggested retitling the Palmer story "The Devil's Filly" ("It's punchy, sexy and ties in nicely with the story. If you don't agree, what do you think of 'The Devil's a Rough Lover'?"). It soon became apparent that nobody had much heart for this momentary fling with saucy sf, and the story was finally retitled "A Bride for the Devil," a graceful and apt enough title, but one which, even in 1949, must have been at least a light-year short of "sexy." This marked the end of sex as a topic of editorial discussion until the 1960s, when science fiction (surely literature's last holdout) fell with us all under the onslaught of the sexual revolution.

Science fiction was to remain around for a long time, however, indeed to this day. McComas wrote that he had found an "excellent sf short, done by a well-known man in the field, that combines not-too-difficult science with sharply satiric fiction." The author was Theodore Sturgeon, and his story was "The Hurkle is a Happy Beast," the first in a long and distinguished roster of science fiction stories in F&SF.

---

† Publishers of *Astounding Science Fiction,* now *Analog.*

In late March of 1949 Joe Ferman scheduled the first issue: it would be dated Fall 1949 and would be published in September. The designer he chose was George Salter, a highly regarded book designer with a distinctive style that was perfectly suited for fantasy and horror. The cover of the first issue illustrated "A Bride for the Devil" and combined artwork and photography: there was a photo of an attractive woman wearing a strapless (but unsexy) gown and a drawing by Salter of a devil-beast. Salter tried the art/photo combination in one subsequent issue and then abandoned photography entirely. All F&SF covers since then have been drawings.

Although the cover art was well under way, there was still some indecision about the magazine's title. So in May, Joe Ferman wrote McComas suggesting that they go with simply: *The Magazine of Fantasy*. McComas replied:

> Tony and I heartily approve of the new title. It's less pulpish than the other—avoiding the use of the word "terror"‡ will eliminate the risk of frightening off women readers—who love light fantasy but scare easily. Then too, not using "terror" will keep us from the attention of those self-appointed guardians of the public weal—the vigilante groups in all too many communities who have taken over censorship of the newsstands.

Publication date for the first issue was set for October 7, and to celebrate the occasion, the publishers planned a luncheon at the Waldorf. The public relations firm that was hired to promote the magazine and to plan the luncheon felt it was necessary to tie the event in with some more significant happening. At first they selected September 29, which was the 160th anniversary of the formation of the Regular Army. This sounds hilarious now, but it should be remembered that it was 1949, and to the general public science fiction was in large measure equated with weapons of war, especially the atomic bomb.

Larry Spivak suggested that instead of serving food in the usual way, "we might serve the luncheon in fantastic molds, so that no dish would be recognized for what it is."

Apparently no one was up to executing this interesting proposal, since I have in front of me the menu for the occasion. It includes such down-to-Earth fare as: "Martinis, Manhattans, Scotch, Rye and Bour-

---

‡ It had been so long since the choice of the original title that McComas had apparently forgotten that the word was not "terror" but "horror."

bon Highballs passed by Waiters; Breast of Chicken; Nest of Souffle Potatoes, Tiny Stringbeans Saute au Beurre," and so on.

The fortuitous discovery that October 6 marked the one hundredth anniversary of the death of Edgar Allan Poe led to the creation of a Poe Centennial Fantasy and Science Fiction Committee, the tie-in that the PR people were so fond of, and an apt one. The luncheon party came off successfully on October 6. Fifty-three guests attended; the total cost was $265. The speakers included master of ceremonies Basil Rathbone, Lieutenant Colonel Albert Cassevant (from the U. S. Army Signal Corps), Willy Ley, Richard Hoffmann (a well-known psychiatrist), Larry Spivak and Tony Boucher.

And so here we are now, some thirty years and 340 issues later. The book you hold in your hands is our celebration of F&SF's thirtieth anniversary. Immediately following are some introductory comments from Isaac Asimov, F&SF's most prolific and valued contributor, and then our party begins, this time with a truly fantastic menu.

F&SF at 30

Isaac Asimov

THIRTY YEARS isn't much in the lifetime of the universe, but it is a good deal in the lifetime of a human being or a magazine.

Thirty years is about a generation. It is the length of time that, on the average, separates parents from their children. With the passage of thirty years infants become parents; young adults become middle-aged; middle-aged become elderly.

Or, to get down to cases, an experimental magazine becomes an established pillar of the field, whose existence seems, in the minds of its young readers, to have been eternal.

The Magazine of Fantasy and Science Fiction (F&SF) first came into being in the fall of 1949, and it was not quite like anything else in the field. Its editors, Anthony Boucher and J. Francis McComas, intended, as far as possible, to stress literary quality and to lift it above the pulp inheritance of magazine science fiction.

To do this, they published not only the best new stories they could find, but also classic science fiction from other countries and from the non-magazine past. They published new and classic fantasies as well, for at no time did they neglect that allied field. Indeed, the first issue of the magazine, dated Fall 1949 was entitled simply *The Magazine of Fantasy*. It was only with the second issue that it became F&SF.

There was no certainty that the magazine would succeed. In fact, any sensible gambler would have given odds it wouldn't.

For one thing, fantasy magazines (as distinguished from science fiction magazines) did not usually prosper. The most venerable of the fantasy magazines, *Weird Tales,* did well enough when it was alone in the field, but it began a long, sad decline once science fiction magazines established themselves in the late 1920s.

The most unusual of the fantasy magazines, *Unknown,* driven with all the force of the legendary John W. Campbell, Jr., never did as well as its sister magazine *Astounding Science Fiction*. After twenty-two issues it was forced to go bimonthly and after seventeen more issues it died.

Other efforts in the 1950s had even less luck. Horace Gold's *Beyond Fantasy Fiction* had to drop the word "Fantasy" in its title after eight issues and died after two more.

As for putting out a magazine that dealt with both fantasy *and* science fiction, that had never been properly tried, and one would naturally have thought it would fall between two stools. Surely the enthusiasts for one of those fields would be impatient with the other.

Finally, the attempt to inject literary values into the field, a cynic might have believed, would have limited the readership, and this in itself would be enough to ensure failure.

Boucher and McComas were, however, determined to stick to their guns, and they received the unwavering support of Joseph W. Ferman, the publisher.

F&SF, having spent its first year as a quarterly, went bimonthly with the December 1950 issue, and monthly with the August 1952 issue. It has never wavered since.

When the October 1979 F&SF was published—the thirtieth anniversary issue—it was whole number 341, and in F&SF's pages had appeared, all told, nearly four thousand stories and articles.

It is a source of considerable pride to me that some of those stories were mine. It is a source of even greater pride that the last 252 issues, about 74 per cent of the total, and without one gap in the list, have each carried a science essay by me.

If thirty years is a long time chronologically, it is even longer in terms of the rapidly changing world of our times. Consider that day in 1949 when F&SF's first issue appeared.

World War II had ended only four years before, and the Korean War had not yet begun. Stalin was still alive, the Berlin blockade had just ended, and the Cold War was moving into high gear.

Harry Truman was President of the United States, still a klutz in the eyes of most Americans and not yet the honest hero he was to become in nostalgic minds later on. Dwight D. Eisenhower, still unaware that he was to spend eight years vegetating as President of the United States, was vegetating as president of Columbia University. And no one had yet heard of a junior senator from Wisconsin named Joseph McCarthy.

The Soviet Union was about to explode its first nuclear bomb, ending the American monopoly. The Chinese Communists had completed their conquest of the mainland, and the Nationalists had fled to Taiwan. A young man on the make had completed his task of working out the downfall of Alger Hiss and began his triumphant climb toward a far greater downfall of his own.

Cuba was safely in the vest pocket of the United States, and virtually no one in the United States had ever heard of Vietnam.

But that's just the world generally. For a *real* taste of how far we have come, consider the status of science in 1949.

It was still possible to write stories set on the dark side of Mercury, where the nearby Sun was never seen, and where mounds of frozen gases could be used to supply human settlers—and to cite astronomical chapter and verse to prove that the story was scientifically accurate.

The dank, warm swamps and forests of Venus were still home to Mesozoic monsters, and web-footed natives could rebel against Earthly domination.

The canals of Mars crisscrossed the cool desert, and an old and decadent civilization (gentle, perhaps, or fiendish) was going down to its inevitable end, or was planning a strike across space against the lushness of Earth.

Or perhaps the Martians had already established a base on the far side of the Moon. There, invisible to humanity, they could take advantage of a lunar hemisphere with an altitude generally lower than the one that faced us, a hemisphere where there were wisps of air, bits of water, and even a thin scattering of native life.

Jupiter lacked a magnetosphere (and so, for that matter, did Earth), and there was no solar wind, in any case, to supply the energetic subatomic particles of the magnetosphere.

The large satellites of Jupiter were ripe for colonization, and there was no danger, other than gravitational, in approaching the giant planet. Even the gravitation was no great problem if the spaceship was atomic-powered.

Uranus had no rings. Jupiter had no rings. Pluto was as large as the Earth and had no satellites.

There were no flying saucers, no ancient astronauts, no Velikovskian fantasies—except what a writer could make up out of his own head.

Farther out in space there were normal stars, white dwarfs, and red giants, but that was all. There were no pulsars or neutron stars. There were no black holes and no dust clouds full of complicated molecules.

The galaxies were tame, too. None exploded and there were no central black holes. There were no galactic cores sizzling in x-ray and gamma-ray radiation and humming with a dense array of microwave radiation.

Rather, the central nuclei, where the stars were strewn thickly, was the natural home of any Galactic Empire. There, under a star-lit sky, pyrotechnically shining with half the brightness of our Moon, you would find the world-cities.

There were no Seyfert galaxies, no distant quasars with their mysterious floods of energies. There were no white holes or worm tunnels or accretion disks.

On Earth itself, atomic doom could not long be deferred—because as soon as the Soviet Union got the bomb there would be a nuclear war, and Earth would be inhabited by mutants with tails on each rump and two heads on each neck.

If the nuclear war could be avoided in some way, there would be a glowing atomic future in which every house could power its furnace with a tiny pellet of uranium that would last for seventy years.

There was no fusion bomb, of course, no artificial satellites, no weather satellites, no communications satellites. If people went out into space, it was non-stop to the Moon, flying by the seat of one's pants.

There were no detectable neutrinos, no hyperons, no strange particles, no charmed particles, no colored particles, no quarks. Nor were there holograms, masers or lasers—just disintegrator guns.

There were no tachyons, though hyperspace and subspace were at everyone's beck and call, with hyperatomic motors to take advantage of it.

Robots were intelligent, but had platinum-iridium brains that had nothing to do with computers and were powered by a sliver of a battery whose disintegrating atoms lasted for a hundred years.

How could robots have anything to do with computers when these were vast indeed and whole mountains had to be hollowed out to hold all the millions of vacuum tubes needed to keep a really big one going?

There was no double helix, no recombinant-DNA, no broad-spectrum antibiotics, no hallucinogens, no chlorofluorocarbon-powered spray cans to endanger the ozone layer.

And yet there are those who think that with the years it has become impossible to write science fiction—who think that science has killed all our plots by either making them come true or showing them to be false.

Quite the reverse!

Think back on the universe of 1949 when F&SF came into being and think how deprived we were.

Imagine writing about Mars without those volcanoes and canyons and dry riverbeds, and with satellites whose measurements and appearance were completely unknown.

Imagine a trip across the galaxy, with no mini-black holes to encounter, no tachyonic drive to help you on your way.

Imagine writing about the twenty-first century, with no space settlements in lunar orbit, with no mass-drivers, with no solar power stations turning their large glittering wings to the Sun, with no genetic engineering of any account.

Imagine exploring the solar system without ever sighting Chiron pursuing its lonely course between the orbits of Saturn and Uranus, or the thin rings that glint darkly about Jupiter and Uranus, or the small double-planet of Pluto-Charon, or the thin, vast cloud of drifting ice-balls, a light-year from the Sun, that are the parents of the occasional comets that come flashing through the inner solar system.

Has science consumed our plots?

Nonsense! Science has *given* us plots. For every 1949 notion that has vanished, we have anywhere from two to twenty 1979 notions we can use instead.

In a way, then, an anthology of thirty years of a good science fiction magazine is not only a history of the magazine, but is a history of science, too, one that offers tantalizing glimpses, here and there, of the way in which advancing knowledge has offered the clever writer endless opportunities to do better, and to probe more deeply into the universe, into the human condition, and into the future of both.

The Magazine of
FANTASY and SCIENCE FICTION
A 30-YEAR RETROSPECTIVE

Fondly Fahrenheit

Alfred Bester

HE DOESN'T KNOW which of us I am these days, but they know one truth. You must own nothing but yourself. You must make your own life, live your own life and die your own death . . . or else you will die another's.

The rice fields on Paragon III stretch for hundreds of miles like checkerboard tundras, a blue and brown mosaic under a burning sky of orange. In the evening, clouds whip like smoke, and the paddies rustle and murmur.

A long line of men marched across the paddies the evening we escaped from Paragon III. They were silent, armed, intent; a long rank of silhouetted statues looming against the smoking sky. Each man carried a gun. Each man wore a walkie-talkie belt pack, the speaker button in his ear, the microphone bug clipped to his throat, the glowing view-screen strapped to his wrist like a green-eyed watch. The multitude of screens showed nothing but a multitude of individual paths through the paddies. The annunciators uttered no sound but the rustle and splash of steps. The men spoke infrequently, in heavy grunts, all speaking to all.

"Nothing here."

"FONDLY FAHRENHEIT," *first published in the August 1954 issue, is an SFWA Hall of Fame story. Its author, formerly F&SF's book reviewer, broke into the sf field in 1939 with a story called "The Broken Axiom" and has been contributing distinguished short fiction and novels ever since. His best-known books are* The Demolished Man *and* The Stars My Destination.

"Where's here?"

"Jenson's fields."

"You're drifting too far west."

"Close in the line there."

"Anybody covered the Grimson paddy?"

"Yeah. Nothing."

"She couldn't have walked this far."

"Could have been carried."

"Think she's alive?"

"Why should she be dead?"

The slow refrain swept up and down the long line of beaters advancing toward the smoky sunset. The line of beaters wavered like a writhing snake, but never ceased its remorseless advance. One hundred men spaced fifty feet apart. Five thousand feet of ominous search. One mile of angry determination stretching from east to west across a compass of heat. Evening fell. Each man lit his search lamp. The writhing snake was transformed into a necklace of wavering diamonds.

"Clear here. Nothing."

"Nothing here."

"Nothing."

"What about the Allen paddies?"

"Covering them now."

"Think we missed her?"

"Maybe."

"We'll beat back and check."

"This'll be an all-night job."

"Allen paddies clear."

"God damn! We've got to find her!"

"We'll find her."

"Here she is. Sector seven. Tune in."

The line stopped. The diamonds froze in the heat. There was silence. Each man gazed into the glowing green screen on his wrist, tuning to sector seven. All tuned to one. All showed a small nude figure awash in the muddy water of a paddy. Alongside the figure an owner's stake of bronze read: VANDALEUR. The ends of the line converged toward the Vandaleur field. The necklace turned into a cluster of stars. One hundred men gathered around a small nude body, a child dead in a rice paddy. There was no water in her mouth. There were fingermarks on her throat. Her innocent face was battered. Her body was torn. Clotted blood on her skin was crusted and hard.

"Dead three-four hours at least."

"Her mouth is dry."

"She wasn't drowned. Beaten to death."

In the dark evening heat the men swore softly. They picked up the body. One stopped the others and pointed to the child's fingernails. She had fought her murderer. Under the nails were particles of flesh and bright drops of scarlet blood, still liquid, still uncoagulated.

"That blood ought to be clotted too."

"Funny."

"Not so funny. What kind of blood don't clot?"

"Android."

"Looks like she was killed by one."

"Vandaleur owns an android."

"She couldn't be killed by an android."

"That's android blood under her nails."

"The police better check."

"The police'll prove I'm right."

"But androids can't kill."

"That's android blood, ain't it?"

"Androids can't kill. They're made that way."

"Looks like one android was made wrong."

"Jesus!"

And the thermometer that day registered 92.9° gloriously Fahrenheit.

So there we were aboard the *Paragon Queen* enroute for Megaster V, James Vandaleur and his android. James Vandaleur counted his money and wept. In the second-class cabin with him was his android, a magnificent synthetic creature with classic features and wide blue eyes. Raised on its forehead in a cameo of flesh were the letters MA, indicating that this was one of the rare multiple aptitude androids, worth $57,000 on the current exchange. There we were, weeping and counting and calmly watching.

"Twelve, fourteen, sixteen. Sixteen hundred dollars," Vandaleur wept. "That's all. Sixteen hundred dollars. My house was worth ten thousand. The land was worth five. There was furniture, cars, my paintings, etchings, my plane, my—— And nothing to show for everything but sixteen hundred dollars. Christ!"

I leaped up from the table and turned on the android. I pulled a strap from one of the leather bags and beat the android. It didn't move.

"I must remind you," the android said, "that I am worth fifty-seven thousand dollars on the current exchange. I must warn you that you are endangering valuable property."

"You damned crazy machine," Vandaleur shouted.

"I am not a machine," the android answered. "The robot is a machine. The android is a chemical creation of synthetic tissue."

"What got into you?" Vandaleur cried. "Why did you do it? Damn you!" He beat the android savagely.

"I must remind you that I cannot be punished," I said. "The pleasure-pain syndrome is not incorporated in the android synthesis."

"Then why did you kill her?" Vandaleur shouted. "If it wasn't for kicks, why did you——"

"I must remind you," the android said, "that the second-class cabins in these ships are not soundproofed."

Vandaleur dropped the strap and stood panting, staring at the creature he owned.

"Why did you do it? Why did you kill her?" I asked.

"I don't know," I answered.

"First it was malicious mischief. Small things. Petty destruction. I should have known there was something wrong with you then. Androids can't destroy. They can't harm. They——"

"There is no pleasure-pain syndrome incorporated in the android synthesis."

"Then it got to arson. Then serious destruction. Then assault . . . that engineer on Rigel. Each time worse. Each time we had to get out faster. Now it's murder. Christ! What's the matter with you? What's happened?"

"There are no self-check relays incorporated in the android brain."

"Each time we had to get out of it was a step downhill. Look at me. In a second-class cabin. Me. James Paleologue Vandaleur. There was a time when my father was the wealthiest—— Now, sixteen hundred dollars in the world. That's all I've got. And you. Christ damn you!"

Vandaleur raised the strap to beat the android again, then dropped it and collapsed on a berth, sobbing. At last he pulled himself together.

"Instructions," he said.

The multiple aptitude android responded at once. It arose and awaited orders.

"My name is now Valentine. James Valentine. I stopped off on Paragon III for only one day to transfer to this ship for Megaster V.

My occupation: Agent for one privately owned MA android which is for hire. Purpose of visit: To settle on Megaster V. Fix the papers."

The android removed Vandaleur's passport and papers from a bag, got pen and ink and sat down at the table. With an accurate, flawless hand—an accomplished hand that could draw, write, paint, carve, engrave, etch, photograph, design, create and build—it meticulously forged new credentials for Vandaleur. Its owner watched me miserably.

"Create and build," I muttered. "And now destroy. Oh, God! What am I going to do? Christ! If I could only get rid of you. If I didn't have to live off you. God! If only I'd inherited some guts instead of you."

Dallas Brady was Megaster's leading jewelry designer. She was short, stocky, amoral and a nymphomaniac. She hired Vandaleur's multiple aptitude android and put me to work in her shop. She seduced Vandaleur. In her bed one night, she asked abruptly: "Your name's Vandaleur, isn't it?"

"Yes," I murmured. Then: "No! No! It's Valentine. James Valentine."

"What happened on Paragon?" Dallas Brady asked. "I thought androids couldn't kill or destroy property. Prime Directives and Inhibitions set up for them when they're synthesized. Every company guarantees they can't."

"Valentine!" Vandaleur insisted.

"Oh, come off it," Dallas Brady said. "I've known for a week. I haven't hollered copper, have I?"

"The name is Valentine."

"You want to prove it? You want I should call the cops?" Dallas reached out and picked up the phone.

"For God's sake, Dallas!" Vandaleur leaped up and struggled to take the phone from her. She fended him off, laughing at him, until he collapsed and wept in shame and helplessness.

"How did you find out?" he asked at last.

"The papers are full of it. And Valentine was a little too close to Vandaleur. That wasn't smart, was it?"

"I guess not. I'm not very smart."

"Your android's got quite a record, hasn't it? Assault. Arson. Destruction. What happened on Paragon?"

"It kidnaped a child. Took her out into the rice fields and murdered her."

"Raped her?"

"I don't know."

"They're going to catch up with you."

"Don't I know it? Christ! We've been running for two years now. Seven planets in two years. I must have abandoned fifty thousand dollars worth of property in two years."

"You better find out what's wrong with it."

"How can I? Can I walk into a repair clinic and ask for an overhaul? What am I going to say? 'My android's just turned killer. Fix it.' They'd call the police right off." I began to shake. "They'd have that android dismantled inside one day. I'd probably be booked as accessory to murder."

"Why didn't you have it repaired before it got to murder?"

"I couldn't take the chance," Vandaleur explained angrily. "If they started fooling around with lobotomies and body chemistry and endocrine surgery, they might have destroyed its aptitudes. What would I have left to hire out? How would I live?"

"You could work yourself. People do."

"Work at what? You know I'm good for nothing. How could I compete with specialist androids and robots? Who can, unless he's got a terrific talent for a particular job?"

"Yeah. That's true."

"I lived off my old man all my life. Damn him! He had to go bust just before he died. Left me the android and that's all. The only way I can get along is living off what it earns."

"You better sell it before the cops catch up with you. You can live off fifty grand. Invest it."

"At 3 per cent? Fifteen hundred a year? When the android returns 15 per cent on its value? Eight thousand a year. That's what it earns. No, Dallas. I've got to go along with it."

"What are you going to do about its violence kick?"

"I can't do anything . . . except watch it and pray. What are you going to do about it?"

"Nothing. It's none of my business. Only one thing . . . I ought to get something for keeping my mouth shut."

"What?"

"The android works for me for free. Let somebody else pay you, but I get it for free."

The multiple aptitude android worked. Vandaleur collected its fees. His expenses were taken care of. His savings began to mount. As the warm spring of Megaster V turned to hot summer, I began investigating farms and properties. It would be possible, within a year or two, for us to settle down permanently, provided Dallas Brady's demands did not become rapacious.

On the first hot day of summer, the android began singing in Dallas Brady's workshop. It hovered over the electric furnace which, along with the weather, was broiling the shop, and sang an ancient tune that had been popular half a century before.

> Oh, it's no feat to beat the heat.
> All reet! All reet!
> So jeet your seat
> Be fleet be fleet
> Cool and discreet
> Honey . . .

It sang in a strange, halting voice, and its accomplished fingers were clasped behind its back, writhing in a strange rumba all their own. Dallas Brady was surprised.

"You happy or something?" she asked.

"I must remind you that the pleasure-pain syndrome is not incorporated in the android synthesis," I answered. "All reet! All reet! Be fleet be fleet, cool and discreet, honey . . ."

Its fingers stopped their writhing and picked up a heavy pair of iron tongs. The android poked them into the glowing heart of the furnace, leaning far forward to peer into the lovely heat.

"Be careful, you damned fool!" Dallas Brady exclaimed. "You want to fall in?"

"I must remind you that I am worth fifty-seven thousand dollars on the current exchange," I said. "It is forbidden to endanger valuable property. All reet! All reet! Honey . . ."

It withdrew a crucible of glowing gold from the electric furnace, turned, capered hideously, sang crazily, and splashed a sluggish gobbet of molten gold over Dallas Brady's head. She screamed and collapsed, her hair and clothes flaming, her skin crackling. The android poured again while it capered and sang.

"Be fleet be fleet, cool and discreet, honey . . ." It sang and slowly poured and poured the molten gold. Then I left the workshop and rejoined James Vandaleur in his hotel suite. The android's charred clothes and squirming fingers warned its owner that something was very much wrong.

Vandaleur rushed to Dallas Brady's workshop, stared once, vomited and fled. I had enough time to pack one bag and raise nine hundred dollars on portable assets. He took a third class cabin on the *Megaster Queen* which left that morning for Lyra Alpha. He took me with him. He wept and counted his money and I beat the android again.

And the thermometer in Dallas Brady's workshop registered 98.1° beautifully Fahrenheit.

On Lyra Alpha we holed up in a small hotel near the university. There, Vandaleur carefully bruised my forehead until the letters MA were obliterated by the swelling and the discoloration. The letters would reappear again, but not for several months, and in the meantime Vandaleur hoped the hue and cry for an MA android would be forgotten. The android was hired out as a common laborer in the university power plant. Vandaleur, as James Venice, eked out life on the android's small earnings.

I wasn't too unhappy. Most of the other residents in the hotel were university students, equally hard up, but delightfully young and enthusiastic. There was one charming girl with sharp eyes and a quick mind. Her name was Wanda, and she and her beau, Jed Stark, took a tremendous interest in the killing android which was being mentioned in every paper in the galaxy.

"We've been studying the case," she and Jed said at one of the casual student parties which happened to be held this night in Vandaleur's room. "We think we know what's causing it. We're going to do a paper." They were in a high state of excitement.

"Causing what?" somebody wanted to know.

"The android rampage."

"Obviously out of adjustment, isn't it? Body chemistry gone haywire. Maybe a kind of synthetic cancer, yes?"

"No." Wanda gave Jed a look of suppressed triumph.

"Well, what is it?"

"Something specific."

"What?"

"That would be telling."

"Oh, come on."

"Nothing doing."

"Won't you tell us?" I asked intently. "I . . . We're very much interested in what could go wrong with an android."

"No, Mr. Venice," Wanda said. "It's a unique idea and we've got to protect it. One thesis like this and we'll be set up for life. We can't take the chance of somebody stealing it."

"Can't you give us a hint?"

"No. Not a hint. Don't say a word, Jed. But I'll tell you this much, Mr. Venice. I'd hate to be the man who owns that android."

"You mean the police?" I asked.

"I mean projection, Mr. Venice. Projection! That's the danger . . . and I won't say any more. I've said too much as is."

I heard steps outside, and a hoarse voice singing softly: "Be fleet be fleet cool and discreet, honey . . ." My android entered the room, home from its tour of duty at the university power plant. It was not introduced. I motioned to it and I immediately responded to the command and went to the beer keg and took over Vandaleur's job of serving the guests. Its accomplished fingers writhed in a private rumba of their own. Gradually they stopped their squirming, and the strange humming ended.

Androids were not unusual at the university. The wealthier students owned them along with cars and planes. Vandaleur's android provoked no comment, but young Wanda was sharp-eyed and quick-witted. She noted my bruised forehead and she was intent on the history-making thesis she and Jed Stark were going to write. After the party broke up, she consulted with Jed walking upstairs to her room.

"Jed, why'd that android have a bruised forehead?"

"Probably hurt itself, Wanda. It's working in the power plant. They fling a lot of heavy stuff around."

"That all?"

"What else?"

"It could be a convenient bruise."

"Convenient for what?"

"Hiding what's stamped on its forehead."

"No point to that, Wanda. You don't have to see marks on a forehead to recognize an android. You don't have to see a trademark on a car to know it's a car."

"I don't mean it's trying to pass as a human. I mean it's trying to pass as a lower grade android."

"Why?"

"Suppose it had MA on its forehead."

"Multiple aptitude? Then why in hell would Venice waste it stoking furnaces if it could earn more—— Oh. Oh! You mean it's—?"

Wanda nodded.

"Jesus!" Stark pursed his lips. "What do we do? Call the police?"

"No. We don't know if it's an MA for a fact. If it turns out to be an MA and the killing android, our paper comes first anyway. This is our big chance, Jed. If it's *that* android we can run a series of controlled tests and——"

"How do we find out for sure?"

"Easy. Infrared film. That'll show what's under the bruise. Borrow a camera. Buy some film. We'll sneak down to the power plant tomorrow afternoon and take some pictures. Then we'll know."

They stole down into the university power plant the following afternoon. It was a vast cellar, deep under the earth. It was dark, shadowy, luminous with burning light from the furnace doors. Above the roar of the fires they could hear a strange voice shouting and chanting in the echoing vault: "All reet! All reet! So jeet your seat. Be fleet be fleet, cool and discreet, honey . . ." And they could see a capering figure dancing a lunatic rumba in time to the music it shouted. The legs twisted. The arms waved. The fingers writhed.

Jed Stark raised the camera and began shooting his spool of infrared film, aiming the camera sights at that bobbing head. Then Wanda shrieked, for I saw them and came charging down on them, brandishing a polished steel shovel. It smashed the camera. It felled the girl and then the boy. Jed fought me for a desperate hissing moment before he was bludgeoned into helplessness. Then the android dragged them to the furnace and fed them to the flames, slowly, hideously. It capered and sang. Then it returned to my hotel.

The thermometer in the power plant registered 100.9° murderously Fahrenheit. All reet! All reet!

We bought steerage on the *Lyra Queen* and Vandaleur and the android did odd jobs for their meals. During the night watches, Vandaleur would sit alone in the steerage head with a cardboard portfolio on his lap, puzzling over its contents. That portfolio was all he had managed to bring with him from Lyra Alpha. He had stolen it from Wanda's room. It was labeled ANDROID. It contained the secret of my sickness.

And it contained nothing but newspapers. Scores of newspapers from all over the galaxy, printed, microfilmed, engraved, etched, offset, photostated . . . Rigel *Star-Banner* . . . Paragon *Picayune* . . . Megaster *Times-Leader* . . . Lalande *Herald* . . . Lacaille *Journal* . . . Indi *Intelligencer* . . . Eridani *Telegram-News*. All reet! All reet!

Nothing but newspapers. Each paper contained an account of one crime in the android's ghastly career. Each paper also contained news, domestic and foreign, sports, society, weather, shipping news, stock exchange quotations, human interest stories, features, contests, puzzles. Somewhere in that mass of uncollated facts was the secret Wanda and Jed Stark had discovered. Vandaleur pored over the papers helplessly. It was beyond him. So jeet your seat!

"I'll sell you," I told the android. "Damn you. When we land on Terra, I'll sell you. I'll settle for 3 per cent on whatever you're worth."

"I am worth fifty-seven thousand dollars on the current exchange," I told him.

"If I can't sell you, I'll turn you in to the police," I said.

"I am valuable property," I answered. "It is forbidden to endanger valuable property. You won't have me destroyed."

"Christ damn you!" Vandaleur cried. "What? Are you arrogant? Do you know you can trust me to protect you? Is that the secret?"

The multiple aptitude android regarded him with calm accomplished eyes. "Sometimes," it said, "it is a good thing to be property."

It was 3 below zero when the *Lyra Queen* dropped at Croydon Field. A mixture of ice and snow swept across the field, fizzing and exploding into steam under the *Queen*'s tail jets. The passengers trotted numbly across the blackened concrete to customs inspection, and thence to the airport bus that was to take them to London. Vandaleur and the android were broke. They walked.

By midnight they reached Piccadilly Circus. The December ice storm had not slackened and the statue of Eros was encrusted with ice. They turned right, walked down to Trafalgar Square and then along the Strand toward Soho, shaking with cold and wet. Just above Fleet Street, Vandaleur saw a solitary figure coming from the direction of St. Paul's. He drew the android into an alley.

"We've got to have money," he whispered. He pointed at the approaching figure. "He has money. Take it from him."

"The order cannot be obeyed," the android said.

"Take it from him," Vandaleur repeated. "By force. Do you understand? We're desperate."

"It is contrary to my prime directive," I said. "I cannot endanger life or property. The order cannot be obeyed."

"For God's sake!" Vandaleur burst out. "You've attacked, destroyed, murdered. Don't gibber about prime directives. You haven't any left. Get his money. Kill him if you have to. I tell you, we're desperate!"

"It is contrary to my prime directive," the android repeated. "The order cannot be obeyed."

I thrust the android back and leaped out at the stranger. He was tall, austere, competent. He had an air of hope curdled by cyncism. He carried a cane. I saw he was blind.

"Yes?" he said. "I hear you near me. What is it?"

"Sir . . ." Vandaleur hesitated. "I'm desperate."

"We are all desperate," the stranger replied. "Quietly desperate."

"Sir . . . I've got to have some money."

"Are you begging or stealing?" The sightless eyes passed over Vandaleur and the android.

"I'm prepared for either."

"Ah. So are we all. It is the history of our race." The stranger motioned over his shoulder. "I have been begging at St. Paul's, my friend. What I desire cannot be stolen. What is it you desire that you are lucky enough to be able to steal?"

"Money," Vandaleur said.

"Money for what? Come, my friend, let us exchange confidences. I will tell you why I beg, if you will tell me why you steal. My name is Blenheim."

"My name is . . . Vole."

"I was not begging for sight at St. Paul's, Mr. Vole. I was begging for a number."

"A number?"

"Ah yes. Numbers rational, numbers irrational. Numbers imaginary. Positive integers. Negative integers. Fractions, positive and negative. Eh? You have never heard of Blenheim's immortal treatise on Twenty Zeros, or The Differences in Absence of Quantity?" Blenheim smiled bitterly. "I am the wizard of the Theory of Number, Mr. Vole, and I have exhausted the charm of number for myself. After fifty years of wizardry, senility approaches and the appetite vanishes. I have been praying in St. Paul's for inspiration. Dear God, I prayed, if You exist, send me a number."

Vandaleur slowly lifted the cardboard portfolio and touched Blenheim's hand with it. "In here," he said, "is a number. A hidden number. A secret number. The number of a crime. Shall we exchange, Mr. Blenheim? Shelter for a number?"

"Neither begging nor stealing, eh?" Blenheim said. "But a bargain.

So all life reduces itself to the banal." The sightless eyes again passed over Vandaleur and the android. "Perhaps the All-Mighty is not God but a merchant. Come home with me."

On the top floor of Blenheim's house we shared a room—two beds, two closets, two washstands, one bathroom. Vandaleur bruised my forehead again and sent me out to find work, and while the android worked, I consulted with Blenheim and read him the papers from the portfolio, one by one. All reet! All reet!

Vandaleur told him so much and no more. He was a student, I said, attempting a thesis on the murdering android. In these papers which he had collected were the facts that would explain the crimes of which Blenheim had heard nothing. There must be a correlation, a number, a statistic, something which would account for my derangement, I explained, and Blenheim was piqued by the mystery, the detective story, the human interest of number.

We examined the papers. As I read them aloud, he listed them and their contents in his blind, meticulous writing. And then I read his notes to him. He listed the papers by type, by type face, by fact, by fancy, by article, spelling, words, theme, advertising, pictures, subject, politics, prejudices. He analyzed. He studied. He meditated. And we lived together in that top floor, always a little cold, always a little terrified, always a little closer . . . brought together by our fear of it, our hatred between us. Like a wedge driven into a living tree and splitting the trunk, only to be forever incorporated into the scar tissue, we grew together. Vandaleur and the android. Be fleet be fleet!

And one afternoon Blenheim called Vandaleur into his study and displayed his notes. "I think I've found it," he said, "but I can't understand it."

Vandaleur's heart leaped.

"Here are the correlations," Blenheim continued. "In fifty papers there are accounts of the criminal android. What is there, outside the depredations, that is also in fifty papers?"

"I don't know, Mr. Blenheim."

"It was a rhetorical question. Here is the answer. The weather."

"What?"

"The weather." Blenheim nodded. "Each crime was committed on a day when the temperature was above 90 degrees Fahrenheit."

"But that's impossible," Vandaleur exclaimed. "It was cool on Lyra Alpha."

"We have no record of any crime committed on Lyra Alpha. There is no paper."

"No. That's right. I——" Vandaleur was confused. Suddenly he exclaimed. "No. You're right. The furnace room. It was hot there. Hot! Of course. My God, yes! That's the answer. Dallas Brady's electric furnace . . . The rice deltas on Paragon. So jeet your seat. Yes. But why? Why? My God, why?"

I came into the house at that moment, and passing the study, saw Vandaleur and Blenheim. I entered, awaiting commands, my multiple aptitudes devoted to service.

"That's the android, eh?" Blenheim said after a long moment.

"Yes," Vandaleur answered, still confused by the discovery. "And that explains why it refused to attack you that night on the Strand. It wasn't hot enough to break the prime directive. Only in the heat . . . The heat, all reet!" He looked at the android. A lunatic command passed from man to android. I refused. It is forbidden to endanger life. Vandaleur gestured furiously, then seized Blenheim's shoulders and yanked him back out of his desk chair to the floor. Blenheim shouted once. Vandaleur leaped on him like a tiger, pinning him to the floor and sealing his mouth with one hand.

"Find a weapon," he called to the android.

"It is forbidden to endanger life."

"This is a fight for self-preservation. Bring me a weapon!" He held the squirming mathematician with all his weight. I went at once to a cupboard where I knew a revolver was kept. I checked it. It was loaded with five cartridges. I handed it to Vandaleur. I took it, rammed the barrel against Blenheim's head and pulled the trigger. He shuddered once.

We had three hours before the cook returned from her day off. We looted the house. We took Blenheim's money and jewels. We packed a bag with clothes. We took Blenheim's notes, destroyed the newspapers; and we left, carefully locking the door behind us. In Blenheim's study we left a pile of crumpled papers under a half inch of burning candle. And we soaked the rug around it with kerosene. No, I did all that. The android refused. I am forbidden to endanger life or property.

All reet!

They took the tubes to Leicester Square, changed trains and rode to the British Museum. There they got off and went to a small Georgian house just off Russell Square. A shingle in the window read: NAN WEBB, PSYCHOMETRIC CONSULTANT. Vandaleur had made a note of the address some weeks earlier. They went into the house. The android waited in the foyer with the bag. Vandaleur entered Nan Webb's office.

She was a tall woman with gray shingled hair, very fine English complexion and very bad English legs. Her features were blunt, her expression acute. She nodded to Vandaleur, finished a letter, sealed it and looked up.

"My name," I said, "is Vanderbilt. James Vanderbilt."

"Quite."

"I'm an exchange student at London University."

"Quite."

"I've been researching on the killing android, and I think I've discovered something very interesting. I'd like your advice on it. What is your fee?"

"What is your college at the university?"

"Why?"

"There is a discount for students."

"Merton College."

"That will be two pounds, please."

Vandaleur placed two pounds on the desk and added to the fee Blenheim's notes. "There is a correlation," he said, "between the crimes of the android and the weather. You will note that each crime was committed when the temperature rose above 90 degrees Fahrenheit. Is there a psychometric answer for this?"

Nan Webb nodded, studied the notes for a moment, put down the sheets of paper and said: "Synesthesia, obviously."

"What?"

"Synesthesia," she repeated. "When a sensation, Mr. Vanderbilt, is interpreted immediately in terms of a sensation from a different sense organ from the one stimulated, it is called synesthesia. For example: A sound stimulus gives rise to a simultaneous sensation of definite color. Or color gives rise to a sensation of taste. Or a light stimulus gives rise to a sensation of sound. There can be confusion or short circuiting of any sensation of taste, smell, pain, pressure, temperature and so on. D'you understand?"

"I think so."

"Your research has uncovered the fact that the android most probably reacts to temperature stimulus above the 90-degree level synesthetically. Most probably there is an endocrine response. Probably a temperature linkage with the android adrenal surrogate. High temperature brings about a response of fear, anger, excitement and violent physical activity . . . all within the province of the adrenal gland."

"Yes. I see. Then if the android were to be kept in cold climates . . ."

"There would be neither stimulus nor response. There would be no crimes. Quite."

"I see. What is projection?"

"How do you mean?"

"Is there any danger of projection with regard to the owner of the android?"

"Very interesting. Projection is a throwing forward. It is the process of throwing out upon another the ideas or impulses that belong to oneself. The paranoid, for example, projects upon others his conflicts and disturbances in order to externalize them. He accuses, directly or by implication, other men of having the very sicknesses with which he is struggling himself."

"And the danger of projection?"

"It is the danger of believing what is implied. If you live with a psychotic who projects his sickness upon you, there is a danger of falling into his psychotic pattern and becoming virtually psychotic yourself. As, no doubt, is happening to you, Mr. Vandaleur."

Vandaleur leaped to his feet.

"You are an ass," Nan Webb went on crisply. She waved the sheets of notes. "This is no exchange student's writing. It's the unique cursive of the famous Blenheim. Every scholar in England knows this blind writing. There is no Merton College at London University. That was a miserable guess. Merton is one of the Oxford colleges. And you, Mr. Vandaleur, are so obviously infected by association with your deranged android . . . by projection, if you will . . . that I hesitate between calling the Metropolitan Police and the Hospital for the Criminally Insane."

I took the gun and shot her.

Reet!

"Antares II, Alpha Aurigae, Acrux IV, Pollux IX, Rigel Centaurus," Vandaleur said. "They're all cold. Cold as a witch's kiss. Mean temperatures of 40 degrees Fahrenheit. Never get hotter than 70. We're in business again. Watch that curve."

The multiple aptitude android swung the wheel with its accomplished hands. The car took the curve sweetly and sped on through the northern marshes, the reeds stretching for miles, brown and dry, under the cold English sky. The sun was sinking swiftly. Overhead, a lone flight of bustards flapped clumsily eastward. High above the flight, a lone helicopter drifted toward home and warmth.

"No more warmth for us," I said. "No more heat. We're safe when we're cold. We'll hole up in Scotland, make a little money, get across to Norway, build a bankroll and then ship out. We'll settle on Pollux. We're safe. We've licked it. We can live again."

There was a startling *bleep* from overhead, and then a ragged roar: "ATTENTION JAMES VANDALEUR AND ANDROID. ATTENTION JAMES VANDALEUR AND ANDROID!"

Vandaleur started and looked up. The lone helicopter was floating above them. From its belly came amplified commands: "YOU ARE SURROUNDED. THE ROAD IS BLOCKED. YOU ARE TO STOP YOUR CAR AT ONCE AND SUBMIT TO ARREST. STOP AT ONCE!"

I looked at Vandaleur for orders.

"Keep driving," Vandaleur snapped.

The helicopter dropped lower: "ATTENTION ANDROID. YOU ARE IN CONTROL OF THE VEHICLE. YOU ARE TO STOP AT ONCE. THIS IS A STATE DIRECTIVE SUPERSEDING ALL PRIVATE COMMANDS."

"What the hell are you doing?" I shouted.

"A state directive supersedes all private commands," the android answered. "I must point out to you that——"

"Get the hell away from the wheel," Vandaleur ordered. I clubbed the android, yanked him sideways and squirmed over him to the wheel. The car veered off the road in that moment and went churning through the frozen mud and dry reeds. Vandaleur regained control and continued westward through the marshes toward a parallel highway five miles distant.

"We'll beat their God damned block," he grunted.

The car pounded and surged. The helicopter dropped even lower. A searchlight blazed from the belly of the plane.

"ATTENTION JAMES VANDALEUR AND ANDROID. SUBMIT TO ARREST. THIS IS A STATE DIRECTIVE SUPERSEDING ALL PRIVATE COMMANDS."

"He can't submit," Vandaleur shouted wildly. "There's no one to submit to. He can't and I won't."

"Christ!" I muttered. "We'll beat them yet. We'll beat the block. We'll beat the heat. We'll——"

"I must point out to you," I said, "that I am required by my prime

directive to obey state directives which supersede all private commands.
I must submit to arrest."

"Who says it's a state directive?" Vandaleur said. "Them? Up in that
plane? They've got to show credentials. They've got to prove it's state
authority before you submit. How d'you know they're not crooks trying
to trick us?"

Holding the wheel with one arm, he reached into his side pocket to
make sure the gun was still in place. The car skidded. The tires
squealed on frost and reeds. The wheel was wrenched from his grasp
and the car yawed up a small hillock and overturned. The motor roared
and the wheels screamed. Vandaleur crawled out and dragged the
android with him. For the moment we were outside the circle of light
boring down from the helicopter. We blundered off into the marsh, into
the blackness, into concealment . . . Vandaleur running with a pound-
ing heart, hauling the android along.

The helicopter circled and soared over the wrecked car, searchlight
peering, loudspeaker braying. On the highway we had left, lights appeared as the pursuing and blocking parties gathered and followed
radio directions from the plane. Vandaleur and the android continued
deeper and deeper into the marsh, working their way toward the parallel road and safety. It was night by now. The sky was a black matte.
Not a star showed. The temperature was dropping. A southeast night
wind knifed us to the bone.

Far behind there was a dull concussion. Vandaleur turned, gasping.
The car's fuel had exploded. A geyser of flame shot up like a lurid
fountain. It subsided into a low crater of burning reeds. Whipped by
the wind, the distant hem of flame fanned up into a wall, ten feet high.
The wall began marching down on us, crackling fiercely. Above it, a
pall of oily smoke surged forward. Behind it, Vandaleur could make
out the figures of men . . . a mass of beaters searching the marsh.

"Christ!" I cried and searched desperately for safety. He ran, dragging me with him, until their feet crunched through the surface ice of a
pool. He trampled the ice furiously, then flung himself down in the
numbing water, pulling the android with us.

The wall of flame approached. I could hear the crackle and feel the
heat. He could see the searchers clearly. Vandaleur reched into his
side pocket for the gun. The pocket was torn. The gun was gone. He
groaned and shook with cold and terror. The light from the marsh fire
was blinding. Overhead, the helicopter floated helplessly to one side,

unable to fly through the smoke and flames and aid the searchers who were beating far to the right of us.

"They'll miss us," Vandaleur whispered. "Keep quiet. That's an order. They'll miss us. We'll beat them. We'll beat the fire. We'll——"

Three distinct shots sounded less than a hundred feet from the fugitives. *Blam! Blam! Blam!* They came from the last three cartridges in my gun as the marsh fire reached it where it had dropped, and exploded the shells. The searchers turned toward the sound and began working directly toward us. Vandaleur cursed hysterically and tried to submerge even deeper to escape the intolerable heat of the fire. The android began to twitch.

The wall of flame surged up to them. Vandaleur took a deep breath and prepared to submerge until the flame passed over them. The android shuddered and burst into an ear-splitting scream.

"All reet! All reet!" it shouted. "Be fleet be fleet!"

"Damn you!" I shouted. I tried to drown it.

"Damn you!" I cursed him. I smashed his face.

The android battered Vandaleur, who fought it off until it exploded out of the mud and staggered upright. Before I could return to the attack, the live flames captured it hypnotically. It danced and capered in a lunatic rumba before the wall of fire. Its legs twisted. Its arms waved. The fingers writhed in a private rumba of their own. It shrieked and sang and ran in a crooked waltz before the embrace of the heat, a muddy monster silhouetted against the brilliant sparkling flare.

The searchers shouted. There were shots. The android spun around twice and then continued its horrid dance before the face of the flames. There was a rising gust of wind. The fire swept around the capering figure and enveloped it for a roaring moment. Then the fire swept on, leaving behind it a sobbing mass of synthetic flesh oozing scarlet blood that would never coagulate.

The thermometer would have registered 1200° wondrously Fahrenheit.

Vandaleur didn't die. I got away. They missed him while they watched the android caper and die. But I don't know which of us he is these days. Projection, Wanda warned me. Projection, Nan Webb told him. If you live with a crazy man or a crazy machine long enough, I become crazy too. Reet!

But we know one truth. We know they were wrong. The new robot and Vandaleur know that because the new robot's started twitching too.

Reet! Here on cold Pollux, the robot is twitching and singing. No heat, but my fingers writhe. No heat, but it's taken the little Talley girl off for a solitary walk. A cheap labor robot. A servo-mechanism . . . all I could afford . . . but it's twitching and humming and walking alone with the child somewhere and I can't find them. Christ! Vandaleur can't find me before it's too late. Cool and discreet, honey, in the dancing frost while the thermometer registers 10° fondly Fahrenheit.

And Now the News...
Theodore Sturgeon

THE MAN'S NAME was MacLyle, which by looking at him you can tell wasn't his real name, but let's say this is fiction, shall we? MacLyle had a good job in—well—a soap concern. He worked hard and made good money and got married to a girl called Esther. He bought a house in the suburbs and after it was paid for he rented it to some people and bought a home a little farther out and a second car and a freezer and a power mower and a book on landscaping, and settled down to the worthy task of giving his kids all the things he never had.

He had habits and he had hobbies, like everybody else and (like everybody else) his were a little different from anybody's. The one that annoyed his wife the most, until she got used to it, was the news habit, or maybe hobby. MacLyle read a morning paper on the 8:14 and an evening paper on the 6:10, and the local paper his suburb used for its lost dogs and auction sales took up forty after-dinner minutes. And when he read a paper he read it, he didn't mess with it. He read Page 1 first and Page 2 next, and so on all the way through. He didn't care too much for books but he respected them in a mystical sort of way, and he used to say a newspaper was a kind of book, and so would raise particular hell if a section was missing or in upside down, or if the pages

THEODORE STURGEON *had a story, "The Hurkle Is a Happy Beast," in the first issue of F&SF, Fall 1949. I chose "And Now the News . . ." for this volume because I liked the story a bit better and believe it is more representative of the author's work. Sturgeon produced some of his best writing in the mid-fifties, including the classic novel* More Than Human.

were out of line. He also heard the news on the radio. There were three stations in town with hourly broadcasts, one on the hour, one on the half-hour, and one five minutes before the hour, and he was usually able to catch them all. During these five-minute periods he would look you right in the eye while you talked to him and you'd swear he was listening to you, but he wasn't. This was a particular trial to his wife, but only for five years or so. Then she stopped trying to be heard while the radio talked about floods and murders and scandal and suicide. Five more years, and she went back to talking right through the broadcasts, but by the time people are married ten years, things like that don't matter; they talk in code anyway, and nine tenths of their speech can be picked up anytime like ticker tape. He also caught the 7:30 news on Channel 2 and the 7:45 news on Channel 4 on television.

Now it might be imagined from all this that MacLyle was a crotchety character with fixed habits and a neurotic neatness, but this was far from the case. MacLyle was basically a reasonable guy who loved his wife and children and liked his work and pretty much enjoyed being alive. He laughed easily and talked well and paid his bills. He justified his preoccupation with the news in a number of ways. He would quote Donne: ". . . *any man's death diminishes me, because I am involved in mankind . . .*" which is pretty solid stuff and hard to argue down. He would point out that he made his trains and his trains made him punctual, but that because of them he saw the same faces at the same time day after endless day, before, during, and after he rode those trains, so that his immediate world was pretty circumscribed, and only a constant awareness of what was happening all over the earth kept him conscious of the fact that he lived in a bigger place than a thin straight universe with his house at one end, his office at the other, and a railway track in between.

It's hard to say just when MacLyle started to go to pieces, or even why, though it obviously had something to do with all that news he exposed himself to. He began to react, very slightly at first; that is, you could tell he was listening. He'd *shh!* you, and if you tried to finish what you were saying he'd run and stick his head in the speaker grille. His wife and kids learned to shut up when the news came on, five minutes before the hour until five after (with MacLyle switching stations) and every hour on the half-hour, and from 7:30 to 8 for the TV, and during the forty minutes it took him to read the local paper. He was not so obvious about it when he read his paper, because all he did was freeze over the pages like a catatonic, gripping the top corners until the sheets shivered, knotting his jaw and breathing from his nostrils with a strangled whistle.

Naturally all this was a weight on his wife Esther, who tried her best to reason with him. At first he answered her, saying mildly that a man has to keep in touch, you know; but very quickly he stopped responding altogether, giving her the treatment a practiced suburbanite gets so expert in, as when someone mentions a lawn mower just too damn early on Sunday morning. You don't say yes and you don't say no, you don't even grunt, and you don't move your head or even your eyebrows. After a while your interlocutor goes away. Pretty soon you don't hear these ill-timed annoyances any more than you appear to.

It needs to be said again here that MacLyle was, outside his peculiarity, a friendly and easygoing character. He liked people and invited them and visited them, and he was one of those adults who can really listen to a first-grade child's interminable adventures and really care. He never forgot things like the slow leak in the spare tire or antifreeze or anniversaries, and he always got the storm windows up in time, but he didn't rub anyone's nose in his reliability. The first thing in his whole life he didn't take as a matter of course was this news thing that started so small and grew so quickly.

So after a few weeks of it his wife took the bull by the horns and spent the afternoon hamstringing every receiver in the house. There were three radios and two TV sets, and she didn't understand the first thing about them, but she had a good head and she went to work with a will and the can-opening limb of a pocket knife. From each receiver she removed one tube, and one at a time, so as not to get them mixed up, she carried them into the kitchen and meticulously banged their bases against the edge of the sink, being careful to crack no glass and bend no pins until she could see the guts of the tube rolling around loose inside. Then she replaced them and got the back panels on the sets again.

MacLyle came home and put the car away and kissed her and turned on the living-room radio and then went to hang up his hat. When he returned the radio should have been warmed up but it wasn't. He twisted the knobs for a while and bumped it and rocked it back and forth a little, grunting, and then noticed the time. He began to feel a little frantic, and raced back to the kitchen and turned on the little ivory radio on the shelf. It warmed up quickly and cheerfully and gave him a clear sixty-cycle hum, but that was all. He behaved badly from then on, roaring out the information that the sets didn't work, either of them, as if that wasn't pretty evident by that time, and flew upstairs to the boys' room, waking them explosively. He turned on their radio and got another sixty-cycle note, this time with a shattering microphonic when he rapped the case, which he did four times, whereupon the set went dead altogether.

Esther had planned the thing up to this point, but no further, which was the way her mind worked. She figured she could handle it, but she figured wrong. MacLyle came downstairs like a pallbearer, and he was silent and shaken until 7:30, time for the news on TV. The living-room set wouldn't peep, so up he went to the boys' room again, waking them just as they were nodding off again, and this time the little guy started to cry. MacLyle didn't care. When he found out there was no picture on the set, he almost started to cry too, but then he heard the sound come in. A TV set has an awful lot of tubes in it and Esther didn't know audio from video. MacLyle sat down in front of the dark screen and listened to the news. *"Everything seemed to be under control in the riot-ridden border country in India,"* said the TV set. Crowd noises and a background of Beethoven's "Turkish March." *"And then——"* Cut music. Crowd noise up: gabble-wurra and a scream. Announcer over: *"Six hours later, this was the scene."* Dead silence, going on so long that MacLyle reached out and thumped the TV set with the heel of his hand. Then, slow swell, Ketelbey's "In a Monastery Garden." *"On a more cheerful note, here are the six finalists in the Miss Continuum contest."* Background music, "Blue Room," interminably, interrupted only once, when the announcer said through a childish chuckle *". . . and she meant it!"* MacLyle pounded himself on the temples. The little guy continued to sob. Esther stood at the foot of the stairs wringing her hands. It went on for thirty minutes like this. All MacLyle said when he came downstairs was that he wanted the paper—that would be the local one. So Esther faced the great unknown and told him frankly she hadn't ordered it and wouldn't again, which of course led to a full and righteous confession of her activities of the afternoon.

Only a woman married better than fourteen years can know a man well enough to handle him so badly. She was aware that she was wrong but that was quite overridden by the fact that she was logical. It would not be logical to continue her patience, so patience was at an end. That which offendeth thee, cast it out, yea, even thine eye and thy right hand. She realized too late that the news was so inextricably part of her husband that in casting it out she cast him out too. And out he went, while whitely she listened to the rumble of the garage door, the car door speaking its sharp syllables, clear as *Exit* in a playscript; the keen of a starter, the mourn of a motor. She said she was glad and went in the kitchen and tipped the useless ivory radio off the shelf and retired, weeping.

And yet, because true life offers few clean cuts, she saw him once more. At seven minutes to three in the morning she became aware of faint music from somewhere; unaccountably it frightened her, and she tiptoed about the house looking for it. It wasn't in the house, so she pulled on MacLyle's trench coat and crept down the steps into the garage. And there, just outside in the driveway, where steel beams couldn't interfere with radio reception, the car stood where it had been all along, and MacLyle was in the driver's seat dozing over the wheel. The music came from the car radio. She drew the coat tighter around her and went to the car and opened the door and spoke his name. At just that moment the radio said ". . . *and now the news*" and MacLyle sat bolt upright and *shh*'d furiously. She fell back and stood a moment in a strange transition from unconditional surrender to total defeat. Then he shut the car door and bent forward, his hand on the volume control, and she went back into the house.

After the news report was over and he had recovered himself from the stab wounds of a juvenile delinquent, the grinding agonies of a derailed train, the terrors of the near-crash of a C-119, and the fascination of a cabinet officer, charter member of the We Don't Trust Nobody Club, saying in exactly these words that there's a little bit of good in the worst of us and a little bit of bad in the best of us, all of which he felt keenly, he started the car (by rolling it down the drive because the battery was almost dead) and drove as slowly as possible into town.

At an all-night garage he had the car washed and greased while he waited, after which the automat was open and he sat in it for three hours drinking coffee, holding his jaw set until his back teeth ached, and making occasional, almost inaudible noises in the back of his throat. At nine he pulled himself together. He spent the entire day with his astonished attorney, going through all his assets, selling, converting, establishing, until when he was finished he had a modest packet of cash and his wife would have an adequate income until the children went to college, at which time the house would be sold, the tenants in the older house evicted, and Esther would be free to move to the smaller home with the price of the larger one added to the basic capital. The lawyer might have entertained fears for MacLyle except for the fact that he was jovial and loquacious throughout, behaving like a happy man—a rare form of insanity, but acceptable. It was hard work but they did it in a day, after which MacLyle wrung the lawyer's hand and thanked him profusely and checked into a hotel.

When he awoke the following morning he sprang out of bed, feeling years younger, opened the door, scooped up the morning paper and glanced at the headlines.

He couldn't read them.

He grunted in surprise, closed the door gently, and sat on the bed with paper in his lap. His hands moved restlessly on it, smoothing and smoothing until the palms were shadowed and the type hazed. The shouting symbols marched across the page like a parade of strangers in some unrecognized lodge uniform, origins unknown, destination unknown, and the occasion for marching only to be guessed at. He traced the letters with his little finger, he measured the length of a word between his index finger and thumb and lifted them up to hold them before his wondering eyes. Suddenly he got up and crossed to the desk, where signs and placards and printed notes were trapped like a butterfly collection under glass—the breakfast menu, something about valet service, something about checking out. He remembered them all and had an idea of their significance—but he couldn't read them. In the drawer was stationery, with a picture of the building and no other buildings around it, which just wasn't so, and an inscription which might have been in Cyrillic for all he knew. Telegram blanks, a bus schedule, a blotter, all bearing hieroglyphs and runes, as far as he was concerned. A phone book full of strangers' names in strange symbols.

He requested of himself that he recite the alphabet. "A," he said clearly, and "Eh?" because it didn't sound right and he couldn't imagine what would. He made a small foolish grin and shook his head slightly and rapidly, but grin or no, he felt frightened. He felt glad, or relieved—mostly happy anyway, but still a little frightened.

He called the desk and told them to get his bill ready, and dressed and went downstairs. He gave the doorman his parking check and waited while they brought the car round. He got in and turned the radio on and started to drive west.

He drove for some days, in a state of perpetual, cold, and (for all that) happy fright—roller-coaster fright, horror-movie fright—remembering the significance of a stop sign without being able to read the word STOP across it, taking caution from the shape of a railroad-crossing notice. Restaurants look like restaurants, gas stations like gas stations; if Washington's picture denotes a dollar and Lincoln's five, one doesn't need to read them. MacLyle made out just fine. He drove until he was well into one of those square states with all the mountains and cruised until he recognized the section where, years before he was married, he had spent a hunting vacation. Avoiding the lodge he had used, he took back roads until, sure enough, he came to that deserted cabin in which he had sheltered one night, standing yet, rotting a bit but only around the edges. He wandered in and out of it for a long time, memorizing details because he could not make a list, and then got back into his car and drove to the nearest town, not very near and not very much of a town. At the general store he bought shingles and flour and nails and paint—all sorts of paint, in little cans, as well as big containers of house paint—and canned goods and tools. He ordered a knock-down windmill and a generator, eighty pounds of modeling clay, two loaf pans and a mixing bowl, and a war-surplus jungle hammock. He paid cash and promised to be back in two weeks for the things the store didn't stock, and wired (because it could be done over the phone) his lawyer to arrange for the predetermined eighty dollars a month which was all he cared to take for himself from his assets. Before he left he stood in wonder before a monstrous piece of musical plumbing called an ophicleide which stood, dusty and majestic, in a corner. (While it might be easier on the reader to make this a French horn or a sousaphone—which would answer narrative purposes quite as well— we're done telling lies here. MacLyle's real name is concealed, his home town cloaked, and his occupation disguised, and dammit it really was a twelve-keyed, 1824, fifty-inch, obsolete brass ophicleide.) The storekeeper explained how his great-grandfather had brought it over from the old country and nobody had played it for two generations except an itinerant tuba player who had turned pale green on the first three notes and put it down as if it was full of percussion caps. MacLyle asked how it sounded and the man told him, terrible. Two weeks later MacLyle was back to pick up the rest of his stuff, nodding and smiling and saying not a word. He still couldn't read and now he couldn't speak. Even more, he had lost the power to understand speech. He had paid for the purchases with a hundred-dollar bill and a wistful expression, and then another hundred-dollar bill, and the storekeeper, thinking he had turned deaf and dumb, cheated him roundly but at the same time felt so sorry for him that he gave him the ophicleide. MacLyle loaded up his car happily and left. And that's the first part of the story about MacLyle's being in a bad way.

MacLyle's wife Esther found herself in a peculiar position. Friends and neighbors offhandedly asked her questions to which she did not know the answers, and the only person who had any information at all —MacLyle's attorney—was under bond not to tell her anything. She had not, in the full and legal sense, been deserted, since she and the children were provided for. She missed MacLyle, but in a specialized way; she missed the old reliable MacLyle, and he had, in effect, left her long before that perplexing night when he had driven away. She wanted the old MacLyle back again, not this untrolleyed stranger with the grim and spastic preoccupation with the news. Of the many unpleasant facets of this stranger's personality, one glowed brightest, and that was that he was the sort of man who would walk out the way he did and stay away as long as he had. Ergo, he was that undesirable person just as long as he stayed away, and tracking him down would, if it returned him against his will, return to her only a person who was not the person she missed.

Yet she was dissatisfied with herself, for all that she was the injured party and had wounds less painful than the pangs of conscience. She had always prided herself on being a good wife, and had done many things in the past which were counter to her reason and her desires purely because they were consistent with being a good wife. So as time went on she gravitated away from the "what shall I do?" area into the "what ought a good wife to do?" spectrum, and after a great deal of careful thought, went to se a psychiatrist.

He was a fairly intelligent psychiatrist which is to say he caught on to the obvious a little faster than most people. For example he became aware in only four minutes of conversation that MacLyle's wife Esther had not come to him on her own behalf, and further, decided to hear her out completely before resolving to treat her. When she had quite finished and he had dug out enough corroborative detail to get the picture, he went into a long silence and cogitated. He matched the broad pattern of MacLyle's case with his reading and his experience, recognized the challenge, the clinical worth of the case, the probable value of the heirloom diamond pendant worn by his visitor. He placed his finger tips together, lowered his fine young head, gazed through his eyebrows at MacLyle's wife Esther, and took up the gauntlet. At the prospects of getting her husband back safe and sane, she thanked him quietly and left the office with mixed emotions. The fairly intelligent psychiatrist drew a deep breath and began making arrangements with another headshrinker to take over his other patients, both of them, while he was away, because he figured to be away quite a while.

It was appallingly easy for him to trace MacLyle. He did not go near the lawyer. The solid foundation of all skip tracers and Bureaus of Missing Persons, in their *modus operandi*, is the piece of applied psychology which dictates that a man might change his name and his address, but he will seldom—can seldom—change the things he does, particularly the things he does to amuse himself. The ski addict doesn't skip to Florida, though he might make Banff instead of an habitual Mount Tremblant. A philatelist is not likely to mount butterflies. Hence when the psychiatrist found, among MacLyle's papers, some snapshots and brochures, dating from college days, of the towering Rockies, of bears feeding by the roadside, and especially of season after season's souvenirs of a particular resort to which he had never brought his wife and which he had not visited since he married her, it was worth a feeler, which went out in the form of a request to that state's police for information on a man of such-and-such a description driving so-and-so with out-of-state plates, plus a request that the man not be detained nor warned, but only that he, the fairly intelligent psychiatrist, be notified. He threw out other lines, too, but this is the one that hooked the fish. It was a matter of weeks before a state patrol car happened by MacLyle's favorite general store: after that it was a matter of minutes before the information was in the hands of the psychiatrist. He said nothing to MacLyle's wife Esther except good-by for a while, and this bill is payable now, and then took off, bearing with him a bag of tricks.

He rented a car at the airport nearest MacLyle's hideout and drove a long, thirsty, climbing way until he came to the general store. There he interviewed the proprietor, learning some eighteen hundred items about how bad business could get, how hot it was, how much rain hadn't fallen and how much was needed, the tragedy of being blamed for high markups when anyone with the brains God gave a goose ought to know it cost plenty to ship things out here, especially in the small quantities necessitated by business being so bad and all; and betwixt and between, he learned eight or ten items about MacLyle—the exact location of his cabin, the fact that he seemed to have turned into a deaf-mute who was also unable to read, and that he must be crazy because who but a crazy man would want eighty-four different half-pint cans of house paint or, for that matter, live out here when he didn't have to?

The psychiatrist got loose after a while and drove off, and the country got higher and dustier and more lost every mile, until he began to pray that nothing would go wrong with the car, and sure enough, ten minutes later something had. Any car that made a noise like the one he began to hear was strictly a shotrod, and he pulled over to the side to worry about it. He turned off the motor and the noise went right on, and he began to realize that the sound was not in the car or even near it, but came from somewhere uphill. There was a mile and a half more of the hill to go, and he drove it in increasing amazement, because that sound got louder and more impossible all the time. It was sort of like music, but like no music currently heard on this or any other planet. It was a solo voice, brass, with muscles. The upper notes, of which there seemed to be about two octaves, were wild and unmusical, the middle was rough, but the low tones were like the speech of these mountains themselves, big up to the sky, hot, and more natural than anything ought to be, basic as a bear's fang. Yet all the notes were perfect—their intervals were perfect—this awful noise was tuned like an electronic organ. The psychiatrist had a good ear, though for a while he wondered how long he'd have any ears at all, and he realized all these things about the sound, as well as the fact that it was rendering one of the more primitive fingering studies from Czerny, Book One, the droning little horror that goes: *do mi fa sol la sol fa mi, re fa sol la ti la sol fa, mi sol la* . . . etcetera, inchworming up the scale and then descending hand over hand.

He saw blue sky almost under his front tires and wrenched the wheel hard over, and found himself in the grassy yard of a made-over prospector's cabin, but that he didn't notice right away because sitting in front of it was what he described to himself, startled as he was out of his professional detachment, as the craziest-looking man he had ever seen.

He was sitting under a parched, wind-warped Engelmann spruce. He was barefoot up to the armpits. He wore the top half of a skivvy shirt and a hat the shape of one of those conical Boy Scout tents when one of the Boy Scouts has left the pole home. And he was playing, or anyway practicing, the ophicleide, and on his shoulders was a little moss of spruce needles, a small shower of which descended from the tree every time he hit on or under the low B♭. Only a mouse trapped inside a tuba during band practice can know precisely what it's like to stand that close to an operating ophicleide.

It was MacLyle all right, looming well fed and filled out. When he saw the psychiatrist's car he went right on playing, but, catching the psychiatrist's eye, he winked, smiled with the small corner of lip which showed from behind the large cup of the mouthpiece, and twiddled three fingers of his right hand, all he could manage of a wave without stopping. And he didn't stop either until he had scaled the particular octave he was working on and let himself down the other side. Then he put the ophicleide down carefully and let it lean against the spruce tree, and got up. The psychiatrist had become aware, as the last stupendous notes rolled away down the mountain, of his extreme isolation with this offbeat patient, of the unconcealed health and vigor of the man, and of the presence of the precipice over which he had almost driven his car a moment before, and had rolled up his window and buttoned the door lock and was feeling grateful for them. But the warm good humor and genuine welcome on MacLyle's sunburned face drove away fright and even caution, and almost before he knew what he was doing the psychiatrist had the door open and was stooping up out of the car, thinking, merry is a disused word but that's what he is, by God, a merry man. He called him by name but either MacLyle did not hear him or didn't care; he just put out a big warm hand and the psychiatrist took it. He could feel hard flat calluses in MacLyle's hand, and the controlled strength an elephant uses to lift a bespangled child in its trunk; he smiled at the image, because after all MacLyle was not a particularly large man, there was just that feeling about him. And once the smile found itself there it wouldn't go away.

He told MacLyle that he was a writer trying to soak up some of this magnificent country and had just been driving wherever the turn of the road led him, and here he was; but before he was half through he became conscious of MacLyle's eyes, which were in some indescribable way very much on him but not at all on anything he said; it was precisely as if he had stood there and hummed a tune. MacLyle seemed to be willing to listen to the sound until it was finished, and even to enjoy it, but that enjoyment was going to be all he got out of it. The psychiatrist finished anyway and MacLyle waited a moment as if to see if there would be any more, and when there wasn't he gave out more of that luminous smile and cocked his head toward the cabin. MacLyle led the way, with his visitor bringing up the rear with some platitudes about nice place you got here. As they entered, he suddenly barked at that unresponsive back, "Can't you hear me?" and MacLyle, without turning, only waved him on.

They walked into such a clutter and clabber of colors that the psychiatrist stopped dead, blinking. One wall had been removed and replaced with glass panes; it overlooked the precipice and put the little building afloat on haze. All the walls were hung with clean white chenille bedspreads, and the floor was white, and there seemed to be much more light indoors here than outside. Opposite the large window was an oversized easel made of peeled poles, notched and lashed together with baling wire, and on it was a huge canvas, most non-objective, in the purest and most uncompromising colors. Part of it was unquestionably this room, or at least its air of colored confusion here and all infinity yonder. The ophicleide was in the picture, painstakingly reproduced, looking like the hopper of some giant infernal machine, and in the foreground, some flowers; but the central figure repulsed him—more, it repulsed everything which surrounded it. It did not look exactly like anything familiar and, in a disturbed way, he was happy about that.

Stacked on the floor on each side of the easel were other paintings some daubs, some full of ruled lines and overlapping planes, but all in this achingly pure color. He realized what was being done with the dozens of colors of house paint in little cans which had so intrigued the storekeeper.

In odd places around the room were clay sculptures, most mounted on pedestals made of sections of tree trunks large enough to stand firmly on their sawed ends. Some of the pedestals were peeled, some painted, and in some the bark texture or the bulges or clefts in the wood had been carried right up into the model, and in others clay had been knived or pressed into the bark all the way down to the floor. Some of the clay was painted, some not, some ought to have been. There were free forms and gollywogs, a marsupial woman and a guitar with legs, and some, but not an overweening number, of the symbolisms which preoccupy even fairly intelligent psychiatrists. Nowhere was there any furniture per se. There were shelves at all levels and of varying lengths, bearing nail kegs, bolts of cloth, canned foods, tools and cooking untensils. There was a sort of table but it was mostly a workbench, with a vise at one end and at the other, half finished, a crude but exceedingly ingenious foot-powered potter's wheel.

He wondered where MacLyle slept, so he asked him, and again MacLyle reacted as if the words were not words, but a series of pleasant sounds, cocking his head and waiting to see if there would be any more. So the psychiatrist resorted to sign language, making a pillow of his two hands, laying his head on it, closing his eyes. He opened them to see MacLyle nodding eagerly, then going to the white-draped wall.

From behind the chenille he brought a hammock, one end of which was fastened to the wall. The other end he carried to the big window and hung on a hook screwed to a heavy stud between the panes. To lie in that hammock would be to swing between heaven and earth like Mahomet's tomb, with all that sky and scenery virtually surrounding the sleeper. His admiration for this idea ceased as MacLyle began making urgent indications for him to get into the hammock. He backed off warily, expostulating, trying to convey to MacLyle that he only wondered, he just wanted to know: no, *no,* he wasn't tired, dammit; but MacLyle became so insistent that he picked the psychiatrist up like a child sulking at bedtime and carried him to the hammock. Any impulse to kick or quarrel was quenched by the nature of this and all other hammocks to be intolerant of shifting burdens, and by the proximity of the large window, which he now saw was built leaning outward, enabling one to look out of the hammock straight down a minimum of four hundred and eighty feet. So all right, he concluded, if you say so. I'm sleepy.

So for the next two hours he lay in the hammock watching MacLyle putter about the place, thinking more or less professional thoughts.

He doesn't or can't speak (he diagnosed): aphasia, motor. He doesn't or can't understand speech: aphasia, sensory. He won't or can't read and write: alexia. And what else?

He looked at all that art—if it *was* art, and any that was, was art by accident—and the gadgetry: the chuntering windmill outside, the sashweight door closer. He let his eyes follow a length of clothesline dangling unobtrusively down the leaning center post to which his hammock was fastened, and the pulley and fittings from which it hung, and its extension clear across the ceiling to the back wall, and understood finally that it would, when pulled, open two long, narrow horizontal hatches for through ventilation. A small door behind the chenille led to what he correctly surmised was a primitive powder room, built to overhang the precipice, the most perfect no-plumbing solution for that convenience he had ever seen.

He watched MacLyle putter. That was the only word for it, and his actions were the best example of puttering he had ever seen. MacLyle lifted, shifted, and put things down, backed off to judge, returned to lay an approving hand on the thing he had moved. Net effect, nothing tangible—yet one could not say there was no effect, because of the intense satisfaction the man radiated. For minutes he would stand, head cocked, smiling slightly, regarding the half-finished potter's wheel, then explode into activity, sawing, planing, drilling. He would add the finished piece to the cranks and connecting rods already completed, pat it as if it were an obedient child, and walk away, leaving the rest of the job for some other time. With a wood-rasp he carefully removed the nose from one of his dried clay figures, and meticulously put on a new one. Always there was this absorption in his own products and processes, and the air of total reward in everything. And there was time, there seemed to be time enough for everything, and always would be.

Here is a man, thought the fairly intelligent psychiatrist, in retreat, but in a retreat the like of which my science has not yet described. For observe: he has reacted toward the primitive in terms of supplying himself with his needs with his own hands and by his own ingenuity, and yet there is nothing primitive in those needs themselves. He works constantly to achieve the comforts which his history has conditioned him to in the past—electric lights, cross-ventilation, trouble-free waste disposal. He exhibits a profound humility in the low rates he pays himself for his labor: he is building a potter's wheel apparently in order to make his own cooking vessels, and since wood is cheap and clay free, his vessel can only cost him less than engine-turned aluminum by a very low evaluation of his own efforts.

His skills are less than his energy (mused the psychiatrist). His carpentry, like his painting and sculpture, shows considerable intelligence, but only moderate training; he can construct but not beautify, draw but not draft, and reach the artistically pleasing only by not erasing the random shake, the accidental cut; so that real creation in his work is, like any random effect, rare and unpredictable. Therefore his reward is in the area of satisfaction—about as wide a generalization as one can make.

What satisfaction? Not in possessions themselves, for this man could have bought better for less. Not in excellence in itself, for he obviously could be satisfied with less than perfection. Freedom, perhaps, from routine, from dominations of work? Hardly, because for all that complexity of this cluttered cottage, it had its order and its system; the presence of an alarm clock conveyed a good deal in this area. He wasn't dominated by regularity—he used it. And his satisfaction? Why, it must lie in this closed circle, himself to himself, and in the very fact of non-communication!

Retreat . . . retreat. Retreat to savagery and you don't engineer your cross-ventilation or adjust a five-hundred-foot gravity flush for your john. Retreat into infancy and you don't design and build a potter's wheel. Retreat from people and you don't greet a stranger like . . .

Wait.

Maybe a stranger who had something to communicate, or some way of communication, wouldn't be so welcome. An unsettling thought, that. Running the risk of doing something MacLyle didn't like would be, possibly, a little more unselfish than the challenge warranted.

MacLyle began to cook.

Watching him, the psychiatrist reflected suddenly that this withdrawn and wordless individual was a happy one, in his own matrix; further, he had fulfilled all his obligations and responsibilities and was bothering no one.

It was intolerable.

It was intolerable because it was a violation of the prime directive of psychiatry—at least, of that school of psychiatry which he professed, and he was not going to confuse himself by considerations of other, less-tried theories—*It is the function of psychiatry to adjust the aberrate to society, and to restore or increase his usefulness to it.* To yield, to rationalize this man's behavior as balance, would be to fly in the face of science itself; for this particular psychiatry finds its most successful approaches in the scientific method, and it is unprofitable to debate whether or not it is or is not a science. To its practitioner it is, and that's that; it has to be. Operationally speaking, what has been found true, even statistically, must be Truth, and all other things, even Possible, kept the hell out of the toolbox. No known Truth allowed a social entity to secede this way, and, for one, this fairly intelligent psychiatrist was not going to give this—this *suicide* his blessing.

He must, then, find a way to communicate with MacLyle, and when he had found it, he must communicate to him the error of his ways. Without getting thrown over the cliff.

He became aware that MacLyle was looking at him, twinkling. He smiled back before he knew what he was doing, and obeyed MacLyle's beckoning gesture. He eased himself out of the hammock and went to the workbench, where a steaming stew was set out in earthenware bowls. The bowls stood on large plates and were surrounded by a band of carefully sliced tomatoes. He tasted them. They were obviously vine-ripened and had been speckled with a dark green paste which, after studious attention to its aftertaste, he identified as fresh basil mashed with fresh garlic and salt. The effect was symphonic.

He followed suit when MacLyle picked up his own bowl and they went outside and squatted under the old Engelmann spruce to eat. It was a quiet and pleasant occasion, and during it the psychiatrist had plenty of opportunity to size up his man and plan his campaign. He was quite sure now how to proceed, and all he needed was opportunity, which presented itself when MacLyle rose, stretched, smiled, and went indoors. The psychiatrist followed him to the door and saw him crawl into the hammock and fall almost instantly asleep.

The psychiatrist went to his car and got out his bag of tricks. And so it was late in the afternoon, when MacLyle emerged stretching and yawning from his nap, he found his visitor under the spruce tree, hefting the ophicleide and twiddling its keys in a perplexed and investigatory fashion. MacLyle strode over to him and lifted the ophicleide away with a pleasant I'll-show-you smile, got the monstrous contraption into position, and ran his tongue around the inside of the mouthpiece, large as a demitasse. He had barely time to pucker up his lips at the strange taste there before his irises rolled up completely out of sight and he collapsed like a grounded parachute. The psychiatrist was able only to snatch away the ophicleide in time to keep the mouthpiece from knocking out MacLyle's front teeth.

He set the ophicleide carefully against the tree and straightened MacLyle's limbs. He concentrated for a moment on the pulse, and turned the head to one side so saliva would not drain down the flaccid throat, and then went back to his bag of tricks. He came back and knelt, and MacLyle did not even twitch at the bite of the hypodermics: a careful blend of the non-soporific tranquilizers Frenquel, chlorpromazine and Reserpine, and a judicious dose of scopolamine, a hypnotic.

The psychiatrist got water and carefully sponged out the man's mouth, not caring to wait out another collapse the next time he swallowed. Then there was nothing to do but wait, and plan.

Exactly on schedule, according to the psychiatrist's wrist watch, MacLyle groaned and coughed weakly. The psychiatrist immediately and in a firm quiet voice told him not to move. Also not to think. He stayed out of the immediate range of MacLyle's unfocused eyes and explained that MacLyle must trust him, because he was there to help, and not to worry about feeling mixed-up or disoriented. "You don't know where you are or how you got here," he informed MacLyle. He also told MacLyle, who was past forty, that he was thirty-seven years old, but he knew what he was doing.

MacLyle just lay there obediently and thought these things over and waited for more information. He didn't know where he was or how he had gotten here. He did know that he must trust this voice, the owner of which was here to help him; that he was thirty-seven years old; and his name. In these things he lay and marinated. The drugs kept him conscious, docile, submissive and without guile. The psychiatrist observed and exulted: oh you azacyclonol, he chanted silently to himself, you pretty piperidyl, handsome hydrochloride, subtle Serpasil . . . Confidently he left MacLyle and went into the cabin where, after due search, he found some decent clothes and some socks and shoes and brought them out and wrapped the supine patient in them. He helped MacLyle across the clearing and into his car, humming as he did so, for there is none so happy as an expert faced with excellence in his specialty. MacLyle sank back into the cushions and gave one wondering glance at the cabin and at the blare of late light from the bell of the ophicleide; but the psychiatrist told him firmly that these things had nothing to do with him, nothing at all, and MacLyle smiled relievedly and fell to watching the scenery go by, passive as a Pekingese. As they passed the general store MacLyle stirred, but said nothing about it. Instead he asked the psychiatrist if the Ardsmere station was open yet, whereupon the psychiatrist could barely answer him for the impulse to purr like a cat: the Ardsmere station, two stops before MacLyle's suburban town, had burned down and been rebuilt almost six years ago; so now he knew for sure that MacLyle was living in a time preceding his difficulties—a time during which, of course, MacLyle had been able to talk. He crooned his appreciation for chlorpromazine (which had helped MacLyle be tranquil) and he made up a silent song, o doll o' mine, scopolamine, which had made him so very suggestible. But all of this the psychiatrist kept to himself, and answered gravely that yes, they had the Ardsmere station operating again. And did he have anything else on his mind?

MacLyle considered this carefully, but since all the immediate questions were answered—unswervingly, he *knew* he was safe in the hands of this man, whoever he was; he knew (he thought) his correct age and that he was expected to feel disoriented; he was also under a command not to think—he placidly shook his head and went back to watching the road unroll under their wheels. "Fallen Rock Zone," he murmured as they passed a sign. The psychiatrist drove happily down the mountain and across the flats, back to the city where he had hired the car. He left it at the railroad station ("Rail Crossing Road," murmured MacLyle) and made reservations for a compartment on the train, aircraft being too open and public for his purposes and far too fast for the hourly rate he suddenly decided to apply.

They had time for a silent and companionable dinner before train

time, and then at last they were aboard, solid ground beneath, a destination ahead, and the track joints applauding.

The psychiatrist turned off all but one reading lamp and leaned forward. MacLyle's eyes dilated readily to the dimmer light, and the psychiatrist leaned back comfortably and asked him how he felt. He felt
fine and said so. The psychiatrist asked him how old he was and
MacLyle told him, thirty-seven, but he sounded doubtful.

Knowing that the scopolamine was wearing off but the other drugs,
the tranquilizers, would hang on for a bit, the psychiatrist drew a deep
breath and removed the suggestion; he told MacLyle the truth about his
age, and brought him up to the here and now. MacLyle just looked
puzzled for a few minutes and then his features settled into an expression that can only be described as not unhappy. "Porter," was all he
said, gazing at the push button on the partition with its little metal sign,
and announced that he could read now.

The psychiatrist nodded sagely and offered no comment, being quite
willing to let a patient stew in his own juice as long as he produced essence.

MacLyle abruptly demanded to know why he had lost the powers of
speech and reading. The psychiatrist raised his eyebrows a little and his
shoulders a good deal and smiled one of those "You-tell-me" smiles,
and then got up and suggested they sleep on it. He got the porter in to
fix the beds and as an afterthought told the man to come back with the
evening papers. Nothing can orient a cultural expatriate better than the
evening papers. The man did. MacLyle paid no attention to this, one
way or the other. He just climbed into the psychiatrist's spare pajamas
thoughtfully and they went to bed.

The psychiatrist didn't know if MacLyle had awakened him on purpose or whether the train's slowing down for a watering stop had done
it, or both; anyway he awoke about three in the morning to find
MacLyle standing beside his bunk looking at him fixedly. He closed his
eyes and screwed them tight and opened them again, and MacLyle was
still there, and now he noticed that MacLyle's reading lamp was lit and
the papers were scattered all over the floor. MacLyle said, "You're
some kind of a doctor," in a flat voice.

The psychiatrist admitted it.

MacLyle said, "Well, this ought to make some sense to you. I was
skiing out here years ago when I was a college kid. Accident, fellow I
was with broke his leg. Compound. Made him comfortable as I could
and went for help. Came back, he'd slid down the mountain, thrashing

around, I guess. Crevasse, down in the bottom; took two days to find him, three days to get him out. Frostbite. Gangrene."

The psychiatrist tried to look as if he was following this.

MacLyle said, "The one thing I always remember, him pulling back the bandages all the time to look at his leg. Knew it was gone, couldn't keep himself from watching the stuff spread around and upward. Didn't like to; *had* to. Tried to stop him, finally had to help him or he'd hurt himself. Every ten, fifteen minutes all the way down to the lodge, fifteen hours, looking under the bandages."

The psychiatrist tried to think of something to say and couldn't, so he looked wise and waited.

MacLyle said, "That Donne, that John Donne I used to spout, I always believed that."

The psychiatrist began to misquote the thing about send not to ask for whom the bell . . .

"Yeah, that, but especially '*any man's death diminishes me, because I am involved in mankind.*' I believed that," MacLyle repeated. "I believed more than that. Not only death. Damn foolishness diminishes me because I am involved. People all the time pushing people around diminishes me. Everybody hungry for a fast buck diminishes me." He picked up a sheet of newspaper and let it slip away; it flapped off to the corner of the compartment like a huge grave-moth. "I was getting diminished to death and I had to watch it happening to me like that kid with the gangrene, so that's why." The train, crawling now, lurched suddenly and yielded. MacLyle's eyes flicked to the window, where neon beer signs and a traffic light were reluctantly being framed. MacLyle leaned close to the psychiatrist. "I just had to get un-involved with mankind before I got diminished altogether, everything mankind did was my fault. So I did and now here I am involved again." MacLyle abruptly went to the door. "And for that, thanks."

From a dusty throat the psychiatrist asked him what he was going to do.

"Do?" asked MacLyle cheerfully. "Why, I'm going out there and diminish mankind right back." He was out in the corridor with the door closed before the psychiatrist so much as sat up. He banged it open again and leaned in. He said in the sanest of all possible voices, "Now mind you, doctor, this is only one man's opinion," and was gone. He killed four people before they got him.

Through Time and Space with Ferdinand Feghoot

Grendel Briarton

IN 2778, Ferdinand Feghoot landed on Dallas XIX, a previously unknown planet. He and his crew were immediately seized by the natives, trussed, and carried to a nearby veterinary hospital for investigation.

Lying there in the operating theater, the horrified crew saw a Dallasian nine feet high towering over their captain. He (the Dallasian) was as shaggy as a Kodiak bear. From the crown of his mushroom-shaped head grew a hand-like appendage holding a huge hypodermic full of fuming green fluids.

They started to scream out a warning. But they suddenly stopped—their captain had chuckled! They stared at him open-mouthed. He grinned back.

"No need to get scared," said Ferdinand Feghoot. "It's just a furry with a syringe on top."

Not with a Bang
Damon Knight

TEN MONTHS after the last plane passed over, Rolf Smith knew beyond doubt that only one other human being had survived. Her name was Louise Oliver, and he was sitting opposite her in a department-store cafe in Salt Lake City. They were eating canned Vienna sausages and drinking coffee.

Sunlight struck through a broken pane, lying like a judgment on the cloudy air of the room. Inside and outside, there was no sound; only a stifling rumor of absence. The clatter of dishware in the kitchen, the heavy rumble of streetcars: never again. There was sunlight; and silence; and the watery, astonished eyes of Louise Oliver.

He leaned forward, trying to capture the attention of those fishlike eyes for a second. "Darling," he said, "I respect your views, naturally. But I've got to make you see that they're impractical."

She looked at him with faint surprise, then away again. Her head shook slightly: No. *No, Rolf. I will not live with you in sin.*

Smith thought of the women of France, of Russia, of Mexico, of the South Seas. He had spent three months in the ruined studios of a radio station in Rochester, listening to the voices until they stopped. There had been a large colony in Sweden, including an English cabinet minister. They reported that Europe was gone. Simply gone; there was

DAMON KNIGHT *has been a short story writer, novelist, editor and critic (he is a former book reviewer for F&SF and won a Hugo for his criticism in 1956). This story appeared in F&SF's second issue (Winter–Spring 1950) and should have closed the door forever on last-man-on-Earth stories. Of course it didn't.*

not an acre that had not been swept clean by radioactive dust. They had two planes and enough fuel to take them anywhere on the Continent; but there was nowhere to go. Three of them had the plague; then eleven; then all.

There was a bomber pilot who had fallen near a government radio in Palestine. He did not last long, because he had broken some bones in the crash; but he had seen the vacant waters where the Pacific Islands should have been. It was his guess that the Arctic ice-fields had been bombed. He did not know whether that had been a mistake or not.

There were no reports from Washington, from New York, from London, Paris, Moscow, Chungking, Sydney. You could not tell who had been destroyed by disease, who by the dust, who by bombs.

Smith himself had been a laboratory assistant in a team that was trying to find an antibiotic for the plague. His superiors had found one that worked sometimes, but it was a little too late. When he left, Smith took along with him all there was of it—forty ampoules, enough to last him for years.

Louise had been a nurse in a genteel hospital near Denver. According to her, something rather odd had happened to the hospital as she was approaching it the morning of the attack. She was quite calm when she said this, but a vague look came into her eyes and her shattered expression seemed to slip a little more. Smith did not press her for an explanation.

Like himself, she had found a radio station which still functioned, and when Smith discovered that she had not contracted the plague, he agreed to meet her. She was, apparently, naturally immune. There must have been others, a few at least; but the bombs and the dust had not spared them.

It seemed very awkward to Louise that not one Protestant minister was left alive.

The trouble was, she really meant it. It had taken Smith a long time to believe it, but it was true. She would not sleep in the same hotel with him, either; she expected, and received, the utmost courtesy and decorum. Smith had learned his lesson. He walked on the outside of the rubble-heaped sidewalks; he opened doors for her, when there were still doors; he held her chair; he refrained from swearing. He courted her.

Louise was forty or thereabouts, at least five years older than Smith. He often wondered how old she thought she was. The shock of seeing whatever it was that had happened to the hospital, the patients she had cared for, had sent her mind scuttling back to her childhood. She tacitly admitted that everyone else in the world was dead, but she seemed to regard it as something one did not mention.

A hundred times in the last three weeks, Smith had felt an almost irresistible impulse to break her thin neck and go his own way. But there was no help for it; she was the only woman in the world, and he needed her. If she died, or left him, he died. *Old bitch!* he thought to himself furiously, and carefully kept the thought from showing on his face.

"Louise, honey," he told her gently, "I want to spare your feelings as much as I can. You know that."

"Yes, Rolf," she said, staring at him with the face of a hypnotized chicken.

Smith forced himself to go on. "We've got to face the facts, unpleasant as they may be. Honey, we're the only man and the only woman there are. We're like Adam and Eve in the Garden of Eden."

Louise's face took on a slightly disgusted expression. She was obviously thinking of fig-leaves.

"Think of the generations unborn," Smith told her, with a tremor in his voice. *Think about me for once. Maybe you're good for another ten years, maybe not.* Shuddering, he thought of the second stage of the disease—the helpless rigidity, striking without warning. He'd had one such attack already, and Louise had helped him out of it. Without her, he would have stayed like that till he died, the hypodermic that would save him within inches of his rigid hand. He thought desperately, *If I'm lucky, I'll get at least two kids out of you before you croak. Then I'll be safe.*

He went on, "God didn't mean for the human race to end like this. He spared us, you and me, to—" He paused; how could he say it without offending her? "Parents" wouldn't do—too suggestive. "—to carry on the torch of life," he ended. There. That was sticky enough.

Louise was staring vaguely over his shoulder. Her eyelids blinked regularly, and her mouth made little rabbit-like motions in the same rhythm.

Smith looked down at his wasted thighs under the tabletop. *I'm not strong enough to force her,* he thought. *Christ, if I were strong enough!*

He felt the futile rage again, and stifled it. He had to keep his head, because this might be his last chance. Louise had been talking lately, in the cloudy language she used about everything, of going up in the mountains to pray for guidance. She had not said, "alone," but it was easy enough to see that she pictured it that way. He had to argue her around before her resolve stiffened. He concentrated furiously, and tried once more.

The pattern of words went by like a distant rumbling. Louise heard a phrase here and there; each of them fathered chains of thought, binding her revery tighter. "Our duty to humanity . . ." Mama had often said —that was in the old house on Waterbury Street of course, before Mama had taken sick—she had said, "Child, your duty is to be clean, polite, and God-fearing. Pretty doesn't matter. There's a plenty of plain women that have got themselves good, Christian husbands."

Husbands . . . To have and to hold . . . Orange blossoms, and the bridesmaids; the organ music. Through the haze, she saw Rolf's lean, wolfish face. Of course, he was the only one she'd ever get; *she* knew that well enough. Gracious, when a girl was past twenty-five, she had to take what she could get.

But I sometimes wonder if he's really a nice *man,* she thought.

". . . in the eyes of God . . ." She remembered the stained-glass windows in the old First Episcopalian Church, and how she always thought God was looking down at her through that brilliant transparency. Perhaps He was still looking at her, though it seemed sometimes that He had forgotten. Well, of course she realized that marriage customs changed, and if you couldn't have a regular minister. . . . But it was really a shame, an outrage almost, that if she were actually going to marry this man, she couldn't have all those nice things . . . There wouldn't even be any wedding presents. Not even that. But of course Rolf would give her anything she wanted. She saw his face again, noticed the narrow black eyes staring at her with ferocious purpose, the thin mouth that jerked in a slow, regular tic, the hairy lobes of the ears below the tangle of black hair.

He oughtn't to let his hair grow so long, she thought, *it isn't quite decent.* Well, she could change all that. If she did marry him, she'd certainly make him change his ways. It was no more than her duty.

He was talking now about a farm he'd seen outside town—a good big house and a barn. There was no stock, he said, but they could get some later. And they'd plant things, and have their own food to eat, not go to restaurants all the time.

She felt a touch on her hand, lying pale before her on the table. Rolf's brown, stubby fingers, black-haired above and below the knuckles, were touching hers. He had stopped talking for a moment, but now he was speaking again, still more urgently. She drew her hand away.

He was saying, ". . . and you'll have the finest wedding dress you ever saw, with a bouquet. Everything you want, Louise, everything . . ."

A wedding dress! And flowers, even if there couldn't be any minister! Well, why hadn't the fool said so before?

Rolf stopped halfway through a sentence, aware that Louise had said quite clearly, "Yes, Rolf, I will marry you if you wish."

Stunned, he wanted her to repeat it, but dared not ask, "What did you say?" for fear of getting some fantastic answer, or none at all. He breathed deeply. He said, "Today, Louise?"

She said, "Well, *today* . . . I don't know quite . . . Of course, if you think you can make all the arrangements in time, but it does seem . . ."

Triumph surged through Smith's body. He had the advantage now, and he'd ride it. "Say you will, dear," he urged her; "say yes, and make me the happiest man . . ."

Even then, his tongue balked at the rest of it; but it didn't matter. She nodded submissively. "Whatever you think best, Rolf."

He rose, and she allowed him to kiss her pale, sapless cheek. "We'll leave right away," he said. "If you'll excuse me for just a minute, dear?"

He waited for her "Of course" and then left her, making footprints in the furred carpet of dust down toward the end of the room. Just a few more hours he'd have to speak to her like that, and then, in her eyes, she'd be committed to him forever. Afterwards, he could do with her as he liked—beat her when he pleased, submit her to any proof of his scorn and revulsion, use her. Then it would not be too bad, being the last man on Earth—not bad at all. She might even have a daughter . . .

He found the washroom door and entered. He took a step inside, and froze, balanced by a trick of motion, upright but helpless. Panic struck at his throat as he tried to turn his head and failed; tried to scream, and failed. Behind him, he was aware of a tiny click as the door, cushioned by the hydraulic check, shut forever. It was not locked; but its other side bore the warning: MEN.

Flowers for Algernon
Daniel Keyes

progris riport 1—martch 5 1965

DR. STRAUSS SAYS I shud rite down what I think and evrey thing that happins to me from now on. I dont know why but he says its importint so they will see if they will use me. I hope they use me. Miss Kinnian says maybe they can make me smart. I want to be smart. My name is Charlie Gordon. I am 37 years old and 2 weeks ago was my birthday. I have nuthing more to rite now so I will close for today.

progris riport 2—martch 6

I had a test today. I think I faled it. and I think that maybe now they wont use me. What happind is a nice young man was in the room and he had some white cards with ink spillled all over them. He sed Charlie what do you see on this card. I was very skared even tho I had my rabits foot in my pockit because when I was a kid I always faled tests in school and I spillled ink to.

I told him I saw a inkblot. He said yes and it made me feel good. I thot that was all but when I got up to go he stopped me. He said now

---

"FLOWERS FOR ALGERNON" (*April 1959*) *is perhaps the most famous story F&SF has ever published. It won a Hugo award in 1960 and was later developed into a novel (*Nebula Award winner in 1966*), a teleplay and a film (*retitled as* Charly) *which won Cliff Robertson an Academy Award as Best Actor of 1968. It has recently been produced as a stage musical which opened in June 1979 in London.*

sit down Charlie we are not thru yet. Then I dont remember so good but he wantid me to say what was in the ink. I dint see nuthing in the ink but he said there was picturs there other pepul saw some picturs. I coudnt see any picturs. I reely tryed to see. I held the card close up and then far away. Then I said if I had my glases I coud see better I usally only ware my glases in the movies or TV but I said they are in the closit in the hall. I got them. Then I said let me see that card agen I bet Ill find it now.

I tryed hard but I still coudnt find the picturs I only saw the ink. I told him maybe I need new glases. He rote somthing down on a paper and I got skared of faling the test. I told him it was a very nice inkblot with littel points al around the eges. He looked very sad so that wasnt it. I said please let me try agen. Ill get it in a few minits becaus Im not so fast somtimes. Im a slow reeder too in Miss Kinnians class for slow adults but I'm trying very hard.

He gave me a chance with another card that had 2 kinds of ink spillled on it red and blue.

He was very nice and talked slow like Miss Kinnian does and he explained it to me that it was a *raw shok*. He said pepul see things in the ink. I said show me where. He said think. I told him I think a inkblot but that wasnt rite eather. He said what does it remind you—pretend something. I closd my eyes for a long time to pretend. I told him I pretned a fowntan pen with ink leeking all over a table cloth. Then he got up and went out.

I dont think I passd the *raw shok* test.

progris report 3—martch 7

Dr Strauss and Dr Nemur say it dont matter about the inkblots. I told them I dint spill the ink on the cards and I coudnt see anything in the ink. They said that maybe they will still use me. I said Miss Kinnian never gave me tests like that one only spelling and reading. They said Miss Kinnian told that I was her bestist pupil in the adult nite scool becaus I tryed the hardist and I reely wantid to lern. They said how come you went to the adult nite scool all by yourself Charlie. How did you find it. I said I askd pepul and sumbody told me where I shud go to lern to read and spell good. They said why did you want to. I told them becaus all my life I wantid to be smart and not dumb. But its very hard to be smart. They said you know it will probly be tempirery. I said yes. Miss Kinnian told me. I dont care if it herts.

Later I had more crazy tests today. The nice lady who gave it me told me the name and I asked her how do you spellit so I can rite it in my progris riport. THEMATIC APPERCEPTION TEST. I dont know the frist 2 words but I know what *test* means. You got to pass it or you get bad marks. This test lookd easy becaus I coud see the picturs. Only this time she dint want me to tell her the picturs. That mixd me up. I said the man yesterday said I shoud tell him what I saw in the ink she said that dont make no difrence. She said make up storys about the pepul in the picturs.

I told her how can you tell storys about pepul you never met. I said why shud I make up lies. I never tell lies any more becaus I always get caut.

She told me this test and the other one the raw-shok was for getting personalty. I laffed so hard. I said how can you get that thing from inkblots and fotos. She got sore and put her picturs away. I dont care. It was sily. I gess I faled that test too.

Later some men in white coats took me to a difernt part of the hospitil and gave me a game to play. It was like a race with a white mouse. They called the mouse Algernon. Algernon was in a box with a lot of twists and turns like all kinds of walls and they gave me a pencil and a paper with lines and lots of boxes. On one side it said START and on the other end it said FINISH. They said it was *amazed* and that Algernon and me had the same *amazed* to do. I dint see how we could have the same *amazed* if Algernon had a box and I had a paper but I dint say nothing. Anyway there wasnt time because the race started.

One of the men had a watch he was trying to hide so I woudnt see it so I tryed not to look and that made me nervus.

Anyway that test made me feel worser than all the others because they did it over 10 times with difernt *amazeds* and Algernon won every time. I dint know that mice were so smart. Maybe thats because Algernon is a white mouse. Maybe white mice are smarter then other mice.

progris riport 4—Mar 8

Their going to use me! Im so exited I can hardly write. Dr Nemur and Dr Strauss had a argament about it first. Dr Nemur was in the office when Dr Strauss brot me in. Dr Nemur was worryed about using me but Dr Strauss told him Miss Kinnian rekemmended me the best from all the people who she was teaching. I like Miss Kinnian becaus shes a very smart teacher. And she said Charlie your going to have a second chance. If you volenteer for this experament you mite get smart. They dont know if it will be perminint but theirs a chance. Thats why I said ok even when I was scared because she said it was an operashun. She said dont be scared Charlie you done so much with so little I think you deserv it most of all.

So I got scaird when Dr Nemur and Dr Strauss argud about it. Dr Strauss said I had something that was very good. He said I had a good *motor-vation*. I never even knew I had that. I felt proud when he said that not every body with an eye-q of 68 had that thing. I dont know what it is or where I got it but he said Algernon had it too. Algernons *motor-vation* is the cheese they put in his box. But it cant be that because I didnt eat any cheese this week.

Then he told Dr Nemur something I dint understand so while they were talking I wrote down some of the words.

He said Dr Nemur I know Charlie is not what you had in mind as the first of your new brede of intelek** (coudnt get the word) superman. But most people of his low ment** are host** and uncoop** they are usualy dull apath** and hard to reach. He has a good natcher hes intristed and eager to please.

Dr Nemur said remember he will be the first human beeng ever to have his intelijence trippled by surgicle meens.

Dr Strauss said exakly. Look at how well hes lerned to read and write for his low mentel age its as grate an acheve** as you and I lerning einstines therey of **vity without help. That shows the intenss motorvation. Its comparat** a tremen** achev** I say we use Charlie.

I dint get all the words and they were talking to fast but it sounded like Dr. Strauss was on my side and like the other one wasnt.

Then Dr Nemur nodded he said all right maybe your right. We will use Charlie. When he said that I got so exited I jumped up and shook his hand for being so good to me. I told him thank you doc you wont be sorry for giving me a second chance. And I mean it like I told him. After the operashun Im gonna try to be smart. Im gonna try awful hard.

progris ript 5—Mar 10

Im skared. Lots of people who work here and the nurses and the people who gave me the tests came to bring me candy and wish me luck. I hope I have luck. I got my rabits foot and my lucky penny and my horse shoe. Only a black cat crossed me when I was comming to the hospitil. Dr Strauss says dont be supersitis Charlie this is sience. Anyway Im keeping my rabits foot with me.

I asked Dr Strauss if Ill beat Algernon in the race after the operashun and he said maybe. If the operashun works Ill show that mouse I can be as smart as he is. Maybe smarter. Then Ill be abel to read better and spell the words good and know lots of things and be like other people. I want to be smart like other people. If it works perminint they will make everybody smart all over the wurld.

They dint give me anything to eat this morning. I dont know what that eating has to do with getting smart. Im very hungry and Dr Nemur took away my box of candy. That Dr Nemur is a grouch. Dr Strauss says I can have it back after the operashun. You cant eat befor a operashun . . .

Progress Report 6—Mar 15

The operashun dint hurt. He did it while I was sleeping. They took off the bandijis from my eyes and my head today so I can make a PROGRESS REPORT. Dr Nemur who looked at some of my other ones says I spell PROGRESS wrong and he told me how to spell it and REPORT too. I got to try and remember that.

I have a very bad memary for spelling. Dr Strauss says its ok to tell about all the things that happin to me but he says I shoud tell more about what I feel and what I think. When I told him I dont know how to think he said try. All the time when the bandijis were on my eyes I tryed to think. Nothing happened. I dont know what to think about. Maybe if I ask him he will tell me how I can think now that Im suppose to get smart. What do smart people think about. Fancy things I suppose. I wish I knew some fancy things alredy.

Progress Report 7—mar 19

Nothing is happining. I had lots of tests and different kinds of races with Algernon. I hate that mouse. He always beats me. Dr Strauss said I got to play those games. And he said some time I got to take those tests over again. Thse inkblots are stupid. And those pictures are stupid too. I like to draw a picture of a man and a woman but I wont make up lies about people.

I got a headache from trying to think so much. I thot Dr Strauss was my frend but he dont help me. He dont tell me what to think or when Ill get smart. Miss Kinnian dint come to see me. I think writing these progress reports are stupid too.

Progress Report 8—Mar 23

Im going back to work at the factery. They said it was better I shud go back to work but I cant tell anyone what the operashun was for and I have to come to the hospitil for an hour evry night after work. They are gonna pay me mony every month for lerning to be smart.

Im glad Im going back to work because I miss my job and all my frends and all the fun we have there.

Dr Strauss says I shud keep writing things down but I dont have to do it every day just when I think of something or something speshul happins. He says dont get discoridged because it takes time and it happins slow. He says it took a long time with Algernon before he got 3 times smarter than he was before. Thats why Algernon beats me all the time because he had that operashun too. That makes me feel better. I coud probly do that *amazed* faster than a reglar mouse. Maybe some day Ill beat Algernon. Boy that would be something. So far Algernon looks like he mite be smart perminent.

Mar 25 (I dont have to write PROGRESS REPORT on top any more just when I hand it in once a week for Dr Nemur to read. I just have to put the date on. That saves time)

We had a lot of fun at the factery today. Joe Carp said hey look where Charlie had his operashun what did they do Charlie put some brains in. I was going to tell him but I remembered Dr Strauss said no. Then Frank Reilly said what did you do Charlie forget your key and open your door the hard way. That made me laff. Their really my friends and they like me.

Sometimes somebody will say hey look at Joe or Frank or George he really pulled a Charlie Gordon. I dont know why they say that but they always laff. This morning Amos Borg who is the 4 man at Donnegans used my name when he shouted at Ernie the office boy. Ernie lost a packige. He said Ernie for godsake what are you trying to be a Charlie Gordon. I dont understand why he said that. I never lost any packiges.

Mar 28 Dr Strauss came to my room tonight to see why I dint come in like I was suppose to. I told him I dont like to race with Algernon any more. He said I dont have to for a while but I shud come in. He had a present for me only it wasnt a present but just for lend. I thot it was a little television but it wasnt. He said I got to turn it on when I go to sleep. I said your kidding why shud I turn it on when Im going to sleep. Who ever herd of a thing like that. But he said if I want to get smart I got to do what he says. I told him I dint think I was going to get smart and he put his hand on my sholder and said Charlie you dont know it yet but your getting smarter all the time. You wont notice for a while. I think he was just being nice to make me feel good because I dont look any smarter.

Oh yes I almost forgot. I asked him when I can go back to the class at Miss Kinnians school. He said I wont go their. He said that soon Miss Kinnian will come to the hospitil to start and teach me speshul. I was mad at her for not comming to see me when I got the operashun but I like her so maybe we will be frends again.

Mar 29 That crazy TV kept me up all night. How can I sleep with something yelling crazy things all night in my ears. And the nutty pictures. Wow. I dont know what it says when Im up so how am I going to know when Im sleeping.

Dr Strauss says its ok. He says my brains are lerning when I sleep and that will help me when Miss Kinnian starts my lessons in the hospitl (only I found out it isnt a hospitil its a labatory). I think its all crazy. If you can get smart when your sleeping why do people go to school. That thing I dont think will work. I use to watch the late show and the late late show on TV all the time and it never made me smart. Maybe you have to sleep while you watch it.

PROGRESS REPORT 9—*April 3*

Dr Strauss showed me how to keep the TV turned low so now I can sleep. I dont hear a thing. And I still dont understand what it says. A few times I play it over in the morning to find out what I lerned when I was sleeping and I dont think so. Miss Kinnian says Maybe its another langwidge or something. But most times it sounds american. It talks so fast faster then even Miss Gold who was my teacher in 6 grade and I remember she talked so fast I coudnt understand her.

I told Dr Strauss what good is it to get smart in my sleep. I want to be smart when Im awake. He says its the same thing and I have two minds. Theres the *subconscious* and the *conscious* (thats how you spell it). And one dont tell the other one what its doing. They dont even talk to each other. Thats why I dream. And boy have I been having crazy dreams. Wow. Ever since that night TV. The late late late late late show.

I forgot to ask him if it was only me or if everybody had those two minds.

(I just looked up the word in the dictionary Dr Strauss gave me. The word is *subconscious. adj. Of the nature of mental operations yet not present in consciousness; as, subconscious conflict of desires.*) Theres more but I still don't know what it means. This isnt a very good dictionary for dumb people like me.

Anyway the headache is from the party. My frends from the factery Joe Carp and Frank Reilly invited me to go with them to Muggsys Saloon for some drinks. I dont like to drink but they said we will have lots of fun. I had a good time.

Joe Carp said I shoud show the girls how I mop out the toilet in the factory and he got me a mop. I showed them and everyone laffed when I told that Mr Donnegan said I was the best janiter he ever had because I like my job and do it good and never come late or miss a day except for my operashun.

I said Miss Kinnian always said Charlie be proud of your job because you do it good.

Everybody laffed and we had a good time and they gave me lots of drinks and Joe said Charlie is a card when hes potted. I dont know what that means but everybody likes me and we have fun. I cant wait to be smart like my best frends Joe Carp and Frank Reilly.

I dont remember how the party was over but I think I went out to buy a newspaper and coffe for Joe and Frank and when I came back there was no one their. I looked for them all over till late. Then I dont remember so good but I think I got sleepy or sick. A nice cop brot me back home. Thats what my landlady Mrs Flynn says.

But I got a headache and a big lump on my head and black and blue all over. I think maybe I fell but Joe Carp says it was the cop they beat up drunks some times. I don't think so. Miss Kinnian says cops are to help people. Anyway I got a bad headache and Im sick and hurt all over. I dont think Ill drink anymore.

April 6 I beat Algernon! I dint even know I beat him until Burt the tester told me. Then the second time I lost because I got so exited I fell off the chair before I finished. But after that I beat him 8 more times. I must be getting smart to beat a smart mouse like Algernon. But I dont *feel* smarter.

I wanted to race Algernon some more but Burt said thats enough for one day. They let me hold him for a minit. Hes not so bad. Hes soft like a ball of cotton. He blinks and when he opens his eyes their black and pink on the eges.

I said can I feed him because I felt bad to beat him and I wanted to be nice and make frends. Burt said no Algernon is a very specshul mouse with an operashun like mine, and he was the first of all the animals to stay smart so long. He told me Algernon is so smart that every day he has to solve a test to get his food. Its a thing like a lock on a door that changes every time Algernon goes in to eat so he has to lern something new to get his food. That made me sad because if he coudnt lern he woud be hungry.

I dont think its right to make you pass a test to eat. How woud Dr Nemur like it to have to pass a test every time he wants to eat. I think Ill be frends with Algernon.

April 9 Tonight after work Miss Kinnian was at the laboratory. She looked like she was glad to see me but scared. I told her dont worry Miss Kinnian Im not smart yet and she laffed. She said I have confidence in you Charlie the way you struggled so hard to read and right better than all the others. At werst you will have it for a littel wile and your doing somthing for sience.

We are reading a very hard book. I never read such a hard book before. Its called *Robinson Crusoe* about a man who gets merooned on a dessert Iland. Hes smart and figers out all kinds of things so he can have a house and food and hes a good swimmer. Only I feel sorry because hes all alone and has no frends. But I think their must be somebody else on the iland because theres a picture with his funny umbrella looking at footprints. I hope he gets a frend and not be lonly.

April 10 Miss Kinnian teaches me to spell better. She says look at a word and close your eyes and say it over and over until you remember. I have lots of truble with *through* that you say *threw* and *enough* and *tough* that you dont say *enew* and *tew*. You got to say *enuff* and *tuff*. Thats how I use to write it before I started to get smart. Im confused but Miss Kinnian says theres no reason in spelling.

Apr 14 Finished *Robinson Crusoe*. I want to find out more about what happens to him but Miss Kinnian says thats all there is. *Why*

Apr 15 Miss Kinnian says Im lerning fast. She read some of the Progress Reports and she looked at me kind of funny. She says Im a fine person and Ill show them all. I asked her why. She said never mind but I shoudnt feel bad if I find out that everybody isnt nice like I think. She said for a person who god gave so little to you done more then a lot of people with brains they never even used. I said all my frends are smart people but there good. They like me and they never did anything that wasnt nice. Then she got something in her eye and she had to run out to the ladys room.

Apr 16 Today, I lerned, the *comma,* this is a comma (,) a period, with a tail, Miss Kinnian, says its important, because, it makes writing, better, she said, sombeody, could lose, a lot of money, if a comma, isnt, in the, right place, I dont have, any money, and I dont see, how a comma, keeps you, from losing it,

But she says, everybody, uses commas, so Ill use, them too,

Apr 17 I used the comma wrong. Its punctuation. Miss Kinnian told me to look up long words in the dictionary to lern to spell them. I said whats the difference if you can read it anyway. She said its part of your education so now on Ill look up all the words Im not sure how to spell. It takes a long time to write that way but I think Im remembering. I only have to look up once and after that I get it right. Anyway thats how come I got the word *punctuation* right. (Its that way in the dictionary). Miss Kinnian says a period is punctuation too, and there are lots of other marks to lern. I told her I thot all the periods had to have tails but she said no.

You got to mix them up, she showed? me" how. to mix! them(up,. and now; I can! mix up all kinds" of punctuation, in! my writing? There, are lots! of rules? to lern; but Im gettin'g them in my head.

One thing I? like about, Dear Miss Kinnian: (thats the way it goes in a business letter if I ever go into business) is she, always gives me' a reason" when—I ask. She's a gen'ius! I wish! I cou'd be smart" like, her;

(Punctuation, is; fun!)

April 18 What a dope I am! I didn't even understand what she was talking about. I read the grammar book last night and it explanes the whole thing. Then I saw it was the same way as Miss Kinnian was try-ing to tell me, but I didn't get it. I got up in the middle of the night, and the whole thing straightened out in my mind.

Miss Kinnian said that the TV working in my sleep helped out. She said I reached a plateau. Thats like the flat top of a hill.

After I figgered out how punctuation worked, I read over all my old Progress Reports from the beginning. Boy, did I have crazy spelling and punctuation! I told Miss Kinnian I ought to go over the pages and fix all the mistakes but she said, "No, Charlie, Dr. Nemur wants them just as they are. That's why he let you keep them after they were photostated, to see your own progress. You're coming along fast, Charlie."

That made me feel good. After the lesson I went down and played with Algernon. We don't race any more.

April 20 I feel sick inside. Not sick like for a doctor, but inside my chest it feels empty like getting punched and a heartburn at the same time.

I wasn't going to write about it, but I guess I got to, because it's im-portant. Today was the first time I ever stayed home from work.

Last night Joe Carp and Frank Reilly invited me to a party. There were lots of girls and some men from the factory. I remembered how sick I got last time I drank too much, so I told Joe I didn't want any-thing to drink. He gave me a plain Coke instead. It tasted funny, but I thought it was just a bad taste in my mouth.

We had a lot of fun for a while. Joe said I should dance with Ellen and she would teach me the steps. I fell a few times and I couldn't un-derstand why because no one else was dancing besides Ellen and me. And all the time I was tripping because somebody's foot was always sticking out.

Then when I got up I saw the look on Joe's face and it gave me a funny feeling in my stomack. "He's a scream," one of the girls said. Ev-erybody was laughing.

Frank said, "I ain't laughed so much since we sent him off for the newspaper that night at Muggsy's and ditched him."

"Look at him. His face is red."

"He's blushing. Charlie is blushing."

"Hey, Ellen, what'd you do to Charlie? I never saw him act like that before."

I didn't know what to do or where to turn. Everyone was looking at me and laughing and I felt naked. I wanted to hide myself. I ran out into the street and I threw up. Then I walked home. It's a funny thing I never knew that Joe and Frank and the others liked to have me around all the time to make fun of me.

Now I know what it means when they say "to pull a Charlie Gordon."

I'm ashamed.

PROGRESS REPORT 11

April 21 Still didn't go into the factory. I told Mrs. Flynn my landlady to call and tell Mr. Donnegan I was sick. Mrs. Flynn looks at me very funny lately like she's scared of me.

I think it's a good thing about finding out how everybody laughs at me. I thought about it a lot. It's because I'm so dumb and I don't even know when I'm doing something dumb. People think it's funny when a dumb person can't do things the same way they can.

Anyway, now I know I'm getting smarter every day. I know punctuation and I can spell good. I like to look up all the hard words in the dictionary and I remember them. I'm reading a lot now, and Miss Kinnian says I read very fast. Sometimes I even understand what I'm reading about, and it stays in my mind. There are times when I can close my eyes and think of a page and it all comes back like a picture.

Besides history, geography, and arithmetic, Miss Kinnian said I should start to learn a few foreign languages. Dr. Strauss gave me some more tapes to play while I sleep. I still don't understand how that conscious and unconscious mind works, but Dr. Strauss says not to worry yet. He asked me to promise that when I start learning college subjects next week I wouldn't read any books on psychology—that is, until he gives me permission.

I feel a lot better today, but I guess I'm still a little angry that all the time people were laughing and making fun of me because I wasn't so smart. When I become intelligent like Dr. Strauss says, with three times my I.Q. of 68, then maybe I'll be like everyone else and people will like me and be friendly.

I'm not sure what an I.Q. is. Dr. Nemur said it was something that measured how intelligent you were—like a scale in the drugstore weighs pounds. But Dr. Strauss had a big argument with him and said an I.Q. didn't weigh intelligence at all. He said an I.Q. showed how much intelligence you could get, like the numbers on the outside of a measuring cup. You still had to fill the cup up with stuff.

Then when I asked Burt, who gives me my intelligence tests and works with Algernon, he said that both of them were wrong (only I had to promise not to tell them he said so). Burt says that the I.Q. measures a lot of different things including some of the things you learned already, and it really isn't any good at all.

So I still don't know what I.Q. is except that mine is going to be over 200 soon. I didn't want to say anything, but I don't see how if they don't know *what* it is, or *where* it is—I don't see how they know *how much* of it you've got.

Dr. Nemur says I have to take a *Rorshach Test* tomorrow. I wonder what *that* is.

April 22 I found out what a *Rorshach* is. It's the test I took before the operation—the one with the inkblots on the pieces of cardboard. The man who gave me the test was the same one.

I was scared to death of those inkblots. I knew he was going to ask me to find the pictures and I knew I wouldn't be able to. I was thinking to myself, if only there was some way of knowing what kind of pictures were hidden there. Maybe there weren't any pictures at all. Maybe it was just a trick to see if I was dumb enough to look for something that wasn't there. Just thinking about that made me sore at him.

"All right, Charlie," he said, "you've seen these cards before, remember?"

"Of course I remember."

The way I said it, he knew I was angry, and he looked surprised. "Yes, of course. Now I want you to look at this one. What might this be? What do you see on this card? People see all sorts of things in these inkblots. Tell me what it might be for you—what it makes you think of."

I was shocked. That wasn't what I had expected him to say at all. "You mean there are no pictures hidden in those inkblots?"

He frowned and took off his glasses. "What?"

"Pictures. Hidden in the inkblots. Last time you told me that everyone could see them and you wanted me to find them too."

He explained to me that the last time he had used almost the exact same words he was using now. I didn't believe it, and I still have the suspicion that he misled me at the time just for the fun of it. Unless—I don't know any more—could I have been *that* feebleminded?

We went through the cards slowly. One of them looked like a pair of bats tugging at something. Another one looked like two men fencing with swords. I imagined all sorts of things. I guess I got carried away. But I didn't trust him any more, and I kept turning them around and even looking on the back to see if there was anything there I was supposed to catch. While he was making his notes, I peeked out of the corner of my eye to read it. But it was all in code that looked like this:

WF+A DdF-Ad orig. WF-A SF+obj

The test still doesn't make sense to me. It seems to me that anyone could make up lies about things that they didn't really see. How could he know I wasn't making a fool of him by mentioning things that I didn't really imagine? Maybe I'll understand it when Dr. Strauss lets me read up on psychology.

April 25 I figured out a new way to line up the machines in the factory, and Mr. Donnegan says it will save him ten thousand dollars a year in labor and increased production. He gave me a twenty-five-dollar bonus.

I wanted to take Joe Carp and Frank Reilly out to lunch to celebrate, but Joe said he had to buy some things for his wife, and Frank said he was meeting his cousin for lunch. I guess it'll take a little time for them to get used to the changes in me. Everybody seems to be frightened of me. When I went over to Amos Borg and tapped him on the shoulder, he jumped up in the air.

People don't talk to me much any more or kid around the way they used to. It makes the job kind of lonely.

April 27 I got up the nerve today to ask Miss Kinnian to have dinner with me tomorrow night to celebrate my bonus.

At first she wasn't sure it was right, but I asked Dr. Strauss and he said it was okay. Dr. Strauss and Dr. Nemur don't seem to be getting along so well. They're arguing all the time. This evening when I came in to ask Dr. Strauss about having dinner with Miss Kinnian, I heard them shouting. Dr. Nemur was saying that it was *his* experiment and *his* research, and Dr. Strauss was shouting back that he contributed just as much, because he found me through Miss Kinnian and he performed the operation. Dr. Strauss said that someday thousands of neurosurgeons might be using his technique all over the world.

Dr. Nemur wanted to publish the results of the experiment at the end of this month. Dr. Strauss wanted to wait a while longer to be sure. Dr.

Strauss said that Dr. Nemur was more interested in the Chair of Psychology at Princeton than he was in the experiment. Dr. Nemur said that Dr. Strauss was nothing but an opportunist who was trying to ride to glory on *his* coattails.

When I left afterwards, I found myself trembling. I don't know why for sure, but it was as if I'd seen both men clearly for the first time. I remember hearing Burt say that Dr. Nemur had a shrew of a wife who was pushing him all the time to get things published so that he could became famous. Burt said that the dream of her life was to have a big-shot husband.

Was Dr. Strauss really trying to ride on his coattails?

April 28 I don't understand why I never noticed how beautiful Miss Kinnian really is. She has brown eyes and feathery brown hair that comes to the top of her neck. She's only thirty-four! I think from the beginning I had the feeling that she was an unreachable genius—and very, very old. Now, every time I see her she grows younger and more lovely.

We had dinner and a long talk. When she said that I was coming along so fast that soon I'd be leaving her behind, I laughed.

"It's true, Charlie. You're already a better reader than I am. You can read a whole page at a glance while I can take in only a few lines at a time. And you remember every single thing you read. I'm lucky if I can recall the main thoughts and the general meaning."

"I don't feel intelligent. There are so many things I don't understand."

She took out a cigarette and I lit it for her. "You've got to be a *little* patient. You're accomplishing in days and weeks what it takes normal people to do in half a lifetime. That's what makes it so amazing. You're like a giant sponge now, soaking things in. Facts, figures, general knowledge. And soon you'll begin to connect them, too. You'll see how the different branches of learning are related. There are many levels, Charlie, like steps on a giant ladder that take you up higher and higher to see more and more of the world around you.

"I can see only a little bit of that, Charlie, and I won't go much higher than I am now, but you'll keep climbing up and up, and see more and more, and each step will open new worlds that you never even knew existed." She frowned. "I hope . . . I just hope to God—"

"What?"

"Never mind, Charles. I just hope I wasn't wrong to advise you to go into this in the first place."

I laughed. "How could that be? It worked, didn't it? Even Algernon is still smart."

We sat there silently for a while and I knew what she was thinking about as she watched me toying with the chain of my rabbit's foot and my keys. I didn't want to think of that possibility any more than elderly people want to think of death. I *knew* that this was only the beginning. I knew what she meant about levels because I'd seen some of them already. The thought of leaving her behind made me sad.

I'm in love with Miss Kinnian.

PROGRESS REPORT 12

April 30 I've quit my job with Donnegan's Plastic Box Company. Mr. Donnegan insisted that it would be better for all concerned if I left. What did I do to make them hate me so?

The first I knew of it was when Mr. Donnegan showed me the petition. Eight hundred and forty names, everyone connected with the factory, except Fanny Girden. Scanning the list quickly, I saw at once that hers was the only missing name. All the rest demanded that I be fired.

Joe Carp and Frank Reilly wouldn't talk to me about it. No one else would either, except Fanny. She was one of the few people I'd known who set her mind to something and believed it no matter what the rest of the world proved, said, or did—and Fanny did not believe that I should have been fired. She had been against the petition on principle and despite the pressure and threats she'd held out.

"Which don't mean to say," she remarked, "that I don't think there's something mighty strange about you, Charlie. Them changes. I don't know. You used to be a good, dependable, ordinary man—not too bright maybe, but honest. Who knows what you done to yourself to get so smart all of a sudden. Like everybody around here's been saying, Charlie, it's not right."

"But how can you say that, Fanny? What's wrong with a man becoming intelligent and wanting to acquire knowledge and understanding of the world around him?"

She stared down at her work and I turned to leave. Without looking at me, she said: "It was evil when Eve listened to the snake and ate from the tree of knowledge. It was evil when she saw that she was naked. If not for that none of us would ever have to grow old and sick, and die."

Once again now I have the feeling of shame burning inside me. This intelligence has driven a wedge between me and all the people I once knew and loved. Before, they laughed at me and despised me for my ignorance and dullness; now, they hate me for my knowledge and understanding. What in God's name do they want of me?

They've driven me out of the factory. Now I'm more alone than ever before . . .

May 15 Dr. Strauss is very angry at me for not having written any progress reports in two weeks. He's justified because the lab is now paying me a regular salary. I told him I was too busy thinking and reading. When I pointed out that writing was such a slow process that it made me impatient with my poor handwriting, he suggested that I learn to type. It's much easier to write now because I can type nearly seventy-five words a minute. Dr. Strauss continually reminds me of the need to speak and write simply so that people will be able to understand me.

I'll try to review all the things that happened to me during the last two weeks. Algernon and I were presented to the American Psychological Association sitting in convention with the World Psychological Association last Tuesday. We created quite a sensation. Dr. Nemur and Dr. Strauss were proud of us.

I suspect that Dr. Nemur, who is sixty—ten years older than Dr. Strauss—finds it necessary to see tangible results of his work. Undoubtedly the result of pressure by Mrs. Nemur.

Contrary to my earlier impressions of him, I realize that Dr. Nemur is not at all a genius. He has a very good mind, but it struggles under the spectre of self-doubt. He wants people to take him for a genius. Therefore, it is important for him to feel that his work is accepted by the world. I believe that Dr. Nemur was afraid of further delay because he worried that someone else might make a discovery along these lines and take the credit from him.

Dr. Strauss on the other hand might be called a genius, although I feel that his areas of knowledge are too limited. He was educated in the tradition of narrow specialization; the broader aspects of background were neglected far more than necessary—even for a neurosurgeon.

I was shocked to learn that the only ancient languages he could read were Latin, Greek, and Hebrew, and that he knows almost nothing of mathematics beyond the elementary levels of the calculus of variations. When he admitted this to me, I found myself almost annoyed. It was as if he'd hidden this part of himself in order to deceive me, pretending— as do many people I've discovered—to be what he is not. No one I've ever known is what he appears to be on the surface.

Dr. Nemur appears to be uncomfortable around me. Sometimes when I try to talk to him, he just looks at me strangely and turns away. I was angry at first when Dr. Strauss told me I was giving Dr. Nemur an inferiority complex. I thought he was mocking me and I'm oversensitive at being made fun of.

How was I to know that a highly respected psychoexperimentalist like Nemur was unacquainted with Hindustani and Chinese? It's absurd when you consider the work that is being done in India and China today in the very field of this study.

I asked Dr. Strauss how Nemur could refute Rahajamati's attack on his method and results if Nemur couldn't even read them in the first place. That strange look on Dr. Strauss' face can mean only one of two things. Either he doesn't want to tell Nemur what they're saying in India, or else—and this worries me—Dr. Strauss doesn't know either. I must be careful to speak and write clearly and simply so that people won't laugh.

May 18 I am very disturbed. I saw Miss Kinnian last night for the first time in over a week. I tried to avoid all discussions of intellectual concepts and to keep the conversation on a simple, everyday level, but she just stared at me blankly and asked me what I meant about the mathematical variance equivalent in Dorbermann's *Fifth Concerto*.

When I tried to explain she stopped me and laughed. I guess I got angry, but I suspect I'm approaching her on the wrong level. No matter what I try to discuss with her, I am unable to communicate. I must review Vrostadt's equations on *Levels of Semantic Progression*. I find that I don't communicate with people much any more. Thank God for books and music and things I can think about. I am alone in my apartment at Mrs. Flynn's boardinghouse most of the time and seldom speak to anyone.

May 20 I would not have noticed the new dishwasher, a boy of about sixteen, at the corner diner where I take my evening meals if not for the incident of the broken dishes.

They crashed to the floor, shattering and sending bits of white china under the tables. The boy stood there, dazed and frightened, holding the empty tray in his hand. The whistles and catcalls from the customers (the cries of "hey, there go the profits!" . . . "*Mazeltov!*" . . . and "well, *he* didn't work here very long . . ." which invariably seems to follow the breaking of glass or dishware in a public restaurant) all seemed to confuse him.

When the owner came to see what the excitement was about, the boy cowered as if he expected to be struck and threw up his arms as if to ward off the blow.

"All right! All right, you dope," shouted the owner, "don't just stand there! Get the broom and sweep that mess up. A broom . . . a broom, you idiot! It's in the kitchen. Sweep up all the pieces."

The boy saw that he was not going to be punished. His frightened expression disappeared and he smiled and hummed as he came back with the broom to sweep the floor. A few of the rowdier customers kept up the remarks, amusing themselves at his expense.

"Here, sonny, over here there's a nice piece behind you . . ."

"C'mon, do it again . . ."

"He's not so dumb. It's easier to break 'em than to wash 'em . . ."

As his vacant eyes moved across the crowd of amused onlookers, he slowly mirrored their smiles and finally broke into an uncertain grin at the joke which he obviously did not understand.

I felt sick inside as I looked at his dull, vacuous smile, the wide, bright eyes of a child, uncertain but eager to please. They were laughing at him because he was mentally retarded.

And I had been laughing at him too.

Suddenly, I was furious at myself and all those who were smirking at him. I jumped up and shouted, "Shut up! Leave him alone! It's not his fault he can't understand! He can't help what he is! But for God's sake . . . he's still a human being!"

The room grew silent. I cursed myself for losing control and creating a scene. I tried not to look at the boy as I paid my check and walked out without touching my food. I felt ashamed for both of us.

How strange it is that people of honest feelings and sensibility, who would not take advantage of a man born without arms or legs or eyes— how such people think nothing of abusing a man born with low intelligence. It infuriated me to think that not too long ago I, like this boy, had foolishly played the clown.

And I had almost forgotten.

I'd hidden the picture of the old Charlie Gordon from myself because now that I was intelligent it was something that had to be pushed out of my mind. But today in looking at that boy, for the first time I saw what I had been. *I was just like him!*

Only a short time ago, I learned that people laughed at me. Now I can see that unknowingly I joined with them in laughing at myself. That hurts most of all.

I have often reread my progress reports and seen the illiteracy, the childish naïveté, the mind of low intelligence peering from a dark room, through the keyhole, at the dazzling light outside. I see that even in my dullness I knew that I was inferior, and that other people had something I lacked—something denied me. In my mental blindness, I thought that it was somehow connected with the ability to read and write, and I was sure that if I could get those skills I would automatically have intelligence too.

Even a feeble-minded man wants to be like other men.

A child may not know how to feed itself, or what to eat, yet it knows of hunger.

This then is what I was like, I never knew. Even with my gift of intellectual awareness, I never really knew.

This day was good for me. Seeing the past more clearly, I have decided to use my knowledge and skills to work in the field of increasing human intelligence levels. Who is better equipped for this work? Who else has lived in both worlds? These are my people. Let me use my gift to do something for them.

Tomorrow, I will discuss with Dr. Strauss the manner in which I can work in this area. I may be able to help him work out the problems of widespread use of the technique which was used on me. I have several good ideas of my own.

There is so much that might be done with this technique. If I could be made into a genius, what about thousands of others like myself? What fantastic levels might be achieved by using this technique on normal people? On *geniuses?*

There are so many doors to open. I am impatient to begin.

PROGRESS REPORT 13

May 23 It happened today. Algernon bit me. I visited the lab to see him as I do occasionally, and when I took him out of his cage, he snapped at my hand. I put him back and watched him for a while. He was unusually disturbed and vicious.

May 24   Burt, who is in charge of the experimental animals, tells me that Algernon is changing. He is less co-operative; he refuses to run the maze any more; general motivation has decreased. And he hasn't been eating. Everyone is upset about what this may mean.

May 25   They've been feeding Algernon, who now refuses to work the shifting-lock problem. Everyone identifies me with Algernon. In a way we're both the first of our kind. They're all pretending that Algernon's behavior is not necessarily significant for me. But it's hard to hide the fact that some of the other animals who were used in this experiment are showing strange behavior.

Dr. Strauss and Dr. Nemur have asked me not to come to the lab any more. I know what they're thinking but I can't accept it. I am going ahead with my plans to carry their research forward. With all due respect to both of these fine scientists, I am well aware of their limitations. If there is an answer, I'll have to find it out for myself. Suddenly, time has become very important to me.

May 29   I have been given a lab of my own and permission to go ahead with the research. I'm on to something. Working day and night. I've had a cot moved into the lab. Most of my writing time is spent on the notes which I keep in a separate folder, but from time to time I feel it necessary to put down my moods and my thoughts out of sheer habit.

I find the *calculus of intelligence* to be a fascinating study. Here is the place for the application of all the knowledge I have acquired. In a sense it's the problem I've been concerned with all my life.

May 31   Dr. Strauss thinks I'm working too hard. Dr. Nemur says I'm trying to cram a lifetime of research and thought into a few weeks. I know I should rest, but I'm driven on by something inside that won't let me stop. I've got to find the reason for the sharp regression in Algernon. I've got to know *if* and *when* it will happen to me.

June 4
LETTER TO DR. STRAUSS (*copy*)
Dear Dr. Strauss:
Under separate cover I am sending you a copy of my report entitled, "The Algernon-Gordon Effect: A Study of Structure and Function of Increased Intelligence," which I would like to have you read and have published.

As you see, my experiments are completed. I have included in my report all of my formulae, as well as mathematical analysis in the appendix. Of course, these should be verified.

Because of its importance to both you and Dr. Nemur (and need I say to myself, too?) I have checked and rechecked my results a dozen times in the hope of finding an error. I am sorry to say the results must stand. Yet for the sake of science, I am grateful for the little bit that I here add to the knowledge of the function of the human mind and of the laws governing the artificial increase of human intelligence.

I recall your once saying to me that an experimental *failure* or the *disproving* of a theory was as important to the advancement of learning as a success would be. I know now that this is true. I am sorry, however, that my own contribution to the field must rest upon the ashes of the work of two men I regard so highly.

Yours truly,
Charles Gordon

encl.: rept.

June 5 I must not become emotional. The facts and the results of my experiments are clear, and the more sensational aspects of my own rapid climb cannot obscure the fact that the tripling of intelligence by the surgical technique developed by Drs. Strauss and Nemur must be viewed as having little or no practical applicability (at the present time) to the increase of human intelligence.

As I review the records and data on Algernon, I see that although he is still in his physical infancy, he has regressed mentally. Motor activity is impaired; there is a general reduction of glandular activity; there is an accelerated loss of co-ordination.

There are also strong indications of progressive amnesia.

As will be seen by my report, these and other physical and mental deterioration syndromes can be predicted with statistically significant results by the application of my formula.

The surgical stimulus to which we were both subjected has resulted in an intensification and acceleration of all mental processes. The unforeseen development, which I have taken the liberty of calling the *Algernon-Gordon Effect,* is the logical extension of the entire intelligence speed-up. The hypothesis here proven may be described simply in the following terms: Artificially increased intelligence deteriorates at a rate of time directly proportional to the quantity of the increase.

I feel that this, in itself, is an important discovery.

As long as I am able to write, I will continue to record my thoughts in these progress reports. It is one of my few pleasures. However, by all indications, my own mental deterioration will be very rapid.

I have already begun to notice signs of emotional instability and forgetfulness, the first symptoms of the burnout.

June 10 Deterioration progressing. I have become absentminded. Algernon died two days ago. Dissection shows my predictions were right. His brain had decreased in weight and there was a general smoothing out of cerebral convolutions as well as a deepening and broadening of brain fissures.

I guess the same thing is or will soon be happening to me. Now that it's definite, I don't want it to happen.

I put Algernon's body in a cheese box and buried him in the back yard. I cried.

June 15 Dr. Strauss came to see me again. I wouldn't open the door and I told him to go away. I want to be left to myself. I have become touchy and irritable. I feel the darkness closing in. It's hard to throw off thoughts of suicide. I keep telling myself how important this introspective journal will be.

It's a strange sensation to pick up a book that you've read and enjoyed just a few months ago and discover that you don't remember it. I remembered how great I thought John Milton was, but when I picked up *Paradise Lost* I couldn't understand it at all. I got so angry I threw the book across the room.

I've got to try to hold on to some of it. Some of the things I've learned. Oh, God, please don't take it all away.

June 19 Sometimes, at night, I go out for a walk. Last night I couldn't remember where I lived. A policeman took me home. I have the strange feeling that this has all happened to me before—a long time ago. I keep telling myself I'm the only person in the world who can describe what's happening to me.

June 21 Why can't I remember? I've got to fight. I lie in bed for days and I don't know who or where I am. Then it all comes back to me in a flash. Fugues of amnesia. Symptoms of senility—second childhood. I can watch them coming on. It's so cruelly logical. I learned so much and so fast. Now my mind is deteriorating rapidly. I won't let it happen. I'll fight it. I can't help thinking of the boy in the restaurant, the blank expression, the silly smile, the people laughing at him. No—please—not that again . . .

June 22 I'm forgetting things that I learned recently. It seems to be following the classic pattern—the last things learned are the first things forgotten. Or is that the pattern? I'd better look it up again . . .

I reread my paper on the *Algernon-Gordon Effect* and I get the strange feeling that it was written by someone else. There are parts I don't even understand.

Motor activity impaired. I keep tripping over things, and it becomes increasingly difficult to type.

June 23 I've given up using the typewriter completely. My co-ordination is bad. I feel that I'm moving slower and slower. Had a terrible shock today. I picked up a copy of an article I used in my research, Krueger's *Uber psychische Ganzheit,* to see if it would help me understand what I had done. First I thought there was something wrong with my eyes. Then I realized I could no longer read German. I tested myself in other languages. All gone.

June 30 A week since I dared to write again. It's slipping away like sand through my fingers. Most of the books I have are too hard for me now. I get angry with them because I know that I read and understood them just a few weeks ago.

I keep telling myself I must keep writing these reports so that somebody will know what is happening to me. But it gets harder to form the words and remember spellings. I have to look up even simple words in the dictionary now and it makes me impatient with myself.

Dr. Strauss comes around almost every day, but I told him I wouldn't see or speak to anybody. He feels guilty. They all do. But I don't blame anyone. I knew what might happen. But how it hurts.

July 7 I don't know where the week went. Todays Sunday I know because I can see through my window people going to church. I think I stayed in bed all week but I remember Mrs. Flynn bringing food to me a few times. I keep saying over and over Ive got to do something but then I forget or maybe its just easier not to do what I say Im going to do.

I think of my mother and father a lot these days. I found a picture of them with me taken at a beach. My father has a big ball under his arm and my mother is holding me by the hand. I dont remember them the way they are in the picture. All I remember is my father drunk most of the time and arguing with mom about money.

He never shaved much and he used to scratch my face when he hugged me. My mother said he died but Cousin Miltie said he heard his mom and dad say that my father ran away with another woman. When I asked my mother she slapped my face and said my father was dead. I dont think I ever found out which was true but I don't care much. (He said he was going to take me to see cows on a farm once but he never did. He never kept his promises . . .)

July 10   My landlady Mrs Flynn is very worried about me. She says the way I lay around all day and dont do anything I remind her of her son before she threw him out of the house. She said she doesnt like loafers. If Im sick its one thing, but if Im a loafer thats another thing and she wont have it. I told her I think Im sick.

I try to read a little bit every day, mostly stories, but sometimes I have to read the same thing over and over again because I dont know what it means. And its hard to write. I know I should look up all the words in the dictionary but its so hard and Im so tired all the time.

Then I got the idea that I would only use the easy words instead of the long hard ones. That saves time. I put flowers on Algernons grave about once a week. Mrs Flynn thinks Im crazy to put flowers on a mouses grave but I told her that Algernon was special.

July 14   Its sunday again. I dont have anything to do to keep me busy now because my television set is broke and I dont have any money to get it fixed. (I think I lost this months check from the lab. I dont remember)

I get awful headaches and asperin doesnt help me much. Mrs Flynn knows Im really sick and she feels very sorry for me. Shes a wonderful woman whenever someone is sick.

July 22   Mrs Flynn called a strange doctor to see me. She was afraid I was going to die. I told the doctor I wasnt too sick and that I only forget sometimes. He asked me did I have any friends or relatives and I said no I dont have any. I told him I had a friend called Algernon once but he was a mouse and we used to run races together. He looked at me kind of funny like he thought I was crazy.

He smiled when I told him I used to be a genius. He talked to me like I was a baby and he winked at Mrs Flynn. I got mad and chased him out because he was making fun of me the way they all used to.

July 24 I have no more money and Mrs Flynn says I got to go to work somewhere and pay the rent because I havent paid for over two months. I dont know any work but the job I used to have at Donnegans Plastic Box Company. I dont want to go back there because they all knew me when I was smart and maybe theyll laugh at me. But I dont know what else to do to get money.

July 25 I was looking at some of my old progress reports and its very funny but I cant read what I wrote. I can make out some of the words but they dont make sense.

Miss Kinnian came to the door but I said go away I dont want to see you. She cried and I cried too but I wouldnt let her in because I didnt want her to laugh at me. I told her I didn't like her any more. I told her I didnt want to be smart any more. Thats not true. I still love her and I still want to be smart but I had to say that so shed go away. She gave Mrs Flynn money to pay the rent. I dont want that. I got to get a job.

Please . . . please let me not forget how to read and write . . .

July 27 Mr Donnegan was very nice when I came back and asked him for my old job of janitor. First he was very suspicious but I told him what happened to me then he looked very sad and put his hand on my shoulder and said Charlie Gordon you got guts.

Everybody looked at me when I came downstairs and started working in the toilet sweeping it out like I used to. I told myself Charlie if they make fun of you dont get sore because you remember their not so smart as you once thot they were. And besides they were once your friends and if they laughed at you that doesnt mean anything because they liked you too.

One of the new men who came to work there after I went away made a nasty crack he said hey Charlie I hear your a very smart fella a real quiz kid. Say something intelligent. I felt bad but Joe Carp came over and grabbed him by the shirt and said leave him alone you lousy cracker or Ill break your neck. I didnt expect Joe to take my part so I guess hes really my friend.

Later Frank Reilly came over and said Charlie if anybody bothers you or trys to take advantage you call me or Joe and we will set em straight. I said thanks Frank and I got choked up so I had to turn around and go into the supply room so he wouldnt see me cry. Its good to have friends.

July 28 I did a dumb thing today I forgot I wasnt in Miss Kinnians class at the adult center any more like I use to be. I went in and sat down in my old seat in the back of the room and she looked at me funny and she said Charles. I dint remember she ever called me that before only Charlie so I said hello Miss Kinnian Im redy for my lesin today only I lost my reader that we was using. She startid to cry and run out of the room and everybody looked at me and I saw they wasnt the same pepul who used to be in my class.

Then all of a suddin I rememberd some things about the operashun and me getting smart and I said holy smoke I reely pulled a Charlie Gordon that time. I went away before she come back to the room.

Thats why Im going away from New York for good. I dont want to do nothing like that agen. I dont want Miss Kinnian to feel sorry for me. Evry body feels sorry at the factery and I dont want that eather so Im going someplace where nobody knows that Charlie Gordon was once a genus and now he cant even reed a book or rite good.

Im taking a cuple of books along and even if I cant reed them Ill practise hard and maybe I wont forget every thing I lerned. If I try reel hard maybe Ill be a littel bit smarter than I was before the operashun. I got my rabits foot and my luky penny and maybe they will help me.

If you ever reed this Miss Kinnian dont be sorry for me Im glad I got a second chanse to be smart becaus I lerned a lot of things that I never even new were in this world and Im grateful that I saw it all for a littel bit. I dont know why Im dumb agen or what I did wrong maybe its becaus I dint try hard enuff. But if I try and practis very hard maybe Ill get a littl smarter and know what all the words are. I remember a littel bit how nice I had a feeling with the blue book that has the torn cover when I red it. Thats why Im gonna keep trying to get smart so I can have that feeling agen. Its a good feeling to know things and be smart. I wish I had it rite now if I did I would sit down and reed all the time. Anyway I bet Im the first dumb person in the world who ever found out something importent for sience. I remember I did somthing but I dont remember what. So I gess its like I did it for all the dumb pepul like me.

Good-by Miss Kinnian and Dr. Strauss and evreybody. And P.S. please tell Dr Nemur not to be such a grouch when pepul laff at him and he woud have more frends. Its easy to make frends if you let pepul laff at you. Im going to have lots of frends where I go.

P.P.S. Please if you get a chanse put some flowrs on Algernons grave in the bak yard . . .

A Canticle for Leibowitz
Walter M. Miller, Jr.

BROTHER FRANCIS GERARD OF UTAH would never have discovered the sacred document, had it not been for the pilgrim with girded loins who appeared during that young monk's Lenten fast in the desert. Never before had Brother Francis actually seen a pilgrim with girded loins, but that this one was the bona fide article he was convinced at a glance. The pilgrim was a spindly old fellow with a staff, a basket hat, and a brushy beard, stained yellow about the chin. He walked with a limp and carried a small waterskin over one shoulder. His loins truly were girded with a ragged piece of dirty burlap, his only clothing except for hat and sandals. He whistled tunelessly on his way.

The pilgrim came shuffling down the broken trail out of the north, and he seemed to be heading toward the Brothers of Leibowitz Abbey six miles to the south. The pilgrim and the monk noticed each other across an expanse of ancient rubble. The pilgrim stopped whistling and stared. The monk, because of certain implications of the rule of solitude for fast days, quickly averted his gaze and continued about his business of hauling large rocks with which to complete the wolf-proofing of his temporary shelter. Somewhat weakened by a ten-day

---

"A CANTICLE FOR LEIBOWITZ" was first published in the April 1955 issue and, along with its two sequels, "And the Light Is Risen" and "The Last Canticle," was later expanded into a novel that has sold millions of copies and is on everyone's list of ten best sf novels ever written. In 1961 it won a Hugo Award, beating out Poul Anderson's The High Crusade, *Algis Budrys'* Rogue Moon *and Theodore Sturgeon's* Venus Plus X. *Has there ever been a greater year for sf novels?*

diet of cactus fruit, Brother Francis found the work made him exceedingly dizzy; the landscape had been shimmering before his eyes and
dancing with black specks, and he was at first uncertain that the
bearded apparition was not a mirage induced by hunger, but after a
moment it called to him cheerfully, *"Ola allay!"*

It was a pleasant musical voice.

The rule of silence forbade the young monk to answer, except by
smiling shyly at the ground.

"Is this here the road to the abbey?" the wanderer asked.

The novice nodded at the ground and reached down for a chalklike
fragment of stone. The pilgrim picked his way toward him through the
rubble. "What you doing with all the rocks?" he wanted to know.

The monk knelt and hastily wrote the words "Solitude & Silence" on
a large flat rock, so that the pilgrim—if he could read, which is statistically unlikely—would know that he was making himself an occasion
of sin for the penitent and would perhaps have the grace to leave in
peace.

"Oh, well," said the pilgrim. He stood there for a moment, looking
around, then rapped a certain large rock with his staff. *"That* looks like
a handy crag for you," he offered helpfully, then added: "Well, good
luck. And may you find a Voice, as y' seek."

Now Brother Francis had no immediate intuition that the stranger
meant "Voice" with a capital V, but merely assumed that the old fellow
had mistaken him for a deaf mute. He glanced up once again as the pilgrim shuffled away whistling, sent a swift silent benediction after him
for safe wayfaring, and went back to his rock-work, building a coffin-
sized enclosure in which he might sleep at night without offering himself as wolf-bait.

A sky-herd of cumulus clouds, on their way to bestow moist blessings
on the mountains after having cruelly tempted the desert, offered welcome respite from the searing sunlight, and he worked rapidly to finish
before they were gone again. He punctuated his labors with whispered
prayers for the certainty of a true Vocation, for this was the purpose of
his inward quest while fasting in the desert.

At last he hoisted the rock which the pilgrim had suggested.

The color of exertion drained quickly from his face. He backed away
a step and dropped the stone as if he had uncovered a serpent.

A rusted metal box lay half crushed in the rubble . . . only a rusted
metal box.

He moved toward it curiously, then paused. There were things, and then there were Things. He crossed himself hastily, and muttered brief Latin at the heavens. Thus fortified, he readdressed himself to the box.

"Apage Satanas!"

He threatened it with the heavy crucifix of his rosary.

"Depart, O Foul Seductor!"

He sneaked a tiny aspergillum from his robes and quickly spattered the box with holy water before it could realize what he was about.

"If thou be creature of the Devil, begone!"

The box showed no signs of withering, exploding, melting away. It exuded no blasphemous ichor. It only lay quietly in its place and allowed the desert wind to evaporate the sanctifying droplets.

"So be it," said the brother, and knelt to extract it from its lodging. He sat down on the rubble and spent nearly an hour battering it open with a stone. The thought crossed his mind that such an archeological relic—for such it obviously was—might be the Heaven-sent sign of his vocation but he suppressed the notion as quickly as it occurred to him. His abbot had warned him sternly against expecting any direct personal Revelation of a spectacular nature. Indeed, he had gone forth from the abbey to fast and do penance for forty days that he might be rewarded with the inspiration of a calling to Holy Orders, but to expect a vision or a voice crying "Francis, where art thou?" would be a vain presumption. Too many novices had returned from their desert vigils with tales of omens and signs and visions in the heavens, and the good abbot had adopted a firm policy regarding these. Only the Vatican was qualified to decide the authenticity of such things. "An attack of sunstroke is no indication that you are fit to profess the solemn vows of the order," he had growled. And certainly it was true that only rarely did a call from Heaven come through any device other than the *inward* ear, as a gradual congealing of inner certainty.

Nevertheless, Brother Francis found himself handling the old metal box with as much reverence as was possible while battering at it.

It opened suddenly, spilling some of its contents. He stared for a long time before daring to touch, and a cool thrill gathered along his spine. Here was antiquity indeed! And as a student of archeology, he could scarcely believe his wavering vision. Brother Jeris would be frantic with envy, he thought, but quickly repented this unkindness and murmured his thanks to the sky for such a treasure.

He touched the articles gingerly—they were real enough—and began sorting through them. His studies had equipped him to recognize a screwdriver—an instrument once used for twisting threaded bits of metal into wood—and a pair of cutters with blades no longer than his thumbnail, but strong enough to cut soft bits of metal or bone. There was an odd tool with a rotted wooden handle and a heavy copper tip to which a few flakes of molten lead had adhered, but he could make nothing of it. There was a toroidal roll of gummy black stuff, too far deteriorated by the centuries for him to identify. There were strange bits of metal, broken glass, and an assortment of tiny tubular things with wire whiskers of the type prized by the hill pagans as charms and amulets, but thought by some archeologists to be remnants of the legendary *machina analytica*, supposedly dating back to the Deluge of Flame.

All these and more he examined carefully and spread on the wide flat stone. The documents he saved until last. The documents, as always, were the real prize, for so few papers had survived the angry bonfires of the Age of Simplification, when even the sacred writings had curled and blackened and withered into smoke while ignorant crowds howled vengeance.

Two large folded papers and three hand-scribbled notes constituted his find. All were cracked and brittle with age, and he handled them tenderly, shielding them from the wind with his robe. They were scarcely legible and scrawled in the hasty characters of pre-Deluge English—a tongue now used, together with Latin, only by monastics and in the Holy Ritual. He spelled it out slowly, recognizing words but uncertain of meanings. One note said: *Pound pastrami, can kraut, six bagels, for Emma.* Another ordered: *Don't forget to pick up form 1040 for Uncle Revenue.* The third note was only a column of figures with a circled total from which another amount was subtracted and finally a percentage taken, followed by the word *damn!* From this he could deduce nothing, except to check the arithmetic, which proved correct.

Of the two larger papers, one was tightly rolled and began to fall to pieces when he tried to open it; he could make out the words RACING FORM, but nothing more. He laid it back in the box for later restorative work.

The second large paper was a single folded sheet, whose creases were so brittle that he could only inspect a little of it by parting the folds and peering between them as best he could.

A diagram . . . a web of white lines on dark paper!

Again the cool thrill gathered along his spine. It was a *blueprint*—that exceedingly rare class of ancient document most prized by students of antiquity, and usually most challenging to interpreters and searchers for meaning.

And, as if the find itself were not enough of a blessing, among the words written in a block at the lower corner of the document was the name of the founder of his order—of the Blessed Leibowitz *himself!*

His trembling hands threatened to tear the paper in their happy agitation. The parting words of the pilgrim tumbled back to him: "May you find a Voice, as y' seek." Voice indeed, with V capitalized and formed by the wings of a descending dove and illuminated in three colors against a background of gold leaf. *V* as in *Vere dignum* and *Vidi aquam* at the head of a page of the Missal. *V,* he saw quite clearly, as in Vocation.

He stole another glance to make certain it was so, then breathed, *"Beate Leibowitz, ora pro me. . . . Sancte Leibowitz, exaudi me,"* the second invocation being a rather daring one, since the founder of his order had not yet been declared a saint.

Forgetful of his abbot's warning, he climbed quickly to his feet and stared across the shimmering terrain to the south in the direction taken by the old wanderer of the burlap loincloth. But the pilgrim had long since vanished. Surely an angel of God, if not the Blessed Leibowitz himself, for had he not revealed this miraculous treasure by pointing out the rock to be moved and murmuring that prophetic farewell?

Brother Francis stood basking in his awe until the sun lay red on the hills and evening threatened to engulf him in its shadows. At last he stirred, and reminded himself of the wolves. His gift included no guarantee of charismata for subduing the wild beast, and he hastened to finish his enclosure before darkness fell on the desert. When the stars came out, he rekindled his fire and gathered his daily repast of the small purple cactus fruit, his only nourishment except the handful of parched corn brought to him by the priest each Sabbath. Sometimes he found himself staring hungrily at the lizards which scurried over the rocks, and was troubled by gluttonous nightmares.

But tonight his hunger was less troublesome than an impatient urge to run back to the abbey and announce his wondrous encounter to his brethren. This, of course, was unthinkable. Vocation or no, he must remain here until the end of Lent, and continue as if nothing extraordinary had occurred.

A cathedral will be built upon this site, he thought dreamily as he sat by the fire. He could see it rising from the rubble of the ancient village, magnificent spires visible for miles across the desert. . . .

But cathedrals were for teeming masses of people. The desert was home for only scattered tribes of huntsmen and the monks of the abbey. He settled in his dreams for a shrine, attracting rivers of pilgrims with girded loins. . . . He drowsed. When he awoke, the fire was reduced to glowing embers. Something seemed amiss. Was he quite alone? He blinked about at the darkness.

From beyond the bed of reddish coals, the dark wolf blinked back. The monk yelped and dived for cover.

The yelp, he decided as he lay trembling within his den of stones, had not been a serious breach of the rule of silence. He lay hugging the metal box and praying for the days of Lent to pass swiftly, while the sound of padded feet scratched about the enclosure.

Each night the wolves prowled about his camp, and the darkness was full of their howling. The days were glaring nightmares of hunger, heat, and scorching sun. He spent them at prayer and wood-gathering, trying to suppress his impatience for the coming of Holy Saturday's high noon, the end of Lent and of his vigil.

But when at last it came, Brother Francis found himself too famished for jubilation. Wearily he packed his pouch, pulled up his cowl against the sun, and tucked his precious box beneath one arm. Thirty pounds lighter and several degrees weaker than he had been on Ash Wednesday, he staggered the six-mile stretch to the abbey where he fell exhausted before its gates. The brothers who carried him in and bathed him and shaved him and anointed his desiccated tissues reported that he babbled incessantly in his delirium about an apparition in a burlap loincloth, addressing it at times as an angel and again as a saint, frequently invoking the name of Leibowitz and thanking him for a revelation of sacred relics and a racing form.

Such reports filtered through the monastic congregation and soon reached the ears of the abbot, whose eyes immediately narrowed to slits and whose jaw went rigid with the rock of policy.

"Bring him," growled that worthy priest in a tone that sent a recorder scurrying.

The abbot paced and gathered his ire. It was not that he objected to miracles, as such, if duly investigated, certified, and sealed; for miracles —even though always incompatible with administrative efficiency, and the abbot was administrator as well as priest—were the bedrock stuff on which his faith was founded. But last year there had been Brother Noyen with his miraculous hangman's noose, and the year before that,

Brother Smirnov, who had been mysteriously cured of the gout upon handling a probable relic of the Blessed Leibowitz, and the year before that . . . *Faugh!* The incidents had been too frequent and outrageous to tolerate. Ever since Leibowitz' beatification, the young fools had been sniffing around after shreds of the miraculous like a pack of good-natured hounds scratching eagerly at the back gate of Heaven for scraps.

It was quite understandable, but also quite unbearable. Every monastic order is eager for the canonization of its founder, and delighted to produce any bit of evidence to serve the cause in advocacy. But the abbot's flock was getting out of hand, and their zeal for miracles was making the Albertian Order of Leibowitz a laughingstock at New Vatican. He had determined to make any new bearers of miracles suffer the consequences, either as a punishment for impetuous and impertinent credulity, or as payment in penance for a gift of grace in case of later verification.

By the time the young novice knocked at his door, the abbot had projected himself into the desired state of carnivorous expectancy beneath a bland exterior.

"Come in, my son," he breathed softly.

"You sent for . . ." The novice paused, smiling happily as he noticed the familiar metal box on the abbot's table. ". . . for me, Father Juan?" he finished.

"Yes . . ." The abbot hesitated. His voice smiled with a withering acid, adding: "Or perhaps you would prefer that I come to *you*, hereafter, since you've become such a famous personage."

"Oh, no, Father!" Brother Francis reddened and gulped.

"You are seventeen, and plainly an idiot."

"That is undoubtedly true, Father."

"What improbable excuse can you propose for your outrageous vanity in believing yourself fit for Holy Orders?"

"I can offer none, my ruler and teacher. My sinful pride is unpardonable."

"To imagine that it is so great as to be unpardonable is even a vaster vanity," the priest roared.

"Yes, Father. I am indeed a worm."

The abbot smiled icily and resumed his watchful calm. "And you are now ready to deny your feverish ravings about an angel appearing to reveal to you this . . ." He gestured contemptuously at the box. ". . . this assortment of junk?"

Brother Francis gulped and closed his eyes. "I—I fear I cannot deny it, my master."

"What?"

"I cannot deny what I have seen, Father."

"Do you know what is going to happen to you now?"

"Yes, Father."

"Then prepare to take it!"

With a patient sigh, the novice gathered up his robes about his waist and bent over the table. The good abbot produced his stout hickory ruler from the drawer and whacked him soundly ten times across the bare buttocks. After each whack, the novice dutifully responded with a *"Deo Gratias!"* for this lesson in the virtue of humility.

"Do you *now* retract it?" the abbot demanded as he rolled down his sleeve.

"Father, I cannot."

The priest turned his back and was silent for a moment. "Very well," he said tersely. "Go. But do not expect to profess your solemn vows this season with the others."

Brother Francis returned to his cell in tears. His fellow novices would join the ranks of the professed monks of the order, while he must wait another year—and spend another Lenten season among the wolves in the desert, seeking a vocation which he felt had already been granted to him quite emphatically. As the weeks passed, however, he found some satisfaction in noticing that Father Juan had not been entirely serious in referring to his find as "an assortment of junk." The archeological relics aroused considerable interest among the brothers, and much time was spent at cleaning the tools, classifying them, restoring the documents to a pliable condition, and attempting to ascertain their meaning. It was even whispered among the novices that Brother Francis had discovered true relics of the Blessed Leibowitz—especially in the form of the blueprint bearing the legend OP COBBLESTONE, REQ LEIBOWITZ & HARDIN, which was stained with several brown splotches which might have been his blood—or equally likely, as the abbot pointed out, might be stains from a decayed apple core. But the print was dated in the Year of Grace 1956, which was—as nearly as could be determined—during that venerable man's lifetime, a lifetime now obscured by legend and myth, so that it was hard to determine any but a few facts about the man.

It was said that God, in order to test mankind, had commanded wise men of that age, among them the Blessed Leibowitz, to perfect diabolic weapons and give them into the hands of latter-day Pharaohs. And with such weapons Man had, within the span of a few weeks, destroyed most of his civilization and wiped out a large part of the population. After the Deluge of Flame came the plagues, the madness, and the bloody inception of the Age of Simplification when the furious remnants of humanity had torn politicians, technicians, and men of learning limb from limb, and burned all records that might contain information that could once more lead into paths of destruction. Nothing had been so fiercely hated as the written word, the learned man. It was during this time that the word "simpleton" came to mean "honest, upright, virtuous citizen," a concept once denoted by the term "common man."

To escape the righteous wrath of the surviving simpletons, many scientists and learned men fled to the only sanctuary which would try to offer them protection. Holy Mother Church received them, vested them in monks' robes, tried to conceal them from the mobs. Sometimes the sanctuary was effective; more often it was not. Monasteries were invaded, records and sacred books were burned, refugees seized and hanged. Leibowitz had fled to the Cistercians, professed their vows, become a priest, and after twelve years had won permission from the Holy See to found a new monastic order to be called "the Albertians," after St. Albert the Great, teacher of Aquinas and patron saint of scientists. The new order was to be dedicated to the preservation of knowledge, secular and sacred, and the duty of the brothers was to memorize such books and papers as could be smuggled to them from all parts of the world. Leibowitz was at last identified by simpletons as a former scientist, and was martyred by hanging; but the order continued, and when it became safe again to possess written documents, many books were transcribed from memory. Precedence, however, had been given to sacred writings, to history, the humanities, and social sciences—since the memories of the memorizers were limited, and few of the brothers were trained to understand the physical sciences. From the vast store of human knowledge, only a pitiful collection of handwritten books remained.

Now, after six centuries of darkness, the monks still preserved it, studied it, recopied it, and waited. It mattered not in the least to them that the knowledge they saved was useless—and some of it even incomprehensible. The knowledge was there, and it was their duty to save it, and it would still be with them if the darkness in the world lasted ten thousand years.

Brother Francis Gerard of Utah returned to the desert the following year and fasted again in solitude. Once more he returned, weak and emaciated, to be confronted by the abbot, who demanded to know if he claimed further conferences with members of the Heavenly Host, or was prepared to renounce his story of the previous year.

"I cannot help what I have seen, my teacher," the lad repeated.

Once more did the abbot chastise him in Christ, and once more did he postpone his profession. The document, however, had been forwarded to a seminary for study, after a copy had been made. Brother Francis remained a novice, and continued to dream wistfully of the shrine which might someday be built upon the site of his find.

"Stubborn boy!" fumed the abbot. "Why didn't somebody else see his silly pilgrim, if the slovenly fellow was heading for the abbey as he said? One more escapade for the Devil's Advocate to cry hoax about. Burlap loincloth indeed!"

The burlap had been troubling the abbot, for tradition related that Leibowitz had been hanged with a burlap bag for a hood.

Brother Francis spent seven years in the novitiate, seven Lenten vigils in the desert, and became highly proficient in the imitation of wolf calls. For the amusement of his brethren, he would summon the pack to the vicinity of the abbey by howling from the walls after dark. By day, he served in the kitchen, scrubbed the stone floors, and continued his studies of the ancients.

Then one day a messenger from the seminary came riding to the abbey on an ass, bearing tidings of great joy. "It is known," said the messenger, "that the documents found near here are authentic as to date of origin, and that the blueprint was somehow connected with your founder's work. It's being sent to New Vatican for further study."

"Possibly a true relic of Leibowitz, then?" the abbot asked calmly.

But the messenger could not commit himself to that extent, and only raised a shrug of one eyebrow. "It is said that Leibowitz was a widower at the time of his ordination. If the name of his deceased wife could be discovered . . ."

The abbot recalled the note in the box concerning certain articles of food for a woman, and he too shrugged an eyebrow.

Soon afterwards, he summoned Brother Francis into his presence. "My boy," said the priest, actually beaming. "I believe the time has come for you to profess your solemn vows. And may I commend you for your patience and persistence. We shall speak no more of your, ah

. . . encounter with the ah desert wanderer. You are a good simpleton. You may kneel for my blessing, if you wish."

Brother Francis sighed and fell forward in a dead faint. The abbot blessed him and revived him, and he was permitted to profess the solemn vows of the Albertian Brothers of Leibowitz, swearing himself to perpetual poverty, chastity, obedience, and observance of the rule.

Soon afterwards, he was assigned to the copying room, apprentice under an aged monk named Horner, where he would undoubtedly spend the rest of his days illuminating the pages of algebra texts with patterns of olive leaves and cheerful cherubim.

"You have five hours a week," croaked his aged overseer, "which you may devote to an approved project of your own choosing, if you wish. If not, the time will be assigned to copying the *Summa Theologica* and such fragmentary copies of the Britannica as exist."

The young monk thought it over, then asked: "May I have the time for elaborating a beautiful copy of the Leibowitz blueprint?"

Brother Horner frowned doubtfully. "I don't know, son—our good abbot is rather sensitive on this subject. I'm afraid . . ."

Brother Francis begged him earnestly.

"Well, perhaps," the old man said reluctantly. "It seems like a rather brief project, so—I'll permit it."

The young monk selected the finest lambskin available and spent many weeks curing it and stretching it and stoning it to a perfect surface, bleached to a snowy whiteness. He spent more weeks at studying copies of his precious document in every detail, so that he knew each tiny line and marking in the complicated web of geometric markings and mystifying symbols. He pored over it until he could see the whole amazing complexity with his eyes closed. Additional weeks were spent searching painstakingly through the monastery's library for any information at all that might lead to some glimmer of understanding of the design.

Brother Jeris, a young monk who worked with him in the copy room and who frequently teased him about miraculous encounters in the desert, came to squint at it over his shoulder and asked: "What, pray, is the meaning of *Transistorized Control System for Unit Six-B?*"

"Clearly, it is the name of the thing which this diagram represents," said Francis, a trifle crossly since Jeris had merely read the title of the document aloud.

"Surely," said Jeris. "But what is the thing the diagram represents?"

"The transistorized control system for unit six-B, obviously."

Jeris laughed mockingly.

Brother Francis reddened. "I should imagine," said he, "that it represents an abstract concept, rather than a concrete *thing*. It's clearly not a recognizable picture of an object, unless the form is so stylized as to require special training to see it. In my opinion, *Transistorized Control System* is some high abstraction of transcendental value."

"Pertaining to what field of learning?" asked Jeris, still smiling smugly.

"Why . . ." Brother Francis paused. "Since our Beatus Leibowitz was an electronicist prior to his profession and ordination, I suppose the concept applies to the lost art called *electronics*."

"So it is written. But what was the subject matter of that art, Brother?"

"That too is written. The subject matter of electronics was the Electron, which one fragmentary source defines as a Negative Twist of Nothingness."

"I am impressed by your astuteness," said Jeris. "Now perhaps you can tell me how to negate nothingness?"

Brother Francis reddened slightly and squirmed for a reply.

"A negation of nothingness should yield somethingness, I suppose," Jeris continued. "So the Electron must have been a twist of *something*. Unless the negation applies to the 'twist,' and then we would be 'Untwisting Nothing,' eh?" He chuckled. "How clever they must have been, these ancients. I suppose if you keep at it, Francis, you will learn how to untwist a nothing, and then we shall have the Electron in our midst. Where would we put it? On the high altar, perhaps?"

"I couldn't say," Francis answered stiffly. "But I have a certain faith that the Electron must have existed at one time, even though I can't say how it was constructed or what it might have been used for."

The iconoclast laughed mockingly and returned to his work. The incident saddened Francis, but did not turn him from his devotion to his project.

As soon as he had exhausted the library's meager supply of information concerning the lost art of the Albertians' founder, he began preparing preliminary sketches of the designs he meant to use on the lambskin. The diagram itself, since its meaning was obscure, would be redrawn precisely as it was in the blueprint, and penned in coal-black lines. The lettering and numbering, however, he would translate into a more decorative and colorful script than the plain block letters used by the ancients. And the text contained in a square block marked SPECIFI-

CATIONS would be distributed pleasingly around the borders of the document, upon scrolls and shields supported by doves and cherubim. He would make the black lines of the diagram less stark and austere by imagining the geometric tracery to be a trellis, and decorate it with green vines and golden fruit, birds and perhaps a wily serpent. At the very top would be a representation of the Triune God, and at the bottom the coat of arms of the Albertian Order. Thus was the Transistorized Control System of the Blessed Leibowitz to be glorified and rendered appealing to the eye as well as to the intellect.

When he had finished the preliminary sketch, he showed it shyly to Brother Horner for suggestions or approval. "I can see," said the old man a bit remorsefully, "that your project is not to be as brief as I had hoped. But . . . continue with it anyhow. The design is beautiful, beautiful indeed."

"Thank you, Brother."

The old man leaned close to wink confidentially. "I've heard the case for Blessed Leibowitz' canonization has been speeded up, so possibly our dear abbot is less troubled by you-know-what than he previously was."

The news of the speed-up was, of course, happily received by all monastics of the order. Leibowitz' beatification had long since been effected, but the final step in declaring him to be a saint might require many more years, even though the case was under way; and indeed there was the possibility that the Devil's Advocate might uncover evidence to prevent the canonization from occurring at all.

Many months after he had first conceived the project, Brother Francis began actual work on the lambskin. The intricacies of scrollwork, the excruciatingly delicate work of inlaying the gold leaf, the hair-fine detail, made it a labor of years; and when his eyes began to trouble him, there were long weeks when he dared not touch it at all for fear of spoiling it with one little mistake. But slowly, painfully, the ancient diagram was becoming a blaze of beauty. The brothers of the abbey gathered to watch and murmur over it, and some even said that the inspiration of it was proof enough of his alleged encounter with the pilgrim who might have been Blessed Leibowitz.

"I can't see why you don't spend your time on a *useful* project," was Brother Jeris' comment, however. The skeptical monk had been using his own free-project time to make and decorate sheepskin shades for the oil lamps in the chapel.

Brother Horner, the old master copyist, had fallen ill. Within weeks, it became apparent that the well-loved monk was on his deathbed. In the midst of the monastery's grief, the abbot quietly appointed Brother Jeris as master of the copy room.

A Mass of Burial was chanted early in Advent, and the remains of the holy old man were committed to the earth of their origin. On the following day, Brother Jeris informed Brother Francis that he considered it about time for him to put away the things of a child and start doing a man's work. Obediently, the monk wrapped his precious project in parchment, protected it with heavy board, shelved it, and began producing sheepskin lampshades. He made no murmur of protest, and contented himself with realizing that someday the soul of Brother Jeris would depart by the same road as that of Brother Horner, to begin the life for which this copy room was but the staging ground; and afterwards, please God, he might be allowed to complete his beloved document.

Providence, however, took an earlier hand in the matter. During the following summer, a monsignor with several clerks and a donkey train came riding into the abbey and announced that he had come from New Vatican, as Leibowitz advocate in the canonization proceedings, to investigate such evidence as the abbey could produce that might have bearing on the case, including an alleged apparition of the beatified which had come to one Francis Gerard of Utah.

The gentleman was warmly greeted, quartered in the suite reserved for visiting prelates, lavishly served by six young monks responsive to his every whim, of which he had very few. The finest wines were opened, the huntsman snared the plumpest quail and chaparral cocks, and the advocate was entertained each evening by fiddlers and a troupe of clowns, although the visitor persisted in insisting that life go on as usual at the abbey.

On the third day of his visit, the abbot sent for Brother Francis "Monsignor di Simone wishes to see you," he said. "If you let your imagination run away with you, boy, we'll use your gut to string a fiddle, feed your carcass to the wolves, and bury the bones in unhallowed ground. Now get along and see the good gentleman."

Brother Francis needed no such warning. Since he had awakened from his feverish babblings after his first Lenten fast in the desert, he had never mentioned the encounter with the pilgrim except when asked about it, nor had he allowed himself to speculate any further concerning the pilgrim's identity. That the pilgrim might be a matter for high ecclesiastical concern frightened him a little, and his knock was timid at the monsignor's door.

His fright proved unfounded. The monsignor was a suave and diplomatic elder who seemed keenly interested in the small monk's career.

"Now about your encounter with our blessed founder," he said after some minutes of preliminary amenities.

"Oh, but I never said he was our Blessed Leibo——"

"Of course you didn't, my son. Now I have here an account of it, as gathered from other sources, and I would like you to read it, and either confirm it or correct it." He paused to draw a scroll from his case and handed it to Francis. "The sources for this version, of course, had it on hearsay only," he added, "and only *you* can describe it first hand, so I want you to edit it *most* scrupulously."

"Of course. What happened was really very simple, Father."

But it was apparent from the fatness of the scroll that the hearsay account was not so simple. Brother Francis read with mounting apprehension which soon grew to the proportions of pure horror.

"You look white, my son. Is something wrong?" asked the distinguished priest.

"This . . . this . . . it wasn't like this *at all!*" gasped Francis. "He didn't say more than a few words to me. I only saw him once. He just asked me the way to the abbey and tapped the rock where I found the relics."

"No heavenly choir?"

"Oh, no!"

"And it's not true about the nimbus and the carpet of roses that grew up along the road where he walked?"

"As God is my judge, nothing like that happened at all!"

"Ah, well," sighed the advocate. "Travelers' stories are always exaggerated."

He seemed saddened, and Francis hastened to apologize, but the advocate dismissed it as of no great importance to the case. "There are other miracles, carefully documented," he explained, "and anyway—there is one bit of good news about the documents you discovered. We've unearthed the name of the wife who died before our founder came to the order."

"Yes?"

"Yes. It was Emily."

Despite his disappointment with Brother Francis' account of the pilgrim, Monsignor di Simone spent five days at the site of the find. He was accompanied by an eager crew of novices from the abbey, all armed with picks and shovels. After extensive digging, the advocate returned with a small assortment of additional artifacts, and one bloated tin can that contained a desiccated mess which might once have been sauerkraut.

Before his departure, he visited the copy room and asked to see Brother Francis' copy of the famous blueprint. The monk protested that it was really nothing, and produced it with such eagerness his hands trembled.

"Zounds!" said the monsignor, or an oath to such effect. "Finish it, man, finish it!"

The monk looked smilingly at Brother Jeris. Brother Jeris swiftly turned away; the back of his neck gathered color. The following morning, Francis resumed his labors over the illuminated blueprint, with gold leaf, quills, brushes, and dyes.

And then came another donkey train from New Vatican, with a full complement of clerks and armed guards for defense against highwaymen, this time headed by a monsignor with small horns and pointed fangs (or so several novices would later have testified), who announced that he was the *Advocatus Diaboli,* opposing Leibowitz' canonization, and he was here to investigate—and perhaps fix responsibility, he hinted—for a number of incredible and hysterical rumors filtering out of the abbey and reaching even high officials at New Vatican. He made it clear that he would tolerate no romantic nonsense.

The abbot greeted him politely and offered him an iron cot in a cell with a south exposure, after apologizing for the fact that the guest suite had been recently exposed to smallpox. The monsignor was attended by his own staff, and ate mush and herbs with the monks in refectory.

"I understand you are susceptible to fainting spells," he told Brother Francis when the dread time came. "How many members of your family have suffered from epilepsy or madness?"

"None, Excellency."

"I'm not an 'Excellency,'" snapped the priest. "Now we're going to get the truth out of you." His tone implied that he considered it to be a simple straightforward surgical operation which should have been performed years ago.

"Are you aware that documents can be aged artificially?" he demanded.

Francis was not so aware.

"Did you know that Leibowitz' wife was named Emily, and that Emma is *not* a diminutive for Emily?"

Francis had not known it, but recalled from childhood that his own parents had been rather careless about what they called each other. "And if Blessed Leibowitz chose to call her Emma, then I'm sure . . ."

The monsignor exploded, and tore into Francis with semantic tooth and nail, and left the bewildered monk wondering whether he had ever really seen a pilgrim at all.

Before the advocate's departure, he too asked to see the illuminated copy of the print, and this time the monk's hands trembled with fear as he produced it, for he might again be forced to quit the project. The monsignor only stood gazing at it however, swallowed slightly, and forced himself to nod. "Your imagery is vivid," he admitted, "but then, of course, we all knew that, didn't we?"

The monsignor's horns immediately grew shorter by an inch, and he departed the same evening for New Vatican.

The years flowed smoothly by, seaming the faces of the once young and adding gray to the temples. The perpetual labors of the monastery continued, supplying a slow trickle of copied and recopied manuscript to the outside world. Brother Jeris developed ambitions of building a printing press, but when the abbot demanded his reasons, he could only reply, "So we can mass-produce."

"Oh? And in a world that's smug in its illiteracy, what do you intend to do with the stuff? Sell it as kindling paper to the peasants?"

Brother Jeris shrugged unhappily, and the copy room continued with pot and quill.

Then one spring, shortly before Lent, a messenger arrived with glad tidings for the order. The case for Leibowitz was complete. The College of Cardinals would soon convene, and the founder of the Albertian Order would be enrolled in the Calendar of Saints. During the time of rejoicing that followed the announcement, the abbot—now withered and in his dotage—summoned Brother Francis into his presence, and wheezed:

"His Holiness commands your presence during the canonization of Isaac Edward Leibowitz. Prepare to leave.

"Now don't faint on me again," he added querulously.

The trip to New Vatican would take at least three months, perhaps longer, the time depending on how far Brother Francis could get before the inevitable robber band relieved him of his ass, since he would be going unarmed and alone. He carried with him only a begging bowl and the illuminated copy of the Leibowitz print, praying that ignorant robbers would have no use for the latter. As a precaution, however, he wore a black patch over his right eye, for the peasants, being a superstitious lot, could often be put to flight by even a hint of the evil eye. Thus armed and equipped, he set out to obey the summons of his high priest.

Two months and some odd days later he met his robber on a mountain trail that was heavily wooded and far from any settlement. His robber was a short man, but heavy as a bull, with a glazed knob of a pate and a jaw like a block of granite. He stood in the trail with his legs spread wide and his massive arms folded across his chest, watching the approach of the little figure on the ass. The robber seemed alone, and armed only with a knife which he did not bother to remove from his belt thong. His appearance was a disappointment, since Francis had been secretly hoping for another encounter with the pilgrim of long ago.

"Get off," said the robber.

The ass stopped in the path. Brother Francis tossed back his cowl to reveal the eye patch, and raised a trembling finger to touch it. He began to lift the patch slowly as if to reveal something hideous that might be hidden beneath it. The robber threw back his head and laughed a laugh that might have sprung from the throat of Satan himself. Francis muttered an exorcism, but the robber seemed untouched.

"You black-sacked jeebers wore that one out years ago," he said. "Get off."

Francis smiled, shrugged, and dismounted without protest.

"A good day to you, sir," he said pleasantly. "You may take the ass. Walking will improve my health, I think." He smiled again and started away.

"Hold it," said the robber. "Strip to the buff. And let's see what's in that package."

Brother Francis touched his begging bowl and made a helpless gesture, but this brought only another scornful laugh from the robber.

"I've seen that alms-pot trick before too," he said. "The last man with a begging bowl had half a heklo of gold in his boot. Now strip."

Brother Francis displayed his sandals, but began to strip. The robber searched his clothing, found nothing, and tossed it back to him.

"Now let's see inside the package."

"It is only a document, sir," the monk protested. "Of value to no one but its owner."

"Open it."

Silently Brother Francis obeyed. The gold leaf and the colorful design flashed brilliantly in the sunlight that filtered through the foliage. The robber's craggy jaw dropped an inch. He whistled softly.

"What a pretty! Now wouldn't me woman like it to hang on the shanty wall!"

He continued to stare while the monk went slowly sick inside. *If Thou has sent him to test me, O Lord,* he pleaded inwardly, *then help me to die like a man, for he'll get it over the dead body of Thy servant, if take it he must.*

"Wrap it up for me," the robber commanded, clamping his jaw in sudden decision.

The monk whimpered softly. "Please, sir, you would not take the work of a man's lifetime. I spent fifteen years illuminating this manuscript, and . . ."

"Well! Did it yourself, did you?" The robber threw back his head and howled again.

Francis reddened. "I fail to see the humor, sir . . ."

The robber pointed at it between guffaws. "You! Fifteen years to make a paper bauble. So that's what you do. Tell me why. Give me one good reason. For fifteen years. Ha!"

Francis stared at him in stunned silence and could think of no reply that would appease his contempt.

Gingerly, the monk handed it over. The robber took it in both hands and made as if to rip it down the center.

"Jesus, Mary, Joseph!" the monk screamed, and went to his knees in the trail. "For the love of God, sir!"

Softening slightly, the robber tossed it on the ground with a snicker. "Wrestle you for it."

"Anything, sir, anything!"

They squared off. The monk crossed himself and recalled that wrestling had once been a divinely sanctioned sport—and with grim faith, he marched into battle.

Three seconds later, he lay groaning on the flat of his back under a short mountain of muscle. A sharp rock seemed to be severing his spine.

"Heh-heh," said the robber, and arose to claim his document.

Hands folded as if in prayer, Brother Francis scurried after him on his knees, begging at the top of his lungs.

The robber turned to snicker. "I believe you'd kiss a boot to get it back."

Francis caught up with him and fervently kissed his boot.

This proved too much for even such a firm fellow as the robber. He flung the manuscript down again with a curse and climbed aboard the monk's donkey. The monk snatched up the precious document and trotted along beside the robber, thanking him profusely and blessing him repeatedly while the robber rode away on the ass. Francis sent a glowing cross of benediction after the departing figure and praised God for the existence of such selfless robbers.

And yet when the man had vanished among the trees, he felt an aftermath of sadness. Fifteen years to make a paper bauble . . . The taunting voice still rang in his ears. Why? Tell one good reason for fifteen years.

He was unaccustomed to the blunt ways of the outside world, to its harsh habits and curt attitudes. He found his heart deeply troubled by the mocking words, and his head hung low in the cowl as he plodded along. At one time he considered tossing the document in the brush and leaving it for the rains—but Father Juan had approved his taking it as a gift, and he could not come with empty hands. Chastened, he traveled on.

The hour had come. The ceremony surged about him as a magnificent spectacle of sound and stately movement and vivid color in the majestic basilica. And when the perfectly infallible Spirit had finally been invoked, a monsignor—it was di Simone, Francis noticed, the advocate for the saint—arose and called upon Peter to speak, through the person of Leo XXII, commanding the assemblage to hearken.

Whereupon, the Pope quietly proclaimed that Isaac Edward Leibowitz was a saint, and it was finished. The ancient and obscure technician was of the heavenly hagiarchy, and Brother Francis breathed a dutiful prayer to his new patron as the choir burst into the *Te Deum*.

The Pontiff strode quickly into the audience room where the little monk was waiting, taking Brother Francis by surprise and rendering him briefly speechless. He knelt quickly to kiss the Fisherman's ring and receive the blessing. As he arose, he found himself clutching the beautiful document behind him as if ashamed of it. The Pope's eyes caught the motion, and he smiled.

"You have brought us a gift, our son?" he asked.

The monk gulped, nodded stupidly, and brought it out. Christ's Vicar stared at it for a long time without apparent expression. Brother Francis' heart went sinking deeper as the seconds drifted by.

"It is a nothing," he blurted, "a miserable gift. I am ashamed to have wasted so much time at . . ." He choked off.

The Pope seemed not to hear him. "Do you understand the meaning of Saint Isaac's symbology?" he asked, peering curiously at the abstract design of the circuit.

Dumbly the monk shook his head.

"Whatever it means . . ." the Pope began, but broke off. He smiled and spoke of other things. Francis had been so honored not because of any official judgment concerning his pilgrim. He had been honored for his role in bringing to light such important documents and relics of the saint, for such they had been judged, regardless of the manner in which they had been found.

Francis stammered his thanks. The Pontiff gazed again at the colorful blaze of his illuminated diagram. "Whatever it means," he breathed once more, "this bit of learning, though dead, will live again." He smiled up at the monk and winked. "And we shall guard it till that day."

For the first time, the little monk noticed that the Pope had a hole in his robe. His clothing, in fact, was threadbare. The carpet in the audience room was worn through in spots, and plaster was falling from the ceiling.

But there were books on the shelves along the walls. Books of painted beauty, speaking of incomprehensible things, copied by men whose business was not to understand but to save. And the books were waiting.

"Goodby, beloved son."

And the small keeper of the flame of knowledge trudged back toward his abbey on foot. His heart was singing as he approached the robber's outpost. And if the robber happened to be taking the day off, the monk meant to sit down and wait for his return. This time he had an answer.

Love Letters from Mars
John Clardi

Dear cell, the Martian winter ends.
The tubes run green again, and green
the hydroponic hills are seen
without their glass. Our ship ascends
through a new vapor. And the Frogs
grow restless in their locks. Unrest
is on us all. This gravity
works through me. No psychometry
keeps its adjustment. Everywhere
the Frogs are hating us, hating us.
(Can we shut out what we shut in?)
Sometimes I tense myself to tear
my filter off, gulp, and be damned.
"A lot of extra-sensory fuss,"
I tell myself, but can't command
the balance of my mood. My dear,
something is happening to Spring:
we've come too far from everything.

One Ordinary Day, with Peanuts

Shirley Jackson

MR. JOHN PHILIP JOHNSON shut his front door behind him and came down his front steps into the bright morning with a feeling that all was well with the world on this best of all days, and wasn't the sun warm and good, and didn't his shoes feel comfortable after the resoling, and he knew that he had undoubtedly chosen the precise very tie which belonged with the day and the sun and his comfortable feet, and, after all, wasn't the world just a wonderful place? In spite of the fact that he was a small man, and the tie was perhaps a shade vivid, Mr. Johnson irradiated this feeling of well-being as he came down the steps and onto the dirty sidewalk, and he smiled at people who passed him, and some of them even smiled back. He stopped at the newsstand on the corner and bought his paper, saying *"Good* morning" with real conviction to the man who sold him the paper and the two or three other people who were lucky enough to be buying papers when Mr. Johnson skipped up. He remembered to fill his pockets with candy and peanuts, and then he set out to get himself uptown. He stopped in a flower shop and bought

---

SHIRLEY JACKSON *was a well-known novelist (and practicing amateur witch!) who died in 1965. Her novels include* The Haunting of Hill House *and* We Have Always Lived in the Castle. *Her short fiction includes the famous story "The Lottery" and the lesser-known but equally distinguished story that appears below. It was first published in F&SF's January 1955 issue.*

a carnation for his buttonhole, and stopped almost immediately afterward to give the carnation to a small child in a carriage, who looked at him dumbly, and then smiled, and Mr. Johnson smiled, and the child's mother looked at Mr. Johnson for a minute and then smiled too.

When he had gone several blocks uptown, Mr. Johnson cut across the avenue and went along a side street, chosen at random; he did not follow the same route every morning, but preferred to pursue his eventful way in wide detours, more like a puppy than a man intent upon business. It happened this morning that halfway down the block a moving van was parked, and the furniture from an upstairs apartment stood half on the sidewalk, half on the steps, while an amused group of people loitered, examining the scratches on the tables and the worn spots on the chairs, and a harassed woman, trying to watch a young child and the movers and the furniture all at the same time, gave the clear impression of endeavoring to shelter her private life from the people staring at her belongings. Mr. Johnson stopped, and for a moment joined the crowd, and then he came forward and, touching his hat civilly, said, "Perhaps I can keep an eye on your little boy for you?"

The woman turned and glared at him distrustfully, and Mr. Johnson added hastily, "We'll sit right here on the steps." He beckoned to the little boy, who hesitated and then responded agreeably to Mr. Johnson's genial smile. Mr. Johnson brought out a handful of peanuts from his pocket and sat on the steps with the boy, who at first refused the peanuts on the grounds that his mother did not allow him to accept food from strangers; Mr. Johnson said that probably his mother had not intended peanuts to be included, since elephants at the circus ate them, and the boy considered, and then agreed solemnly. They sat on the steps cracking peanuts in a comradely fashion, and Mr. Johnson said, "So you're moving?"

"Yep," said the boy.

"Where you going?"

"Vermont."

"Nice place. Plenty of snow there. Maple sugar, too; you like maple sugar?"

"Sure."

"Plenty of maple sugar in Vermont. You going to live on a farm?"

"Going to live with Grandpa."

"Grandpa like peanuts?"

"Sure."

"Ought to take him some," said Mr. Johnson, reaching into his pocket. "Just you and Mommy going?"

"Yep."

"Tell you what," Mr. Johnson said. "You take some peanuts to eat on the train."

The boy's mother, after glancing at them frequently, had seemingly decided that Mr. Johnson was trustworthy, because she had devoted herself wholeheartedly to seeing that the movers did not—what movers rarely do, but every housewife believes they will—crack a leg from her good table, or set a kitchen chair down on a lamp. Most of the furniture was loaded by now, and she was deep in that nervous stage when she knew there was something she had forgotten to pack—hidden away in the back of a closet somewhere, or left at a neighbor's and forgotten, or on the clothesline—and was trying to remember under stress what it was.

"This all, lady?" the chief mover said, completing her dismay.

Uncertainly, she nodded.

"Want to go on the truck with the furniture, sonny?" the mover asked the boy, and laughed. The boy laughed too and said to Mr. Johnson, "I guess I'll have a good time at Vermont."

"Fine time," said Mr. Johnson, and stood up. "Have one more peanut before you go," he said to the boy.

The boy's mother said to Mr. Johnson. "Thank you so much; it was a great help to me."

"Nothing at all," said Mr. Johnson gallantly. "Where in Vermont are you going?"

The mother looked at the little boy accusingly, as though he had given away a secret of some importance, and said unwillingly, "Greenwich."

"Lovely town," said Mr. Johnson. He took out a card, and wrote a name on the back. "Very good friend of mine lives in Greenwich," he said. "Call on him for anything you need. His wife makes the best doughnuts in town," he added soberly to the little boy.

"Swell," said the little boy.

"Goodbye," said Mr. Johnson.

He went on, stepping happily with his new-shod feet, feeling the warm sun on his back and on the top of his head. Halfway down the block he met a stray dog and fed him a peanut.

At the corner, where another wide avenue faced him, Mr. Johnson decided to go on uptown again. Moving with comparative laziness, he was passed on either side by people hurrying and frowning, and people brushed past him going the other way, clattering along to get somewhere quickly. Mr. Johnson stopped on every corner and waited patiently for the light to change, and he stepped out of the way of anyone who seemed to be in any particular hurry, but one young lady came too fast for him, and crashed wildly into him when he stooped to pat a kitten which had run out onto the sidewalk from an apartment house and was now unable to get back through the rushing feet.

"Excuse me," said the young lady, trying frantically to pick up Mr. Johnson and hurry on at the same time, "terribly sorry."

The kitten, regardless now of danger, raced back to its home. "Perfectly all right," said Mr. Johnson, adjusting himself carefully. "You seem to be in a hurry."

"Of course I'm in a hurry," said the young lady. "I'm late."

She was extremely cross and the frown between her eyes seemed well on its way to becoming permanent. She had obviously awakened late, because she had not spent any extra time in making herself look pretty, and her dress was plain and unadorned with collar or brooch, and her lipstick was noticeably crooked. She tried to brush past Mr. Johnson, but, risking her suspicious displeasure, he took her arm and said, "Please wait."

"Look," she said ominously, "I ran into you and your lawyer can see my lawyer and I will gladly pay all damages and all inconveniences suffered therefrom but please this minute let me go because *I am late*."

"Late for what?" said Mr. Johnson; he tried his winning smile on her but it did no more than keep her, he suspected, from knocking him down again.

"Late for work," she said between her teeth. "Late for my employment. I have a job and if I am late I lose exactly so much an hour and I cannot really afford what your pleasant conversation is costing me, be it *ever* so pleasant."

"I'll pay for it," said Mr. Johnson. Now these were magic words, not necessarily because they were true, or because she seriously expected Mr. Johnson to pay for anything, but because Mr. Johnson's flat statement, obviously innocent of irony, could not be, coming from Mr. Johnson, anything but the statement of a responsible and truthful and respectable man.

"What *do* you mean?" she asked.

"I said that since I am obviously responsible for your being late I shall certainly pay for it."

"Don't be silly," she said, and for the first time the frown disappeared. *"I* wouldn't expect you to pay for anything—a few minutes ago I was offering to pay *you.* Anyway," she added, almost smiling, "it *was* my fault."

"What happens if you don't go to work?"

She stared. "I don't get paid."

"Precisely," said Mr. Johnson.

"What do you mean, precisely? If I don't show up at the office exactly twenty minutes ago I lose a dollar and twenty cents an hour, or two cents a minute or . . ." She thought. ". . . Almost a dime for the time I've spent talking to you."

Mr. Johnson laughed, and finally she laughed, too. "You're late already," he pointed out. "Will you give me another four cents worth?"

"I don't understand why."

"You'll see," Mr. Johnson promised. He led her over to the side of the walk, next to the buildings, and said, "Stand here," and went out into the rush of people going both ways. Selecting and considering, as one who must make a choice involving perhaps whole years of lives, he estimated the people going by. Once he almost moved, and then at the last minute thought better of it and drew back. Finally, from half a block away, he saw what he wanted, and moved out into the center of the traffic to intercept a young man, who was hurrying, and dressed as though he had awakened late, and frowning.

"Oof," said the young man, because Mr. Johnson had thought of no better way to intercept anyone than the one the young woman had unwittingly used upon him. "Where do you think you're going?" the young man demanded from the sidewalk."

"I want to speak to you," said Mr. Johnson ominously.

The young man got up nervously, dusting himself and eying Mr. Johnson. "What for?" he said. "What'd *I* do?"

"That's what bothers me most about people nowadays," Mr. Johnson complained broadly to the people passing. "No matter whether they've done anything or not, they always figure someone's after them. About what you're going to do," he told the young man.

"Listen," said the young men, trying to brush past him, "I'm late, and I don't have any time to listen. Here's a dime, now get going."

"Thank you," said Mr. Johnson, pocketing the dime. "Look," he said, "what happens if you stop running?"

"I'm late," said the young man, still trying to get past Mr. Johnson, who was unexpectedly clinging.

"How much you make an hour?" Mr. Johnson demanded.

"A communist, are you?" said the young man. "Now will you please let me——"

"No," said Mr. Johnson insistently, *"how* much?"

"Dollar fifty," said the young man. "And *now* will you——"

"You like adventure?"

The young man stared, and, staring, found himself caught and held by Mr. Johnson's genial smile; he almost smiled back and then repressed it and made an effort to tear away. "I got to *hurry,*" he said.

"Mystery? Like surprises? Unusual and exciting events?"

"You selling something?"

"Sure," said Mr. Johnson. "You want to take a chance?"

The young man hesitated, looked longingly up the avenue toward what might have been his destination and then, when Mr. Johnson said, "I'll pay for it," with his own peculiar convincing emphasis, turned and said, "Well, okay. But I got to *see* it first, what I'm buying."

Mr. Johnson, breathing hard, led the young man over to the side where the girl was standing; she had been watching with interest Mr. Johnson's capture of the young man and now, smiling timidly, she looked at Mr. Johnson as though prepared to be surprised at nothing.

Mr. Johnson reached into his pocket and took out his wallet. "Here," he said, and handed a bill to the girl. "This about equals your day's pay."

"But no," she said, surprised in spite of herself. "I mean, I *couldn't.*"

"Please do not interrupt," Mr. Johnson told her. "And *here,*" he said to the young man, "this will take care of *you.*" The young man accepted the bill dazedly, but said, "Probably counterfeit," to the young woman out of the side of his mouth. "Now," Mr. Johnson went on, disregarding the young man, "what is your name, miss?"

"Kent," she said helplessly. "Mildred Kent."

"Fine," said Mr. Johnson. "And you, sir?"

"Arthur Adams," said the young man stiffly.

"Splendid," said Mr. Johnson. "Now, Miss Kent, I would like you to meet Mr. Adams. Mr. Adams, Miss Kent."

Miss Kent stared, wet her lips nervously, made a gesture as though she might run, and said, "How do you do?"

Mr. Adams straightened his shoulders, scowled at Mr. Johnson, made a gesture as though he might run, and said, "How do you do?"

"Now *this,*" said Mr. Johnson, taking several bills from his wallet, "should be enough for the day for both of you. I would suggest, perhaps, Coney Island—although I personally am not fond of the place—or perhaps a nice lunch somewhere, and dancing, or a matinee, or even a movie, although take care to choose a really *good* one; there are so many bad movies these days. You might," he said, struck with an inspiration, "visit the Bronx Zoo, or the Planetarium. Anywhere, as a matter of fact," he concluded, "that you would like to go. Have a nice time."

As he started to move away Arthur Adams, breaking from his dumfounded stare, said, "But see here, mister, you *can't* do this. Why—how do you know—I mean, *we* don't even know—I mean, how do you know we won't just take the money and not do what you said?"

"You've taken the money," Mr. Johnson said. "You don't have to follow any of my suggestions. You may know something you prefer to do—perhaps a museum, or something."

"But suppose I just run away with it and leave her here?"

"I know you won't," said Mr. Johnson gently, "because you remembered to ask *me* that. Goodbye," he added, and went on.

As he stepped up the street, conscious of the sun on his head and his good shoes, he heard from somewhere behind him the young man saying, "Look, you know you don't *have* to if you don't want to," and the girl saying. "But unless *you* don't want to . . ." Mr. Johnson smiled to himself and then thought that he had better hurry along; when he wanted to he could move very quickly, and before the young woman had gotten around to saying, "Well, I will if *you* will," Mr. Johnson was several blocks away and had already stopped twice, once to help a lady lift several large packages into a taxi and once to hand a peanut to a seagull. By this time he was in an area of large stores and many more people and he was buffeted constantly from either side by people hurrying and cross and late and sullen. Once he offered a peanut to a man who asked him for a dime, and once he offered a peanut to a bus driver who had stopped his bus at an intersection and had opened the window next to his seat and put out his head as though longing for fresh air and the comparative quiet of the traffic. The man wanting a dime took the peanut because Mr. Johnson had wrapped a dollar bill around it, but the bus driver took the peanut and asked ironically, "You want a transfer, Jack?"

On a busy corner Mr. Johnson encountered two young people—for one minute he thought they might be Mildred Kent and Arthur Adams —who were eagerly scanning a newspaper, their backs pressed against a storefront to avoid the people passing, their heads bent together. Mr.

Johnson, whose curiosity was insatiable, leaned onto the storefront next to them and peeked over the man's shoulder; they were scanning the "Apartments Vacant" columns.

Mr. Johnson remembered the street where the woman and her little boy were going to Vermont and he tapped the man on the shoulder and said amiably, "Try down on West Seventeen. About the middle of the block, people moved out this morning."

"Say, what do you——" said the man, and then, seeing Mr. Johnson clearly. "Well, thanks. Where did you say?"

"West Seventeen," said Mr. Johnson. "About the middle of the block." He smiled again and said, "Good luck."

"Thanks," said the man.

"Thanks," said the girl, as they moved off.

"Goodbye," said Mr. Johnson.

He lunched alone in a pleasant restaurant, where the food was rich, and only Mr. Johnson's excellent digestion could encompass two of their whipped-cream-and-chocolate-and-rum-cake pastries for dessert. He had three cups of coffee, tipped the waiter largely, and went out into the street again into the wonderful sunlight, his shoes still comfortable and fresh on his feet. Outside he found a beggar staring into the windows of the restaurant he had left and, carefully looking through the money in his pocket, Mr. Johnson approached the beggar and pressed some coins and a couple of bills into his hand. "It's the price of the veal cutlet lunch plus tip," said Mr. Johnson. "Goodbye."

After his lunch he rested; he walked into the nearest park and fed peanuts to the pigeons. It was late afternoon by the time he was ready to start back downtown, and he had refereed two checker games and watched a small boy and girl whose mother had fallen asleep and awakened with surprise and fear which turned to amusement when she saw Mr. Johnson. He had given away almost all of his candy, and had fed all the rest of his peanuts to the pigeons, and it was time to go home. Although the late afternoon sun was pleasant, and his shoes were still entirely comfortable, he decided to take a taxi downtown.

He had a difficult time catching a taxi, because he gave up the first three or four empty ones to people who seemed to need them more; finally, however, he stood alone on the corner and—almost like netting a frisky fish—he hailed desperately until he succeeded in catching a cab which had been proceeding with haste uptown and seemed to draw in towards Mr. Johnson against its own will.

"Mister," the cab driver said as Mr. Johnson climbed in, "I figured you was an omen, like. I wasn't going to pick you up at all."

"Kind of you," said Mr. Johnson ambiguously.

"If I'd of let you go it would of cost me ten bucks," said the driver.

"Really?" said Mr. Johnson.

"Yeah," said the driver. "Guy just got out of the cab, he turned around and give me ten bucks, said take this and bet it in a hurry on a horse named Vulcan, right away."

"Vulcan?" said Mr. Johnson, horrified. "A fire sign on a Wednesday?"

"What?" said the driver. "Anyway, I said to myself if I got no fare between here and there I'd bet the ten, but if anyone looked like they needed the cab I'd take it as an omen and I'd take the ten home to the wife."

"You were very right," said Mr. Johnson heartily. "This is Wednesday, you would have lost your money. Monday, yes, or even Saturday. But never never never a fire sign on a Wednesday. Sunday would have been good, now."

"Vulcan don't run on Sunday," said the driver.

"You wait till another day," said Mr. Johnson. "Down this street, please, driver. I'll get off on the next corner."

"He *told* me Vulcan, though," said the driver.

"I'll tell you," said Mr. Johnson, hesitating with the door of the cab half open. "You take that ten dollars and I'll give you another ten dollars to go with it, and you go right ahead and bet that money on any Thursday on any horse that has a name indicating . . . let me see, Thursday . . . well, grain. Or any growing food."

"Grain?" said the driver. "You mean a horse named, like, Wheat or something?"

"Certainly," said Mr. Johnson. "Or, as a matter of fact, to make it even easier, any horse whose name includes the letters, C, R, L. Perfectly simple."

"Tall corn?" said the driver, a light in his eye. "You mean a horse named, like, Tall Corn?"

"Absolutely," said Mr. Johnson. "Here's your money."

"Tall Corn," said the driver. "Thank *you*, mister."

"Goodbye," said Mr. Johnson.

He was on his own corner and went straight up to his apartment. He let himself in and called "Hello?" and Mrs. Johnson answered from the kitchen, "Hello, dear, aren't you early?"

"Took a taxi home," Mr. Johnson said. "I remembered the cheese-cake, too. What's for dinner?"

Mrs. Johnson came out of the kitchen and kissed him; she was a comfortable woman, and smiling as Mr. Johnson smiled. "Hard day?" she asked.

"Not very," said Mr. Johnson, hanging his coat in the closet. "How about you?"

"So-so," she said. She stood in the kitchen doorway while he settled into his easy chair and took off his good shoes and took out the paper he had bought that morning. "Here and there," she said.

"I didn't do so badly," Mr. Johnson said. "Couple young people."

"Fine," she said. "I had a little nap this afternoon, took it easy most of the day. Went into a department store this morning and accused the woman next to me of shoplifting, and had the store detective pick her up. Sent three dogs to the pound—*you* know, the usual thing. Oh, and listen," she added, remembering.

"What?" asked Mr. Johnson.

"Well," she said, "I got onto a bus and asked the driver for a transfer, and when he helped someone else first I said that he was impertinent, and quarreled with him. And then I said why wasn't he in the army, and I said it loud enough for everyone to hear, and I took his number and I turned in a complaint. Probably got him fired."

"Fine," said Mr. Johnson. "But you do look tired. Want to change over tomorrow?"

"I *would* like to," she said. "I could do with a change."

"Right," said Mr. Johnson. "What's for dinner?"

"Veal cutlet."

"Had it for lunch," said Mr. Johnson.

The Women
Men Don't See

James Tiptree, Jr.

I SEE HER FIRST while the Mexicana 727 is barreling down to Cozumel Island. I come out of the can and lurch into her seat, saying "Sorry," at a double female blur. The near blur nods quietly. The younger one in the window seat goes on looking out. I continue down the aisle, registering nothing. Zero. I never would have looked at them or thought of them again.

Cozumel airport is the usual mix of panicky Yanks dressed for the sand pile and calm Mexicans dressed for lunch at the Presidente. I am a used-up Yank dressed for serious fishing; I extract my rods and duffel from the riot and hike across the field to find my charter pilot. One Captain Estéban has contracted to deliver me to the bonefish flats of Bélise three hundred kilometers down the coast.

Captain Estéban turns out to be four feet nine of mahogany Maya *puro*. He is also in a somber Maya snit. He tells me my Cessna is grounded somewhere and his Bonanza is booked to take a party to Chetumal.

Well, Chetumal is south; can he take me along and go on to Bélise

---

"JAMES TIPTREE, *Jr.*" *is a pen name for Alice Sheldon, a psychologist who started writing science fiction in the late 1960s. She has won several Nebula and Hugo awards in recent years and is considered one of the most innovative writers in the field. "The Women Men Don't See," a Nebula Award nominee, appeared in the December 1973 issue.*

after he drops them? Gloomily he concedes the possibility—*if* the other party permits, and *if* there are not too many *equipajes*.

The Chetumal party approaches. It's the woman and her young companion—daughter?—neatly picking their way across the gravel and yucca apron. Their Ventura two-suiters, like themselves, are small, plain and neutral-colored. No problem. When the captain asks if I may ride along, the mother says mildly "Of course," without looking at me.

I think that's when my inner tilt-detector sends up its first faint click. How come this woman has already looked me over carefully enough to accept on her plane? I disregard it. Paranoia hasn't been useful in my business for years, but the habit is hard to break.

As we clamber into the Bonanza, I see the girl has what could be an attractive body if there was any spark at all. There isn't. Captain Estéban folds a serape to sit on so he can see over the cowling and runs a meticulous check-down. And then we're up and trundling over the turquoise Jello of the Caribbean into a stiff south wind.

The coast on our right is the territory of Quintana Roo. If you haven't seen Yucatan, imagine the world's biggest absolutely flat green-grey rug. An empty-looking land. We pass the white ruin of Tulum and the gash of the road to Chichen Itza, a half-dozen coconut plantations, and then nothing but reef and low scrub jungle all the way to the horizon, just about the way the conquistadores saw it four centuries back.

Long strings of cumulus are racing at us, shadowing the coast. I have gathered that part of our pilot's gloom concerns the weather. A cold front is dying on the henequen fields of Mérida to west, and the south wind has piled up a string of coastal storms: what they call *llovisnas*. Estéban detours methodically around a couple of small thunderheads. The Bonanza jinks, and I look back with a vague notion of reassuring the women. They are calmly intent on what can be seen of Yucatan. Well, they were offered the copilot's view, but they turned it down. Too shy?

Another *llovisna* puffs up ahead. Estéban takes the Bonanza upstairs, rising in his seat to sight his course. I relax for the first time in too long, savoring the latitudes between me and my desk, the week of fishing ahead. Our captain's classic Maya profile attracts my gaze: forehead sloping back from his predatory nose, lips and jaw stepping back below it. If his slant eyes had been any more crossed, he couldn't have made his license. That's a handsome combination, believe it or not. On the little Maya chicks in their minishifts with iridescent gloop on those cockeyes, it's also highly erotic. Nothing like the oriental doll thing;

these people have stone bones. Captain Estéban's old grandmother could probably tow the Bonanza . . .

I'm snapped awake by the cabin hitting my ear. Estéban is barking into his headset over a drumming racket of hail; the windows are dark grey.

One important noise is missing—the motor. I realize Estéban is fighting a dead plane. Thirty-six hundred; we've lost two thousand feet!

He slaps tank switches as the storm throws us around; I catch something about *gasolina* in a snarl that shows his big teeth. The Bonanza reels down. As he reaches for an overhead toggle, I see the fuel gauges are high. Maybe a clogged gravity feed line; I've heard of dirty gas down here. He drops the set. It's a million to one nobody can read us through the storm at this range anyway. Twenty-five hundred—going down.

His electric feed pump seems to have cut in: the motor explodes—quits—explodes—and quits again for good. We are suddenly out of the bottom of the clouds. Below us is a long white line almost hidden by rain: The reef. But there isn't any beach behind it, only a big meandering bay with a few mangrove flats—and it's coming up at us fast.

This is going to be bad, I tell myself with great unoriginality. The women behind me haven't made a sound. I look back and see they're braced down with their coats by their heads. With a stalling speed around eighty, all this isn't much use, but I wedge myself in.

Estéban yells some more into his set, flying a falling plane. He is doing one jesus job, too—as the water rushes up at us he dives into a hair-raising turn and hangs us into the wind—with a long pale ridge of sandbar in front of our nose.

Where in hell he found it I never know. The Bonanza mushes down, and we belly-hit with a tremendous tearing crash—bounce—hit again—and everything slews wildly as we flat-spin into the mangroves at the end of the bar. Crash! Clang! The plane is wrapping itself into a mound of strangler fig with one wing up. The crashing quits with us all in one piece. And no fire. Fantastic.

Captain Estéban prys open his door, which is now in the roof. Behind me a woman is repeating quietly, "Mother. Mother." I climb up the floor and find the girl trying to free herself from her mother's embrace. The woman's eyes are closed. Then she opens them and suddenly lets go, sane as soap. Estéban starts hauling them out. I grab the Bonanza's aid kit and scramble out after them into brilliant sun and wind. The storm that hit us is already vanishing up the coast.

"Great landing, Captain."

"Oh, *yes!* It was beautiful." The women are shaky, but no hysteria. Estéban is surveying the scenery with the expression his ancestors used on the Spaniards.

If you've been in one of these things, you know the slow-motion inanity that goes on. Euphoria, first. We straggle down the fig tree and out onto the sandbar in the roaring hot wind, noting without alarm that there's nothing but miles of crystalline water on all sides. It's only a foot or so deep, and the bottom is the olive color of silt. The distant shore around us is all flat mangrove swamp, totally uninhabitable.

"Bahia Espiritu Santo." Estéban confirms my guess that we're down in that huge water wilderness. I always wanted to fish it.

"What's all that smoke?" The girl is pointing at the plumes blowing around the horizon.

"Alligator hunters," says Estéban. Maya poachers have left burn-offs in the swamps. It occurs to me that any signal fires we make aren't going to be too conspicuous. And I now note that our plane is well-buried in the mound of fig. Hard to see it from the air.

Just as the question of how the hell we get out of here surfaces in my mind, the older woman asks composedly, "If they didn't hear you, Captain, when will they start looking for us? Tomorrow?"

"Correct," Estéban agrees dourly. I recall that air-sea rescue is fairly informal here. Like, keep an eye open for Mario, his mother says he hasn't been home all week.

It dawns on me we may be here quite some while.

Furthermore, the diesel-truck noise on our left is the Caribbean piling back into the mouth of the bay. The wind is pushing it at us, and the bare bottoms on the mangroves show that our bar is covered at high tide. I recall seeing a full moon this morning in—believe it, St. Louis—which means maximal tides. Well, we can climb up in the plane. But what about drinking water?

There's a small splat! behind me. The older woman has sampled the bay. She shakes her head, smiling ruefully. It's the first real expression on either of them; I take it as the signal for introductions. When I say I'm Don Fenton from St. Louis, she tells me their name is Parsons, from Bethesda, Maryland. She says it so nicely I don't at first notice we aren't being given first names. We all compliment Captain Estéban again.

His left eye is swelled shut, an inconvenience beneath his attention as a Maya, but Mrs. Parsons spots the way he's bracing his elbow in his ribs.

"You're hurt, Captain."

"*Roto*—I think is broken." He's embarrassed at being in pain. We get him to peel off his Jaime shirt, revealing a nasty bruise in his superb dark-bay torso.

"Is there tape in that kit, Mr. Fenton? I've had a little first-aid training."

She begins to deal competently and very impersonally with the tape. Miss Parsons and I wander to the end of the bar and have a conversation which I am later to recall acutely.

"Roseate spoonbills," I tell her as three pink birds flap away.

"They're beautiful," she says in her tiny voice. They both have tiny voices. "He's a Mayan Indian, isn't he? The pilot, I mean."

"Right. The real thing, straight out of the Bonampak murals. Have you seen Chichén and Uxmal?"

"Yes. We were in Mérida. We're going to Tikal in Guatemala . . . I mean, we were."

"You'll get there." It occurs to me the girl needs cheering up. "Have they told you that Maya mothers used to tie a board on the infant's forehead to get that slant? They also hung a ball of tallow over its nose to make its eyes cross. It was considered aristocratic."

She smiles and takes another peek at Estéban. "People seem different in Yucatan," she says thoughtfully. "Not like the Indians around Mexico City. More, I don't know, independent."

"Comes from never having been conquered. Mayas got massacred and chased a lot, but nobody ever really flattened them. I bet you didn't know that the last Mexican-Maya war ended with a negotiated truce in nineteen thirty-five?"

"No!" Then she says seriously, "I like that."

"So do I."

"The water is really rising very fast," says Mrs. Parsons gently from behind us.

It is, and so is another *llovisna*. We climb back into the Bonanza. I try to rig my parka for a rain catcher, which blows loose as the storm hits fast and furious. We sort a couple of malt bars and my bottle of Jack Daniels out of the jumble in the cabin and make ourselves reasonably comfortable. The Parsons take a sip of whiskey each, Estéban and I considerably more. The Bonanza begins to bump soggily.

Estéban makes an ancient one-eyed Maya face at the water seeping into his cabin and goes to sleep. We all nap.

When the water goes down, the euphoria has gone with it, and we're very, very thirsty. It's also damn near sunset. I get to work with a bait-casting rod and some treble hooks and manage to foul-hook four small mullets. Estéban and the women tie the Bonanza's midget life raft out in the mangroves to catch rain. The wind is parching hot. No planes go by.

Finally another shower comes over and yields us six ounces of water apiece. When the sunset envelops the world in golden smoke, we squat on the sandbar to eat wet raw mullet and Instant Breakfast crumbs. The women are now in shorts, neat but definitely not sexy.

"I never realized how refreshing raw fish is," Mrs. Parsons says pleasantly. Her daughter chuckles, also pleasantly. She's on Mamma's far side away from Estéban and me. I have Mrs. Parsons figured now; Mother Hen protecting only chick from male predators. That's all right with me. I came here to fish.

But something is irritating me. The damn women haven't complained once, you understand. Not a peep, not a quaver, no personal manifestations whatever. They're like something out of a manual.

"You really seem at home in the wilderness, Mrs. Parsons. You do much camping?"

"Oh goodness no." Diffident laugh. "Not since my girl scout days. Oh, look—are those man-of-war birds?"

Answer a question with a question. I wait while the frigate birds sail nobly into the sunset.

"Bethesda . . . Would I be wrong in guessing you work for Uncle Sam?"

"Why, yes. You must be very familiar with Washington, Mr. Fenton. Does your work bring you there often?"

Anywhere but on our sandbar the little ploy would have worked. My hunter's gene twitches.

"Which agency are you with?"

She gives up gracefully. "Oh, just GSA records. I'm a librarian."

Of course, I know her now, all the Mrs. Parsonses in records divisions, accounting sections, research branches, personnel and administration offices. Tell Mrs. Parsons we need a recap on the external service contracts for fiscal '73. So Yucatan is on the tours now? Pity . . . I offer her the tired little joke. "You know where the bodies are buried."

She smiles deprecatingly and stands up. "It does get dark quickly, doesn't it?"

Time to get back into the plane.

A flock of ibis are circling us, evidently accustomed to roosting in our fig tree. Estéban produces a machete and a Maya hammock. He proceeds to sling it between tree and plane, refusing help. His machete stroke is noticeably tentative.

The Parsons are taking a pee behind the tail vane. I hear one of them slip and squeal faintly. When they come back over the hull, Mrs. Parsons asks, "Might we sleep in the hammock, Captain?"

Estéban splits an unbelieving grin. I protest about rain and mosquitoes.

"Oh, we have insect repellent and we do enjoy fresh air."

The air is rushing by about force five and colder by the minute.

"We have our raincoats," the girl adds cheerfully.

Well, okay, ladies. We dangerous males retire inside the damp cabin. Through the wind I hear the women laugh softly now and then, apparently cosy in their chilly ibis roost. A private insanity, I decide. I know myself for the least threatening of men; my non-charisma has been in fact an asset jobwise, over the years. Are they having fantasies about Estéban? Or maybe they really are fresh-air nuts . . . Sleep comes for me in invisible diesels roaring by on the reef outside.

We emerge dry-mouthed into a vast windy salmon sunrise. A diamond chip of sun breaks out of the sea and promptly submerges in cloud. I go to work with the rod and some mullet bait while two showers detour around us. Breakfast is a strip of wet barracuda apiece.

The Parsons continue stoic and helpful. Under Estéban's direction they set up a section of cowling for a gasoline flare in case we hear a plane, but nothing goes over except one unseen jet droning toward Panama. The wind howls, hot and dry and full of coral dust. So are we.

"They look first in the sea," Estéban remarks. His aristocratic frontal slope is beaded with sweat; Mrs. Parsons watches him concernedly. I watch the cloud blanket tearing by above, getting higher and dryer and thicker. While that lasts nobody is going to find us, and the water business is now unfunny.

Finally I borrow Estéban's machete and hack a long light pole. There's stream coming in there, I saw it from the plane. Can't be more than two, three miles."

"I'm afraid the raft's torn." Mrs. Parsons shows me the cracks in the orange plastic; irritatingly, it's a Delaware label.

"All right," I hear myself announce. "The tide's going down. If we cut the good end of that air tube, I can haul water back in it. I've waded flats before."

Even to me it sounds crazy.

"Stay by plane," Estéban says. He's right, of course. He's also clearly running a fever. I look at the overcast and taste grit and old barracuda. The hell with the manual.

When I start cutting up the raft, Estéban tells me to take the serape. "You stay one night." He's right about that, too; I'll have to wait out the tide.

"I'll come with you," says Mrs. Parsons calmly.

I simply stare at her. What new madness has got into Mother Hen? Does she imagine Estéban is too battered to be functional? While I'm being astounded, my eyes take in the fact that Mrs. Parsons is now quite rosy around the knees, with her hair loose and a sunburn starting on her nose. A trim, in fact a very neat shading-forty.

"Look, that stuff is horrible going. Mud up to your ears and water over your head."

"I'm really quite fit and I swim a great deal. I'll try to keep up. Two would be much safer, Mr. Fenton, and we can bring more water."

She's serious. Well, I'm about as fit as a marshmallow at this time of winter, and I can't pretend I'm depressed by the idea of company. So be it.

"Let me show Miss Parsons how to work this rod."

Miss Parsons is even rosier and more windblown, and she's not clumsy with my tackle. A good girl, Miss Parsons, in her nothing way. We cut another staff and get some gear together. At the last minute Estéban shows how sick he feels: he offers me the machete. I thank him, but, no; I'm used to my Wirkkala knife. We tie some air into the plastic tube for a float and set out along the sandiest looking line.

Estéban raises one dark palm. *"Buen viaje."* Miss Parsons has hugged her mother and gone to cast from the mangrove. She waves. We wave.

An hour later we're barely out of waving distance. The going is purely god-awful. The sand keeps dissolving into silt you can't walk on or swim through, and the bottom is spiked with dead mangrove spears. We flounder from one pothole to the next, scaring up rays and turtles and hoping to god we don't kick a moray eel. Where we're not soaked in slime, we're desiccated, and we smell like the Old Cretaceous.

Mrs. Parsons keeps up doggedly. I only have to pull her out once. When I do so, I notice the sandbar is now out of sight.

Finally we reach the gap in the mangrove line I thought was the creek. It turns out to open into another arm of the bay, with more mangroves ahead. And the tide is coming in.

"I've had the world's lousiest idea."

Mrs. Parsons only says mildly, "It's so different from the view from the plane."

I revise my opinion of the girl scouts, and we plow on past the mangroves toward the smoky haze that has to be shore. The sun is setting in our faces, making it hard to see. Ibises and herons fly up around us, and once a big hermit spooks ahead, his fin cutting a rooster tail. We fall into more potholes. The flashlights get soaked. I am having fantasies of the mangrove as universal obstacle; it's hard to recall I ever walked down a street, for instance, without stumbling over or under or through mangrove roots. And the sun is dropping, down, down.

Suddenly we hit a ledge and fall over it into a cold flow.

"The stream! It's fresh water!"

We guzzle and gargle and douse our heads; it's the best drink I remember. "Oh my, oh my—!" Mrs. Parsons is laughing right out loud.

"That dark place over to the right looks like real land."

We flounder across the flow and follow a hard shelf, which turns into solid bank and rises over our heads. Shortly there's a break beside a clump of spiny bromels, and we scramble up and flop down at the top, dripping and stinking. Out of sheer reflex my arms goes around my companion's shoulder—but Mrs. Parsons isn't there; she's up on her knees peering at the burnt-over plain around us.

"Its so good to see land one can walk on!" The tone is too innocent. *Noli me tangere.*

"Don't try it." I'm exasperated; the muddy little woman, what does she think? "That ground out there is a crust of ashes over muck, and it's full of stubs. You can go in over your knees."

"It seems firm here."

"We're in an alligator nursery. That was the slide we came up. Don't worry, by now the old lady's doubtless on her way to be made into handbags."

"What a shame."

"I better set a line down in the stream while I can still see."

I slide back down and rig a string of hooks that may get us breakfast. When I get back Mrs. Parsons is wringing muck out of the serape.

"I'm glad you warned me, Mr. Fenton. It *is* treacherous."

"Yeah." I'm over my irritation; god knows I don't want to *tangere* Mrs. Parsons, even if I weren't beat down to mush. "In its quiet way, Yucatan is a tough place to get around in. You can see why the Mayas built roads. Speaking of which—look!"

The last of the sunset is silhouetting a small square shape a couple of kilometers inland: a Maya *ruina* with a fig tree growing out of it.

"Lot of those around. People think they were guard towers."

"What a deserted-feeling land."

"Let's hope it's deserted by mosquitoes."

We slump down in the 'gator nursery and share the last malt bar, watching the stars slide in and out of the blowing clouds. The bugs aren't too bad; maybe the burn did them in. And it isn't hot any more, either—in fact, it's not even warm, wet as we are. Mrs. Parsons continues tranquilly interested in Yucatan and unmistakably uninterested in togetherness.

Just as I'm beginning to get aggressive notions about how we're going to spend the night if she expects me to give her the serape, she stands up, scuffs at a couple of hummocks and says, "I expect this is as good a place as any, isn't it, Mr. Fenton?"

With which she spreads out the raft bag for a pillow and lies down on her side in the dirt with exactly half the serape over her and the other corner folded neatly open. Her small back is toward me.

The demonstration is so convincing that I'm halfway under my share of serape before the preposterousness of it stops me.

"By the way. My name is Don."

"Oh, of course." Her voice is graciousness itself. "I'm Ruth."

I get in not quite touching her, and we lie there like two fish on a plate, exposed to the stars and smelling the smoke in the wind and feeling things underneath us. It is absolutely the most intimately awkward moment I've had in years.

The woman doesn't mean one thing to me, but the obtrusive recessiveness of her, the defiance of her little rump eight inches from my fly—for two pesos I'd have those shorts down and introduce myself. If I were twenty years younger. If I wasn't so bushed . . . But the twenty years and the exhaustion are there, and it comes to me wryly that Mrs. Ruth Parsons has judged things to a nicety. If I *were* twenty years younger, she wouldn't be here. Like the butterfish that float around a sated barracuda, only to vanish away the instant his intent changes,

Mrs. Parsons knows her little shorts are safe. Those firmly filled little shorts, so close . . .

A warm nerve stirs in my groin—and just as it does I become aware of a silent emptiness beside me. Mrs. Parsons is imperceptibly inching away. Did my breathing change? Whatever, I'm perfectly sure that if my hand reached, she'd be elsewhere—probably announcing her intention to take a dip. The twenty years bring a chuckle to my throat, and I relax.

"Good night, Ruth."

"Good night, Don."

And believe it or not, we sleep, while the armadas of the wind roar overhead.

Light wakes me—a cold white glare.

My first thought is 'gator hunters. Best to manifest ourselves as *turistas* as fast as possible. I scramble up, noting that Ruth has dived under the bromel clump.

"*Quien estas? A secorro!* Help, *senores!*"

No answer except the light goes out, leaving me blind.

I yell some more in a couple of languages. It stays dark. There's a vague scrabbling, whistling sound somewhere in the burn-off. Liking everything less by the minute, I try a speech about our plane having crashed and we need help.

A very narrow pencil of light flicks over us and snaps off.

"Eh-ep," says a blurry voice and something metallic twitters. They for sure aren't locals. I'm getting unpleasant ideas.

"Yes, help!"

Something goes crackle-crackle whish-whish, and all sounds fade away.

"What the holy hell!" I stumble toward where they were.

"Look." Ruth whispers behind me. "Over by the ruin."

I look and catch a multiple flicker which winks out fast.

"A camp?"

And I take two more blind strides; my leg goes down through the crust, and a spike spears me just where you stick the knife in to unjoint a drumstick. By the pain that goes through my bladder I recognize that my trick kneecap has caught it.

For instant basket case you can't beat kneecaps. First you discover your knee doesn't bend any more, and so you try putting some weight on it, and a bayonet goes up your spine and unhinges your jaw. Little grains of gristle have got into the sensitive bearing surface. The knee tries to buckle and can't, and mercifully you fall down.

Ruth helps me back to the serape.

"What a fool, what a god-forgotten imbecile—"

"Not at all, Don. It was perfectly natural." We strike matches; her fingers push mine aside, exploring. "I think it's in place, but it's swelling fast. I'll lay a wet handkerchief on it. We'll have to wait for morning to check the cut. Were they poachers, do you think?"

"Probably," I lie. What I think they were is smugglers.

She comes back with a soaked bandanna and drapes it on. "We must have frightened them. That light . . . it seemed so bright."

"Some hunting party. People do crazy things around here."

"Perhaps they'll come back in the morning."

"Could be."

Ruth pulls up the wet serape, and we say goodnight again. Neither of us are mentioning how we're going to get back to the plane without help.

I lie staring south where Alpha Centauri is blinking in and out of the overcast and cursing myself for the sweet mess I've made. My first idea is giving way to an even less pleasing one.

Smuggling, around here, is a couple of guys in an outboard meeting a shrimp boat by the reef. They don't light up the sky or have some kind of swamp buggy that goes whoosh. Plus a big camp . . . paramilitary-type equipment?

I've seen a report of Guévarista infiltrators operating on the British Honduran border, which is about a hundred kilometers—sixty miles—south of here. Right under those clouds. If that's what looked us over, I'll be more than happy if they don't come back . . .

I wake up in pelting rain, alone. My first move confirms that my leg is as expected—a giant misplaced erection bulging out of my shorts. I raise up painfully to see Ruth standing by the bromels, looking over the bay. Solid wet nimbus is pouring out of the south.

"No planes today."

"Oh, good morning, Don. Should we look at that cut now?"

"It's minimal." In fact the skin is hardly broken, and no deep puncture. Totally out of proportion to the havoc inside.

"Well, they have water to drink," Ruth says tranquilly. "Maybe those hunters will come back. I'll go see if we have a fish—that is, can I help you in any way, Don?"

Very tactful. I emit an ungracious negative, and she goes off about her private concerns.

They certainly are private, too; when I recover from my own sanitary efforts, she's still away. Finally I hear splashing.

"It's a big fish!" More splashing. Then she climbs up the bank with a three-pound mangrove snapper—and something else.

It isn't until after the messy work of filleting the fish that I begin to notice.

She's making a smudge of chaff and twigs to singe the fillets, small hands very quick, tension in that female upper lip. The rain has eased off for the moment; we're sluicing wet but warm enough. Ruth brings me my fish on a mangrove skewer and sits back on her heels with an odd breathy sigh.

"Aren't you joining me?"

"Oh, of course." She gets a strip and picks at it, saying quickly. "We either have too much salt or too little, don't we? I should fetch some brine." Her eyes are roving from nothing to noplace.

"Good thought." I hear another sigh and decide the girl scouts need an assist. "Your daughter mentioned you've come from Mérida. Seen much of Mexico?"

"Not really. Last year we went to Mazatlan and Cuernavaca . . ." She puts the fish down, frowning.

"And you're going to see Tikál. Going to Bonampak too?"

"No." Suddenly she jumps up brushing rain off her face. "I'll bring you some water, Don."

She ducks down the slide, and after a fair while comes back with a full bromel stalk.

"Thanks." She's standing above me, staring restlessly round the horizon.

"Ruth, I hate to say it, but those guys are not coming back and it's probably just as well. Whatever they were up to, we looked like trouble. The most they'll do is tell someone we're here. That'll take a day or two to get around, we'll be back at the plane by then."

"I'm sure you're right, Don." She wanders over to the smudge fire.

"And quit fretting about your daughter. She's a big girl."

"Oh, I'm sure Althea's all right . . . They have plenty of water now." Her fingers drum on her thigh. It's raining again.

"Come on, Ruth. Sit down. Tell me about Althea. Is she still in college?"

She gives that sighing little laugh and sits. "Althea got her degree last year. She's in computer programming.

"I'm in Foreign Procurement Archives." She smiles mechanically, but her breathing is shallow. "It's very interesting."

"I know a Jack Wittig in Contracts, maybe you know him?"

It sounds pretty absurd, there in the 'gator slide.

"Oh, I've met Mr. Wittig. I'm sure he wouldn't remember me."

"Why not?"

"I'm not very memorable."

Her voice is purely factual. She's perfectly right, of course. Who was that woman, Mrs. Jannings, Janny, who coped with my per diem for years? Competent, agreeable, impersonal. She had a sick father or something. But dammit, Ruth is a lot younger and better-looking. Comparatively speaking.

"Maybe Mrs. Parsons doesn't want to be memorable."

She makes a vague sound, and I suddenly realize Ruth isn't listening to me at all. Her hands are clenched around her knees, she's staring inland at the ruin.

"Ruth, I tell you our friends with the light are in the next county by now. Forget it, we don't need them."

Her eyes come back to me as if she'd forgotten I was there, and she nods slowly. It seems to be too much effort to speak. Suddenly she cocks her head and jumps up again.

"I'll go look at the line, Don. I thought I heard something—" She's gone like a rabbit.

While she's away I try getting up onto my good leg and the staff. The pain is sickening; knees seem to have some kind of hot line to the stomach. I take a couple of hops to test whether the Demerol I have in my belt would get me walking. As I do so, Ruth comes up the bank with a fish flapping in her hands.

"Oh, no, Don! *No!*" She actually clasps the snapper to her breast.

"The water will take some of my weight. I'd like to give it a try."

"You mustn't!" Ruth says quite violently and instantly modulates down. "Look at the bay, Don. One can't see a thing."

I teeter there, tasting bile and looking at the mingled curtains of sun and rain driving across the water. She's right, thank god. Even with two good legs we could get into trouble out there.

"I guess one more night won't kill us."

I let her collapse me back onto the gritty plastic, and she positively bustles around, finding me a chunk to lean on, stretching the serape on both staffs to keep rain off me, bringing another drink, grubbing for dry tinder.

"I'll make us a real bonfire as soon as it lets up, Don. They'll see our smoke, they'll know we're all right. We just have to wait." Cheery smile. "Is there any way we can make you more comfortable?"

Holy Saint Sterculius: playing house in a mud puddle. For a fatuous moment I wonder if Mrs. Parsons has designs on me. And then she lets out another sigh and sinks back onto her heels with that listening look. Unconsciously her rump wiggles a little. My ear picks up the operative word: *wait.*

Ruth Parsons is waiting. In fact, she acts as if she's waiting so hard it's killing her. For what? For someone to get us out of here, what else? . . . But why was she so horrified when I got up to try to leave? Why all this tension?

My paranoia stirs. I grab it by the collar and start idly checking back. Up to when whoever it was showed up last night, Mrs. Parsons was, I guess, normal. Calm and sensible, anyway. Now she's humming like a high wire. And she seems to want to stay here and wait. Just as an intellectual pastime, why?

Could she have intended to come here? No way. Where she planned to be was Chetumal, which is on the border. Come to think, Chetumal is an odd way round to Tikál. Let's say the scenario was that she's meeting somebody in Chetumal. Somebody who's part of an organisation. So now her contact in Chetumal knows she's overdue. And when those types appeared last night, something suggests to her that they're part of the same organisation. And she hopes they'll put one and one together and come back for her?

"May I have the knife, Don? I'll clean the fish."

Rather slowly I pass the knife, kicking my subconscious. Such a decent ordinary little woman, a good girl scout. My trouble is that I've bumped into too many professional agilities under the careful stereotypes. *I'm not very memorable . . .*

What's in Foreign Procurement Archives? Wittig handles classified contacts. Lots of money stuff; foreign currency negotiations, commodity price schedules, some industrial technology. Or—just as a hypothesis—it could be as simple as a wad of bills back in that modest beige Ventura, to be exchanged for a packet from say, Costa Rica. If she were a courier, they'd want to get at the plane. And then what about me and maybe Estéban? Even hypothetically, not good.

I watch her hacking at the fish, forehead knotted with effort, teeth in her lip. Mrs. Ruth Parsons of Bethesda, this thrumming, private woman. How crazy can I get? *They'll see our smoke* . . .

"Here's your knife, Don. I washed it. Does the leg hurt very badly?"

I blink away the fantasies and see a scared little woman in a mangrove swamp.

"Sit down, rest. You've been going all out."

She sits obediently, like a kid in a dentist chair.

"You're stewing about Althea. And she's probably worried about you. We'll get back tomorrow under our own steam, Ruth."

"Honestly I'm not worried at all, Don." The smile fades; she nibbles her lip, frowning out at the bay.

"Ruth, you know you surprised me when you offered to come along. Not that I don't appreciate it. But I rather thought you'd be concerned about leaving Althea. Alone with our good pilot, I mean. Or was it only me?"

This gets her attention at last.

"I believe Captain Estéban is a very fine type of man."

The words surprise me a little. Isn't the correct line more like "I trust Althea," or even, indignantly, "Althea is a good girl"?

"He's a man. Althea seemed to think he was interesting."

She goes on staring at the bay. And then I notice her tongue flick out and lick that prehensile upper lip. There's a flush that isn't sunburn around her ears and throat too, and one hand is gently rubbing her thigh. What's she seeing, out there in the flats?

Captain Estéban's mahogany arms clasping Miss Althea Parsons' pearly body. Captain Estéban's archaic nostrils snuffling in Miss Parsons' tender neck. Captain Estéban's copper buttocks pumping into Althea's creamy upturned bottom . . . The hammock, very bouncy. Mayas know all about it.

Well, well. So Mother Hen has her little quirks.

I feel fairly silly and more than a little irritated. *Now* I find out . . . But even vicarious lust has much to recommend it, here in the mud and rain. I settle back, recalling that Miss Althea the computer programmer had waved good-bye very composedly. Was she sending her mother to flounder across the bay with me so she can get programmed in Maya? The memory of Honduran mahogany logs drifting in and out of the opalescent sand comes to me. Just as I am about to suggest that Mrs. Parsons might care to share my rain shelter, she remarks serenely, "The Mayas seem to be a very fine type of people. I believe you said so to Althea."

The implications fall on me with the rain. *Type.* As in breeding, bloodline, sire. Am I supposed to have certified Estéban not only as a stud but as a genetic donor?

"Ruth, are you telling me you're prepared to accept a half-Indian grandchild?"

"Why, Don, that's up to Althea, you know."

Looking at the mother, I guess it is. Oh, for mahogany gonads.

Ruth has gone back to listening to the wind, but I'm not about to let her off that easy. Not after all that *noli me tangere* jazz.

"What will Althea's father think?"

Her face snaps around at me, genuinely startled.

"Althea's father?" Complicated semismile. "He won't mind."

"He'll accept it too, eh?" I see her shake her head as if a fly were bothering her, and add with a cripple's malice: "Your husband must be a very fine type of a man."

Ruth looks at me, pushing her wet hair back abruptly. I have the impression that mousy Mrs. Parsons is roaring out of control, but her voice is quiet.

"There isn't any Mr. Parsons, Don. There never was. Althea's father was a Danish medical student . . . I believe he has gained considerable prominence."

"Oh." Something warns me not to say I'm sorry. "You mean he doesn't know about Althea?"

"No." She smiles, her eyes bright and cuckoo.

"Seems like rather a rough deal for her."

"I grew up quite happily under the same circumstances."

Bang, I'm dead. Well, well, well. A mad image blooms in my mind: generations of solitary Parsons women selecting sires, making impregnation trips. Well, I hear the world is moving their way.

"I better look at the fish line."

She leaves. The glow fades. *No.* Just no, no contact. Good-bye, Captain Estéban. My leg is very uncomfortable. The hell with Mrs. Parsons' long-distance orgasm.

We don't talk much after that, which seems to suit Ruth. The odd day drags by. Squall after squall blows over us. Ruth singes up some more fillets, but the rain drowns her smudge; it seems to pour hardest just as the sun's about to show.

Finally she comes to sit under my sagging serape, but there's no warmth there. I doze, aware of her getting up now and then to look around. My subconscious notes that she's still twitchy. I tell my subconscious to knock it off.

Presently I wake up to find her penciling on the water-soaked pages of a little notepad.

"What's that, a shopping list for alligators?"

Automatic polite laugh. "Oh, just an address. In case we—I'm being silly, Don."

"Hey." I sit up, wincing. "Ruth, quit fretting. I mean it. We'll all be out of this soon. You'll have a great story to tell."

She doesn't look up. "Yes . . . I guess we will."

"Come on, we're doing fine. There isn't any real danger here, you know. Unless you're allergic to fish?"

Another good-little-girl laugh, but there's a shiver in it.

"Sometimes I think I'd like to go . . . really far away."

To keep her talking I say the first thing in my head.

"Tell me, Ruth. I'm curious why you would settle for that kind of lonely life, there in Washington? I mean, a woman like you—"

"Should get married?" She gives a shaky sigh, pushing the notebook back in her wet pocket.

"Why not? It's the normal source of companionship. Don't tell me you're trying to be some kind of professional man-hater."

"Lesbian, you mean?" Her laugh sounds better. "With my security rating? No, I'm not."

"Well, then. Whatever trauma you went through, these things don't last forever. You can't hate all men."

The smile is back. "Oh, there wasn't any trauma, Don, and I *don't* hate men. That would be as silly as—as hating the weather." She glances wryly at the blowing rain.

"I think you have a grudge. You're even spooky of me."

Smooth as a mouse bite she says, "I'd love to hear about your family, Don?"

Touché. I give her the edited version of how I don't have one any more, and she says she's sorry, how sad. And we chat about what a good life a single person really has, and how she and her friends enjoy plays and concerts and travel, and one of them is head cashier for Ringling Brothers, how about that?

But it's coming out jerkier and jerkier like a bad tape, with her eyes going round the horizon in the pauses and her face listening for something that isn't my voice. What's wrong with her? Well, what's wrong with any furtively unconventional middle-aged woman with an empty bed. And a security clearance. An old habit of mind remarks unkindly that Mrs. Parsons represents what is known as the classic penetration target.

"—so much more opportunity now." Her voice trails off.

"Hurrah for women's lib, eh?"

"The lib?" Impatiently she leans forward and tugs the serape straight. "Oh, that's doomed."

The word apocalyptic jars my attention.

"What do you mean, doomed?"

She glances at me as if I weren't hanging straight either and says vaguely, "Oh . . ."

"Come on, why doomed? Didn't they get that equal rights bill?"

Long hesitation. When she speaks again her voice is different.

"Women have no rights, Don, except what men allow us. Men are more aggressive and powerful, and they run the world. When the next real crisis upsets them, our so-called rights will vanish like—like that smoke. We'll be back where we always were: property. And whatever has gone wrong will be blamed on our freedom, like the fall of Rome was. You'll see."

Now all this is delivered in a grey tone of total conviction. The last time I heard that tone, the speaker was explaining why he had to keep his file drawers full of dead pigeons.

"Oh, come on. You and your friends are the backbone of the system; if you quit, the country would come to a screeching halt before lunch."

No answering smile.

"That's fantasy." Her voice is still quiet. "Women don't work that way. We're a—a toothless world." She looks around as if she wanted to stop talking. "What women do is survive. We live by ones and twos in the chinks of your world-machine."

"Sounds like a guerrilla operation." I'm not really joking, here in the 'gator den. In fact, I'm wondering if I spent too much thought on maghogany logs.

"Guerrillas have something to hope for." Suddenly she switches on the jolly smile. "Think of opossums, Don. Did you know there are opossums living all over? Even in New York City."

I smile back with my neck prickling. I thought I was the paranoid one.

"Men and women aren't different species, Ruth. Women do everything men do."

"Do they?" Our eyes meet, but she seems to be seeing ghosts between us in the rain. She mutters something that could be "My Lai" and looks away. "All the endless wars . . ." Her voice is a whisper, "All the huge authoritarian organizations for doing unreal things. Men live to struggle against each other; we're just part of the battlefields. It'll never change unless you change the whole world. I dream sometimes of—of going away—" She checks and abruptly changes voice. "Forgive me, Don, it's so stupid saying all this."

"Men hate wars too, Ruth," I say as gently as I can.

"I know." She shrugs and climbs to her feet. "But that's your problem, isn't it?"

End of communication. Mrs. Ruth Parsons isn't even living in the same world with me.

I watch her move around restlessly, head turning toward the ruins. Alienation like that can add up to dead pigeons, which would be GSA's problem. It could also lead to believing some joker who's promising to change the world. Which could just probably be my problem if one of them was over in that camp last night, where she keeps looking. *Guerrillas have something to hope for . . . ?*

Nonsense. I try another position and see that the sky seems to be clearing as the sun sets. The wind is quieting down at last too. Insane to think this little woman is acting out some fantasy in this swamp. But that equipment last night was no fantasy; if those lads have some connection with her, I'll be in the way. You couldn't find a handier spot to dispose of a body . . . Maybe some Guévarista is a fine type of man?

Absurd. Sure . . . The only thing more absurd would be to come through the wars and get myself terminated by a mad librarian's boyfriend on a fishing trip.

A fish flops in the stream below us. Ruth spins around so fast she hits the serape. "I better start the fire," she says, her eyes still on the plain and her head cocked, listening.

All right, let's test.

"Expecting company?"

It rocks her. She freezes, and her eyes come swiveling around at me like a film take captioned Fright. I can see her decide to smile.

"Oh, one never can tell!" She laughs weirdly, the eyes not changed. "I'll get the—the kindling." She fairly scuttles into the brush.

Nobody, paranoid or not, could call *that* a normal reaction.

Ruth Parsons is either psycho or she's expecting something to happen —and it has nothing to do with me; I scared her pissless.

Well, she could be nuts. And I could be wrong, but there are some mistakes you only make once. Reluctantly I unzip my body belt, telling myself that if I think what I think, my only course is to take something for my leg and get as far as possible from Mrs. Ruth Parsons before whoever she's waiting for arrives.

In my belt also is a .32 caliber asset Ruth doesn't know about—and it's going to stay there. My longevity program leaves the shoot-outs to TV and stresses being somewhere else when the roof falls in. I can spend a perfectly safe and also perfectly horrible night out in one of those mangrove flats . . . am I insane?

At this moment Ruth stands up and stares blatantly inland with her hand shading her eyes. Then she tucks something into her pocket, buttons up and tightens her belt.

That does it.

I dry-swallow two 100 mg tabs, which should get me ambulatory and still leave me wits to hide. Give it a few minutes. I make sure my compass and some hooks are in my own pocket and sit waiting while Ruth fusses with her smudge fire, sneaking looks away when she thinks I'm not watching.

The flat world around us is turning into an unearthly amber and violet light show as the first numbness seeps into my leg. Ruth has crawled under the bromels for more dry stuff; I can see her foot. Okay. I reach for my staff.

Suddenly the foot jerks, and Ruth yells—or rather, her throat makes that *Uh-uh-uhhh* that means pure horror. The foot disappears in a rattle of bromel stalks.

I lunge upright on the crutch and look over the bank at a frozen scene.

Ruth is crouching sideways on the ledge, clutching her stomach. They are about a yard below, floating on the river in a skiff. While I was making up my stupid mind, her friends have glided right under my ass. There are three of them.

They are tall and white. I try to see them as men in some kind of white jumpsuits. The one nearest the bank is stretching out a long white arm toward Ruth. She jerks and scuttles further away.

The arm stretches after her. It stretches and stretches. It stretches two yards and stays hanging in air. Small black things are wiggling from its tip.

I look where their faces should be and see black hollow dishes with vertical stripes. The stripes move slowly . . .

There is no more possibility of their being human—or anything else I've ever seen. What has Ruth conjured up?

The scene is totally silent. I blink, blink—this cannot be real. The two in the far end of the skiff are writhing those arms around an apparatus on a tripod. A weapon? Suddenly I hear the same blurry voice I heard in the night.

"Guh-give," it groans. "G-give . . ."

"Dear god, it's real, whatever it is. I'm terrified. My mind is trying not to form a word.

And Ruth—Jesus, of course—Ruth is terrified too; she's edging along the bank away from them, gaping at the monsters in the skiff, who are obviously nobody's friends. She's hugging something to her body. Why doesn't she get over the bank and circle back behind me?

"G-g-give." That wheeze is coming from the tripod. "Pee-eeze give." The skiff is moving upstream below Ruth, following her. The arm undulates out at her again, its black digits looping. Ruth scrambles to the top of the bank.

"Ruth!" My voice cracks. "Ruth, get over here behind me!"

She doesn't look at me, only keeps sidling farther away. My terror detonates into anger.

"Come back here!" With my free hand I'm working the .32 out of my belt. The sun has gone down.

She doesn't turn but straightens up warily, still hugging the thing. I see her mouth working. Is she actually trying to *talk* to them?

"Please . . ." She swallows. "Please speak to me. I need your help."

"RUTH!"

At this moment the nearest white monster whips into a great S-curve and sails right onto the bank at her, eight feet of snowy rippling horror.

And I shoot Ruth.

I don't know that for a minute—I've yanked the gun up so fast that my staff slips and dumps me as I fire. I stagger up, hearing Ruth scream "No! No! No!"

The creature is back down by his boat, and Ruth is still farther away, clutching herself. Blood is running down her elbow.

"Stop it, Don! They aren't attacking you!"

"For god's sake! Don't be a fool, I can't help you if you won't get away from them!"

No reply. Nobody moves. No sound except the drone of a jet passing far above. In the darkening stream below me the three white figures shift uneasily; I get the impression of radar dishes focusing. The word spells itself in my head: *Aliens.*

Extraterrestrials.

What do I do, call the President? Capture them single-handed with my peashooter? . . . I'm alone in the arse end of nowhere with one leg and my brain cuddled in meperidine hydrochloride.

"Prrr-eese," their machine blurs again. "Wa-wat hep . . ."

"Our plane fell down," Ruth says in a very distinct, eerie voice. She points up at the jet, out towards the bay. "My—my child is there. Please take us *there* in your boat."

Dear god. While she's gesturing. I get a look at the thing she's hugging in her wounded arm. It's metallic, like a big glimmering distributor head. What—?

Wait a minute. This morning: when she was gone so long, she could have found that thing. Something they left behind. Or dropped. And she hid it, not telling me. That's why she kept going under that bromel clump—she was peeking at it. Waiting. And the owners came back and caught her. They want it. She's trying to bargain, by god.

"—Water," Ruth is pointing again. "Take us. Me. And him."

The black faces turn toward me, blind and horrible. Later on I may be grateful for that "us." Not now.

"Throw your gun away, Don. They'll take us back." Her voice is weak.

"Like hell I will. You—who are you? What are you doing here?"

"Oh god, does it matter? He's frightened," she cries to them. "Can you understand?"

She's as alien as they, there in the twilight. The beings in the skiff are twittering among themselves. Their box starts to moan.

"Ss-stu-dens," I make out. "S-stu-ding . . . not-huh-arm-ing . . . w-we . . . buh . . ." It fades into garble and then says "G-give . . . we . . . g-go . . ."

Peace-loving cultural-exchange students—on the interstellar level now. Oh, no.

"Bring that thing here, Ruth—right now!"

But she's starting down the bank toward them saying. "Take me."

"Wait! You need a tourniquet on that arm."

"I know. Please put the gun down, Don."

She's actually at the skiff, right by them. They aren't moving.

"Jesus Christ." Slowly, reluctantly I drop the .32. When I start down the slide, I find I'm floating; adrenaline and Demerol are a bad mix.

The skiff comes gliding toward me, Ruth in the bow clutching the thing and her arm. The aliens stay in the stern behind their tripod, away from me. I note the skiff is camouflaged tan and green. The world around us is deep shadowy blue.

"Don, bring the water bag!"

As I'm dragging down the plastic bag, it occurs to me that Ruth really is cracking up, the water isn't needed now. But my own brain seems to have gone into overload. All I can focus on is a long white rubbery arm with black worms clutching the far end of the orange tube, helping me fill it. This isn't happening.

"Can you get in, Don?" As I hoist my numb legs up, two long white pipes reach for me. *No you don't.* I kick and tumble in beside Ruth. She moves away.

A creaky hum starts up, it's coming from a wedge in the center of the skiff. And we're in motion, sliding toward dark mangrove files.

I stare mindlessly at the wedge. Alien technological secrets? I can't see any, the power source is under that triangular cover, about two feet long. The gadgets on the tripod are equally cryptic, except that one has a big lens. Their light?

As we hit the open bay, the hum rises and we start planing faster and faster still. Thirty knots? Hard to judge in the dark. Their hull seems to be a modified trihedral much like ours, with a remarkable absence of slap. Say twenty-two feet. Schemes of capturing it swirl in my mind: I'll need Estéban.

Suddenly a huge flood of white light fans out over us from the tripod, blotting out the aliens in the stern. I see Ruth pulling at a belt around her arm, which is still hugging the gizmo.

"I'll tie that for you."

"It's all right."

The alien device is twinkling or phosphorescing slightly. I lean over to look, whispering, "Give that to me, I'll pass it to Estéban."

"No!" She scoots away, almost over the side. "It's theirs, they need it!"

"What? Are you crazy?" I'm so taken aback by this idiocy I literally stammer. "We have to, we—"

"They haven't hurt us. I'm sure they could." Her eyes are watching me with feral intensity; in the light her face has a lunatic look. Numb as I am, I realize that the wretched woman is poised to throw herself over the side if I move. With the gizmo.

"I think they're gentle," she mutters.

"For Christ's sake, Ruth, they're *aliens!*"

"I'm used to it," she says absently. "There's the island! Stop! Stop here!"

The skiff slows, turning. A mound of foliage is tiny in the light. Metal glints—the plane.

"Althea! Althea! Are you all right?"

Yells, movement on the plane. The water is high, we're floating over the bar. The aliens are keeping us in the lead with the light hiding them. I see one pale figure splashing toward us and a dark one behind, coming more slowly. Estéban must be puzzled by that light.

"Mr. Fenton is hurt, Althea. These people brought us back with the water. Are you all right?"

"A-okay." Althea flounders up, peering excitedly. "You all right? Whew, that light!" Automatically I start handing her the idiotic water bag.

"Leave that for the captain," Ruth says sharply. "Althea, can you climb in the boat? Quickly, it's important."

"Coming!"

"No, no!" I protest, but the skiff tilts as Althea swarms in. The aliens twitter, and their voice box starts groaning. "Gu-give . . . now . . . give . . ."

"*Que llega?*" Estéban's face appears beside me, squinting fiercely into the light.

"Grab it, get it from her—that thing she has—" but Ruth's voice rides over mine. "Captain, lift Mr. Fenton out of the boat. He's hurt his leg. Hurry, please."

"Goddamn it, wait!" I shout, but an arm has grabbed my middle. When a Maya boosts you, you go. I hear Althea saying, "Mother, your arm!" and fall onto Estéban. We stagger around in water up to my waist; I can't feel my feet at all.

When I get steady, the boat is yards away, the two women, head-to-head, murmuring.

"Get them!" I tug loose from Estéban and flounder forward. Ruth stands up in the boat facing the invisible aliens.

"Take us with you. Please. We want to go with you, away from here."

"Ruth! Estéban, get that boat!" I lunge and lose my feet again. The aliens are chirruping madly behind their light.

"Please take us. We don't mind what your planet is like; we'll learn

—we'll do anything! We won't cause any trouble. Please. Oh *please*."
The skiff is drifting farther away.

"Ruth! Althea! You're crazy, wait—" But I can only shuffle night-marelike in the ooze, hearing that damn voice box wheeze, "N-not come . . . more . . . not come . . ." Althea's face turns to it, open-mouthed grin.

"Yes, we understand," Ruth cries. "We don't want to come back. Please let us go with you!"

I shout and Estéban splashes past me shouting too, something about radio.

"Yes-s-s" groans the voice.

Ruth sits down suddenly, clutching Althea. At that moment Estéban grabs the edge of the skiff beside her.

"Hold them, Estéban! Don't let her go."

He gives me one slit-eyed glance over his shoulder, and I recognize his total uninvolvement. He's had a good look at that camouflage paint and the absence of fishing gear. I make a desperate rush and slip again. When I come up Ruth is saying, "We're going with these people, Captain. Please take your money out of my purse, it's in the plane. And give this to Mr. Fenton."

She passes him something small; the notebook. He takes it slowly.

"Estéban! Don't!"

He has released the skiff.

"Thank you so much," Ruth says as they float apart. Her voice is shaky; she raises it. "There won't be any trouble, Don. Please send this cable. It's to a friend of mine, she'll take care of everything." Then she adds the craziest touch of the entire night. "She's a grand person; she's director of nursing training at N.I.H."

As the skiff drifts, I hear Althea add something that sounds like "Right on."

Sweet Jesus . . . Next minute the humming has started; the light is receding fast. The last I see of Mrs. Ruth Parsons and Miss Althea Parsons is two small shadows against that light, like two opossums. The light snaps off, the hum deepens—and they're going, going, gone away.

In the dark water beside me Estéban is instructing everybody in general to *chingarse* themselves.

"Friends, or something," I tell him lamely. "She seemed to want to go with them."

He is pointedly silent, hauling me back to the plane. He knows what could be around here better than I do, and Mayas have their own longevity program. His condition seems improved. As we get in I notice the hammock has been repositioned.

In the night—of which I remember little—the wind changes. And at seven thirty next morning a Cessna buzzes the sandbar under cloudless skies.

By noon we're back in Cozumel. Captain Estéban accepts his fees and departs laconically for his insurance wars. I leave the Parsons' bags with the Caribe agent, who couldn't care less. The cable goes to a Mrs. Priscilla Hayes Smith also of Bethesda. I take myself to a medico and by three PM I'm sitting on the Cabañas terrace with a fat leg and a double margharita, trying to believe the whole thing.

The cable said, *Althea and I taking extraordinary opportunity for travel. Gone several years. Please take charge our affairs. Love, Ruth.*

She'd written it that afternoon, you understand.

I order another double, wishing to hell I'd gotten a good look at that gizmo. Did it have a label, Made by Betelgeusians? No matter how weird it was, *how* could a person be crazy enough to imagine—?

Not only that but to hope, to plan? *If I could only go away . . .* That's what she was doing, all day. Waiting, hoping, figuring how to get Althea. To go sight unseen to an alien world . . .

With the third margharita I try to joke about alienated women, but my heart's not in it. And I'm certain there won't be any bother, any trouble at all. Two human women, one of them possibly pregnant, have departed for, I guess, the stars; and the fabric of society will never show a ripple. I brood; do all Mrs. Parsons' friends hold themselves in readiness for any eventuality, including leaving Earth? And will Mrs. Parsons somehow one day contrive to send for Mrs. Priscilla Hayes Smith, that grand person?

I can only send for another cold one, musing on Althea. What suns will Captain Estéban's sloe-eyed offspring, if any, look upon? "Get in, Althea, we're taking off for Orion." "A-okay, Mother." Is that some system of upbringing? *We survive by ones and twos in the chinks of your world-machine . . . I'm used to aliens . . .* She'd meant every word. Insane. How could a woman choose to live among unknown monsters, to say good-bye to her home, her world?

As the margharitas take hold, the whole mad scenario melts down to the image of those two small shapes sitting side by side in the receding alien glare.

Two of our opossums are missing.

Born of Man and Woman

Richard Matheson

X——This day when it had light mother called me a retch. You retch she said. I saw in her eyes the anger. I wonder what it is a retch.

This day it had water falling from upstairs. It fell all around. I saw that. The ground of the back I watched from the little window. The ground it sucked up the water like thirsty lips. It drank too much and it got sick and runny brown. I didn't like it.

Mother is a pretty I know. In my bed place with cold walls around I have a paper things that was behind the furnace. It says on it SCREEN-STARS. I see in the pictures faces like of mother and father. Father says they are pretty. Once he said it.

And also mother he said. Mother so pretty and me decent enough. Look at you he said and didn't have the nice face. I touched his arm and said it is alright father. He shook and pulled away where I couldn't reach.

Today mother let me off the chain a little so I could look out the little window. That's how I saw the water falling from upstairs.

XX——This day it had goldness in the upstairs. As I know, when I looked at it my eyes hurt. After I look at it the cellar is red.

I think this was church. They leave the upstairs. The big machine swallows them and rolls out past and is gone. In the back part is the *lit-*

RICHARD MATHESON *was twenty-three and living in Brooklyn when this story was published in F&SF's Summer 1950 issue. It was his first published story. He now lives in California and is a successful novelist and screenwriter, best-known for* I Am Legend *and* The Shrinking Man *(the basis for the movie).*

tle mother. She is much small than me. I am big. It is a secret but I have pulled the chain out of the wall. I can see out the little window all I like.

In this day when it got dark I had eat my food and some bugs. I hear laughs upstairs. I like to know why there are laughs for. I took the chain from the wall and wrapped it around me. I walked squish to the stairs. They creak when I walk on them. My legs slip on them because I don't walk on stairs. My feet stick to the wood.

I went up and opened a door. It was a white place. White as white jewels that come from upstairs sometime. I went in and stood quiet. I hear the laughing some more. I walk to the sound and look through to the people. More people than I thought was. I thought I should laugh with them.

Mother came out and pushed the door in. It hit me and hurt. I fell back on the smooth floor and the chain made noise. I cried. She made a hissing noise into her and put her hand on her mouth. Her eyes got big.

She looked at me. I heard father call. What fell he called. She said a iron board. Come help pick it up she said. He came and said now is *that* so heavy you need. He saw me and grew big. The anger came in his eyes. He hit me. I spilled some of the drip on the floor from one arm. It was not nice. It made ugly green on the floor.

Father told me to go to the cellar. I had to go. The light it hurt some now in my eyes. It is not so like that in the cellar.

Father tied my legs and arms up. He put me on my bed. Upstairs I heard laughing while I was quiet there looking on a black spider that was swinging down to me. I thought what father said. Ohgod he said. And only eight.

XXX——This day father hit in the chain again before it had light. I have to try pull it out again. He said I was bad to come upstairs. He said never do that again or he would beat me hard. That hurts.

I hurt. I slept the day and rested my head against the cold wall. I thought of the white place upstairs.

XXXX——I got the chain from the wall out. Mother was upstairs. I heard little laughs very high. I looked out the window. I saw all little people like the little mother and little fathers too. They are pretty.

They were making nice noise and jumping around the ground. Their legs was moving hard. They are like mother and father. Mother says all right people look like they do.

One of the little fathers saw me. He pointed at the window. I let go and slid down the wall in the dark. I curled up as they would not see. I heard their talks by the window and foots running. Upstairs there was a door hitting. I heard the little mother call upstairs. I heard heavy steps and I rushed to my bed place. I hit the chain in the wall and lay down on my front.

I heard mother come down. Have you been at the window she said. I heard the anger. *Stay* away from the window. You have pulled the chain out again.

She took the stick and hit me with it. I didn't cry. I can't do that. But the drip ran all over the bed. She saw it and twisted away and made a noise. Oh mygod mygod she said why have you *done* this to me? I heard the stick go bounce on the stone floor. She ran upstairs. I slept the day.

XXXXX——This day it had water again. When mother was upstairs I heard the little one come slow down the steps. I hidded myself in the coal bin for mother would have anger if the little mother saw me.

She had a little live thing with her. It walked on the arms and had pointy ears. She said things to it.

It was all right except the live thing smelled me. It ran up the coal and looked down at me. The hairs stood up. In the throat it made an angry noise. I hissed but it jumped on me.

I didn't want to hurt it. I got fear because it bit me harder than the rat does. I hurt and the little mother screamed. I grabbed the live thing tight. It made sounds I never heard. I pushed it all together. It was all lumpy and red on the black coal.

I hid there when mother called. I was afraid of the stick. She left. I crept over the coal with the thing. I hid it under my pillow and rested on it. I put the chain in the wall again.

X——This is another times. Father chained me tight. I hurt because he beat me. This time I hit the stick out of his hands and made noise. He went away and his face was white. He ran out of my bed place and locked the door.

I am not so glad. All day it is cold in here. The chain comes slow out of the wall. And I have a bad anger with mother and father. I will show them. I will do what I did that once.

I will screech and laugh loud. I will run on the walls. Last I will hang head down by all my legs and laugh and drip green all over until they are sorry they didn't be nice to me.

If they try to beat me again I'll hurt them. I will.

Jeffty Is Five

Harlan Ellison

WHEN I WAS five years old, there was a little kid I played with: Jeffty.
His real name was Jeff Kinzer, and everyone who played with him
called him Jeffty. We were five years old together, and we had good
times playing together.

When I was five, a Clark Bar was as fat around as the gripping end
of a Louisville Slugger, and pretty nearly six inches long, and they used
real chocolate to coat it, and it crunched very nicely when you bit into
the center, and the paper it came wrapped in smelled fresh and good
when you peeled off one end to hold the bar so it wouldn't melt onto
your fingers. Today, a Clark Bar is as thin as a credit card, they use
something artificial and awful-tasting instead of pure chocolate, the
thing is soft and soggy, it costs fifteen or twenty cents instead of a decent, correct nickel, and they wrap it so you think it's the same size it
was twenty years ago, only it isn't; it's slim and ugly and nasty tasting
and not worth a penny, much less fifteen or twenty cents.

When I was that age, five years old, I was sent away to my Aunt Patricia's home in Buffalo, New York, for two years. My father was going
through "bad times," and Aunt Patricia was very beautiful and had
married a stockbroker. They took care of me for two years. When I was

HARLAN ELLISON *wrote three new pieces of fiction for F&SF's Special
Ellison Issue (July 1977). "Jeffty" was the feature story and everybody's favorite. It won a 1977 Nebula Award as well as a Hugo Award
the following year. Except for its being an award winner, it is a somewhat atypical Ellison story.*

seven, I came back home and went to find Jeffty, so we could play together.

I was seven. Jeffty was still five. I didn't notice any difference. I didn't know: I was only seven.

When I was seven years old I used to lie on my stomach in front of our Atwater Kent radio and listen to swell stuff. I had tied the ground wire to the radiator, and I would lie there with my coloring books and my Crayolas (when there were only sixteen colors in the big box), and listen to the NBC red network: Jack Benny on the Jell-O Program, Amos 'n' Andy, Edgar Bergen and Charlie McCarthy on the Chase and Sanborn Program, One Man's Family, First Nighter; the NBC blue network: Easy Aces, the Jergens Program with Walter Winchell, Information Please, Death Valley Days; and best of all, the Mutual Network with The Green Hornet, The Lone Ranger, The Shadow and Quiet Please. Today, I turn on my radio and go from one end of the dial to the other and all I get is 100 strings orchestras, banal housewives and insipid truckers discussing their kinky sex lives with arrogant talk show hosts, country and western drivel and rock music so loud it hurt my ears.

When I was ten, my grandfather died of old age and I was "a troublesome kid," and they sent me off to military school, so I could be "taken in hand."

I came back when I was fourteen. Jeffty was still five.

When I was fourteen years old, I used to go to the movies on Saturday afternoons and a matinee was ten cents and they used real butter on the popcorn and I could always be sure of seeing a western like Lash LaRue, or Wild Bill Elliott as Red Ryder with Bobby Blake as Little Beaver, or Roy Rogers, or Johnny Mack Brown; a scary picture like *House of Horrors* with Rondo Hatton as the Strangler, or *The Cat People*, or *The Mummy*, or *I Married a Witch* with Fredric March and Veronica Lake; plus an episode of a great serial like The Shadow with Victor Jory, or Dick Tracy or Flash Gordon; and three cartoons; a James Fitzpatrick Travel Talk; Movietone News; a singalong and, if I stayed on till evening, Bingo or Keno; and free dishes. Today, I go to movies and see Clint Eastwood blowing people's heads apart like ripe cantaloupes.

At eighteen, I went to college. Jeffty was still five. I came back during the summers, to work at my Uncle Joe's jewelry store. Jeffty hadn't changed. Now I knew there was something different about him, something wrong, something weird. Jeffty was still five years old, not a day older.

At twenty-two I came home for keeps. To open a Sony television franchise in town, the first one. I saw Jeffty from time to time. He was five.

Things are better in a lot of ways. People don't die from some of the old diseases any more. Cars go faster and get you there more quickly on better roads. Shirts are softer and silkier. We have paperback books even though they cost as much as a good hardcover used to. When I'm running short in the bank I can live off credit cards till things even out. But I still think we've lost a lot of good stuff. Did you know you can't buy linoleum any more, only vinyl floor covering? There's no such thing as oilcloth anymore; you'll never again smell that special, sweet smell from your grandmother's kitchen. Furniture isn't made to last thirty years or longer because they took a survey and found that young homemakers like to throw their furniture out and bring in all new color-coded borax every seven years. Records don't feel right; they're not thick and solid like the old ones, they're thin and you can bend them . . . that doesn't seem right to me. Restaurants don't serve cream in pitchers any more, just that artificial glop in little plastic tubs, and one is never enough to get coffee the right color. Everywhere you go, all the towns look the same with Burger Kings and MacDonald's and 7-Elevens and motels and shopping centers. Things may be better, but why do I keep thinking about the past?

What I mean by five years old is not that Jeffty was retarded. I don't think that's what it was. Smart as a whip for five years; very bright, quick, cute, a funny kid.

But he was three feet tall, small for his age, and perfectly formed, no big head, no strange jaw, none of that. A nice, normal-looking five year old kid. Except that he was the same age as I was: twenty-two.

When he spoke, it was with the squeaking, soprano voice of a five year old; when he walked it was with the little hops and shuffles of a five year old; when he talked to you, it was about the concerns of a five year old . . . comic books, playing soldier, using a clothes pin to attach a stiff piece of cardboard to the front fork of his bike so the sound it made when the spokes hit was like a motorboat, asking questions like *why does that thing do that like that,* how high is up, how old is old, why is grass green, what's an elephant look like? At twenty-two, he was five.

Jeffty's parents were a sad pair. Because I was still a friend of

Jeffty's, still let him hang around with me in the store, sometimes took him to the county fair or to the miniature golf or the movies, I wound up spending time with *them*. Not that I much cared for them, because they were so awfully depressing. But then, I suppose one couldn't expect much more from the poor devils. They had an alien thing in their home, a child who had grown no older than five in twenty-two years, who provided the treasure of that special childlike state indefinitely, but who also denied them the joys of watching the child grow into a normal adult.

Five is a wonderful time of life for a little kid . . . or it *can* be, if the child is relatively free of the monstrous beastliness other children indulge in. It is a time when the eyes are wide open and the patterns are not yet set; a time when one has not yet been hammered into accepting everything as immutable and hopeless; a time when the hands can not do enough, the mind cannot learn enough, the world is infinite and colorful and filled with mysteries. Five is a special time before they take the questing, unquenchable, quixotic soul of the young dreamer and thrust it into dreary schoolroom boxes. A time before they take the trembling hands that want to hold everything, touch everything, figure everything out, and make them lie still on desktops. A time before people begin saying "act your age" and "grow up" or "you're behaving like a baby." It is a time when a child who acts adolescent is still cute and responsive and everyone's pet. A time of delight, of wonder, of innocence.

Jeffty had been stuck in that time, just five, just so.

But for his parents it was an ongoing nightmare from which no one —not social workers, not priests, not child psychologists, not teachers, not friends, not medical wizards, not psychiatrists, no one—could slap or shake them awake. For seventeen years their sorrow had grown through stages of parental dotage to concern, from concern to worry, from worry to fear, from fear to confusion, from confusion to anger, from anger to dislike, from dislike to naked hatred, and finally, from deepest loathing and revulsion to a stolid, depressive acceptance.

John Kinzer was a shift foreman at the Balder Tool & Die plant. He was a thirty year man. To everyone but the man living it, his was a spectacularly uneventful life. In no way was he remarkable—save that he had fathered a twenty-two-year-old five year old.

John Kinzer was a small man, soft, with no sharp angles, with pale eyes that never seemed to hold mine for longer than a few seconds. He continually shifted in his chair during conversations, and seemed to see things in the upper corners of the room, things no one else could see . . . or wanted to see. I suppose the word that best suited him was *haunted*. What his life had become . . . well, *haunted* suited him.

Leona Kinzer tried valiantly to compensate. No matter what hour of the day I visited, she always tried to foist food on me. And when Jeffty was in the house she was always at *him* about eating: "Honey, would you like an orange? A nice orange? Or a tangerine? I have tangerines. I could peel a tangerine for you." But there was clearly such fear in her, fear of her own child, that the offers of sustenance always had a faintly ominous tone.

Leona Kinzer had been a tall woman, but the years had bent her. She seemed always to be seeking some area of wallpapered wall or storage niche into which she could fade, adopt some chintz or rose-patterned protective coloration and hide forever in plain sight of the child's big brown eyes, pass her a hundred times a day and never realize she was there, holding her breath, invisible. She always had an apron tied around her waist. And her hands were red from cleaning. As if by maintaining the environment immaculately she could pay off her imagined sin: having given birth to this strange creature.

Neither of them watched television very much. The house was usually dead silent, not even the sibilant whispering of water in the pipes, the creaking of timbers settling, the humming of the refrigerator. Awfully silent, as if time itself had taken a detour around that house.

As for Jeffty, he was inoffensive. He lived in that atmosphere of gentle dread and dulled loathing, and if he understood it, he never remarked in any way. He played, as a child plays, and seemed happy. But he must have sensed, in the way of a five year old, just how alien he was in their presence.

Alien. No, that wasn't right. He was *too* human, if anything. But out of phase, out of synch with the world around him, and resonating to a different vibration than his parents, God knows. Nor would other children play with him. As they grew past him, they found him at first childish, then uninteresting, then simply frightening as their perceptions of aging became clear and they could see he was not affected by time as they were. Even the little ones, his own age, who might wander into the neighborhood, quickly came to shy away from him like a dog in the street when a car backfires.

Thus, I remained his only friend. A friend of many years. Five years.

Twenty-two years. I liked him; more than I can say. And never knew exactly why. But I did, without reserve.

But because we spent time together, I found I was also—polite society—spending time with John and Leona Kinzer. Dinner, Saturday afternoons sometimes, an hour or so when I'd bring Jeffty back from a movie. They were grateful: slavishly so. It relieved them of the embarrassing chore of going out with him, of having to pretend before the world that they were loving parents with a perfectly normal, happy, attractive child. And their gratitude extended to hosting me. Hideous, every moment of their depression, hideous.

I felt sorry for the poor devils, but I despised them for their inability to love Jeffty, who was eminently lovable.

I never let on, even during the evenings in their company that were awkward beyond belief.

We would sit there in the darkening living room—*always* dark or darkening, as if kept in shadow to hold back what the light might reveal to the world outside through the bright eyes of the house—we would sit and silently stare at one another. They never knew what to say to me.

"So how are things down at the plant," I'd say to John Kinzer.

He would shrug. Neither conversation nor life suited him with any ease or grace. "Fine, just fine," he would say, finally.

And we would sit in silence again.

"Would you like a nice piece of coffee cake?" Leona would say. "I made it fresh just this morning." Or deep dish green apple pie. Or milk and toll house cookies. Or a brown betty pudding.

"No, no, thank you, Mrs. Kinzer; Jeffty and I grabbed a couple of cheeseburgers on the way home." And again, silence.

Then, when the stillness and the awkwardness became too much even for them (and who knew how long that total silence reigned when they were alone, with that thing they never talked about any more, hanging between them), Leona Kinzer would say, "I think he's asleep."

John Kinzer would say, "I don't hear the radio playing."

Just so, it would go on like that, until I could politely find excuse to bolt away on some flimsy pretext. Yes, that was the way it would go on, every time, just the same . . . except once.

"I don't know what to do any more," Leona said. She began crying. "There's no change, not one day of peace."

Her husband managed to drag himself out of the old easy chair and went to her. He bent and tried to soothe her, but it was clear from the graceless way in which he touched her graying hair that the ability to be compassionate had been stunned in him. "Shhh, Leona, it's all right. Shhh." But she continued crying. Her hands scraped gently at the antimacassars on the arms of the chair.

Then she said, "Sometimes I wish he had been stillborn."

John looked up into the corners of the room. For the nameless shadows that were always watching him? Was it God he was seeking in those spaces? "You don't mean that," he said to her, softly, pathetically, urging her with body tension and trembling in his voice to recant before God took notice of the terrible thought. But she meant it; she meant it very much.

I managed to get away quickly that evening. They didn't want witnesses to their shame. I was glad to go.

And for a week I stayed away. From them, from Jeffty, from their street, even from that end of town.

I had my own life. The store, accounts, suppliers' conferences, poker with friends, pretty women I took to well-lit restaurants, my own parents, putting anti-freeze in the car, complaining to the laundry about too much starch in the collars and cuffs, working out at the gym, taxes, catching Jan or David (which ever one it was) stealing from the cash register. I had my own life.

But not even *that* evening could keep me from Jeffty. He called me at the store and asked me to take him to the rodeo. We chummed it up as best a twenty-two year old with other interests *could* . . . with a five year old. I never dwelled on what bound us together; I always thought it was simply the years. That, and affection for a kid who could have been the little brother I never had. (Except I *remembered* when we had played together, when we had both been the same age; I *remembered* that period, and Jeffty was still the same.)

And then, one Saturday afternoon, I came to take him to a double feature, and things I should have noticed so many times before, I first began to notice only that afternoon.

I came walking up to the Kinzer house, expecting Jeffty to be sitting on the front porch steps, or in the porch glider, waiting for me. But he was nowhere in sight.

Going inside, into that darkness and silence, in the midst of May sunshine, was unthinkable. I stood on the front walk for a few moments, then cupped my hands around my mouth and yelled, "Jeffty? Hey, Jeffty, come on out, let's go. We'll be late."

His voice came faintly, as if from under the ground.

"Here I am, Donny."

I could hear him, but I couldn't see him. It was Jeffty, no question about it: as Donald H. Horton, President and Sole Owner of The Horton TV & Sound Center, no one but Jeffty called me Donny. He had never called me anything else.

(Actually, it isn't a lie. I *am*, as far as the public is concerned, Sole Owner of the Center. The partnership with my Aunt Patricia is only to repay the loan she made me, to supplement the money I came into when I was twenty-one, left to me when I was ten by my grandfather. It wasn't a very big loan, only eighteen thousand, but I asked her to be a silent partner, because of when she had taken care of me as a child.)

"Where are you, Jeffty?"

"Under the porch in my secret place."

I walked around the side of the porch, and stooped down and pulled away the wicker grating. Back in there, on the pressed dirt, Jeffty had build himself a secret place. He had comics in orange crates, he had a little table and some pillows, it was lit by big fat candles, and we used to hide there when we were both . . . five.

"What'cha up to?" I asked, crawling in and pulling the grate closed behind me. It was cool under the porch, and the dirt smelled comfortable, the candles smelled clubby and familiar. Any kid would feel at home in such a secret place: there's never been a kid who didn't spend the happiest, most productive, most deliciously mysterious times of his life in such a secret place.

"Playin'," he said. He was holding something golden and round. It filled the palm of his little hand.

"You forget we were going to the movies?"

"Nope. I was just waitin' for you here."

"Your mom and dad home?"

"Momma."

I understood why he was waiting under the porch. I didn't push it any further. "What've you got there?"

"Captain Midnight Secret Decoder Badge," he said, showing it to me on his flattened palm.

I realized I was looking at it without comprehending what it was for a long time. Then it dawned on me what a miracle Jeffty had in his hand. A miracle that simply could *not* exist.

"Jeffty," I said softly, with wonder in my voice, "where'd you get that?"

"Came in the mail today. I sent away for it."

"It must have cost a lot of money."

"Not so much. Ten cents an' two inner wax seals from two jars of Ovaltine."

"May I see it?" My voice was trembling, and so was the hand I extended. He gave it to me and I held the miracle in the palm of my hand. It was *wonderful*.

You remember. *Captain Midnight* went on the radio nationwide in 1940. It was sponsored by Ovaltine. And every year they issued a Secret Squadron Decoder Badge. And every day at the end of the program, they would give you a clue to the next day's installment in a code that only kids with the official badge could decipher. They stopped making those wonderful Decoder Badges in 1949. I remember the one I had in 1945; it was beautiful. It had a magnifying glass in the center of the code dial. *Captain Midnight* went off the air in 1950, and though it was a short-lived television series in the mid-Fifties, and though they issued Decoder Badges in 1955 and 1956, as far as the *real* badges were concerned, they never made one after 1949.

The Captain Midnight Code-O-Graph I held in my hand, the one Jeffty said he had gotten in the mail for ten cents (*ten cents!!!*) and two Ovaltine labels, was brand new, shiny gold metal, not a dent or a spot of rust on it like the old ones you can find at exorbitant prices in collectible shoppes from time to time . . . it was a *new* Decoder. And the date on it was *this* year.

But *Captain Midnight* no longer existed. Nothing like it existed on the radio. I'd listened to the one or two weak imitations of old-time radio the networks were currently airing, and the stories were dull, the sound effects bland, the whole feel of it wrong, out of date, cornball. Yet I held a *new* Code-O-Graph.

"Jeffty, tell me about this," I said.

"Tell you what, Donny? It's my new Capt'n Midnight Secret Decoder Badge. I use it to figger out what's gonna happen tomorrow."

"Tomorrow how?"

"On the program."

"*What* program?!"

He stared at me as if I was being purposely stupid. "On Capt'n *Midnight!* Boy!" I was being dumb.

I still couldn't get it straight. It was right there, right out in the open, and I still didn't know what was happening. "You mean one of those records they made of the old-time radio programs? Is that what you mean, Jeffty?"

"What records?" he asked. He didn't know what *I* meant.

We stared at each other, there under the porch. And then I said, very slowly, almost afraid of the answer, "Jeffty, how do you hear *Captain Midnight?*"

"Every day. On the radio. On my radio. Every day at five-thirty."

News. Music, dumb music, and news. That's what was on the radio every day at five-thirty. Not *Captain Midnight*. The Secret Squadron hadn't been on the air in twenty years.

"Can we hear it tonight?" I asked.

"Boy!" he said. I was being dumb. I knew it from the way he said it; but I didn't know *why*. Then it dawned on me: this was Saturday. *Captain Midnight* was on Monday through Friday. Not on Saturday or Sunday.

"We goin' to the movies?"

He had to repeat himself twice. My mind was somewhere else. Nothing definite. No conclusions. No wild assumptions leapt to. Just off somewhere trying to figure it out, and concluding—as *you* would have concluded, as *any*one would have concluded rather than accepting the truth, the impossible and wonderful truth—just finally concluding there was a simple explanation I didn't yet perceive. Something mundane and dull, like the passage of time that steals all good, old things from us, packratting trinkets and plastic in exchange. And all in the name of Progress.

"We goin' to the movies, Donny?"

"You bet your boots we are, kiddo," I said. And I smiled. And I handed him the Code-O-Graph. And he put it in his side pants pocket. And we crawled out from under the porch. And we went to the movies. And neither of us said anything about *Captain Midnight* all the rest of the day. And there wasn't a ten-minute stretch, all the rest of that day, that I didn't think about it.

It was inventory all that next week. I didn't see Jeffty till late Thursday. I confess I left the store in the hands of Jan and David, told them I had some errands to run, and left early. At 4:00. I got to the Kinzer's right around 4:45. Leona answered the door, looking exhausted and distant. "Is Jeffty around?" She said he was upstairs in his room . . .

. . . listening to the radio.

I climbed the stairs two at a time.

All right, I had finally made that impossible, illogical leap. Had the stretch of belief involved anyone but Jeffty, adult or child, I would have reasoned out more explicable answers. But it *was* Jeffty, clearly another kind of vessel of life, and what he might experience should not be expected to fit into the ordered scheme.

I admit it: I *wanted* to hear what I heard.

Even with the door closed, I recognized the program:

"There he goes, Tennessee! Get him!"

There was the heavy report of a rifle shot and the keening whine of the slug ricocheting, and then the same voice yelled triumphantly, *"Got him! D-e-a-a-a-d center!"*

He was listening to the American Broadcasting Company, 790 kilocycles, and he was hearing *Tennessee Jed,* one of my most favorite programs from the Forties, a western adventure I had not heard in twenty years, because it had not existed for twenty years.

I sat down on the top step of the stairs, there in the upstairs hall of the Kinzer home, and I listened to the show. It wasn't a rerun of an old program, because there were occasional references in the body of the drama to current cultural and technological developments, and phrases that had not existed in common usage in the Forties: aerosol spray cans, laseracing of tattoos, Tanzania, the word "uptight."

I could not ignore the fact. Jeffty was listening to a *new* segment of *Tennessee Jed.*

I ran downstairs and out the front door to my car. Leona must have been in the kitchen. I turned the key and punched on the radio and spun the dial to 790 kilocycles. The ABC station. Rock music.

I sat there for a few moments, then ran the dial slowly from one end to the other. Music, news, talk shows. No *Tennessee Jed.* And it was a Blaupunkt, the best radio I could get. I wasn't missing some perimeter station. It simply was not there!

After a few moments I turned off the radio and the ignition and went back upstairs quietly. I sat down on the top step and listened to the entire program. It was *wonderful.*

Exciting, imaginative, filled with everything I remembered as being most innovative about radio drama. But it was modern. It wasn't an antique, re-broadcast to assuage the need of that dwindling listenership who longed for the old days. It was a new show, with all the old voices, but still young and bright. Even the commercials were for currently available products, but they weren't as loud or as insulting as the screamer ads one heard on radio these days.

And when *Tennessee Jed* went off at 5:00, I heard Jeffty spin the dial on his radio till I heard the familiar voice of the announcer Glenn Riggs proclaim, *"Presenting Hop Harrigan! America's ace of the airwaves!"* There was the sound of an airplane in flight. It was a prop plane, *not* a jet! Not the sound kids today have grown up with, but the sound *I* grew up with, the *real* sound of an airplane, the growling, revving, throaty sound of the kind of airplanes G-8 and His Battle Aces flew, the kind Captain Midnight flew, the kind Hop Harrigan flew. And then I heard Hop say, *"CX-4 calling control tower. CX-4 calling control tower. Standing by!"* A pause, then, *"Okay, this is Hop Harrigan . . . coming in!"*

And Jeffty, who had the same problem all of us kids had in the Forties with programming that pitted equal favorites against one another on different stations, having paid his respects to Hop Harrigan and Tank Tinker, spun the dial and went back to ABC where I heard the stroke of a gong, the wild cacophony of nonsense Chinese chatter, and the announcer yelled, *"T-e-e-e-rry and the Pirates!"*

I sat there on the top step and listened to Terry and Connie and Flip Corkin and, so help me God, Agnes Moorehead as The Dragon Lady, all of them in a new adventure that took place in a Red China that had not existed in the days of Milton Caniff's 1937 version of the Orient, with river pirates and Chiang Kai-shek and warlords and the naive Imperialism of American gunboat diplomacy.

Sat, and listened to the whole show, and sat even longer to hear *Superman* and part of *Jack Armstrong, the All-American boy,* and part of *Captain Midnight,* and John Kinzer came home and neither he nor Leona came upstairs to find out what had happened to me, or where Jeffty was, and sat longer, and found I had started crying, and could not stop, just sat there with tears running down my face, into the corners of my mouth, sitting and crying until Jeffty heard me and opened his door and saw me and came out and looked at me in childish confusion as I heard the station break for the Mutual Network and they began the theme music of *Tom Mix,* "When it's Round-up Time in Texas and the Bloom is on the Sage," and Jeffty touched my shoulder and smiled at me and said, "Hi, Donny. Wanna come in an' listen to the radio with me?"

Hume denied the existence of an absolute space, in which each thing has its place; Borges denies the existence of one single time, in which all events are linked.

Jeffty received radio programs from a place that could not, in logic, in the natural scheme of the space-time universe as conceived by Einstein, exist. But that wasn't all he received. He got mail order premiums that no one was manufacturing. He read comic books that had been defunct for three decades. He saw movies with actors who had been dead for twenty years. He was the receiving terminal for endless joys and pleasures of the past that the world had dropped along the way. On its headlong suicidal flight toward New Tomorrows, the world had razed its treasurehouse of simple happiness, had poured concrete over its playgrounds, had abandoned its elfin stragglers, and all of it was being impossibly, miraculously shunted back into the present through Jeffty. Revivified, updated, the traditions maintained but contemporaneous. Jeffty was the unbidding Aladdin whose very nature formed the magic lampness of his reality.

And he took me into his world.

Because he trusted me.

We had breakfast of Quaker Puffed Wheat Sparkies and warm Ovaltine we drank out of *this* year's little Orphan Annie Shake-Up Mugs. We went to the movies and while everyone else was seeing a comedy starring Goldie Hawn and Ryan O'Neal, Jeffty and I were enjoying Humphrey Bogart as the professional thief Parker in John Huston's brilliant adaptation of the Donald Westlake novel, *Slayground*. The second feature was Spencer Tracy, Carole Lombard and Laird Cregar in the Val Lewton-produced film of *Leinengen Versus the Ants*.

Twice a month we went down to the newsstand and bought the current pulp issues of *The Shadow, Doc Savage* and *Startling Stories*. Jeffty and I sat together and I read to him from the magazines. He particularly liked the new short novel by Henry Kuttner, "The Dreams of Achilles," and the new Stanley G. Weinbaum series of short stories set in the subatomic particle universe of Redurna. In September we enjoyed the first installment of the new Robert E. Howard Conan novel, ISLE OF THE BLACK ONES, in *Weird Tales;* and in August were only mildly disappointed by Edgar Rice Burroughs' fourth novella in the Jupiter series featuring John Carter of Barsoom—"Corsairs of

Jupiter." But the editor of *Argosy All-Story Weekly* promised there would be two more stories in the series, and it was such an unexpected revelation for Jeffty and me, that it dimmed our disappointment at the lessened quality of the current story.

We read comics together, and Jeffty and I both decided—separately, before we came together to discuss it—that our favorite characters were Doll Man, Airboy and The Heap. We also adored the George Carlson strips in *Jingle Jangle Comics,* particularly the Pie-Face Prince of Old Pretzleburg stories, which we read together and laughed over, even though I had to explain some of the subtler puns to Jeffty, who was too young to have that kind of subtle wit.

How to explain it? I can't. I had enough physics in college to make some offhand guesses, but I'm more likely wrong than right. The laws of the conservation of energy occasionally break. These are laws that physicists call "weakly violated." Perhaps Jeffty was a catalyst for the weak violation of conservation laws we're only now beginning to realize exist. I tried doing some reading in the area—muon decay of the "forbidden" kind: gamma decay that doesn't include the muon neutrino among its products—but nothing I encountered, not even the latest readings from the Swiss Institute for Nuclear Research near Zurich gave me an insight. I was thrown back on a vague acceptance of the philosophy that the real name for "science" is *magic.*

No explanations, but enormous good times.

The happiest time of my life.

I had the "real" world, the world of my store and my friends and my family, the world of profit & loss, of taxes and evenings with young women who talked about going shopping or the United Nations, of the rising cost of coffee and microwave ovens. And I had Jeffty's world, in which I existed only when I was with him. The things of the past he knew as fresh and new, I could experience only when in his company. And the membrane between the two worlds grew ever thinner, more luminous and transparent. I had the best of both worlds. And knew, somehow, that I could carry nothing from one to the other.

Forgetting that, for just a moment, betraying Jeffty by forgetting, brought an end to it all.

Enjoying myself so much, I grew careless and failed to consider how fragile the relationship between Jeffty's world and my world really was. There is a reason why the present begrudges the existence of the past. I never really understood. Nowhere in the beast books, where survival is shown in battles between claw and fang, tentacle and poison sac, is there recognition of the ferocity the present always brings to bear on the past. Nowhere is there a detailed statement of how the present lies in wait for What-Was, waiting for it to become Now-This-Moment so it can shred it with its merciless jaws.

Who could know such a thing . . . at any age . . . who could understand such a thing?

I'm trying to exculpate myself. I can't. It was my fault.

It was another Saturday afternoon.

"What's playing today?" I asked him, in the car, on the way downtown.

He looked up at me from the other side of the front seat and smiled one of his best smiles. "Ken Maynard in *Bullwhip Justice* an' *The Demolished Man.*" He kept smiling, as if he'd really put one over on me. I looked at him with disbelief.

"You're *kid*ding!" I said, delighted. Bester's THE DEMOLISHED MAN?" He nodded his head, delighted at my being delighted. He knew it was one of my favorite books. "Oh, that's super!"

"Super *duper*," he said.

"Who's in it?"

"Franchot Tone, Evelyn Keyes, Lionel Barrymore and Elisha Cook, Jr." He was much more knowledgeable about movie actors than I'd ever been. He could name the character actors in any movie he'd ever seen. Even the crowd scenes.

"And cartoons?" I asked.

"Three of 'em, a *Little Lulu,* a *Donald Duck* and a *Bugs Bunny.* An' a *Pete Smith Specialty* an' a *Lew Lehr Monkeys is da C-r-r-aziest Peoples.*"

"Oh boy!" I said. I was grinning from ear to ear. And then I looked down and saw the pad of purchase order forms on the seat. I'd forgotten to drop it off at the store.

"Gotta stop by the Center," I said. "Gotta drop off something. It'll only take a minute."

"Okay," Jeffty said. "But we won't be late, will we?"

"Not on your tintype, kiddo," I said.

When I pulled into the parking lot behind the Center, he decided to come in with me and we'd walk over to the theater. It's not a large town. There are only two movie houses, the Utopia and the Lyric. We were going to the Utopia, only three blocks from the Center.

I walked into the store with the pad of forms, and it was bedlam. David and Jan were handling two customers each, and there were people standing around waiting to be helped. Jan turned a look on me and her face was a horror-mask of pleading. David was running from the stockroom to the showroom and all he could murmur as he whipped past was, "Help!" and then he was gone.

"Jeffty," I said, crouching down, "listen, give me a few minutes. Jan and David are in trouble with all these people. We won't be late, I promise. Just let me get rid of a couple of these customers." He looked nervous, but nodded okay.

I motioned to a chair and said, "Just sit down for a while and I'll be right with you."

He went to the chair, good as you please, though he knew what was happening, and he sat down.

I started taking care of people who wanted color television sets. This was the first really substantial batch of units we'd gotten in—color television was only now becoming reasonably priced and this was Sony's first promotion—and it was bonanza time for me. I could see paying off the loan and being out in front for the first time with the Center. It was business.

In my world, good business comes first.

Jeffty sat there and stared at the wall. Let me tell you about the wall.

Stanchion and bracket designs had been rigged from floor to within two feet of the ceiling. Television sets had been stacked artfully on the wall. Thirty-three television sets. All playing at the same time. Black and white, color, little ones, big ones, all going at the same time.

Jeffty sat and watched thirty-three television sets, on a Saturday afternoon. We can pick up a total of thirteen channels including the UHF educational stations. Golf was on one channel; baseball was on a second; celebrity bowling was on a third; the fourth channel was a religious seminar; a teen-age dance show was on the fifth; the sixth was a rerun of a situation comedy; the seventh was a rerun of a police show; eighth was a nature program showing a man flycasting endlessly; ninth was news and conversation; tenth was a stock car race; eleventh was a man doing logarithms on a blackboard; twelfth was a woman in a leotard doing sitting-up exercises; and on the thirteenth channel was a badly-animated cartoon show in Spanish. All but six of the shows were repeated on three sets. Jeffty sat and watched that wall of television on a Saturday afternoon while I sold as fast and as hard as I could, to pay back my Aunt Patricia and stay in touch with my world. It was business.

I should have known better. I should have understood about the present and the way it kills the past. But I was selling with both hands. And when I finally glanced over at Jeffty, half an hour later, he looked like another child.

He was sweating. That terrible fever sweat when you have stomach flu. He was pale, as pasty and pale as a worm, and his little hands were gripping the arms of the chair so tightly I could see his knuckles in bold relief. I dashed over to him, excusing myself from the middle-aged couple looking at the new 21″ Mediterranean model.

"Jeffty!"

He looked at me, but his eyes didn't track. He was in absolute terror. I pulled him out of the chair and started toward the front door with him, but the customers I'd deserted yelled at me, "Hey!" The middle-aged man said, "You wanna sell me this thing or don't you?"

I looked from him to Jeffty and back again. Jeffty was like a zombie. He had come where I'd pulled him. His legs were rubbery and his feet dragged. The past, being eaten by the present, the sound of something in pain.

I clawed some money out of my pants pocket and jammed it into Jeffty's hand. "Kiddo . . . listen to me . . . get out of here right now!" He still couldn't focus properly. *"Jeffty,"* I said as tightly as I could, *"listen* to me!" The middle-aged customer and his wife were walking toward us. "Listen, kiddo, get out of here right this minute. Walk over to the Utopia and buy the tickets. I'll be right behind you." The middle-aged man and his wife were almost on us. I shoved Jeffty through the door and watched him stumble away in the wrong direction, then stop as if gathering his wits, turn and go back past the front of the Center and in the direction of the Utopia. "Yes sir," I said, straightening up and facing them, "yes, ma'am, that is one terrific set with some sen*sa*tional features! If you'll just step back here with me . . ."

There was a terrible sound of something hurting, but I couldn't tell from which channel, or from which set, it was coming.

Most of it I learned later, from the girl in the ticket booth, and from some people I knew who came to me to tell me what had happened. By the time I got to the Utopia, nearly twenty minutes later, Jeffty was already beaten to a pulp and had been taken to the Manager's office.

"Did you see a very little boy, about five years old, with big brown eyes and straight brown hair . . . he was waiting for me?"

"Oh, I think that's the little boy those kids beat up?"

"What!?! *Where is he?*"

"They took him to the Manager's office. No one knew who he was or where to find his parents—"

A young girl wearing an usher's uniform was placing a wet paper towel on his face.

I took the towel away from her and ordered her out of the office. She looked insulted and snorted something rude, but she left. I sat on the edge of the couch and tried to swab away the blood from the lacerations without opening the wounds where the blood had caked. Both his eyes were swollen shut. His mouth was ripped badly. His hair was matted with dried blood.

He had been standing in line behind two kids in their teens. They started selling tickets at 12:30 and the show started at 1:00. The doors weren't opened till 12:45. He had been waiting, and the kids in front of him had had a portable radio. They were listening to the ballgame. Jeffty had wanted to hear some program. God knows what it might have been, *Grand Central Station, Land of the Lost,* God only knows which one it might have been.

He had asked if he could borrow their radio to hear the program for a minute, and it had been a commercial break or something, and the kids had given him the radio, probably out of some malicious kind of courtesy that would permit them to take offense and rag the little boy. He had changed the station . . . and they'd been unable to get it to go back to the ballgame. It was locked into the past, on a station that was broadcasting a program that didn't exist for anyone but Jeffty.

They had beaten him badly . . . as everyone watched.

And then they had run away.

I had left him alone, left him to fight off the present without sufficient weaponry. I had betrayed him for the sale of a 21″ Mediterranean console television, and now his face was pulped meat. He moaned something inaudible and sobbed softly.

"Shhh, it's okay, kiddo, it's Donny. I'm here. I'll get you home, it'll be okay."

I should have taken him straight to the hospital. I don't know why I didn't. I should have. I should have done that.

When I carried him through the door, John and Leona Kinzer just stared at me. They didn't move to take him from my arms. One of his hands was hanging down. He was conscious, but just barely. They stared, there in the semi-darkness of a Saturday afternoon in the present. I looked at them. "A couple of kids beat him up at the theater." I raised him a few inches in my arms and extended him. They stared at me, at both of us, with nothing in their eyes, without movement. "Jesus Christ," I shouted, "he's been beaten! He's your son! Don't you even want to touch him? What the hell kind of people are you?!"

Then Leona moved toward me very slowly. She stood in front of us for a few seconds, and there was a leaden stoicism in her face that was terrible to see. It said, *I have been in this place before, many times, and I cannot bear to be in it again; but I am here now.*

So I gave him to her. God help me, I gave him over to her.

And she took him upstairs to bathe away his blood and his pain.

John Kinzer and I stood in our separate places in the dim living room of their home, and we stared at each other. He had nothing to say to me.

I shoved past him and fell into a chair. I was shaking.

I heard the bath water running upstairs.

After what seemed a very long time Leona came downstairs, wiping her hands on her apron. She sat down on the sofa and after a moment John sat down beside her. I heard the sound of rock music from upstairs.

"Would you like a piece of nice pound cake?" Leona said.

I didn't answer. I was listening to the sound of the music. Rock music. On the radio. There was a table lamp on the end table beside the sofa. It cast a dim and futile light in the shadowed living room. Rock music from the present, on a radio upstairs? I started to say something, and then *knew* . . .

I jumped up just as the sound of hideous crackling blotted out the music, and the table lamp dimmed and dimmed and flickered. I screamed something, I don't know what it was, and ran for the stairs.

Jeffty's parents did not move. They sat there with their hands folded in that place they had been for so many years.

I fell twice rushing up the stairs.

There isn't much on television that can hold my interest. I bought an old cathedral-shaped Philco radio in a second-hand store, and I replaced all the burnt-out parts with the original tubes from old radios I could cannibalize that still worked. I don't use transistors or printed circuits. They wouldn't work. I've sat in front of that set for hours sometimes, running the dial back and forth as slowly as you can imagine, so slowly it doesn't look as if it's moving at all sometimes.

But I can't find *Captain Midnight* or *The Land of the Lost* or *The Shadow* or *Quiet Please.*

So she did love him, still, a little bit, even after all those years. I can't hate them: they only wanted to live in the present world again. That isn't such a terrible thing.

It's a good world, all things considered. It's much better than it used to be, in a lot of ways. People don't die from the old diseases any more. They die from new ones, but that's Progress, isn't it?

Isn't it?

Tell me.

Somebody please tell me.

Ararat

Zenna Henderson

WE'VE HAD TROUBLE with teachers in Cougar Canyon. It's just an Accommodation school anyway, isolated and so unhandy to anything. There's really nothing to hold a teacher. But the way The People bring forth their young, in quantities and with regularity, even our small Group can usually muster the nine necessary for the County School Superintendent to arrange for the schooling for the year.

Of course I'm past school age, Canyon school age, and have been for years, but if the tally came up one short in the Fall, I'd go back for a post-graduate course again. But now I'm working on a college level because Father finished me off for my high school diploma two summers ago. He's promised me that if I do well this year I'll get to go Outside next year and get my training and degree so I can be the teacher and we won't have to go Outside for one any more. Most of the kids would just as soon skip school as not, but the Old Ones don't hold with ignorance and the Old Ones have the last say around here.

Father is the head of the school board. That's how I get in on lots of school things the other kids don't. This summer when he wrote to the County Seat that we'd have more than our nine again this fall and would they find a teacher for us, he got back a letter saying they had exhausted their supply of teachers who hadn't heard of Cougar Canyon

---

SERIES STORIES *are quite common in science fiction and in the pages of F&SF. Probably the most popular series we've ever run was Zenna Henderson's appealing stories about the People (later collected in book form and produced as a television play). "Ararat" was the first of the series, published in October 1952.*

and we'd have to dig up our own teacher this year. That "dig up" sounded like a dirty crack to me since we have the graves of four past teachers in the far corner of our cemetery. They sent us such old teachers, the homeless, the tottering, who were trying to piece out the end of their lives with a year here and a year there in jobs no one else wanted because there's no adequate pension system in the state and most teachers seem to die in harness. And their oldness and their tottering were not sufficient in the Canyon where there are apt to be shocks for Outsiders—unintentional as most of them are.

We haven't done so badly the last few years, though. The Old Ones say we're getting adjusted—though some of the non-conformists say that The Crossing thinned our blood. It might be either or both or the teachers are just getting tougher. The last two managed to last until just before the year ended. Father took them in as far as Kerry Canyon and ambulances took them on in. But they were all right after a while in the sanatorium and they're doing okay now. Before them, though, we usually had four teachers a year.

Anyway, Father wrote to a Teachers Agency on the coast and after several letters each way, he finally found a teacher.

He told us about it at the supper table.

"She's rather young," he said, reaching for a toothpick and tipping his chair back on its hind legs.

Mother gave Jethro another helping of pie and picked up her own fork again. "Youth is no crime," she said, "and it'll be a pleasant change for the children."

"Yes, though it seems a shame." Father prodded at a back tooth and Mother frowned at him. I wasn't sure if it was for picking his teeth or for what he said. I knew he meant it seemed a shame to get a place like Cougar Canyon so early in a career. It isn't that we're mean or cruel, you understand. It's only that they're Outsiders and we sometimes forget—especially the kids.

"She doesn't *have* to come," said Mother. "She could say no."

"Well, now—" Father tipped his chair forward. "Jethro, no more pie. You go on out and help 'Kiah bring in the wood. Karen, you and Lizbeth get started on the dishes. Hop to it, kids."

And we hopped, too. Kids do to fathers in the Canyon, though I understand they don't always Outside. It annoyed me because I knew Father wanted us out of the way so he could talk adult talk to Mother, so I told Lizbeth I'd clear the table and then worked as slowly as I could, and as quietly, listening hard.

"She couldn't get any other job," said Father. "The Agency told me they had placed her twice in the last two years and she didn't finish the year either place."

"Well," said Mother, pinching in her mouth and frowning. "If she's that bad, why on earth did you hire her for the Canyon?"

"We have a choice?" laughed Father. Then he sobered. "No, it wasn't for incompetency. She was a good teacher. The way she tells it, they just fired her out of a clear sky. She asked for recommendations and one place wrote, 'Miss Carmody is a very competent teacher but we dare not recommend her for a teaching position.' "

" 'Dare not'?" asked Mother.

" 'Dare not,' " said Father. "The Agency assured me that they had investigated thoroughly and couldn't find any valid reasons for the dismissals, but she can't seem to find another job anywhere on the coast. She wrote me that she wanted to try another state."

"Do you suppose she's disfigured or deformed?" suggested Mother.

"Not from the neck up!" laughed Father. He took an envelope from his pocket. "Here's her application picture."

By this time I'd got the table cleared and I leaned over Father's shoulder.

"Gee!" I said. Father looked back at me, raising one eyebrow. I knew then that he had known all along that I was listening.

I flushed but stood my ground, knowing I was being granted admission to adult affairs, if only by the back door.

The girl in the picture was lovely. She couldn't have been many years older than I and she was twice as pretty. She had short dark hair curled all over her head and apparently that poreless creamy skin that seems to have an inner light of itself. She had a tentative look about her as though her dark eyebrows were horizontal question marks. There was a droop to the corners of her mouth—not much, just enough to make you wonder why . . . and want to comfort her.

"She'll stir the Canyon for sure," said Father.

"I don't know," Mother frowned thoughtfully. "What will the Old Ones say to a marriageable Outsider in the Canyon?"

"Adonday Veeah!" muttered Father. "That never occurred to me. None of our other teachers were ever of an age to worry about."

"What *would* happen?" I asked. "I mean if one of The Group married an Outsider?"

"Impossible," said Father, so like the Old Ones that I could see why his name was approved in Meeting last Spring.

"Why, there's even our Jemmy," worried Mother. "Already he's saying he'll have to start trying to find another Group. None of the girls here please him. Supposing this Outsider—how old is she?"

Father unfolded the application. "Twenty-three," he said, "Just three years out of college."

"Jemmy's twenty-four," said Mother, pinching her mouth together. "Father, I'm afraid you'll have to cancel the contract. If anything happened— Well, you waited over-long to become an Old One to my way of thinking and it'd be a shame to have something go wrong your first year."

"I can't cancel the contract. She's on her way here. School starts next Monday." Father ruffled his hair forward as he does when he's disturbed. "We're probably making a something of a nothing," he said hopefully.

"Well I only hope we don't have any trouble with this Outsider."

"Or she with us," grinned Father. "Where are my cigarettes?"

"On the book case," said Mother, getting up and folding the table cloth together to hold the crumbs.

Father snapped his fingers and the cigarettes drifted in from the front room.

Mother went on out to the kitchen. The table cloth shook itself over the waste basket and then followed her.

Father drove to Kerry Canyon Sunday night to pick up our new teacher. She was supposed to have arrived Saturday afternoon, but she didn't make bus connections at the County Seat. The road ends at Kerry Canyon. I mean for Outsiders. There's not much of the look of a well-traveled road very far out our way from Kerry Canyon, which is just as well. Tourists leave us alone. Of course *we* don't have much trouble getting our cars to and fro but that's why everything dead-ends at Kerry Canyon and we have to do all our own fetching and carrying —I mean the road being in the condition it is.

All the kids at our house wanted to stay up to see the new teacher, so Mother let them; but by 7:30 the youngest ones began to drop off and by 9 there was only Jethro and 'Kiah, Lizbeth and Jemmy and me. Father should have been home long before and Mother was restless and uneasy. I knew if he didn't arrive soon, she would head for her room and the cedar box under the bed. But at 9:15 we heard the car coughing and sneezing up the draw. Mother's wide relieved smile was reflected on all our faces.

"Of course!" she cried. "I forgot. He has an Outsider in the car. He had to use the *road* and it's terrible across Jackass Flat."

I felt Miss Carmody before she came in the door. I was tingling all over from anticipation already, but all at once I felt her, so plainly that I knew with a feeling of fear and pride that I was of my Grandmother, that soon I would be bearing the burden and blessing of her Gift: the Gift that develops into free access to any mind—one of The People or Outsider—willing or not. And besides the access, the ability to counsel and help, to staighten tangled minds and snarled emotions.

And then Miss Carmody stood in the doorway, blinking a little against the light, muffled to the chin against the brisk fall air. A bright scarf hid her hair but her skin *was* that luminous matt-cream it had looked. She was smiling a little, but scared, too. I shut my eyes and . . . I went in—just like that. It was the first time I had ever sorted anybody. She was all fluttery with tiredness and strangeness and there was a question deep inside her that had the wornness of repetition, but I couldn't catch what it was. And under the uncertainty there was a sweetness and dearness and such a bewildered sorrow that I felt my eyes dampen. Then I looked at her again (sorting takes such a little time) as Father introduced her. I heard a gasp beside me and suddenly I went into Jemmy's mind with a stunning rush.

Jemmy and I have been close all our lives and we don't always need words to talk with one another, but this was the first time I had ever gone in like this and I knew he didn't know what had happened. I felt embarrassed and ashamed to know his emotion so starkly. I closed him out as quickly as possible, but not before I knew that now Jemmy would never hunt for another Group; Old Ones or no Old Ones, he had found his love.

All this took less time than it takes to say "How do you do?" and shake hands. Mother descended with cries and drew Miss Carmody and Father out to the kitchen for coffee and Jemmy swatted Jethro and made him carry the luggage instead of snapping it to Miss Carmody's room. After all, we didn't want to lose our teacher before she even saw the school house.

I waited until everyone was bedded down. Miss Carmody in her cold, cold bed, the rest of us of course with our sheets for warmth—how I pity Outsiders! Then I went to Mother.

She met me in the dark hall and we clung together as she comforted me.

"Oh Mother," I whispered. "I sorted Miss Carmody tonight. I'm afraid."

Mother held me tight again. "I wondered," she said. "It's a great responsibility. You have to be so wise and clear-thinking. Your Grandmother carried the Gift with graciousness and honor. You are of her. You can do it."

"But Mother! To be an Old One!"

Mother laughed. "You have years of training ahead of you before you'll be an Old One. Counselor to the soul is a weighty job."

"Do I have to tell?" I pleaded. "I don't want anyone to know yet. I don't want to be set apart."

"I'll tell the Oldest," she said. "No one else need know." She hugged me again and I went back, comforted, to bed.

I lay in darkness and let my mind clear, not even knowing how I knew how to. Like the gentle reachings of quiet fingers I felt the family about me. I felt warm and comfortable as though I were cupped in the hollow palm of a loving hand. Some day I would belong to the Group as I now belonged to the family. Belong to others? With an odd feeling of panic, I shut the family out. I wanted to be alone—to belong just to me and no one else. I didn't *want* the Gift.

I slept for a while.

Miss Carmody left for the school house an hour before we did. She wanted to get things started a little before school time, her late arrival making it kind of rough on her. 'Kiah, Jethro, Lizbeth and I walked down the lane to the Armisters' to pick up their three kids. The sky was so blue you could taste it, a winey, fallish taste of harvest fields and falling leaves. We were all feeling full of bubbly enthusiasm for the beginning of school. We were light-hearted and light-footed, too, as we kicked along through the cottonwood leaves paving the lane with gold. In fact Jethro felt too light-footed and the third time I hauled him down and made him walk on the ground, I cuffed him good. He was still sniffling when we got to Armisters'.

"She's pretty!" called Lizbeth before the kids got out to the gate, all agog and eager for news of the new teacher.

"She's young," added 'Kiah, elbowing himself ahead of Lizbeth.

"She's littler'n me," sniffed Jethro and we all laughed because he's five-six already even if he isn't twelve yet.

Debra and Rachel Armister linked arms with Lizbeth and scuffled down the lane, heads together, absorbing the details of teacher's hair, dress, nail polish, luggage and night clothes, though goodness knows how Lizbeth knew anything about that.

Jethro and 'Kiah annexed Jeddy and they climbed up on the rail fence that parallels the lane and walked the top rail. Jethro took a tentative step or two above the rail, caught my eye and stepped back in a hurry. He knows as well as any child in the Canyon that a kid his age has no business lifting along a public road.

We detoured at the Mesa Road to pick up the Kroginold boys. More than once Father has sighed over the Kroginolds.

You see, when The Crossing was made, The People got separated in that last wild moment when air was screaming past and the heat was building up so alarmingly. The members of our Group left their ship just seconds before it crashed so devastatingly into the box canyon behind Old Baldy and literally splashed and drove itself into the canyon walls, starting a fire that stripped the hills bare for miles. After The People gathered themselves together from the Life Slips and founded Cougar Canyon, they found that the alloy the ship was made of was a metal much wanted here. Our Group has lived on mining the box canyon ever since, though there's something complicated about marketing the stuff. It has to be shipped out of the country and in again because everyone knows that it doesn't occur in this region.

Anyway, our Group at Cougar Canyon is probably the largest of The People, but we are reasonably sure that at least one Group and maybe two survived along with us. Grandmother in her time sensed two Groups but could never locate them exactly and, since our object is to go unnoticed in this new life, no real effort has ever been made to find them. Father can remember just a little of The Crossing, but some of the Old Ones are blind and crippled from the heat and the terrible effort they put forth to save the others from burning up like falling stars.

But getting back, Father often said that of all The People who could have made up our Group, we had to get the Kroginolds. They're rebels and were even before The Crossing. It's their kids that have been so rough on our teachers. The rest of us usually behave fairly decently and remember that we have to be careful around Outsiders.

Derek and Jake Kroginold were wrestling in a pile of leaves by the front gate when we got there. They didn't even hear us coming, so I leaned over and whacked the nearest rear-end and they turned in a flurry of leaves and grinned up at me for all the world like pictures of Pan in the mythology book at home.

"What kinda old bat we got this time?" asked Derek as he scrabbled in the leaves for his lunch box.

"She's not an old bat," I retorted, madder than need be because Derek annoys me so. "She's young and beautiful."

"Yeah, I'll bet!" Jake emptied the leaves from his cap onto the trio of squealing girls.

"She is so!" retorted 'Kiah. "The nicest teacher we ever had."

"She won't teach me nothing!" yelled Derek, lifting to the top of the cottonwood tree at the turn-off.

"Well, if she won't, I will," I muttered and, reaching for a handful of sun, I platted the twishers so quickly that Derek fell like a rock. He yelled like a catamount, thinking he'd get killed for sure, but I stopped him about a foot from the ground and then let go. Well, the stopping and the thump to the ground pretty well jarred the wind out of him, but he yelled:

"I'll tell the Old Ones! You ain't supposed to platt twishers—!"

"Tell the Old Ones," I snapped, kicking on down the leafy road. "I'll be there and tell them why. And then, old smarty pants, what will be your excuse for lifting?"

And then I was ashamed. I was showing off as bad as a Kroginold —but they make me so mad!

Our last stop before school was at the Clarinades'. My heart always squeezed when I thought of the Clarinade twins. They just started school this year—two years behind the average Canyon kid. Mrs. Kroginold used to say that the two of them, Susie and Jerry, divided one brain between them before they were born. That's unkind and un-true—thoroughly a Kroginold remark—but it is true that by Canyon standards the twins were retarded. They lacked so many of the attri-butes of The People. Father said it might be a delayed effect of The Crossing that they would grow out of, or it might be advance notice of what our children will be like here—what is ahead for The People. It makes me shiver, wondering.

Susie and Jerry were waiting, clinging to one another's hand as they always were. They were shy and withdrawn, but both were radiant be-cause of starting school. Jerry, who did almost all the talking for the two of them, answered our greetings with a shy "Hello."

Then Susie surprised us all by exclaiming, "We're going to school!"

"Isn't it wonderful?" I replied, gathering her cold little hand into mine. "And you're going to have the prettiest teacher we ever had."

But Susie had retired into blushing confusion and didn't say another word all the way to school.

I was worried about Jake and Derek. They were walking apart from us, whispering, looking over at us and laughing. They were cooking up some kind of mischief for Miss Carmody. And more than anything I wanted her to stay. I found right then that there *would* be years ahead of me before I became an Old One. I tried to go in to Derek and Jake to find out what was cooking, but try as I might I couldn't get past the sibilance of the snickers and the hard, flat brightness of their eyes.

We were turning off the road into the school yard when Jemmy, who should have been up at the mine long since, suddenly stepped out of the bushes in front of us, his hands behind him. He glared at Jake and Derek and then at the rest of the children.

"You kids mind your manners when you get to school," he snapped, scowling. "And you Kroginolds—just try anything funny and I'll lift you to Old Baldy and platt the twishers on you. This is one teacher we're going to keep."

Susie and Jerry clung together in speechless terror. The Kroginolds turned red and pushed out belligerent jaws. The rest of us just stared at a Jemmy who never raised his voice and never pushed his weight around.

"I mean it, Jake and Derek. You try getting out of line and the Old Ones will find a few answers they've been looking for—especially about the belfry in Kerry Canyon."

The Kroginolds exchanged looks of dismay and the girls sucked in breaths of astonishment. One of the most rigorously enforced rules of The Group concerns showing off outside the community. If Derek and Jake *had* been involved in ringing that bell all night last Fourth of July . . . well!

"Now you kids, scoot!" Jemmy jerked his head toward the school house and the terrified twins scudded down the leaf-strewn path like a pair of bright leaves themselves, followed by the rest of the children with the Kroginolds looking sullenly back over their shoulders and muttering.

Jemmy ducked his head and scowled. "It's time they got civilized anyway. There's no sense to our losing teachers all the time."

"No," I said noncommittally.

"There's no point in scaring her to death," Jemmy was intent on the leaves he was kicking with one foot.

"No," I agreed, suppressing my smile.

Then Jemmy smiled ruefully in amusement at himself. "I should waste words with you," he said. "Here." He took his hands from behind him and thrust a bouquet of burning bright autumn leaves into my arms. "They're from you to her," he said. "Something pretty for the first day."

"Oh, Jemmy!" I cried through the scarlet and crimson and gold. "They're beautiful. You've been up on Baldy this morning."

"That's right," he said. "But she won't know where they came from." And he was gone.

I hurried to catch up with the children before they got to the door. Suddenly overcome with shyness, they were milling around the porch steps, each trying to hide behind the others.

"Oh, for goodness' sakes!" I whispered to our kids. "You ate breakfast with her this morning. She won't bite. Go on in."

But I found myself shouldered to the front and leading the subdued group into the school room. While I was giving the bouquet of leaves to Miss Carmody, the others with the ease of established habit slid into their usual seats, leaving only the twins, stricken and white, standing alone.

Miss Carmody, dropping the leaves on her desk, knelt quickly beside them, pried a hand of each gently free from their frenzied clutching and held them in hers.

"I'm so glad you came to school," she said in her warm, rich voice. "I need a first grade to make the school work out right and I have a seat that must have been built on purpose for twins."

And she led them over to the side of the room, close enough to the old pot-bellied stove for Outside comfort later and near enough to the window to see out. There, in dusted glory, stood one of the old double desks that The Group must have inherited from some ghost town out in the hills. There were two wooden boxes for footstools for small dangling feet and, spouting like a flame from the old ink well hole, a spray of vivid red leaves—matchmates to those Jemmy had given me.

The twins slid into the desk, never loosing hands, and stared up at Miss Carmody, wide-eyed. She smiled back at them and, leaning forward, poked her finger tip into the deep dimple in each round chin.

"Buried smiles," she said, and the two scared faces lighted up briefly with wavery smiles. Then Miss Carmody turned to the rest of us.

I never did hear her introductory words. I was too busy mulling over the spray of leaves, and how she came to know the identical routine, words and all, that the twins' mother used to make them smile, and how on earth she knew about the old desks in the shed. But by the time we rose to salute the flag and sing our morning song, I had it figured out. Father must have briefed her on the way home last night. The twins were an ever present concern of the whole Group and we were all especially anxious to have their first year a successful one. Also, Father knew the smile routine and where the old desks were stored. As for the spray of leaves, well, some did grow this low on the mountain and frost is tricky at leaf-turning time.

So school was launched and went along smoothly. Miss Carmody was a good teacher and even the Kroginolds found their studies interesting.

They hadn't tried any tricks since Jemmy threatened them. That is, except that silly deal with the chalk. Miss Carmody was explaining something on the board and was groping sideways for the chalk to add to the lesson. Jake was deliberately lifting the chalk every time she almost had it. I was just ready to do something about it when Miss Carmody snapped her fingers with annoyance and grasped the chalk firmly. Jake caught my eye about then and shrank about six inches in girth and height. I didn't tell Jemmy, but Jake's fear that I might kept him straight for a long time.

The twins were really blossoming. They laughed and played with the rest of the kids and Jerry even went off occasionally with the other boys at noon time, coming back as disheveled and wet as the others after a dam-building session in the creek.

Miss Carmody fitted so well into the community and was so well-liked by us kids that it began to look like we'd finally keep a teacher all year. Already she had withstood some of the shocks that had sent our other teachers screaming. For instance . . .

The first time Susie got a robin redbreast sticker on her bookmark for reading a whole page—six lines—perfectly, she lifted all the way back to her seat, literally walking about four inches in the air. I held my breath until she sat down and was caressing the glossy sticker with one finger, then I sneaked a cautious look at Miss Carmody. She was sitting very erect, her hands clutching both ends of her desk as though in the act of rising, a look of incredulous surprise on her face. Then she relaxed, shook her head and smiled, and busied herself with some papers.

I let my breath out cautiously. The last teacher but two went into hysterics when one of the girls absent-mindedly lifted back to her seat because her sore foot hurt. I had hoped Miss Carmody was tougher—and apparently she was.

That same week, one noon hour, Jethro came pelting up to the

school house where Valancy—that's her first name and I call her by it
when we are alone, after all she's only four years older than I—was
helping me with that gruesome Tests and Measurements I was taking
by extension from Teachers College.

"Hey Karen!" he yelled through the window. "Can you come out a
minute?"

"Why?" I yelled back, annoyed at the interruption just when I was
trying to figure what was normal about a normal grade curve.

"There's need," yelled Jethro.

I put my book down. "I'm sorry, Valancy. I'll go see what's eating
him."

"Should I come too?" she asked. "If something's wrong—"

"It's probably just some silly thing," I said, edging out fast. When
one of The People says "There's need," that means Group business.

"Adonday Veeah!" I muttered at Jethro as we rattled down the steep
rocky path to the creek. "What are you trying to do? Get us all in trouble? What's the matter?"

"Look," said Jethro, and there were the boys standing around an
alarmed but proud Jerry and above their heads, poised in the air over a
half-built rock dam, was a huge boulder.

"Who lifted that?" I gasped.

"I did," volunteered Jerry, blushing crimson.

I turned on Jethro. "Well, why didn't you platt the twishers on it?
You didn't have to come running—"

"On *that?*" Jethro squeaked. "You know very well we're not allowed
to *lift* anything that big let alone platt it. Besides," shamefaced, "I can't
remember that dern girl stuff."

"Oh Jethro! You're so stupid sometimes!" I turned to Jerry. "How
on earth did you ever lift anything that big?"

He squirmed. "I watched Daddy at the mine once."

"Does he let you lift at home?" I asked severely.

"I don't know." Jerry squashed mud with one shoe, hanging his head.
"I never lifted anything before."

"Well, you know better. You kids aren't allowed to lift anything an
Outsider your age can't handle alone. And not even that if you can't
platt it afterwards."

"I know it," Jerry was still torn between embarrassment and pride.

"Well, remember it," I said. And taking a handful of sun, I platted
the twishers and set the boulder back on the hillside where it belonged.

Platting does come easier to the girls—sunshine platting, that is. Of

course only the Old Ones do the sun-and-rain one and only the very
Oldest of them all would dare the moonlight-and-dark, that can move
mountains. But that was still no excuse for Jethro to forget and run the
risk of having Valancy see what she musn't see.

It wasn't until I was almost back to the school house that it dawned
on me. Jerry had lifted! Kids his age usually lift play stuff almost from
the time they walk. That doesn't need platting because it's just a matter
of a few inches and a few seconds so gravity manages the return. But
Jerry and Susie never had. They were finally beginning to catch up.
Maybe it *was* just The Crossing that slowed them down—and maybe
only the Clarinades. In my delight, *I* forgot and lifted to the school
porch without benefit of the steps. But Valancy was putting up pictures
on the high, old-fashioned moulding just below the ceiling, so no harm
was done. She was flushed from her efforts and asked me to bring the
step stool so she could finish them. I brought it and steadied it for her—
and then nearly let her fall as I stared. How had she hung those first
four pictures before I got there?

The weather was unnaturally dry all Fall. We didn't mind it much
because rain with an Outsider around is awfully messy. We have to let
ourselves get wet. But when November came and went and Christmas
was almost upon us, and there was practically no rain and no snow at
all, we all began to get worried. The creek dropped to a trickle and
then to scattered puddles and then went dry. Finally the Old Ones had
to spend an evening at the Group Reservoir doing something about our
dwindling water supply. They wanted to get rid of Valancy for the evening, just in case, so Jemmy volunteered to take her to Kerry to the
show. I was still awake when they got home long after midnight. Since I
began to develop the Gift, I have long periods of restlessness when it
seems I have no apartness but am of every person in the Group. The
training I should start soon will help me shut out the others except
when I want them. The only thing is that we don't know who is to train
me. Since Grandmother died there has been no Sorter in our Group and
because of The Crossing, we have no books or records to help.

Anyway, I was awake and leaning on my window sill in the darkness.
They stopped on the porch—Jemmy is bunking at the mine during his
stint there. I didn't have to guess or use a Gift to read the pantomime
before me. I closed my eyes and my mind as their shadows merged.
Under their strong emotion, I could have had free access to their
minds, but I had been watching them all Fall. I knew in a special way

what passed between them, and I knew that Valancy often went to bed in tears and that Jemmy spent too many lonely hours on the Crag that juts out over the canyon from high on Old Baldy, as though he were trying to make his heart as inaccessible to Outsiders as the Crag is. I knew what he felt, but oddly enough I had never been able to sort Valancy since that first night. There was something very un-Outsiderish and also very un-Groupish about her mind and I couldn't figure what.

I heard the front door open and close and Valancy's light steps fading down the hall and then I felt Jemmy calling me outside. I put my coat on over my robe and shivered down the hall. He was waiting by the porch steps, his face still and unhappy in the faint moonlight.

"She won't have me," he said flatly.

"Oh, Jemmy!" I cried. "You asked her—"

"Yes," he said. "She said no."

"I'm so sorry." I huddled down on the top step to cover my cold ankles. "But Jemmy—"

"Yes, I know!" he retorted savagely. "She's an Outsider. I have no business even to want her. Well, if she'd have me, I wouldn't hesitate a minute. This Purity-of-the-Group deal is—"

". . . is fine and right," I said softly, "as long as it doesn't touch you personally? But think for a minute, Jemmy. Would you be able to live a life as an Outsider? Just think of the million and one restraints that you would have to impose on yourself—and for the rest of your life, too, or lose her after all. Maybe it's better to accept *No* now than to try to build something and ruin it completely later. And if there should be children . . ." I paused. *"Could* there be children, Jemmy?"

I heard him draw a sharp breath.

"We don't know," I went on. "We haven't had the occasion to find out. Do you want Valancy to be part of the first experiment?"

Jemmy slapped his hat viciously down on his thigh, then he laughed.

"You have the Gift," he said, though I had never told him. "Have you any idea, sister mine, how little you will be liked when you become an Old One?"

"Grandmother was well-liked," I answered placidly. Then I cried, "Don't *you* set me apart, darn you, Jemmy. Isn't it enough to know that among a different people, *I* am different? Don't *you* desert me now!" I was almost in tears.

Jemmy dropped to the step beside me and thumped my shoulder in his old way. "Pull up your socks, Karen. We have to do what we have to do. I was just taking my mad out on you. What a world." He sighed heavily.

I huddled deeper in my coat, cold of soul.

"But the other one is gone," I whispered. "The Home."

And we sat there sharing the poignant sorrow that is a constant undercurrent among The People, even those of us who never actually saw The Home. Father says it's because of a sort of racial memory.

"But she didn't say no because she doesn't love me," Jemmy went on at last. "She does love me. She told me so."

"Then why not?" Sister-wise I couldn't imagine anyone turning Jemmy down.

Jemmy laughed—a short, unhappy laugh. "Because she is different."

"She's different?"

"That's what she said, as though it was pulled out of her. 'I can't marry,' she said. 'I'm different!' That's pretty good, isn't it, coming from an Outsider!"

"She doesn't know we're The People," I said. "She must feel that she is different from everyone. I wonder why?"

"I don't know. There's something about her, though. A kind of shield or wall that keeps us apart. I've never met anything like it in an Outsider or in one of The People either. Sometimes it's like meshing with one of us and then *bang!* I smash the daylights out of me against that stone wall."

"Yes, I know," I said. "I've felt it, too."

We listened to the silent past-midnight world and then Jemmy stood.

"Well, g'night, Karen. Be seeing you."

I stood up, too. "Good night, Jemmy." I watched him start off in the late moonlight. He turned at the gate, his face hidden in the shadows.

"But I'm not giving up," he said quietly. "Valancy is my love."

The next day was hushed and warm—unnaturally so for December in our hills. There was a kind of ominous stillness among the trees, and, threading thinly against the milky sky, the thin smokes of little brush fires pointed out the dryness of the whole country. If you looked closely you could see piling behind Old Baldy an odd bank of clouds, so nearly the color of the sky that it was hardly discernible, but puffy and summer-thunderheady.

All of us were restless in school, the kids reacting to the weather, Valancy pale and unhappy after last night. I was bruising my mind against the blank wall in hers, trying to find some way I could help her.

Finally the thousand and one little annoyances were climaxed by Jerry and Susie scuffling until Susie was pushed out of the desk onto an open box of wet water colors that Debra for heaven only knows what reason had left on the floor by her desk. Susie shrieked and Debra sputtered and Jerry started a high silly giggle of embarrassment and delight. Valancy, without looking, reached for something to rap for order with and knocked down the old cracked vase full of drooping wildflowers and three-day-old water. The vase broke and flooded her desk with the foul-smelling deluge, ruining the monthly report she had almost ready to send in to the County School Superintendent.

For a stricken moment there wasn't a sound in the room, then Valancy burst into half-hysterical laughter and the whole room rocked with her. We all rallied around doing what we could to clean up Susie and Valancy's desk and then Valancy declared a holiday and decided that it would be the perfect time to go up-canyon to the slopes of Baldy and gather what greenery we could find to decorate our school room for the holidays.

We all take our lunches to school, so we gathered them up and took along a square tarp the boys had brought to help build the dam in the creek. Now that the creek was dry, they couldn't use it and it'd come in handy to sit on at lunch time and would serve to carry our greenery home in, too, stretcher-fashion.

Released from the school room, we were all loud and jubilant and I nearly kinked my neck trying to keep all the kids in sight at once to nip in the bud any thoughtless lifting or other Group activity. The kids were all so wild, they might forget.

We went on up-canyon past the kids' dam and climbed the bare, dry waterfalls that stair-step up to the Mesa. On the Mesa, we spread the tarp and pooled our lunches to make it more picnicky. A sudden hush from across the tarp caught my attention. Debra, Rachel and Lizbeth were staring horrified at Susie's lunch. She was calmly dumping out a half dozen *koomatka* beside her sandwiches.

Koomatka are almost the only plants that lasted through The Crossing. I think four *koomatka* survived in someone's personal effects. They were planted and cared for as tenderly as babies and now every household in The Group has a *koomatka* plant growing in some quiet spot out of casual sight. Their fruit is eaten not so much for nourishment as Earth knows nourishment, but as a last remembrance of all other similar delights that died with The Home. We always save *koomatka* for special occasions. Susie must have sneaked some out when her mother wasn't looking. And there they were—across the table from an Outsider!

Before I could snap them to me or say anything, Valancy turned, too, and caught sight of the softly glowing bluey-green pile. Her eyes widened and one hand went out. She started to say something and then she dropped her eyes quickly and drew her hand back. She clasped her hands tightly together and the girls, eyes intent on her, scrambled the *koomatka* back into the sack and Lizbeth silently comforted Susie who had just realized what she had done. She was on the verge of tears at having betrayed The People to an Outsider.

Just then 'Kiah and Derek rolled across the picnic table fighting over a cupcake. By the time we salvaged our lunch from under them and they had scraped the last of the chocolate frosting off their T-shirts, the *koomatka* incident seemed closed. And yet, as we lay back resting a little to settle our stomachs, staring up at the smothery low-hanging clouds that had grown from the milky morning sky, I suddenly found myself trying to decide about Valancy's look when she saw the fruit. Surely it couldn't have been recognition!

At the end of our brief siesta, we carefully buried the remains of our lunch—the hill was much too dry to think of burning it—and started on again. After a while, the slope got steeper and the stubborn tangle of manzanita tore at our clothes and scratched our legs and grabbed at the rolled-up tarp until we all looked longingly at the free air above it. If Valancy hadn't been with us we could have lifted over the worst and saved all this trouble. But we blew and panted for a while and then struggled on.

After an hour or so, we worked out onto a rocky knoll that leaned against the slope of Baldy and made a tiny island in the sea of manzanita. We all stretched out gratefully on the crumbling granite outcropping, listening to our heart-beats slowing.

Then Jethro sat up and sniffed. Valancy and I alerted. A sudden puff of wind from the little side canyon brought the acrid pungency of burning brush to us. Jethro scrambled along the narrow ridge to the slope of Baldy and worked his way around out of sight into the canyon. He came scrambling back, half lifting, half running.

"Awful!" he panted. "It's awful! The whole canyon ahead is on fire and it's coming this way fast!"

Valancy gathered us together with a glance.

"Why didn't we see the smoke?" she asked tensely. "There wasn't any smoke when we left the school house."

"Can't see this slope from school," he said. "Fire could burn over a dozen slopes and we'd hardly see the smoke. This side of Baldy is a rim fencing in an awful mess of canyons."

"What'll we do?" quavered Lizbeth, hugging Susie to her.

Another gust of wind and smoke set us all to coughing and through my streaming tears, I saw a long lapping tongue of fire reach around the canyon wall.

Valancy and I looked at each other. I couldn't sort her mind, but mine was a panic, beating itself against the fire and then against the terrible tangle of manzanita all around us. Bruising against the possibility of lifting out of danger, then against the fact that none of the kids was capable of sustained progressive self-lifting for more than a minute or so and how could we leave Valancy? I hid my face in my hands to shut out the acres and acres of tinder-dry manzanita that would blaze like a torch at the first touch of fire. If only it would rain! You can't *set* fire to wet manzanita, but after these long months of drought—!

I heard the younger children scream and looked up to see Valancy staring at me with an intensity that frightened me even as I saw fire standing bright and terrible behind her at the mouth of the canyon.

Jake, yelling hoarsely, broke from the group and lifted a yard or two over the manzanita before he tangled his feet and fell helpless into the ugly, angled branches.

"Get under the tarp!" Valancy's voice was a whip-lash. "All of you get under the tarp!"

"It won't do any good," bellowed 'Kiah. "It'll burn like paper!"

"Get—under—the—tarp!" Valancy's spaced, icy words drove us to unfolding the tarp and spreading it to creep under. I lifted (hoping even at this awful moment that Valancy wouldn't see me) over to Jake and yanked him back to his feet. I couldn't lift with him so I pushed and prodded and half-carried him back through the heavy surge of black smoke to the tarp and shoved him under. Valancy was standing, back to the fire, so changed and alien that I shut my eyes against her and started to crawl in with the other kids.

And then she began to speak. The rolling, terrible thunder of her voice shook my bones and I swallowed a scream. A surge of fear swept through our huddled group and shoved me back out from under the tarp.

Till I die, I'll never forget Valancy standing there tense and taller than life against the rolling convulsive clouds of smoke, both her hands outstretched, fingers wide apart as the measured terror of her voice went on and on in words that plague me because I should have known them and didn't. As I watched, I felt an icy cold gather, a paralyzing, unearthly cold that froze the tears on my tensely upturned face.

And then lightning leaped from finger to finger of her lifted hands. And lightning answered in the clouds above her. With a toss of her hands she threw the cold, the lightning, the sullen shifting smoke upward, and the roar of the racing fire was drowned in a hissing roar of down-drenching rain.

I knelt there in the deluge, looking for an eternal second into her drained, despairing, hopeless eyes before I caught her just in time to keep her head from banging on the granite as she pitched forward, inert.

Then as I sat there cradling her head in my lap, shaking with cold and fear, with the terrified wailing of the kids behind me, I heard Father shout and saw him and Jemmy and Darcy Clarinade in the old pick-up, lifting over the steaming streaming manzanita, over the trackless mountain side through the rain to us. Father lowered the truck until one of the wheels brushed a branch and spun lazily, then the three of them lifted all of us up to the dear familiarity of that beat-up old jalopy.

Jemmy received Valancy's limp body into his arms and crouched in back, huddling her in his arms, for the moment hostile to the whole world that had brought his love to such a pass.

We kids clung to Father in an ecstasy of relief. He hugged us all tight to him, then he raised my face.

"Why did it rain?" he asked sternly, every inch an Old One while the cold downpour dripped off the ends of my hair and he stood dry inside his Shield.

"I don't know," I sobbed, blinking my streaming eyes against his sternness. "Valancy did it . . . with lightning . . . it was cold . . . she talked. . . ." Then I broke down completely, plumping down on the rough floor boards and, in spite of my age, howling right along with the other kids.

It was a silent, solemn group that gathered in the school house that evening. I sat at my desk with my hands folded stiffly in front of me, half scared of my own People. This was the first official meeting of the Old Ones I'd ever attended. They all sat in desks, too, except the Oldest who sat in Valancy's chair. Valancy sat stony-faced in the twin's desk, but her nervous fingers shredded one kleenex after another as she waited.

The Oldest rapped the side of the desk with his cane and turned his sightless eyes from one to another of us.

"We're all here," he said, "to inquire——"

"Oh, stop it!" Valancy jumped up from her seat. "Can't you fire me without all this rigmarole? I'm used to it. Just say go and I'll go!" She stood trembling.

"Sit down, Miss Carmody," said the Oldest. And Valancy sat down meekly.

"Where were you born?" asked the Oldest quietly.

"What does it matter?" flared Valancy. Then resignedly, "It's in my application. Vista Mar, California."

"And your parents?"

"I don't know."

There was a stir in the room.

"Why not?"

"Oh, this is so unnecessary!" cried Valancy. "But if you *have* to know, both my parents were foundlings. They were found wandering in the streets after a big explosion and fire in Vista Mar. An old couple who lost everything in the fire took them in. When they grew up, they married. I was born. They died. Can I go now?"

A murmur swept the room.

"Why did you leave your other jobs?" asked Father.

Before Valancy could answer, the door was flung open and Jemmy stalked defiantly in.

"Go!" said the Oldest.

"Please," said Jemmy, deflating suddenly. "Let me stay. It concerns me too."

The Oldest fingered his cane and then nodded. Jemmy half-smiled with relief and sat down in a back seat.

"Go on," said the Oldest One to Valancy.

"All right then," said Valancy. "I lost my first job because I—well— I guess you'd call it levitated—to fix a broken blind in my room. It was stuck and I just . . . went up . . . in the air until I unstuck it. The principal saw me. He couldn't believe it and it scared him so he fired me." She paused expectantly.

The Old Ones looked at one another and my silly, confused mind began to add up columns that only my lack of common sense had kept from giving totals long ago.

"And the other one?" The Oldest leaned his cheek on his doubled-up hand as he bent forward.

"Well," she said hesitantly, "I called my books to me—I mean they were on my desk. . . ."

"We know what you mean," said the Oldest.

"You know!" Valancy looked dazed.

The Oldest stood up.

"Valancy Carmody, open your mind!"

Valancy stared at him and then burst into tears.

"I can't, I can't," she sobbed. "It's been too long. I can't let anyone in. I'm different. I'm alone. Can't you understand? They all died. I'm alien!"

"You are alien no longer, said the Oldest. "You are home now, Valancy." He motioned to me. "Karen, go in to her."

So I did. At first the wall was still there; then with a soundless cry, half anguish and half joy, the wall went down and I was with Valancy. I saw all the secrets that had cankered in her since her parents died— the parents who were of The People.

The had been reared by the old couple who were not only of The People but had been the Oldest of the whole Crossing.

I tasted with her the hidden frightening things—the need for living as an Outsider, the terrible need for concealing all her differences and suppressing all the extra Gifts of The People, the ever present fear of betraying herself and the awful lostness that came when she thought she was the last of The People.

And then suddenly *she* came in to *me* and my mind was flooded with a far greater presence than I had ever before experienced.

My eyes flew open and I saw all of the Old Ones staring at Valancy. Even the Oldest had his face turned to her, wonder written as widely on his scarred face as on the others.

He bowed his head and made The Sign. "The lost persuasions and designs," he murmured. "She has them all."

And then I knew that Valancy, Valancy who had wrapped herself so tightly against the world to which any thoughtless act might betray her that she had lived with us all this time without our knowing about her or she about us, was one of us. Not only one of us but such a one as had not been since Grandmother died—and even beyond that. My incoherent thoughts cleared to one.

Now I would have some one to train me. Now I could become a sorter—but only second to her.

I turned to share my wonder with Jemmy. He was looking at Valancy as The People must have looked at The Home in the last hour. Then he turned to the door.

Before I could draw a breath, Valancy was gone from me and from the Old Ones and Jemmy was turning to her outstretched hands.

Then I bolted for the outdoors and rushed like one possessed down the lane, lifting and running until I staggered up our porch steps and collapsed against Mother, who had heard me coming.

"Oh, Mother!" I cried. "She's one of us! She's Jemmy's love! She's wonderful!" And I burst into noisy sobs in the warm comfort of Mother's arms.

So now I don't have to go Outside to become a teacher. We have a permanent one. But I'm going anyway. I want to be as much like Valancy as I can and she has her degree. Besides I can use the discipline of living Outside for a year.

I have so much to learn and so much training to go through, but Valancy will always be there with me. I won't be set apart alone because of the Gift.

Maybe I shouldn't mention it, but one reason I want to hurry my training is that we're going to try to locate the other People. None of the boys here please me.

Me

Hilbert Schenck, Jr.

I think that I shall never see
A calculator made like me.
A me that likes Martinis dry
And on the rocks, a little rye.
A me that looks at girls and such,
But mostly girls, and very much.
A me that wears an overcoat
And likes a risky anecdote.
A me that taps a foot and grins
Whenever Dixieland begins.
They make computers for a fee,
But only moms can make a me.

Sundance

Robert Silverberg

TODAY YOU LIQUIDATED ABOUT 50,000 Eaters in Sector A, and now you are spending an uneasy night. You and Herndon flew east at dawn, with the green-gold sunrise at your backs, and sprayed the neural pellets over a thousand hectares along the Forked River. You flew on into the prairie beyond the river, where the Eaters have already been wiped out, and had lunch sprawled on that thick, soft carpet of grass where the first settlement is expected to rise. Herndon picked some juiceflowers, and you enjoyed half an hour of mild hallucinations. Then, as you headed toward the copter to begin an afternoon of further pellet spraying, he said suddenly, "Tom, how would you feel about this if it turned out that the Eaters weren't just animal pests? That they were *people* say, with a language and rites and a history and all?"

You thought of how it had been for your own people.

"They aren't," you said.

"Suppose they were. Suppose the Eaters—"

"They aren't. Drop it."

Herndon has this streak of cruelty in him that leads him to ask such

ROBERT SILVERBERG *wrote hundreds of stories and novels in the fifties and early sixties. In the late sixties and early seventies he began to write less, but with better results. In 1974, we published a Special Silverberg Issue, featuring "Born with the Dead," which won a Nebula Award. Since then he has written hardly anything at all, until 1979, when his new novel,* Lord Valentine's Castle, *was completed. "Sundance" appeared in the January 1969 issue.*

questions. He goes for the vulnerabilities; it amuses him. All night now his casual remark has echoed in your mind. Suppose the Eaters . . . Suppose the Eaters . . . Suppose . . . Suppose . . .

You sleep for a while, and dream, and in your dreams you swim through rivers of blood.

Foolishness. A feverish fantasy. You know how important it is to exterminate the Eaters fast, before the settlers get here. They're just animals, and not even harmless animals at that; ecology-wreckers is what they are, devourers of oxygen-liberating plants, and they have to go. A few have been saved for zoological study. The rest must be destroyed. Ritual extirpation of undesirable beings, the old, old story. But let's not complicate our job with moral qualms, you tell yourself. Let's not dream of rivers of blood.

The Eaters don't even *have* blood, none that could flow in rivers, anyway. What they have is, well, a kind of lymph that permeates every tissue and transmits nourishment along the interfaces. Waste products go out the same way, osmotically. In terms of process, it's structurally analogous to your own kind of circulatory system, except there's no network of blood vessels hooked to a master pump. The life-stuff just oozes through their bodies, as though they were amoebas or sponges or some other low-phylum form. Yet they're definitely high-phylum in nervous system, digestive setup, limb-and-organ template, etc. Odd, you think. The thing about aliens is that they're alien, you tell yourself, not for the first time.

The beauty of their biology for you and your companions is that it lets you exterminate them so neatly.

You fly over the grazing grounds and drop the neural pellets. The Eaters find and ingest them. Within an hour the poison has reached all sectors of the body. Life ceases; a rapid breakdown of cellular matter follows, the Eater literally falling apart molecule by molecule the instant that nutrition is cut off, the lymph-like stuff works like acid; a universal lysis occurs; flesh and even the bones, which are cartilaginous, dissolve. In two hours, a puddle on the ground. In four, nothing at all left. Considering how many millions of Eaters you've scheduled for extermination here, it's sweet of the bodies to be self-disposing. Otherwise what a charnel house this world would become!

Suppose the Eaters . . .

Damn Herndon. You almost feel like getting a memory-editing in the

morning. Scrape his stupid speculations out of your head. If you dared.
If you dared.

In the morning he does not dare. Memory-editing frightens him; he
will try to shake free of his new-found guilt without it. The Eaters, he
explains to himself, are mindless herbivores, the unfortunate victims of
human expansionism, but not really deserving of passionate defense.
Their extermination is not tragic; it's just too bad. If Earthmen are to
have this world, the Eaters must relinquish it. There's a difference, he
tells himself, between the elimination of the Plains Indians from the
American prairie in the nineteenth century and the destruction of the
bison on that same prairie. One feels a little wistful about the slaughter
of the thundering herds; one regrets the butchering of millions of the
noble brown woolly beasts, yes. But one feels outrage, not mere wistful
regret, at what was done to the Sioux. There's a difference. Reserve
your passions for the proper cause.

He walks from his bubble at the edge of the camp toward the center
of things. The flagstone path is moist and glistening. The morning fog
has not yet lifted, and every tree is bowed, the long, notched leaves
heavy with droplets of water. He pauses, crouching, to observe a
spider-analog spinning its asymmetrical web. As he watches, a small
amphibian, delicately shaded turquoise, glides as inconspicuously as
possible over the mossy ground. Not inconspicuously enough; he gently
lifts the little creature and puts it on the back of his hand. The gills
flutter in anguish, and the amphibian's sides quiver. Slowly, cunningly,
its color changes until it matches the coppery tone of the hand. The
camouflage is excellent. He lowers his hand and the amphibian scurries
into a puddle. He walks on.

He is forty years old, shorter than most of the other members of the
expedition, with wide shoulders, a heavy chest, dark glossy hair, a
blunt, spreading nose. He is a biologist. This is his third career, for he
has failed as an anthropologist and as a developer of real estate. His
name is Tom Two Ribbons. He has been married twice but has had no
children. His great-grandfather died of alcoholism; his grandfather was
addicted to hallucinogens; his father had compulsively visited cheap
memory-editing parlors. Tom Two Ribbons is conscious that he is
failing a family tradition, but he has not yet found his own mode of
self-destruction.

In the main building he discovers Herndon, Julia, Ellen, Schwartz,

Chang, Michaelson, and Nichols. They are eating breakfast; the others are already at work. Ellen rises and comes to him and kisses him. Her short soft yellow hair tickles his cheeks. "I love you," she whispers. She has spent the night in Michaelson's bubble. "I love you," he tells her, and draws a quick vertical line of affection between her small pale breasts. He winks at Michaelson, who nods, touches the tips of two fingers to his lips, and blows them a kiss. We are all good friends here, Tom Two Ribbons thinks.

"Who drops pellets today?" he asks.

"Mike and Chang," says Julia. "Sector C."

Schwartz says, "Eleven days and we ought to have the whole peninsula clear. Then we can move inland."

"If our pellet supply holds up," Chang points out.

Herndon says, "Did you sleep well, Tom?"

"No," says Tom. He sits down and taps out his breakfast requisition. In the west, the fog is beginning to burn off the mountains. Something throbs in the back of his neck. He has been on this world nine weeks now, and in that time it has undergone its only change of season, shading from dry weather to foggy. The mists will remain for many months. Before the plains parch again, the Eaters will be gone and the settlers will begin to arrive. His food slides down the chute and he seizes it. Ellen sits beside him. She is a little more than half his age; this is her first voyage; she is their keeper of records, but she is also skilled at editing. "You look troubled," Ellen tells him. "Can I help you?"

"No. Thank you."

"I hate it when you get gloomy."

"It's a racial trait," says Tom Two Ribbons.

"I doubt that very much."

"The truth is that maybe my personality reconstruct is wearing thin. The trauma level was so close to the surface. I'm just a walking veneer, you know."

Ellen laughs prettily. She wears only a sprayon halfwrap. Her skin looks damp; she and Michaelson have had a swim at dawn. Tom Two Ribbons is thinking of asking her to marry him, when this job is over. He has not been married since the collapse of the real estate business. The therapist suggested divorce as part of the reconstruct. He sometimes wonders where Terry has gone and whom she lives with now. Ellen says, "You seem pretty stable to me, Tom."

"Thank you," he says. She is young. She does not know.

"If it's just a passing gloom I can edit it out in one quick snip."

"Thank you," he says. "No."

"I forgot. You don't like editing."

"My father—"

"Yes?"

"In fifty years he pared himself down to a thread," Tom Two Ribbons says. "He had his ancestors edited away, his whole heritage, his religion, his wife, his sons, finally his name. Then he sat and smiled all day. Thank you, no editing."

"Where are you working today?" Ellen asks.

"In the compound, running tests."

"Want company? I'm off all morning."

"Thank you, no," he says, too quickly. She looks hurt. He tries to remedy his unintended cruelty by touching her arm lightly and saying, "Maybe this afternoon, all right? I need to commune a while. Yes?"

"Yes," she says, and smiles, and shapes a kiss with her lips.

After breakfast he goes to the compound. It covers a thousand hectares east of the base; they have bordered it with neural-field projectors at intervals of eighty meters, and this is a sufficient fence to keep the captive population of two hundred Eaters from straying. When all the others have been exterminated, this study group will remain. At the southwest corner of the compound stands a lab bubble from which the experiments are run: metabolic, psychological, physiological, ecological. A stream crosses the compound diagonally. There is a low ridge of grassy hills at its eastern edge. Five distinct copses of tightly clustered knifeblade trees are separated by patches of dense savanna. Sheltered beneath the grass are the oxygen-plants, almost completely hidden except for the photosynthetic spikes that jut to heights of three or four meters at regular intervals, and for the lemon-colored respiratory bodies, chest high, that make the grassland sweet and dizzying with exhaled gases. Through the fields move the Eaters in a straggling herd, nibbling delicately at the respiratory bodies.

Tom Two Ribbons spies the herd beside the stream and goes toward it. He stumbles over an oxgen-plant hidden in the grass but deftly recovers his balance and, seizing the puckered orifice of the respiratory body, inhales deeply. His despair lifts. He approaches the Eaters. They are spherical, bulky, slow-moving creatures, covered by masses of coarse orange fur. Saucer-like eyes protrude above narrow rubbery lips. Their legs are thin and scaly, like a chicken's, and their arms are short and held close to their bodies. They regard him with bland lack of curiosity. "Good morning, brothers!" is the way he greets them this time, and he wonders why.

I noticed something strange today. Perhaps I simply sniffed too much oxygen in the fields; maybe I was succumbing to a suggestion Herndon planted; or possibly it's the family masochism cropping out. But while I was observing the Eaters in the compound, it seemed to me, for the first time, that they were behaving intelligently, that they were functioning in a ritualized way.

I followed them around for three hours. During that time they uncovered half a dozen outcroppings of oxygen-plants. In each case they went through a stylized pattern of action before starting to munch. They:

Formed a straggly circle around the plants.

Looked toward the sun.

Looked toward their neighbors on left and right around the circle.

Made fuzzy neighing sounds *only* after having done the foregoing.

Looked toward the sun again.

Moved in and ate.

If this wasn't a prayer of thanksgiving, a saying of grace, then what was it? And if they're advanced enough spiritually to say grace, are we not therefore committing genocide here? Do chimpanzees say grace? Christ, we wouldn't even wipe out chimps the way we're cleaning out the Eaters! Of course, chimps don't interfere with human crops, and some kind of coexistence would be possible, whereas Eaters and human agriculturists simply can't function on the same planet. Nevertheless, there's a moral issue here. The liquidation effort is predicated on the assumption that the intelligence level of the Eaters is about on a par with that of oysters, or, at best, sheep. Our consciences stay clear because our poison is quick and painless and because the Eaters thoughtfully dissolve upon dying, sparing us the mess of incinerating millions of corpses. But if they pray—

I won't say anything to the others just yet. I want more evidence, hard, objective. Films, tapes, record cubes. Then we'll see. What if I can show that we're exterminating intelligent beings? My family knows a little about genocide, after all, having been on the receiving end just a few centuries back. I doubt that I could halt what's going on here. But at the very least I could withdraw from the operation. Head back to Earth and stir up public outcries.

I hope I'm imagining this.

I'm not imagining a thing. They gather in circles; they look to the sun; they neigh and pray. They're only balls of jelly on chicken-legs, but they give thanks for their food. Those big round eyes now seem to stare accusingly at me. Our tame herd here knows what's going on: that we have descended from the stars to eradicate their kind, and that they alone will be spared. They have no way of fighting back or even of communicating their displeasure, but they *know*. And hate us. Jesus, we have killed two million of them since we got here, and in a metaphorical way I'm stained with blood, and what will I do, what can I do?

I must move very carefully, or I'll end up drugged and edited.

I can't let myself seem like a crank, a quack, an agitator. I can't stand up and *denounce!* I have to find allies. Herndon, first. He surely is on to the truth; he's the one who nudged *me* to it, that day we dropped pellets. And I thought he was merely being vicious in his usual way!

I'll talk to him tonight.

He says, "I've been thinking about that suggestion you made. About the Eaters. Perhaps we haven't made sufficiently close psychological studies. I mean, if they really *are* intelligent—"

Herndon blinks. He is a tall man with glossy dark hair, a heavy beard, sharp cheekbones. "Who says they are, Tom?"

"You did. On the far side of the Forked River, you said—"

"It was just a speculative hypothesis. To make conversation."

"No, I think it was more than that. You really believed it."

Herndon looks troubled. "Tom, I don't know what you're trying to start, but don't start it. If I for a moment believed we were killing intelligent creatures, I'd run for an editor so fast I'd start an implosion wave."

"Why did you ask me that thing, then?" Tom Two Ribbons says.

"Idle chatter."

"Amusing yourself by kindling guilts in somebody else? You're a bastard, Herndon. I mean it."

"Well, look, Tom, if I had any idea that you'd get so worked up about a hypothetical suggestion—" Herndon shakes his head. "The

Eaters aren't intelligent beings. Obviously. Otherwise we wouldn't be under orders to liquidate them."

"Obviously," says Tom Two Ribbons.

Ellen said, "No, I don't know what Tom's up to. But I'm pretty sure he needs a rest. It's only a year and a half since his personality reconstruct, and he had a pretty bad breakdown back then."

Michaelson consulted a chart. "He's refused three times in a row to make his pellet-dropping run. Claiming he can't take time away from his research. Hell, we can fill in for him, but it's the idea that he's ducking chores that bothers me."

"What kind of research is he doing?" Nichols wanted to know.

"Not biological," said Julia. "He's with the Eaters in the compound all the time, but I don't see him making any tests on them. He just watches them."

"And talks to them," Chang observed.

"And talks, yes," Julia said.

"About what?" Nichols asked.

"Who knows?"

Everyone looked at Ellen. "You're closest to him," Michaelson said. "Can't you bring him out of it?"

"I've got to know what he's in, first," Ellen said. "He isn't saying a thing."

You know that you must be very careful, for they outnumber you, and their concern for your mental welfare can be deadly. Already they realize you are disturbed, and Ellen has begun to probe for the source of the disturbance. Last night you lay in her arms and she questioned you, obliquely, skillfully, and you knew what she is trying to find out. When the moons appeared she suggested that you and she stroll in the compound, among the sleeping Eaters. You declined, but she sees that you have become involved with the creatures.

You have done probing of your own—subtly, you hope. And you are aware that you can do nothing to save the Eaters. An irrevocable commitment has been made. It is 1876 all over again; these are the bison, these are the Sioux, and they must be destroyed, for the railroad is on its way. If you speak out here, your friends will calm you and pacify you and edit you, for they do not see what you see. If you return to Earth to agitate, you will be mocked and recommended for another reconstruct. You can do nothing. You can do nothing.

You cannot save, but perhaps you can record.

Go out into the prairie. Live with the Eaters; make yourself their friend; learn their ways. Set it down, a full account of their culture, so that at least that much will not be lost. You know the techniques of field anthropology. As was done for your people in the old days, do now for the Eaters.

He finds Michaelson. "Can you spare me for a few weeks?" he asks.

"Spare you, Tom? What do you mean?"

"I've got some field studies to do. I'd like to leave the base and work with Eaters in the wild."

"What's wrong with the ones in the compound?"

"It's the last chance with wild ones, Mike. I've got to go."

"Alone, or with Ellen?"

"Alone."

Michaelson nods slowly. "All right, Tom. Whatever you want. Go. I won't hold you here."

I dance in the prairie under the green-gold sun. About me the Eaters gather. I am stripped; sweat makes my skin glisten; my heart pounds. I talk to them with my feet, and they understand.

They understand.

They have a language of soft sounds. They have a god. They know love and awe and rapture. They have rites. They have names. They have a history. Of all this I am convinced.

I dance on thick grass.

How can I reach them? With my feet, with my hands, with my grunts, with my sweat. They gather by the hundreds, by the thousands, and I dance. I must not stop. They cluster about me and make their sounds. I am a conduit for strange forces. My great-grandfather should see me now! Sitting on his porch in Wyoming, the firewater in his hand, his brain rotting—see me now, old one! See the dance of Tom Two Ribbons! I talk to these strange ones with my feet under a sun that is the wrong color. I dance. I dance.

"Listen to me," I say. "I am your friend, I alone, the only one you can trust. Trust me, talk to me, teach me. Let me preserve your ways, for soon the destruction will come."

I dance, and the sun climbs, and the Eaters murmur.

There is the chief. I dance toward him, back, toward, I bow, I point to the sun, I imagine the being that lives in that ball of flame, I imitate the sounds of these people, I kneel, I rise, I dance. Tom Two Ribbons dances for you.

I summon skills my ancestors forgot. I feel the power flowing in me. As they danced in the days of the bison, I dance now, beyond the Forked River.

I dance, and now the Eaters dance too. Slowly, uncertainly they move toward me, they shift their weight, lift leg and leg, sway about. "Yes, like that!" I cry. "Dance!"

We dance together as the sun reaches noon height.

Now their eyes are no longer accusing. I see warmth and kinship. I am their brother, their red-skinned tribesman, he who dances with them. No longer do they seem clumsy to me. There is a strange ponderous grace in their movements. They dance. They dance. They caper about me. Closer, closer, closer!

We move in holy frenzy.

They sing, now, a blurred hymn of joy. They throw forth their arms, unclench their little claws. In unison they shift weight, left foot forward, right, left, right. Dance, brothers, dance, dance, dance! They press against me. Their flesh quivers; their smell is a sweet one. They gently thrust me across the field, to a part of the meadow where the grass is deep and untrampled. Still dancing, we seek for the oxygen-plants, and find clumps of them beneath the grass, and they make their prayer and seize them with their awkward arms, separating the respiratory bodies from the photosynthetic spikes. The plants, in anguish, release floods of oxygen. My mind reels. I laugh and sing. The Eaters are nibbling the lemon-colored perforated globes, nibbling the stalks as well. They thrust their plants at me. Take from us, eat with us, join with us, this is the body, this is the blood, take, eat, join. I bend forward and put a lemon-colored globe to my lips. I do not bite; I nibble, as they do, my teeth slicing away the skin of the globe. Juice spurts into my mouth, while oxygen drenches my nostrils. The Eaters sing hosannas. I should be in full paint for this, paint of my forefathers, feathers too, meeting their religion in the regalia of what should have been mine. Take, eat, join. The juice of the oxygen-plant flows in my veins. I embrace my brothers. I sing, and as my voice leaves my lips it becomes an arch that glistens like new steel, and I pitch my song lower, and the arch turns to tarnished silver. The Eaters crowd close. The scent of their bodies is fiery red to me. Their soft cries are puffs of steam. The sun is very warm; its rays are tiny jagged pings of puckered sound, close to the top of my range of hearing, plink! plink! plink! The thick grass hums to me, deep and rich, and the wind hurls points of flame along the prairie. I devour another oxygen-plant, and then a third. My brothers laugh and shout. They tell me of their gods, the god of warmth, the god of food, the god of pleasure, the god of death, the god of holiness, the god of wrongness, and the others. The recite for me the names of their kings, and I hear their voices as splashes of green mold on the clean sheet of the sky. They instruct me in their holy rites. I must remember this, I tell myself, for when it is gone it will never come again. I continue to dance. They continue to dance. The color of the hills becomes rough and coarse, like abrasive gas. Take, eat, join. Dance. They are so gentle!

I hear the drone of the copter, suddenly.

It hovers far overhead. I am unable to see who flies in it. "No," I scream. "Not here! Not these people! Listen to me! This is Tom Two Ribbons! Can't you hear me? I'm doing a field study here! You have no right—!"

My voice makes spirals of blue moss edged with red sparks. They drift upward and are scattered by the breeze.

I yell, I shout, I bellow. I dance and shake my fists. From the wings of the copter the jointed arms of the pellet-distributors unfold. The gleaming spigots extend and whirl. The neural pellets rain down into the meadow, each tracing a blazing track that lingers in the sky. The sound of the copter becomes a furry carpet stretching to the horizon, and my shrill voice is lost in it.

The Eaters drift away from me, seeking the pellets, scratching at the roots of the grass to find them. Still dancing, I leap into their midst, striking the pellets from their hands, hurling them into the stream, crushing them to powder. The Eaters growl black needles at me. They turn away and search for more pellets. The copter turns and flies off, leaving a trail of dense oily sound. My brothers are gobbling the pellets eagerly.

There is no way to prevent it.

Joy consumes them and they topple and lie still. Occasionally a limb twitches; then even this stops. They begin to dissolve. Thousands of them melt on the prairie, sinking into shapelessness, losing their spherical forms, flattening, ebbing into the ground. The bonds of the molecules will no longer hold. It is the twilight of protoplasm. They perish. They vanish. For hours I walk the prairie. Now I inhale oxygen; now I eat a lemon-colored globe. Sunset begins with the ringing of leaden chimes. Black clouds make brazen trumpet calls in the east and the deepening wind is a swirl of coaly bristles. Silence comes. Night falls. I dance. I am alone.

The copter comes again, and they find you, and you do not resist as they gather you in. You are beyond bitterness. Quietly you explain what you have done and what you have learned, and why it is wrong to exterminate these people. You describe the plant you have eaten and the way it affects your senses, and as you talk of the blessed synesthesia, the texture of the wind and the sound of the clouds and the timbre of the sunlight, they nod and smile and tell you not to worry, that everything will be all right soon, and they touch something cold to your forearm, so cold that it is almost into the ultraviolet where you cannot see it, and there is a whir and a buzz and the deintoxicant sinks into your vein and soon the ecstasy drains away, leaving only the exhaustion and the grief.

He says, "We never learn a thing, do we? We export all our horrors to the stars. Wipe out the Armenians, wipe out the Jews, wipe out the Tasmanians, wipe out the Indians, wipe out everyone who's in the way, and then come out here and do the same damned murderous thing. You weren't with me out there. You didn't dance with them. You didn't see what a rich, complex culture the Eaters have. Let me tell you about their tribal structure. It's dense: seven levels of matrimonial relationships, to begin with, and an exogamy factor that requires—"

Softly Ellen says, "Tom, darling, nobody's going to harm the Eaters."

"And the religion," he goes on. "Nine gods, each one an aspect of *the* god. Holiness and wrongness both worshiped. They have hymns, prayers, a theology. And we, the emissaries of the god of wrongness—"

"We're not exterminating them," Michaelson says. "Won't you understand that, Tom? This is all a fantasy of yours. You've been under the influence of drugs, but now we're clearing you out. You'll be clean in a little while. You'll have perspective again."

"A fantasy?" he says bitterly. "A drug dream? I stood out in the prairie and saw you drop pellets. And I watched them die and melt away. I didn't dream that."

"How can we convince you?" Chang asks earnestly. "What will make you believe? Shall we fly over the Eater country with you and show you how many millions there are?"

"But how many millions have been destroyed?" he demands.

They insist that he is wrong. Ellen tells him again that no one has ever desired to harm the Eaters. "This is a scientific expedition, Tom.

We're here to *study* them. It's a violation of all we stand for to injure intelligent life-forms."

"You admit that they're intelligent?"

"Of course. That's never been in doubt."

"Then why drop the pellets?" he asks. "Why slaughter them?"

"None of that has happened, Tom," Ellen says. She takes his hand between her cool palms. "Believe us. Believe us."

He says bitterly, "If you want me to believe you, why don't you do the job properly? Get out the editing machine and go to work on me. You can't simply *talk* me into rejecting the evidence of my own eyes."

"You were under drugs all the time," Michaelson says.

"I've never taken drugs! Except for what I ate in the meadow, when I danced—and that came after I had watched the massacre going on for weeks and weeks. Are you saying that it's a retroactive delusion?"

"No, Tom," Schwartz says. "You've had this delusion all along. It's part of your therapy, your reconstruct. You came here programmed with it."

"Impossible," he says.

Ellen kisses his fevered forehead. "It was done to reconcile you to mankind, you see. You had this terrible resentment of the displacement of your people in the nineteenth century. You were unable to forgive the industrial society for scattering the Sioux, and you were terribly full of hate. Your therapist thought that if you could be made to participate in an imaginary modern extermination, if you could come to see it as a necessary operation, you'd be purged of your resentment and able to take your place in society as—"

He thrusts her away. "Don't talk idiocy! If you knew the first thing about reconstruct therapy, you'd realize that no reputable therapist could be so shallow. There are no one-to-one correlations in reconstructs. No, don't touch me. Keep away. Keep away."

He will not let them persuade him that this is merely a drug-born dream. It is no fantasy, he tells himself, and it is no therapy. He rises. He goes out. They do not follow him. He takes a copter and seeks his brothers.

Again I dance. The sun is much hotter today. The Eaters are more numerous. Today I wear paint, today I wear feathers. My body shines with my sweat. They dance with me, and they have a frenzy in them that I have never seen before. We pound the trampled meadow with our feet. We clutch for the sun with our hands. We sing, we shout, we cry. We will dance until we fall.

This is no fantasy. These people are real, and they are intelligent, and they are doomed. This I know.

We dance. Despite the doom we dance.

My great-grandfather comes and dances with us. He too is real. His nose is like a hawk's, not blunt like mine, and he wears the big headdress, and his muscles are like cords under his brown skin. He sings, he shouts, he cries.

Others of my family join us.

We eat the oxygen-plants together. We embrace the Eaters. We know, all of us, what it is to be hunted.

The clouds make music and the wind takes on texture and the sun's warmth has color.

We dance. We dance. Our limbs know no weariness.

The sun grows and fills the whole sky, and I see no Eaters now, only my own people, my father's fathers across the centuries, thousands of gleaming skins, thousands of hawk's noses, and we eat the plants, and we find sharp sticks and thrust them into our flesh, and the sweet blood flows and dries in the blaze of the sun, and we dance, and we dance, and some of us fall from weariness, and we dance, and the prairie is a sea of bobbing headdresses, an ocean of feathers, and we dance, and my heart makes thunder, and my knees become water, and the sun's fire engulfs me, and I dance, and I fall, and I dance, and I fall, and I fall, and I fall.

Again they find you and bring you back. They give you the cool snout on your arm to take the oxygen-plant drug from your veins, and then they give you something else so you will rest. You rest and you are very calm. Ellen kisses you and you stroke her soft skin, and then the others come in and they talk to you, saying soothing things, but you do not listen, for you are searching for realities. It is not an easy search. It is like falling through many trapdoors, looking for the one room whose floor is not hinged. Everything that has happened on this planet is your therapy, you tell yourself, designed to reconcile an embittered aborigine to the white man's conquest; nothing is really being exterminated here. You reject that and fall through and realize that this must be the therapy of your friends; they carry the weight of accumulated centuries of guilts and have come here to shed that load, and you are here to ease them of their burden, to draw their sins into yourself and give them forgiveness. Again you fall through, and see that the Eaters are mere animals who threaten the ecology and must be removed; the culture you imagined for them is your hallucination, kindled out of old churnings. You try to withdraw your objections to this necessary extermination, but you fall through again and discover that there is no extermination except in your mind, which is troubled and disordered by your obsession with the crime against your ancestors, and you sit up, for you wish to apologize to these friends of yours, these innocent scientists whom you have called murderers. And you fall through.

Three Cartoons
Gahan Wilson

GAHAN WILSON, *one of America's most popular cartoonists, has had a cartoon in every issue of F&SF since 1965. His work regularly appears in* Playboy, The New Yorker *and the* National Lampoon, *and his book collections include* I Paint What I See, ". . . And Then We'll Get Him!" *and, most recently,* Nuts.

"This is Willy, and this is Willy's imaginary playmate."

"You can tell she's thinking it over!"

The Gnurrs Come from the Voodvork Out

R. Bretnor

WHEN PAPA SCHIMMELHORN heard about the war with Bobovia, he bought a box-lunch, wrapped his secret weapon in brown paper, and took the first bus straight to Washington. He showed up at the main gate of the Secret Weapons Bureau shortly before midday, complete with box-lunch, beard, and bassoon.

That's right—*bassoon*. He had unwrapped his secret weapon. It looked like a bassoon. The difference didn't show.

Corporal Jerry Colliver, on duty at the gate, didn't know there was a difference. All he knew was that the Secret Weapons Bureau was a mock-up, put there to keep the crackpots out of everybody's hair, and that it was a lousy detail, and that there was the whole afternoon to go before his date with Katie.

"Goot morning, soldier boy!" bellowed Papa Schimmelhorn.

Corporal Colliver winked at the two Pfc's who were sunning themselves with him on the guardhouse steps. "Come back Chris'mus, Santa," he said. "We're closed for inventory."

"No!" Papa Schimmelhorn was annoyed. "I cannot stay so long from vork. Also, I have here a zecret veapon. Ledt me in!"

REG BRETNOR *began contributing to F&SF in its second issue. He is still sending us stories, and we continue to publish everything he sends, ranging from serious fantasy to humorous sf, such as his tales about the mad genius of New Haven, Papa Schimmelhorn. "Gnurrs" (Winter–Spring 1950) was the first of that series.*

The Corporal shrugged. Orders were orders. Crazy or not, you had to let 'em in. He reached back and pressed the loony-button, to alert the psycho's just in case. Then, keys jingling, he walked up to the gate. "A secret weapon, huh?" he said, unlocking it. "Guess you'll have the war all won and over in a week."

"A *veek?*" Papa Schimmelhorn roared with laughter. "Soldier boy, you vait! It is ofer in two days! I am a chenius!"

As he stepped through, Corporal Colliver remembered regulations and asked him sternly if he had any explosives on or about his person.

"Ho-ho-ho! It iss nodt necessary to haff exblosives to vin a var! Zo all right, you zearch me!"

The corporal searched him. He searched the box-lunch, which contained one deviled egg, two pressed-ham sandwiches, and an apple. He examined the bassoon, shaking it and peering down it to make sure that it was empty.

"Okay, Pop," he said, when he had finished. "You can go on in. But you better leave your flute here."

"It iss nodt a fludt," Papa Schimmelhorn corrected him. "It iss a *gnurr-pfeife.* And I must take it because it iss my zecret veapon."

The Corporal, who had been looking forward to an hour or so of trying to tootle "Comin' Through the Rye," shrugged philosophically. "Barney," he said to one of the Pfc's, "take this guy to Section Seven."

As the soldier went off with Papa Schimmelhorn in tow, he pressed the loony-button twice more just for luck. "Don't it beat all," he remarked.

Corporal Colliver, of course, didn't know that Papa Schimmelhorn had spoken only gospel truth. He didn't know that Papa Schimmelhorn really was a genius, or that the gnurrs would end the war in two days, or that Papa Schimmelhorn would win it.

At ten minutes past one, Colonel Powhattan Fairfax Pollard was still mercifully unaware of Papa Schimmelhorn's existence.

Colonel Pollard was long and lean and leathery. He wore Peal boots, spurs, and one of those plum-colored shirts which had been fashionable at Fort Huachuca in the 'twenties. He did not believe in secret weapons. He didn't even believe in atomic bombs and tanks, recoilless rifles and attack aviation. He believed in horses.

The Pentagon had called him back out of retirement to command the Secret Weapons Bureau, and he had been the right man for the job. In the four months of his tenure, only one inventor—a fellow with singularly sound ideas regarding pack-saddles—had been sent on to higher echelons.

Colonel Pollard was seated at his desk, dictating to his blonde WAC secretary from an open copy of Major-General Wardrop's "Modern Pig-sticking." He was accumulating material for a work of his own, to be entitled "Sword and Lance in Future Warfare." Now, in the middle of a quotation outlining the virtues of the Bengal spear, he broke off abruptly. "Miss Hooper!" he announced. "A thought has occurred to me!"

Katie Hooper sniffed. If he had to be formal, why couldn't he just say *sergeant?* Other senior officers had always addressed her as *my dear* or *sweetheart,* at least when they were alone. *Miss* Hooper, indeed! She sniffed again, and said, "Yessir."

Colonel Pollard snorted, apparently to clear his mind. "I can state it as a principle," he began, "that the mania for these so-called scientific weapons is a grave menace to the security of the United States. Flying in the face of the immutable science of war, we are building one unproved weapon after another, counter-weapons against these weapons, counter-counter-weapons, and—and so on. Armed to the teeth with theories and delusions, we soon may stand impotent— Did you hear me, Miss Hooper? *Impotent—*"

Miss Hooper snickered and said, "Yessir."

"—against the onrush of some Attila," shouted the Colonel, "some modern Genghis Khan, as yet unborn, who will sweep away our tinkering technicians like chaff, and carve his empire with cavalry—yes, *cavalry!*"

"Yessir," said his secretary.

"Today," the Colonel thundered, "we have no cavalry! A million mounted moujiks could—"

But the world was not destined to find out just what a million mounted moujiks could or could not do. The door burst open. From the outer office, there came a short, sharp squeal. A plump young officer catapulted across the room, braked to a halt before the Colonel's desk, saluted wildly.

"Oooh!" gasped Katie Hooper, staring with vast blue eyes.

The Colonel's face turned suddenly to stone.

And the young officer caught his breath long enough to cry, "My God, it—it's happened, sir!"

Lieutenant Hanson was no combat soldier; he was a scientist. He had made no appointment. He had entered without knocking, in a most unmilitary manner. And—And—

"MISTER!" roared Colonel Pollard. "WHERE ARE YOUR TROUSERS?"

For Lieutenant Hanson obviously was wearing none. Nor was he wearing socks or shoes. And the tattered tails of his shirt barely concealed his shredded shorts.

"SPEAK UP, DAMMIT!"

Vacantly, the Lieutenant glanced at his lower limbs and back again. He began to tremble. "They—they *ate* them!" he blurted. "That's what I'm trying to tell you! Lord knows how he does it! He's about eighty, and he's a—a foreman in a cuckoo-clock factory! But it's the perfect weapon! And it works, it works, *it works!*" He laughed hysterically. "The gnurrs come from the voodvork out!" he sang, clapping his hands.

Here Colonel Pollard rose from his chair, vaulted his desk, and tried to calm Lieutenant Hanson by shaking him vigorously. "Disgraceful!" he shouted in his ear. "Turn your back!" he ordered the blushing Katie Hooper. "NONSENSE!" he bellowed when the Lieutenant tried to chatter something about gnurrs.

And, "Vot iss nonzense, soldier boy?" enquired Papa Schimmelhorn from the doorway.

The Lieutenant pointed unsteadily at Colonel Pollard. "Gnurrs iss nonzense!" he snickered. *"He* says so."

"Ha!" Papa Schimmelhorn glared. "I show you, soldier boy!"

The Colonel erupted. "Soldier boy? SOLDIER BOY? *Stand at attention when I speak to you! ATTENTION, DAMN YOU!"*

Papa Schimmelhorn, of course, paid no attention whatsoever. He raised his secret weapon to his lips, and the first bars of "Come To The Church In The Wildwood" moaned around the room.

"Mister Hanson!" raged the Colonel. "Arrest that man! Take that thing away from him! I'll prefer charges! I'll—"

At this point, the gnurrs came from the voodvork out.

It isn't easy to describe a gnurr. Can you imagine a mouse-colored, mouse-sized critter shaped like a wild boar, but sort of *shimmery?* With thumbs fore and aft, and a pink, naked tail, and yellow eyes several sizes too large? And with three sets of sharp teeth in its face? You can? Well, that's about it—except that nobody has ever seen *a* gnurr. They don't come that way. When the gnurrs come from the voodvork out, they come *all over*—like lemmings, only more so—millions and millions of them.

And they come eating.

The gnurrs came from the voodvork out just as Papa Schimmelhorn reached ". . . the church in the vale." They covered half the floor, and ate up half the carpet, before he finished "No scene is so dear to my childhood." Then they advanced on Colonel Pollard.

Mounting his desk, the Colonel started slashing around with his riding crop. Katie Hooper climbed a filing case, hoisted her skirt, and screamed. Lieutenant Hanson, secure in his nether nakedness, held his ground and guffawed insubordinately.

Papa Schimmelhorn stopped tootling to shout, "Don'dt vorry, soldier boy!" He started in again, playing something quite unrecognizable—something that didn't sound like a tune at all.

Instantly, the gnurrs halted. They looked over their shoulders apprehensively. They swallowed the remains of the Colonel's chair cushion, shimmered brightly, made a queasy sort of creaking sound, and turning tail, vanished into the wainscoting.

Papa Schimmelhorn stared at the Colonel's boots, which were surprisingly intact, and muttered, "Hmm-m, *zo!*" He leered appreciatively at Katie Hooper, who promptly dropped her skirt. He thumped himself on the chest, and announced "They are vunderful, my gnurrs!"

"Wh—?" The Colonel showed evidences of profound psychic trauma. "Where did they go?"

"Vere they came from," replied Papa Schimmelhorn.

"Where's *that?*"

"It iss yesterday!"

"That—that's absurd!" The Colonel stumbled down and fell into his chair. "They weren't here yesterday!"

Papa Schimmelhorn regarded him pityingly. "Of courze nodt! They *vere* nodt here yesterday because yesterday vas then today. They *are* here yesterday, ven yesterday iss yesterday already. It iss different."

Colonel Pollard cast an appealing glance at Lieutenant Hanson.

"Perhaps I can explain, sir," said the Lieutenant, whose nervous system seemingly had benefited by the second visit of the gnurrs. "May I make my report?"

"Yes, yes, certainly." Colonel Pollard clutched gladly at the straw.

Lieutenant Hanson pulled up a chair, and—as Papa Schimmelhorn walked over to flirt with Katie—he began to talk in a low and very serious voice.

"It's absolutely incredible," he said. "All the routine tests show that he's at best a high grade moron. He quit school when he was eleven, served his apprenticeship, and worked as a clockmaker till he was in his fifties. After that, he was a janitor in the Geneva Institute of Higher Physics until just a few years ago. Then he came to America and got his present job. But it's the Geneva business that's important. They've been concentrating on extensions of Einstein's and Minkowski's work. He must have overheard a lot of it."

"But if he's a moron—" the Colonel had heard of Einstein, and knew that he was very deep indeed "—what good would it do him?"

"That's just the point, sir! He's a moron on the conscious level, but subconsciously he's a genius. Somehow, part of his mind absorbed the stuff, integrated it, and came up with this bassoon thing. It's got a weird little L-shaped crystal in it, impinging on the reed, and when you blow the crystal vibrates. We don't know why it works—but it sure does!"

"You mean the—uh—the fourth dimension?"

"Precisely. Though we've left yesterday behind, the gnurrs have not. They're there *now*. When a day becomes our yesterday, it becomes their today."

"But—but how does he get rid of them?"

"He says he plays the same tune backwards, and reverses the effect."

Papa Schimmelhorn, who had been encouraging Katie Hooper to feel his biceps, turned around. "You vait!" he laughed uproariously. "Soon, vith my *gnurr-pfeife* I broadcast to the enemy! Ve vin the var!"

The Colonel shied. "The thing's untried, unproven! It—er—requires further study—field service—acid test."

"We haven't time, sir. We'd lose the element of surprise!"

"We will make a regular report through channels," declared the Colonel. "It's a damn' machine, isn't it? They're unreliable. Always have been. It would be contrary to the principles of war."

And then Lieutenant Hanson had an inspiration. "But, sir," he argued, "we won't be fighting with the *gnurr-pfeife!* The gnurrs will be our real weapon, and they're not machines—they're animals! The greatest generals used animals in war! The gnurrs aren't interested in living creatures, but they'll devour just about anything else—wool, cotton, leather, even plastics—and their numbers are simply astronomical. If I were you, I'd get through to the Secretary right away!"

For an instant, the Colonel hesitated—but only for an instant. "Hanson," he said decisively, "you've got a point there—a very sound point!"

And he reached for the telephone.

It took less than twenty-four hours to organize *Operation Gnurr*. The Secretary of Defense, after conferring with the President and the General Staff, personally rushed over to direct preliminary tests of Papa Schimmelhorn's secret weapon. By nightfall, it was known that the gnurrs could:

a. Completely blanket everything within two hundred yards of the *gnurr-pfeife* in less than twenty seconds,

b. Strip an entire company of infantry, supported by chemical weapons, to the skin in one minute and eighteen seconds,

c. Ingest the contents of five Quartermaster warehouses in just over two and a half minutes,

and,

d. Come from the voodvork out when the *gnurr-pfeife* was played over a carefully shielded short-wave system.

It had also become apparent that there were only three effective ways to kill a gnurr—by shooting him to death, drenching him with liquid fire, or dropping an atomic bomb on him—and that there were entirely too many gnurrs for any of these methods to be worth a hoot.

By morning, Colonel Powhattan Fairfax Pollard—because he was the only senior officer who had ever seen a gnurr, and because animals were known to be right up his alley—had been made a lieutenant-general and given command of the operation. Lieutenant Hanson, as his aide, had suddenly found himself a major. Corporal Colliver had become a master-sergeant, presumably for being there when the manna fell. And Katie Hooper had had a brief but strenuous date with Papa Schimmelhorn.

Nobody was satisfied. Katie complained that Papa Schimmelhorn and his gnurrs had the same idea in mind, only his technique was different. Jerry Colliver, who had been dating Katie regularly, griped that the old buzzard with the muscles had sent his Hooper rating down to zero. Major Hanson had awakened to the possibility of somebody besides the enemy tuning in on the Papa Schimmelhorn Hour.

Even General Pollard was distressed—

"I could overlook everything, Hanson," he said sourly, "except his calling me 'soldier boy.' I won't stand for it! The science of war cannot tolerate indiscipline. I spoke to him about it, and all he said was, 'It iss all right, soldier boy. You can call me Papa.'"

Major Hanson disciplined his face, and said, "Well, why not call him Papa, sir? After all, it's just such human touches as these that make history."

"Ah, yes—History." The General paused reflectively. "Hmm, perhaps so, perhaps so. They always called Napoleon 'the little Corporal.'"

"The thing that really bothers me, General, is how we're going to get through without our own people listening in. I guess they must've worked out something on it, or they wouldn't have scheduled the—the offensive for five o'clock. That's only four hours off."

"Now that you mention it," said General Pollard, coming out of his reverie, "a memorandum did come through— Oh, Miss Hooper, bring me that memo from G-1, will you?— Thank you. Here it is. It seems that they have decided to—er—scramble the broadcast."

"*Scramble* it, sir?"

"Yes, yes. And I've issued operational orders accordingly. You see, Intelligence reported several weeks ago that the enemy knows how to unscramble anything we transmit that way. When Mr.—ah, 'Papa' Schimmelhorn goes on the air, we will scramble him, but we will not transmit the code key to our own people. It is assumed that from five to fifteen enemy monitors will hear him. His playing of the tune will constitute Phase One. When it is over, the microphones will be switched off, and he will play it backwards. That will be Phase Two, to dispose of such gnurrs as appear locally."

"Seems sound enough." Major Hanson frowned. "And it's pretty smart, if everything goes right. But what if it doesn't? Hadn't we better have an ace up our sleeve?"

He frowned again. Then, as the General didn't seem to have any ideas on the subject, he went about his duties. He made a final inspection of the special sound-proof room in which Papa Schimmelhorn would tootle. He allocated its observation windows—one to the President, the Secretary, and General Pollard; one to the Chief of Staff, with his sea and air counterparts; another to Intelligence liaison; and the last to the functioning staff of Operation Gnurr, himself included. At ten minutes to five, when everything was ready, he was still worrying.

"Look here," he whispered to Papa Schimmelhorn, as he escorted him to the fateful door. "What are we going to do if your gnurrs really get loose here? You couldn't play them back into the voodvork in a month of Sundays!"

"Don'dt vorry, soldier boy!" Papa Schimmelhorn gave him a re-
sounding slap on the back. "I haff yet vun trick I do nodt tell you!"

And with that vague assurance, he closed the door behind him.

"*Ready?*" called General Pollard tensely, at one minute to five.

"*Ready!*" echoed Sergeant Colliver.

The tension mounted. The seconds ticked away. The General's hand
reached for a sabre-hilt that wasn't there. At five exactly—

"*CHARGE!*" the General cried.

A red light flared above the microphones.

And Papa Schimmelhorn started tootling "Come To The Church In
The Wildwood."

The gnurrs, of course, came from the voodvork out.

The gnurrs came from the voodvork out, and a hungry gleam was in
their yellow eyes. They carpeted the floor. They started piling up. They
surged against the massive legs of Papa Schimmelhorn, their tiny elec-
tric-razor sets of teeth going like all get out. His trousers vanished underneath the flood—his checkered coat, his tie, his collar, the fringes of
his beard. And Papa Schimmelhorn, all undismayed, lifted his big bassoon out of gnurrs' way and tootled on. "Come, come, come, come.
Come to the church in the vildvood . . ."

Of course, Major Hanson couldn't hear the *gnurr-pfeife*—but he had
sung the song in Sunday school, and now the words resounded in his
brain. Verse after verse, chorus after chorus— The awful thought
struck him that Papa Schimmelhorn would be overwhelmed, sucked
under, drowned in gnurrs . . .

And then he heard the voice of General Pollard, no longer steady—

"*R-ready, Phase Two?*"

"*R-ready!*" replied Sergeant Colliver.

A green light flashed in front of Papa Schimmelhorn.

For a moment, nothing changed. Then the gnurrs hesitated. Appre-
hensively, they glanced over their hairy shoulders. They shimmered.
The started to recede. Back, back, back they flowed, leaving Papa
Schimmelhorn alone, triumphant, and naked as a jay-bird.

The door was opened, and he emerged—to be congratulated and
re-clothed, and (much to Sergeant Colliver's annoyance) to turn down a
White House dinner invitation in favor of a date with Katie. The active
phases of Operation Gnurr were over.

In far-away Bobovia, however, chaos reigned. Later it was learned
that eleven inquisitive enemy monitors had unscrambled the tootle of

the *gnurr-pfeife*, and that tidal waves of gnurrs had inundated the enemy's eleven major cities. By seven-fifteen, except for a few hysterical outlying stations, Bobovia was off the air. By eight, Bobovian military activity had ceased in every theatre. At twenty after ten, an astounded Press learned that the surrender of Bobovia could be expected momentarily . . . The President had received a message from the Bobovian Marshalissimo, asking permission to fly to Washington with his Chief of Staff, the members of his Cabinet, and several relatives. And would His Excellency the President—the Marshalissimo had radioed—be so good as to have someone meet them at the airport with nineteen pairs of American trousers, new or used?

VE Day wasn't in it. Neither was VJ Day. As soon as the papers hit the streets—BOBOVIA SURRENDERS!—ATOMIC MICE DEVOUR ENEMY!—SWISS GENIUS' STRATEGY WINS WAR!—the crowds went wild. From Maine to Florida, from California to Cape Cod, the lights went on, sirens and bells and auto horns resounded through the night, millions of throats were hoarse from singing "Come To The Church In The Wildwood."

Next day, after massed television cameras had let the entire nation in on the formal signing of the surrender pact, General Pollard and Papa Schimmelhorn were honored at an impressive public ceremony.

Papa Schimmelhorn received a vote of thanks from both Houses of Congress. He was awarded academic honors by Harvard, Princeton, M.I.T., and a number of denominational colleges down in Texas. He spoke briefly about cuckoo-clocks, the gnurrs, and Katie Hooper.

General Pollard, having been presented with a variety of domestic and foreign decorations, spoke at some length on the use of animals in future warfare. He pointed out that the horse, of all animals, was best suited to normal military purposes, and he discussed in detail many of the battles and campaigns in which it had been tried and proven. He was just starting in on swords and lances when the abrupt arrival of Major Hanson cut short the whole affair.

Hanson raced up with sirens screaming. He left his escort of MP's and ran across the platform. Pale and panting, he reached the President —and though he tried to whisper, his voice was loud enough to reach the General's ear. *"The—the gnurrs!"* he choked. *"They're in Los Angeles!"*

Instantly, the General rose to the occasion. "Attention, please!" he shouted at the microphones. "This ceremony is now over. You may consider yourselves—er—ah—DISMISSED!"

Before his audience could react, he had joined the knot of men around the President, and Hanson was briefing them on what had happened. "It was a research unit! They'd worked out a descrambler—new stuff—better than the enemy's. They didn't know. Tried it out on Papa here. Cut a record. Played it back today! Los Angeles is overrun!"

There were long seconds of despairing silence. Then, "Gentlemen," said the President quietly, "we're in the same boat as Bobovia."

The General groaned.

But Papa Schimmelhorn, to everyone's surprise, laughed boisterously. "Oh-ho-ho-ho! Don'dt vorry, soldier boy! You trust old Papa Schimmelhorn. All ofer, in Bobovia, iss gnurrs! Ve haff them only in Los Angeles, vere it does nodt matter! Also, I haff a trick I did nodt tell!" He winked a cunning wink. "Iss vun thing frightens gnurrs—"

"In God's name—*what?*" exclaimed the Secretary.

"Horzes," said Papa Schimmelhorn. "It iss the smell."

"Horses? Did you say *horses?*" The General pawed the ground. His eyes flashed fire. "CAVALRY!" he thundered. "We must have CAVALRY!"

No time was wasted. Within the hour, Lieutenant-General Powhattan Fairfax Pollard, the only senior cavalry officer who knew anything about gnurrs, was promoted to the rank of General of the Armies, and given supreme command. Major Hanson became a brigadier, a change of status which left him slightly dazed. Sergeant Colliver received his warrant.

General Pollard took immediate and decisive action. The entire Air Force budget for the year was commandeered. Anything even remotely resembling a horse, saddle, bridle, or bale of hay was shipped westward in requisitioned trains and trucks. Former cavalry officers and non-com's, ordered to instant duty regardless of age and wear-and-tear, were flown by disgruntled pilots to assembly points in Oregon, Nevada, and Arizona. Anybody and everybody who had ever so much as seen a horse was drafted into service. Mexico sent over several regiments on a lend-lease basis.

The Press had a field day. NUDE HOLLYWOOD STARS FIGHT GNURRS! headlined many a full front page of photographs. *Life* devoted a special issue to General of the Armies Pollard, Jeb Stuart, Marshal Ney, Belisarius, the Charge of the Light Brigade at Balaklava, and AR 50–45, School Of The Soldier Mounted Without Arms. The *Journal-American* reported, on reliable authority, that the ghost of

General Custer had been observed entering the Officers' Club at Fort Riley, Kansas.

On the sixth day, General Pollard had ready in the field the largest cavalry force in all recorded history. Its discipline and appearance left much to be desired. Its horsemanship was, to say the very least, uneven. Still, its morale was high, and—

"Never again," declared the General to correspondents who interviewed him at his headquarters in Phoenix, "must we let politicians and long-haired theorists persuade us to abandon the time-tried principles of war, and trust our national destiny to—to *gadgets*."

Drawing his sabre, the General indicated his operations map. "Our strategy is simple," he announced. "The gnurr forces have by-passed the Mohave Desert in the south, and are invading Arizona. In Nevada, they have concentrated against Reno and Virginia City. Their main offensive, however, appears to be aimed at the Oregon border. As you know, I have more than two million mounted men at my disposal— some three hundred divisions. In one hour, they will move forward. We will force the gnurrs to retreat in three main groups—in the south, in the center, in the north. Then, when the terrain they hold has been sufficiently restricted, Papa—er, that is, Mister—Schimmelhorn will play his instrument over mobile public address systems."

With that, the General indicated that the interview was at an end, and, mounting a splendid bay gelding presented to him by the citizens of Louisville, rode off to emplane for the theatre of operations.

Needless to say, his conduct of the War Against The Gnurrs showed the highest degree of initiative and energy, and a perfect grasp of the immutable principles of strategy and tactics. Even though certain envious elements in the Pentagon afterwards referred to the campaign as "Polly's Round-up," the fact remained that he was able to achieve total victory in five weeks—months before Bobovia even thought of promising its Five Year Plan for re-trousering its population. Inexorably, the terror-stricken gnurrs were driven back. Their queasy creaking could be heard for miles. At night, their shimmering lighted up the sky. In the south, where their deployment had been confined by deserts, three tootlings in reverse sufficed to bring about their downfall. In the center, where the action was heavier than anticipated, seventeen were needed. In the north, a dozen were required to do the trick. In each instance, the sound was carried over an area of several hundred square miles by huge loudspeaker units mounted in escort wagons or carried in pack. Innumerable cases of personal heroism were recorded—and Jerry

Colliver, after having four pairs of breeches shot out from under him, was personally commissioned in the field by General Pollard.

Naturally, a few gnurrs made their escape—but the felines of the state, who had been mewing with frustration, made short work of them. As for the numerous gay instances of indiscipline which occurred as the victorious troops passed through the quite literally denuded towns, these were soon forgiven and forgotten by the joyous populace.

Secretly, to avoid the rough enthusiasm of admiring throngs, General Pollard and Papa Schimmelhorn flew back to Washington—and three full regiments with drawn sabres were needed to clear a way for them. Finally, though, they reached the Pentagon. They walked toward the General's office arm in arm, and then at the door they paused for a moment or two.

"Papa," said General Pollard, pointing at the *gnurr-pfeife* with awe, "we have made History! And, by God, we'll make more of it!"

"*Ja!*" said Papa Schimmelhorn, with an enormous wink. "But tonight, soldier boy, ve vill make vhoopee! I haff a date with Katie. For you she has a girl friend."

General Pollard hesitated. "Wouldn't it—wouldn't it be bad for—er —discipline?"

"Don'dt vorry, soldier boy! Ve don'dt tell anybody!" laughed Papa Schimmelhorn—and threw the door open.

There stood the General's desk. There, at its side, stood Brigadier-General Hanson, looking worried. Against one wall stood Lieutenant Jerry Colliver, smirking loathsomely, with a possessive arm around Katie Hooper's waist. And in the General's chair sat a very stiff old lady, in a very stiff black dress, tapping a very stiff umbrella on the blotting pad.

As soon as she saw Papa Schimmelhorn, she stopped tapping and pointed the umbrella at him. "*So!*" she hissed. "You think you get away? To soil Cousin Anton's beaudtiful bassoon, and play vith mices, and passes at female soldier-girls make?"

She turned to Katie Hooper, and they exchanged a feminine glance of triumph and understanding. "Iss lucky that you phone, so I find out," she said. "You are nice girl. You can see under sheep's clothings."

She rose. As Katie blushed, she strode across the room, and grabbed the *gnurr-pfeife* from Papa Schimmelhorn. Before anyone could stop her, she stripped it of its reed—and ground the L-shaped crystal underfoot. "Now," she exclaimed, "iss no more gnurrs and people-vithout-trousers-monkeyshines!"

While General Pollard stared in blank amazement and Jerry Colliver snickered gloatingly, she took poor Papa Schimmelhorn firmly by the ear. "So ve go home!" she ordered, steering him for the door. "Vere iss no soldier girls, and the house needs painting!"

Looking crestfallen, Papa Schimmelhorn went without resistance. "Gootbye!" he called unhappily. "I must go home vith Mama."

But as he passed by General Pollard, he winked his usual wink. "Don'dt vorry, soldier boy!" he whispered. "I get avay again—I am a chenius!"

Dreaming Is a Private Thing

Isaac Asimov

JESSE WEILL LOOKED UP from his desk. His old spare body, his sharp high-bridged nose, deep-set shadowy eyes and amazing shock of white hair had trademarked his appearance during the years that Dreams, Inc. had become world-famous.

He said, "Is the boy here already, Joe?"

Joe Dooley was short and heavy-set. A cigar caressed his moist lower lip. He took it away for a moment and nodded. "His folks are with him. They're all scared."

"You're sure this is not a false alarm, Joe? I haven't got much time." He looked at his watch. "Government business at two."

"This is a sure thing, Mr. Weill." Dooley's face was a study in earnestness. His jowls quivered with persuasive intensity. "Like I told you, I picked him up playing some kind of basketball game in the school-yard. You should've seen the kid. He stunk. When he had his hands on the ball, his own team had to take it away, and fast, but just the same he had all the stance of a star player. Know what I mean? To me it was a giveaway."

ISAAC ASIMOV'S *author's card lists 285 separate contributions to F&SF. Current readers know him for his regular science essay, which has appeared in every issue since 1958. He has also contributed a fair amount of fiction to the magazine, mostly in its early years. "Dreaming Is a Private Thing" was published in the December 1955 issue.*

"Did you talk to him?"

"Well, sure. I stopped him at lunch. You know me." Dooley gestured expansively with his cigar and caught the severed ash with his other hand. " 'Kid,' I said—"

"And he's dream material?"

"I said, 'Kid, I just came from Africa and—' "

"All right." Weill held up the palm of his hand. "Your word I'll always take. How you do it I don't know, but when you say a boy is a potential dreamer, I'll gamble. Bring him in."

The youngster came in between his parents. Dooley pushed chairs forward and Weill rose to shake hands. He smiled at the youngster in a way that turned the wrinkles of his face into benevolent creases.

"You're Tommy Slutsky?"

Tommy nodded wordlessly. He was about ten and a little small for that. His dark hair was plastered down unconvincingly and his face was unrealistically clean.

Weill said, "You're a good boy?"

The boy's mother smiled at once and patted Tommy's head maternally (a gesture which did not soften the anxious expression on the youngster's face). She said, "He's always a very good boy."

Weill let this dubious statement pass. "Tell me, Tommy," he said, and held out a lollipop which was first hesitantly considered, then accepted. "Do you ever listen to dreamies?"

"Sometimes," said Tommy, in an uncertain treble.

Mr. Slutsky cleared his throat. He was broad-shouldered and thick-fingered, the type of laboring man who, every once in a while, to the confusion of eugenics, sired a dreamer. "We rented one or two for the boy. Real old ones."

Weill nodded. He said, "Did you like them, Tommy?"

"They were sort of silly."

"You think up better ones for yourself, do you?"

The grin that spread over the ten-year-old features had the effect of taking away some of the unreality of the slicked hair and washed face.

Weill went on, gently, "Would you like to make up a dream for me?"

Tommy was instantly embarrassed. "I guess not."

"It won't be hard. It's very easy.—Joe."

Dooley moved a screen out of the way and rolled forward a dream-recorder.

The youngster looked owlishly at it.

Weill lifted the helmet and brought it close to the boy. "Do you know what this is?"

Tommy shrank away. "No."

"It's a thinker. That's what we call it because people think into it. You put it on your head and think anything you want."

"Then what happens?"

"Nothing at all. It feels nice."

"No," said Tommy, "I guess I'd rather not."

His mother bent hurriedly toward him. "It won't hurt, Tommy. You do what the man says." There was an unmistakable edge to her voice.

Tommy stiffened and looked as though he might cry, but he didn't. Weill put the thinker on him.

He did it gently and slowly and let it remain there for some 30 seconds before speaking again, to let the boy assure himself it would do no harm, to let him get used to the insinuating touch of the fibrils against the sutures of his skull (penetrating the skin so finely as to be almost insensible), and finally to let him get used to the faint hum of the alternating field vortices.

Then he said, "Now would you think for us?"

"About what?" Only the boy's nose and mouth showed.

"About anything you want. What's the best thing you would like to do when school is out?"

The boy thought a moment and said, with rising inflection, "Go on a stratojet?"

"Why not? Sure thing. You go on a jet. It's taking off right now." He gestured lightly to Dooley, who threw the freezer into circuit.

Weill kept the boy only five minutes and then let him and his mother be escorted from the office by Dooley. Tommy looked bewildered but undamaged by the ordeal.

Weill said to the father, "Now, Mr. Slutsky, if your boy does well on this test, we'll be glad to pay you five hundred dollars each year until he finishes high school. In that time, all we'll ask is that he spend an hour a week some afternoon at our special school."

"Do I have to sign a paper?" Slutsky's voice was a bit hoarse.

"Certainly. This is business, Mr. Slutsky."

"Well, I don't know. Dreamers are hard to come by, I hear."

"They are. They are. But your son, Mr. Slutsky, is not a dreamer yet. He might never be. Five hundred dollars a year is a gamble for us. It's not a gamble for you. When he's finished high school, it may turn out he's not a dreamer, yet you've lost nothing. You've gained maybe four thousand dollars altogether. If he *is* a dreamer, he'll make a nice living and you certainly haven't lost then."

"He'll need special training, won't he?"

"Oh, yes, most intensive. But we don't have to worry about that till after he's finished high school. Then, after two years with us, he'll be developed. Rely on me, Mr. Slutsky."

"Will you guarantee that special training?"

Weill, who had been shoving a paper across the desk at Slutsky, and punching a pen wrong-side-to at him, put the pen down and chuckled, "Guarantee? No. How can we when we don't know for sure yet if he's a real talent? Still, the five hundred a year will stay yours."

Slutsky pondered and shook his head. "I tell you straight out, Mr. Weill—After your man arranged to have us come here, I called Luster-Think. They said they'll guarantee training."

Weill sighed. "Mr. Slutsky, I don't like to talk against a competitor. If they say they'll guarantee training, they'll do as they say, but they can't make a boy a dreamer if he hasn't got it in him, training or not. If they take a plain boy without the proper talent and put him through a development course, they'll ruin him. A dreamer he won't be, that I guarantee you. And a normal human being he won't be, either. Don't take the chance of doing it to your son.

"Now Dreams, Inc. will be perfectly honest with you. If he can be a dreamer, we'll make him one. If not, we'll give him back to you without having tampered with him and say, 'Let him learn a trade.' He'll be better and healthier that way. I tell you, Mr. Slutsky—I have sons and daughters and grandchildren so I know what I say—I would not allow a child of mine to be pushed into dreaming if he's not ready for it. Not for a million dollars."

Slutsky wiped his mouth with the back of his hand and reached for the pen. "What does this say?"

"This is just an option. We pay you a hundred dollars in cash right now. No strings attached. We'll study the boy's reverie. If we feel it's worth following up, we'll call you in again and make the five hundred dollar a year deal. Leave yourself in my hands, Mr. Slutsky, and don't worry. You won't be sorry."

Slutsky signed.

Weill passed the document through the file slot and handed an envelope to Slutsky.

Five minutes later, alone in the office, he placed the unfreezer over his own head and absorbed the boy's reverie intently. It was a typically childish daydream. First Person was at the controls of the plane, which looked like a compound of illustrations out of the filmed thrillers that still circulated among those who lacked the time, desire or money for dream-cylinders.

When he removed the unfreezer, he found Dooley looking at him.

"Well, Mr. Weill, what do you think?" said Dooley, with an eager and proprietary air.

"Could be, Joe. Could be. He has the overtones and for a ten-year-old boy without a scrap of training it's hopeful. When the plane went through a cloud, there was a distinct sensation of pillows. Also the smell of clean sheets, which was an amusing touch. We can go with him a ways, Joe."

"Good." Joe beamed happily at Weill's approval.

"But I tell you, Joe, what we really need is to catch them still sooner. And why not? Some day, Joe, every child will be tested at birth. A difference in the brain there positively must be and it should be found. Then we could separate the dreamers at the very beginning."

"Hell, Mr. Weill," said Dooley, looking hurt. "What would happen to my job then?"

Weill laughed. "No cause to worry yet, Joe. It won't happen in our lifetimes. In mine, certainly not. We'll be depending on good talent scouts like you for many years. You just watch the playgrounds and the streets"—Weill's gnarled hand dropped to Dooley's shoulder with a gentle, approving pressure—"and find us a few more Hillarys and Janows and Luster-Think won't ever catch us.—Now get out. I want lunch and then I'll be ready for my 2 o'clock appointment. The government, Joe, the government." And he winked portentously.

Jesse Weill's 2 o'clock appointment was with a young man, apple-cheeked, spectacled, sandy-haired and glowing with the intensity of a man with a mission. He presented his credentials across Weill's desk and revealed himself to be John J. Byrne, an agent of the Department of Arts and Sciences.

"Good afternoon, Mr. Byrne," said Weill. "In what way can I be of service?"

"Are we private here?" asked the agent. He had an unexpected baritone.

"Quite private."

"Then, if you don't mind, I'll ask you to absorb this." Byrne produced a small and battered cylinder and held it out between thumb and forefinger.

Weill took it, hefted it, turned it this way and that and said with a denture-revealing smile, "Not the product of Dreams, Inc., Mr. Byrne."

"I didn't think it was," said the agent. "I'd still like you to absorb it. I'd set the automatic cutoff for about a minute, though."

"That's all that can be endured?" Weill pulled the receiver to his desk and placed the cylinder into the unfreeze compartment. He removed it, polished either end of the cylinder with his handkerchief and tried again. "It doesn't make good contact," he said. "An amateurish job."

He placed the cushioned unfreeze helmet over his skull and adjusted the temple contacts, then set the automatic cutoff. He leaned back and clasped his hands over his chest and began absorbing.

His fingers grew rigid and clutched at his jacket. After the cutoff had brought absorption to an end, he removed the unfreezer and looked faintly angry. "A raw piece," he said. "It's lucky I'm an old man so that such things no longer bother me."

Byrne said stiffly, "It's not the worst we've found. And the fad is increasing."

Weill shrugged. "Pornographic dreamies. It's a logical development, I suppose."

The government man said, "Logical or not, it represents a deadly danger for the moral fiber of the nation."

"The moral fiber," said Weill, "can take a lot of beating. Erotica of one form or another has been circulated all through history."

"Not like this, sir. A direct mind-to-mind stimulation is much more effective than smoking-room stories or filthy pictures. Those must be filtered through the senses and lose some of their effect in that way."

Weill could scarcely argue that point. He said, "What would you have me do?"

"Can you suggest a possible source for this cylinder?"

"Mr. Byrne, I'm not a policeman."

"No, no, I'm not asking you to do our work for us. The Department is quite capable of conducting its own investigations. Can you help us, I mean, from your own specialized knowledge? You say your company did not put out that filth. Who did?"

"No reputable dream-distributor. I'm sure of that. It's too cheaply made."

"That could have been done on purpose."

"And no professional dreamer originated it."

"Are you sure, Mr. Weill? Couldn't dreamers do this sort of thing for some small illegitimate concern for money—or for fun?"

"They could, but not this particular one. No overtones. It's two-dimensional. Of course, a thing like this doesn't need overtones."

"What do you mean, overtones?"

Weill laughed gently, "You are not a dreamie fan?"

Byrne tried not to look virtuous and did not entirely succeed. "I prefer music."

"Well, that's all right, too," said Weill, tolerantly, "but it makes it a little harder to explain overtones. Even people who absorb dreamies might not be able to explain if you asked them. Still they'd know a dreamie was no good if the overtones were missing, even if they couldn't tell you why. Look, when an experienced dreamer goes into reverie, he doesn't think a story like in the old-fashioned television or book-films. It's a series of little visions. Each one has several meanings. If you studied them carefully, you'd find maybe five or six. While absorbing them in the ordinary way, you would never notice, but careful study shows it. Believe me, my psychological staff puts in long hours on just that point. All the overtones, the different meanings, blend together into a mass of guided emotion. Without them, everything would be flat, tasteless.

"Now this morning, I tested a young boy. A ten-year-old with possibilities. A cloud to him isn't just a cloud, it's a pillow too. Having the sensations of both, it was more than either. Of course, the boy's very primitive. But when he's through with his schooling, he'll be trained and disciplined. He'll be subjected to all sorts of sensations. He'll store up experience. He'll study and analyze classic dreamies of the past. He'll learn how to control and direct his thoughts, though, mind you, I have always said that when a good dreamer improvises—"

Weill halted abruptly, then proceeded in less impassioned tones, "I shouldn't get excited. All I'm trying to bring out now is that every professional dreamer has his own type of overtones which he can't mask. To an expert it's like signing his name on the dreamie. And I, Mr. Byrne, know all the signatures. Now that piece of dirt you brought me has no overtones at all. It was done by an ordinary person. A little talent, maybe, but like you and me, he can't think."

Byrne reddened a trifle. "Not everyone can't think, Mr. Weill, even if they don't make dreamies."

"Oh, tush," and Weill wagged his hand in the air. "Don't be angry with what an old man says. I don't mean *think* as in *reason*. I mean *think* as in *dream*. We all can dream after a fashion, just like we all can run. But can you and I run a mile in under four minutes? You and I can talk but are we Daniel Websters? Now when I think of a steak, I think of the word. Maybe I have a quick picture of a brown steak on a platter. Maybe you have a better pictorialization of it and you can see the crisp fat and the onions and the baked potato. I don't know. But a *dreamer* . . . He sees it and smells it and tastes it and everything about it, with the charcoal and the satisfied feeling in the stomach and the way the knife cuts through it and a hundred other things all at once. Very sensual. Very sensual. You and I can't do it."

"Well then," said Byrne, "no professional dreamer has done this. That's something anyway." He put the cylinder in his inner jacket pocket. "I hope we'll have your full cooperation in squelching this sort of thing."

"Positively, Mr. Byrne. With a whole heart."

"I hope so." Byrne spoke with a consciousness of power. "It's not up to me, Mr. Weill, to say what will be done and what won't be done, but this sort of thing"—he tapped the cylinder he had brought—"will make it awfully tempting to impose a really strict censorship on dreamies."

He rose. "Good day, Mr. Weill."

"Good day, Mr. Byrne. I'll hope always for the best."

Francis Belanger burst into Jesse Weill's office in his usual steaming tizzy, his reddish hair disordered and his face aglow with worry and a mild perspiration. He was brought up sharply by the sight of Weill's head cradled in the crook of his elbow and bent on the desk until only the glimmer of white hair was visible.

Belanger swallowed. "Boss?"

Weill's head lifted. "It's you, Frank?"

"What's the matter, boss? Are you sick?"

"I'm old enough to be sick, but I'm on my feet. Staggering, but on my feet. A government man was here."

"What did he want?"

"He threatens censorship. He brought a sample of what's going round. Cheap dreamies for bottle parties."

"God damn!" said Belanger, feelingly.

"The only trouble is that morality makes for good campaign fodder. They'll be hitting out everywhere. And to tell the truth, we're vulnerable, Frank."

"*We* are? Our stuff is clean. We play up adventure and romance."

Weill thrust out his lower lip and wrinkled his forehead. "Between us, Frank, we don't have to make believe. Clean? It depends on how you look at it. It's not for publication, maybe, but you know and I know that every dreamie has its Freudian connotations. You can't deny it."

"Sure, if you *look* for it. If you're a psychiatrist—"

"If you're an ordinary person, too. The ordinary observer doesn't know it's there and maybe he couldn't tell a phallic symbol from a mother image even if you pointed them out. Still, his subconscious knows. And it's the connotations that make many a dreamie click."

"All right, what's the government going to do? Clean up the subconscious?"

"It's a problem. I don't know what they're going to do. What we have on our side, and what I'm mainly depending on, is the fact that the public loves its dreamies and won't give them up.—Meanwhile, what did you come in for? You want to see me about something, I suppose?"

Belanger tossed an object onto Weill's desk and shoved his shirt-tail deeper into his trousers.

Weill broke open the glistening plastic cover and took out the enclosed cylinder. At one end was engraved in a too-fancy script in pastel blue: *Along the Himalayan Trail.* It bore the mark of Luster-Think.

"The Competitor's Product." Weill said it with capitals and his lips twitched. "It hasn't been published yet. Where did you get it, Frank?"

"Never mind. I just want you to absorb it."

Weill sighed. "Today, everyone wants me to absorb dreams. Frank, it's not dirty?"

Belanger said testily, "It has your Freudian symbols. Narrow crevasses between the mountain peaks. I hope that won't bother you."

"I'm an old man. It stopped bothering me ten years ago, but that other thing was so poorly done, it hurt.—All right, let's see what you've got here."

Again the recorder. Again the unfreezer over his skull and at the temples. This time, Weill rested back in his chair for fifteen minutes or more, while Francis Belanger went hurriedly through two cigarettes.

When Weill removed the headpiece and blinked dream out of his eyes, Belanger said, "Well, what's your reaction, boss?"

Weill corrugated his forehead. "It's not for me. It was repetitious. With competition like this, Dreams, Inc. doesn't have to worry yet."

"That's your mistake, boss. Luster-Think's going to win with stuff like this. We've got to do something."

"Now, Frank—"

"No, you listen. This is the coming thing."

"This?" Weill stared with half-humorous dubiety at the cylinder. "It's amateurish. It's repetitious. Its overtones are very unsubtle. The snow had a distinct lemon sherbet taste. Who tastes lemon sherbet in snow these days, Frank? In the old days, yes. Twenty years ago, maybe. When Lyman Harrison first made his Snow Symphonies for sale down south, it was a big thing. Sherbet and candy-striped mountain tops and sliding down chocolate-covered cliffs. It's slapstick, Frank. These days it doesn't go."

"Because," said Belanger, "you're not up with the times, boss, I've got to talk to you straight. When you started the dreamie business, when you bought up the basic patents and began putting them out, dreamies were luxury stuff. The market was small and individual. You could afford to turn out specialized dreamies and sell them to people at high prices."

"I know," said Weill, "and we've kept that up. But also we've opened a rental business for the masses."

"Yes, we have and it's not enough. Our dreamies have subtlety, yes. They can be used over and over again. The tenth time you're still finding new things, still getting new enjoyment. But how many people are connoisseurs? And another thing. Our stuff is strongly individualized. They're First Person."

"Well?"

"Well, Luster-Think is opening dream-palaces. They've opened one with three hundred booths in Nashville. You walk in, take your seat, put on your unfreezer and get your dream. Everyone in the audience gets the same one."

"I've heard of it, Frank, and it's been done before. It didn't work the first time and it won't work now. You want to know why it won't work? Because in the first place, dreaming is a private thing. Do you like your neighbor to know what you're dreaming? In the second place, in a dream-palace the dreams have to start on schedule, don't they? So the dreamer has to dream not when he wants to but when some palace manager says he should. Finally, a dream one person likes, another person doesn't like. In those three hundred booths, I guarantee you, a hundred and fifty people are dissatisfied. And if they're dissatisfied, they won't come back."

Slowly, Belanger rolled up his sleeves and opened his collar. "Boss," he said, "you're talking through your hat. What's the use of proving they won't work? They *are* working. The word came through today that Luster-Think is breaking ground for a thousand-booth palace in St. Louis. People can get used to public dreaming, if everyone else in the same room is having the same dream. And they can adjust themselves to having it at a given time, as long as it's cheap and convenient.

"Damn it, boss, it's a social affair. A boy and a girl go to a dream-palace and absorb some cheap romantic thing with stereotyped over-tones and commonplace situations, but still they come out with stars sprinkling their hair. They've had the same dream together. They've gone through identical sloppy emotions. They're *in tune,* boss. You bet they go back to the dream-palace, and all their friends go, too."

"And if they don't like the dream?"

"That's the point. That's the nub of the whole thing. They're bound to like it. If you prepare Hillary specials with wheels within wheels within wheels, with surprise twists on the third-level undertones, with clever shifts of significance and all the other things we're so proud of, why, naturally, it won't appeal to everyone. Specialized dreamies are for specialized tastes. But Luster-Think is turning out simple jobs in Third Person so both sexes can be hit at once. Like what you've just absorbed. Simple, repetitious, commonplace. They're aiming at the lowest common denominator. No one will love it, maybe, but no one will hate it."

Weill sat silent for a long time and Belanger watched him. Then Weill said, "Frank, I started on quality and I'm staying there. Maybe you're right. Maybe dream-palaces are the coming thing. If so we'll open them, but we'll use good stuff. Maybe Luster-Think underes-timates ordinary people. Let's go slowly and not panic. I have based my policies on the theory that there's always a market for quality. Sometimes, my boy, it would surprise you how big a market."

"Boss—"

The sounding of the intercom interrupted Belanger.

"What is it, Ruth?" said Weill.

The voice of his secretary said, "It's Mr. Hillary, sir. He wants to see you right away. He says it's important."

"Hillary?" Weill's voice registered shock. Then, "Wait five minutes, Ruth, then send him in."

Weill turned to Belanger. "Today, Frank, is definitely not one of my good days. A dreamer should be at home with his thinker. And

Hillary's our best dreamer, so he especially should be at home. What do you suppose is wrong with him?"

Belanger, still brooding over Luster-Think and dream-palaces, said shortly, "Call him in and find out."

"In one minute. Tell me, how was his last dream? I haven't absorbed the one that came in last week."

Belanger came down to earth. He wrinkled his nose. "Not so good."

"Why not?"

"It was ragged. Too jumpy. I don't mind sharp transitions for the liveliness, you know, but there's got to be some connection, even if only on a deep level."

"Is it a total loss?"

"No Hillary dream is a *total* loss. It took a lot of editing though. We cut it down quite a bit and spliced in some odd pieces he'd sent us now and then. You know, detached scenes. It's still not Grade A, but it will pass."

"You told him about this, Frank?"

"Think I'm crazy, boss? Think I'm going to say a harsh word to a dreamer?"

And at that point the door opened and Weill's comely young secretary smiled Sherman Hillary into the office.

Sherman Hillary, at the age of 31, could have been recognized as a dreamer by anyone. His eyes, though unspectacled, had nevertheless the misty look of one who either needs glasses or who rarely focuses on anything mundane. He was of average height but underweight, with black hair that needed cutting, a narrow chin, a pale skin and a troubled look.

He muttered, "Hello, Mr. Weill," and half-nodded in hangdog fashion in the direction of Belanger.

Weill said, heartily, "Sherman, my boy, you look fine. What's the matter? A dream is cooking only so-so at home? You're worried about it?—Sit down, sit down."

The dreamer did, sitting at the edge of the chair and holding his thighs stiffly together as though to be ready for instant obedience to a possible order to stand up once more.

He said, "I've come to tell you, Mr. Weill, I'm quitting."

"Quitting?"

"I don't want to dream anymore, Mr. Weill."

Weill's old face looked older now than at any time during the day. "Why, Sherman?"

The dreamer's lips twisted. He blurted out, "Because I'm not *living,* Mr. Weill. Everything passes me by. It wasn't so bad at first. It was even relaxing. I'd dream evenings, weekends when I felt like it or any other time. And when I felt like it I wouldn't. But now, Mr. Weill, I'm an old pro. You tell me I'm one of the best in the business and the industry looks to me to think up new subtleties and new changes on the old reliables like the flying reveries, and the worm-turning skits."

Weill said, "And is anyone better than you, Sherman? Your little sequence on leading an orchestra is selling steadily after ten years."

"All right, Mr. Weill. I've done my part. It's gotten so I don't go out anymore. I neglect my wife. My little girl doesn't know me. Last week we went to a dinner party—Sarah made me—and I don't remember a bit of it. Sarah says I was sitting on the couch all evening just staring at nothing and humming. She said everyone kept looking at me. She cried all night. I'm tired of things like that, Mr. Weill. I want to be a normal person and live in this world. I promised her I'd quit and I will, so it's goodby, Mr. Weill." Hillary stood up and held out his hand awkwardly.

Weill waved it gently away. "If you want to quit, Sherman, it's all right. But do an old man a favor and let me explain something to you."

"I'm not going to change my mind," said Hillary.

"I'm not going to try to make you. I just want to explain something. I'm an old man and even before you were born I was in this business, so I like to talk about it. Humor me, Sherman? Please?"

Hillary sat down. His teeth clamped down on his lower lip and he stared sullenly at his fingernails.

Weill said, "Do you know what a dreamer is, Sherman? Do you know what he means to ordinary people? Do you know what it is to be like me, like Frank Belanger, like your wife Sarah? To have crippled minds that can't imagine, that can't build up thoughts? People like myself, ordinary people, would like to escape just once in a while this life of ours. We can't. We need help.

"In olden times it was books, plays, movies, radio, television. They gave us make-believe, but that wasn't important. What *was* important was that for a little while our own imaginations were stimulated. We could think of handsome lovers and beautiful princesses. We could be attractive, witty, strong, capable—everything we weren't.

"But always the passing of the dream from dreamer to absorber was not perfect. It had to be translated into words in one way or another.

The best dreamer in the world might not be able to get any of it into words. And the best writer in the world could put only the smallest part of his dreams into words. You understand?

"But now, with dream-recording, any man can dream. You, Sherman, and a handful of men like you supply those dreams directly and exactly. It's straight from your head into ours, full strength. You dream for a hundred million people every time you dream. You dream a hundred million dreams at once. This is a great thing, my boy. You give all those people a glimpse of something they could not have by themselves."

Hillary mumbled, "I've done my share." He rose desperately to his feet. "I'm through. I don't care what you say. And if you want to sue me for breaking our contract, go ahead and sue. I don't care."

Weill stood up too. "Would I sue you?—Ruth," he spoke into the intercom, "bring in our copy of Mr. Hillary's contract."

He waited. So did Hillary and Belanger. Weill smiled faintly and his yellowed fingers drummed softly on his desk.

His secretary brought in the contract. Weill took it, showed its face to Hillary and said, "Sherman, my boy, unless you *want* to be with me, it's not right you should stay."

Then before Belanger could make more than the beginning of a horrified gesture to stop him, he tore the contract into four pieces and tossed them down the waste-chute. "That's all."

Hillary's hand shot out to seize Weill's. "Thanks, Mr. Weill," he said, earnestly, his voice husky. "You've always treated me very well, and I'm grateful. I'm sorry it had to be like this."

"It's all right, my boy. It's all right."

Half in tears, still muttering thanks, Sherman Hillary left.

"For the love of Pete, boss, why did you let him go?" demanded Belanger. "Don't you see the game? He'll be going straight to Luster-Think. They've bought him off."

Weill raised his hand. "You're wrong. You're quite wrong. I know the boy and this would not be his style. Besides," he added dryly, "Ruth is a good secretary and she knows what to bring me when I ask for a dreamer's contract. The real contract is still in the safe, believe me.

"Meanwhile, a fine day I've had. I had to argue with a father to give me a chance at new talent, with a government man to avoid censorship, with you to keep from adopting fatal policies, and now with my best dreamer to keep him from leaving. The father I probably won out over. The government man and you, I don't know. Maybe yes, maybe no. But about Sherman Hillary, at least, there is no question. The dreamer will be back."

"How do you know?"

Weill smiled at Belanger and crinkled his cheeks into a network of fine lines. "Frank, my boy, you know how to edit dreamies so you think you know all the tools and machines of the trade. But let me tell you something. The most important tool in the dreamie business is the dreamer himself. He is the one you have to understand most of all, and I understand them.

"Listen. When I was a youngster—there were no dreamies then—I knew a fellow who wrote television scripts. He would complain to me bitterly that when someone met him for the first time and found out who he was, they would say: *Where do you get those crazy ideas?*

"They honestly didn't know. To them it was an impossibility to even think of one of them. So what could my friend say? He used to talk to me about it and tell me: 'Could I say, "I don't know"? When I go to bed I can't sleep for ideas dancing in my head. When I shave I cut myself; when I talk I lose track of what I'm saying; when I drive I take my life in my hands. And always because ideas, situations, dialogs are spinning and twisting in my mind. I can't tell you where I get my ideas. Can you tell me, maybe, your trick of *not* getting ideas, so I, too, can have a little peace?'

"You see, Frank, how it is. *You* can stop work here anytime. So can I. This is our job, not our life. But not Sherman Hillary. Wherever he goes, whatever he does, he'll dream. While he lives, he must think; while he thinks, he must dream. We don't hold him prisoner, our contract isn't an iron wall for him. His own skull is his prisoner. He'll be back. What can he do?"

Belanger shrugged. "If what you say is right, I'm sort of sorry for the guy."

Weill nodded sadly, "I'm sorry for all of them. Through the years, I've found out one thing. It's their business: making people happy. *Other* people."

Poor Little Warrior!
Brian W. Aldiss

CLAUDE FORD KNEW EXACTLY how it was to hunt a brontosaurus. You crawled heedlessly through the mud among the willows, through the little primitive flowers with petals as green and brown as a football field, through the beauty-lotion mud. You peered out at the creature sprawling among the reeds, its body as graceful as a sock full of sand. There it lay, letting the gravity cuddle it nappy-damp to the marsh, running its big rabbit-hole nostrils a foot above the grass in a sweeping semicircle, in a snoring search for more sausagy reeds. It was beautiful: here horror had reached its limits, come full circle and finally disappeared up its own sphincter. Its eyes gleamed with the liveliness of a week-dead corpse's big toe, and its compost breath and the fur in its crude aural cavities were particularly to be recommended to anyone who might otherwise have felt inclined to speak lovingly of the work of Mother Nature.

But as you, little mammal with opposed digit and .65 self-loading, semi-automatic, dual-barrelled, digitally-computed, telescopically sighted, rustless, high-powered rifle gripped in your otherwise-defence-less paws, snide along under the bygone willows, what primarily attracts you is the thunder lizard's hide. It gives off a smell as deeply resonant as the bass note of a piano. It makes the elephant's epidermis look

BRIAN W. ALDISS, *the premier British author of sf, has been a regular contributor to F&SF for more than twenty years. His novels include* Hothouse (*from the F&SF series*), Greybeard, Barefoot in the Head *and* Frankenstein Unbound. *"Poor Little Warrior!" appeared in the April 1958 issue.*

like a sheet of crinkled lavatory paper. It is gray as the Viking seas,
daft-deep as cathedral foundations. What contact possible to bone
could allay the fever of that flesh? Over it scamper—you can see them
from here!—the little brown lice that live in those gray walls and canyons, gay as ghosts, cruel as crabs. If one of them jumped on you, it
would very like break your back. And when one of those parasites
stops to cock its leg against one of the bronto's vertebrae, you can see it
carries in its turn its own crop of easy-livers, each as big as a lobster,
for you're near now, oh, so near that you can hear the monster's primitive heart-organ knocking, as the ventricle keeps miraculous time
with the auricle.

Time for listening to the oracle is past: you're beyond the stage for
omens, you're now headed in for the kill, yours or his; superstition has
had its little day for today, from now on only this windy nerve of yours,
this shaky conglomeration of muscle entangled untraceably beneath the
sweat-shiny carapace of skin, this bloody little urge to slay the dragon,
is going to answer all your opinions.

You could shoot now. Just wait till that tiny steam-shovel head
pauses once again to gulp down a quarry-load of bullrushes, and with
one inexpressibly vulgar bang you can show the whole indifferent
Jurassic world that it's standing looking down the business end of evo-
lution's sex-shooter. You know why you pause, even as you pretend not
to know why you pause; that old worm conscience, long as a baseball
pitch, long-lived as a tortoise, is at work; through every sense it slides,
more monstrous than the serpent. Through the passions: saying here is
a sitting duck, O Englishman! Through the intelligence: whispering that
boredom, the kite-hawk who never feeds, will settle again when the task
is done. Through the nerves: sneering that when the adrenalin currents
cease to flow the vomiting begins. Through the maestro behind the ret-
ina: plausibly forcing the beauty of the view upon you.

Spare us that poor old slipper-slopper of a word, *beauty;* holy mom,
is this a travelogue, nor are we out of it? *"Perched now on this titanic
creature's back, we see a round dozen—and folks let me stress that
round—of gaudily plumaged birds, exhibiting between them all the
colour you might expect to find on lovely, fabled Copacabana Beach.
They're so round because they feed from the droppings that fall from
the rich man's table. Watch this lovely shot now! See the bronto's tail
lift. . . . Oh, lovely, yep, a couple of hayricks-full at least emerging
from his nether end. That sure was a beauty, folks, delivered straight
from consumer to consumer. The birds are fighting over it now. Hey,*

you, there's enough to go round, and anyhow, you're round enough al-
ready. . . . And nothing to do now but hop back up onto the old rump
steak and wait for the next round. And now as the sun sinks in the
Jurassic West, we say 'Fare well on that diet' . . ."

No, you're procrastinating, and that's a life work. Shoot the beast and
put it out of your agony. Taking your courage in your hands, you raise
it to shoulder level and squint down its sights. There is a terrible report;
you are half stunned. Shakily, you look about you. The monster still
munches, relieved to have broken enough wind to unbecalm the Ancient Mariner.

Angered (or is it some subtler emotion?), you now burst from the
bushes and confront it, and this exposed condition is typical of the
straits into which your consideration for yourself and others continually pitches you. Consideration? Or again something subtler? Why
should you be confused just because you come from a confused civili-
sation? But that's a point to deal with later, if there is a later, as these
two hog-wallow eyes pupilling you all over from spitting distance tend
to dispute. Let it not be by jaws alone, O monster, but also by huge
hooves and, if convenient to yourself, by mountainous rollings upon
me! Let death be a saga, sagacious, Beowulfate.

Quarter of a mile distant is the sound of a dozen hippos springing
boisterously in gymslips from the ancestral mud, and next second a
walloping great tail as long as Sunday and as thick as Saturday night
comes slicing over your head. You duck as duck you must, but the
beast missed you anyway because it so happens that its coordination is
no better than yours would be if you had to wave the Woolworth Building at a tarsier. This done, it seems to feel it has done its duty by itself.
It forgets you. You just wish you could forget yourself as easily; that
was, after all, the reason you had to come the long way here. *Get Away*
From It All, said the time travel brochure, which meant for you getting
away from Claude Ford, a husbandman as futile as his name with a
terrible wife called Maude. Maude and Claude Ford. Who could not
adjust to themselves, to each other, or to the world they were born in.
It was the best reason in the as-it-is-at-present-constituted world for
coming back here to shoot giant saurians—if you were fool enough to
think that one hundred and fifty million years either way made an ounce
of difference to the muddle of thoughts in a man's cerebral vortex.

You try and stop your silly, slobbering thoughts, but they have never
really stopped since the coca-collaborating days of your growing up;
God, if adolescence did not exist it would be unnecessary to invent it!

Slightly, it steadies you to look again on the enormous bulk of this ty-
rant vegetarian into whose presence you charged with such a mixed
death-life wish, charged with all the emotion the human orga(ni)sm is
capable of. This time the bogeyman is real, Claude, just as you wanted
it to be, and this time you really have to face up to it before it turns and
faces you again. And so again you lift Ole Equaliser, waiting till you
can spot the vulnerable spot.

The bright birds sway, the lice scamper like dogs, the marsh groans,
as bronto sways over and sends his little cranium snaking down under
the bile-bright water in a forage for roughage. You watch this; you have
never been so jittery before in all your jittered life, and you are counting on this catharsis wringing the last drop of acid fear out of your system for ever. OK, you keep saying to yourself insanely over and over,
your million-dollar twenty-second-century education going for nothing,
OK, OK. And as you say it for the umpteenth time, the crazy head
comes back out of the water like a renegade express and gazes in your
direction.

Grazes in your direction. For as the champing jaw with its big blunt
molars like concrete posts works up and down, you see the swamp
water course out over rimless lips, lipless rims, splashing your feet and
sousing the ground. Reed and root, stalk and stem, leaf and loam, all
are intermittently visible in that masticating maw and, struggling, straggling or tossed among them, minnows, tiny crustaceans, frogs—all destined in that awful, jaw-full movement to turn into bowel movement.
And as the glump-glump-glumping takes place, above it the slime-resist-
ant eyes again survey you.

These beasts live up to two hundred years, says the time travel brochure, and this beast has obviously tried to live up to that, for its gaze
is centuries old, full of decades upon decades of wallowing in its heavy-
weight thoughtlessness until it has grown wise on twitterpatedness. For
you it is like looking into a disturbing misty pool; it gives you a psychic
shock, you fire off both barrels at your own reflection. Bang-bang, the
dum-dums, big as paw-paws, go.

With no indecision, those century-old lights, dim and sacred, go out.
These cloisters are closed till Judgment Day. Your reflection is torn and
bloodied from them for ever. Over their ravaged panes nictitating mem-
branes slide slowly upwards, like dirty sheets covering a cadaver. The
jaw continues to munch slowly, as slowly the head sinks down. Slowly,
a squeeze of cold reptile blood toothpastes down the wrinkled flank of
one cheek. Everything is slow, a creepy Secondary Era slowness like

the drip of water, and you know that if you had been in charge of creation you would have found some medium less heart-breaking than Time
to stage it all in.

Never mind! Quaff down your beakers, lords, Claude Ford has slain
a harmless creature. Long live Claude the Clawed!

You watch breathless as the head touches the ground, the long laugh
of neck touches the ground, the jaws close for good. You watch and
wait for something else to happen, but nothing ever does. Nothing ever
would. You could stand here watching for an hundred and fifty million
years, Lord Claude, and nothing would ever happen here again. Gradually your bronto's mighty carcass, picked loving clean by predators,
would sink into the slime, carried by its own weight deeper; then the
waters would rise, and old Conqueror Sea come in with the leisurely air
of a card-sharp dealing the boys a bad hand. Silt and sediment would
filter down over the mighty grave, a slow rain with centuries to rain in.
Old bronto's bed might be raised up and then down again perhaps
half a dozen times, gently enough not to disturb him, although by now
the sedimentary rocks would be forming thick around him. Finally,
when he was wrapped in a tomb finer than any Indian rajah ever
boasted, the powers of the Earth would raise him high on their shoulders until, sleeping still, bronto would lie in a brow of the Rockies high
above the waters of the Pacific. But little any of that would count with
you, Claude the Sword; once the midget maggot of life is dead in the
creature's skull, the rest is no concern of yours.

You have no emotion now. You are just faintly put out. You expected dramatic thrashing of the ground, or bellowing; on the other
hand, you are glad the thing did not appear to suffer. You are like all
cruel men, sentimental; you are like all sentimental men, squeamish.
You tuck the gun under your arm and walk round the dinosaur to
view your victory.

You prowl past the ungainly hooves, round the septic white of the
cliff of belly, beyond the glistening and how-thought-provoking cavern
of the cloaca, finally posing beneath the switch-back sweep of tail-to-
rump. Now your disappointment is as crisp and obvious as a visiting
card: the giant is not half as big as you thought it was. It is not one half
as large, for example, as the image of you and Maude is in your mind.
Poor little warrior, science will never invent anything to assist the titanic death you want in the contraterrene caverns of your fee-fi-fo
fumblingly fearful id!

Nothing is left to you now but to slink back to your timemobile with a belly full of anticlimax. See, the bright dung-consuming birds have already cottoned on to the true state of affairs; one by one, they gather up their hunched wings and fly disconsolately off across the swamp to other hosts. They know when a good thing turns bad, and do not wait for the vultures to drive them off; all hope abandon, ye who entrail here. You also turn away.

You turn, but you pause. Nothing is left but to go back, no, but 2181 A.D. is not just the home date; it is Maude. It is Claude. It is the whole awful, hopeless, endless business of trying to adjust to an over-complex environment, of trying to turn yourself into a cog. Your escape from it into the *Grand Simplicities of the Jurassic,* to quote the brochure again, was only a partial escape, now over.

So you pause, and as you pause, something lands socko on your back, pitching you face forward into tasty mud. You struggle and scream as lobster claws tear at your neck and throat. You try to pick up the rifle but cannot, so in agony you roll over, and next second the crab-thing is greedying it on your chest. You wrench at its shell, but it giggles and pecks your fingers off. You forgot when you killed the bronto that its parasites would leave it, and that to a little shrimp like you they would be a deal more dangerous than their host.

You do your best, kicking for at least three minutes. By the end of that time there is a whole pack of the creatures on you. Already they are picking your carcass loving clean. You're going to like it up there on top of the Rockies; you won't feel a thing.

Imaginary Numbers
in a Real Garden
Gerald Jonas

Given: one bold mathematician.
Uncertain of his own position,
he drew two lines and at their joint,
where angels danced, he made his •
Then reached into the void and caught
the faceless essence of the 0,
and taught us not to fear ∞
but worship his serene divinity,
whose sacraments at first seem pale;
yet if men hunger for a Grail,
they still may seek, beyond the sun,
the rare $\sqrt{-1}$.

We Can Remember It for You Wholesale

Philip K. Dick

HE AWOKE—and wanted Mars. The valleys, he thought. What would it be like to trudge among them? Great and greater yet: the dream grew as he became fully conscious, the dream and the yearning. He could almost feel the enveloping presence of the other world, which only Government agents and high officials had seen. A clerk like himself? Not likely.

"Are you getting up or not?" his wife Kirsten asked drowsily, with her usual hint of fierce crossness. "If you are, push the hot coffee button on the darn stove."

"Okay," Douglas Quail said, and made his way barefoot from the bedroom of their conapt to the kitchen. There, having dutifully pressed the hot coffee button, he seated himself at the kitchen table, brought out a yellow, small tin of fine Dean Swift snuff. He inhaled briskly, and the Beau Nash mixture stung his nose, burned the roof of his mouth. But still he inhaled; it woke him up and allowed his dreams, his nocturnal desires and random wishes, to condense into a semblance of rationality.

PHILIP K. DICK *first started writing sf in 1952 and is the author of several seminal novels in the field, including* The Man in the High Castle (*Hugo Award, 1963*) Solar Lottery, Eye in the Sky, Ubik *and* Do Androids Dream of Electric Sheep? *"We Can Remember It for You Wholesale" was first published in the April 1966 issue.*

I will go, he said to himself. Before I die I'll see Mars.

It was, of course, impossible, and he knew this even as he dreamed. But the daylight, the mundane noise of his wife now brushing her hair before the bedroom mirror—everything conspired to remind him of what he was. A miserable little salaried employee, he said to himself with bitterness. Kirsten reminded him of this at least once a day and he did not blame her; it was a wife's job to bring her husband down to Earth. Down to Earth, he thought, and laughed. The figure of speech in this was literally apt.

"What are you sniggering about?" his wife asked as she swept into the kitchen, her long busy-pink robe wagging after her. "A dream, I bet. You're always full of them."

"Yes," he said, and gazed out the kitchen window at the hovercars and traffic runnels, and all the little energetic people hurrying to work. In a little while he would be among them. As always.

"I'll bet it has to do with some woman," Kirsten said witheringly.

"No," he said. "A god. The god of war. He has wonderful craters with every kind of plant-life growing deep down in them."

"Listen." Kirsten crouched down beside him and spoke earnestly, the harsh quality momentarily gone from her voice. "The bottom of the ocean—*our* ocean is much more, an infinity of times more beautiful. You know that; everyone knows that. Rent an artificial gill-outfit for both of us, take a week off from work, and we can descend and live down there at one of those year-round aquatic resorts. And in addition —" She broke off. "You're not listening. You should be. Here is something a lot better than that compulsion, that obsession you have about Mars, and you don't even listen!" Her voice rose piercingly. "God in heaven, you're doomed, Doug! What's going to become of you?"

"I'm going to work," he said, rising to his feet, his breakfast forgotten. "That's what's going to become of me."

She eyed him. "You're getting worse. More fanatical every day. Where's it going to lead?"

"To Mars," he said, and opened the door to the closet to get down a fresh shirt to wear to work.

Having descended from the taxi Douglas Quail slowly walked across three densely-populated foot runnels and to the modern, attractively inviting doorway. There he halted, impeding mid-morning traffic, and with caution read the shifting-color neon sign. He had, in the past, scrutinized this sign before . . . but never had he come so close. This was very different; what he did now was something else. Something which sooner or later had to happen.

REKAL, INCORPORATED

Was this the answer? After all, an illusion, no matter how convincing, remained nothing more than an illusion. At least objectively. But subjectively—quite the opposite entirely.

And anyhow he had an appointment. Within the next five minutes.

Taking a deep breath of mildly smog-infested Chicago air, he walked through the dazzling poly-chromatic shimmer of the doorway and up to the receptionist's counter.

The nicely-articulated blonde at the counter, bare-bosomed and tidy, said pleasantly, "Good morning, Mr. Quail."

"Yes," he said. "I'm here to see about a Rekal course. As I guess you know."

"Not 'rekal' but *re*call," the receptionist corrected him. She picked up the receiver of the vid-phone by her smooth elbow and said into it, "Mr. Douglas Quail is here, Mr. McClane. May he come inside, now? Or is it too soon?"

"Giz wetwa wum-wum wamp," the phone mumbled.

"Yes, Mr. Quail," she said. "You may go on in; Mr. McClane is expecting you." As he started off uncertainly she called after him, "Room D, Mr. Quail. To your right."

After a frustrating but brief moment of being lost he found the proper room. The door hung open and inside, at a big genuine walnut desk, sat a genial-looking man, middle-aged, wearing the latest Martian frog-pelt gray suit; his attire alone would have told Quail that he had come to the right person.

"Sit down, Douglas," McClane said, waving his plump hand toward a chair which faced the desk. "So you want to have gone to Mars. Very good."

Quail seated himself, feeling tense. "I'm not so sure this is worth the fee," he said. "It costs a lot and as far as I can see I really get nothing." Costs almost as much as going, he thought.

"You get tangible proof of your trip," McClane disagreed emphatically. "All the proof you'll need. Here; I'll show you." He dug within a drawer of his impressive desk. "Ticket stub." Reaching into a manila folder he produced a small square of embossed cardboard. "It proves you went—and returned. Postcards." He laid out four franked picture 3-D full-color postcards in a neatly-arranged row on the desk for Quail to see. "Film. Shots you took of local sights on Mars with a rented movie camera." To Quail he displayed those, too. "Plus the names of people you met, two hundred poscreds worth of souvenirs, which will arrive—from Mars—within the following month. And passport, certificates listing the shots you received. And more." He glanced up keenly at Quail. "You'll know you went, all right," he said. "You won't remember us, won't remember me or ever having been here. It'll be a real trip in your mind; we guarantee that. A full two weeks of recall; every last piddling detail. Remember this: if at any time you doubt that you really took an extensive trip to Mars you can return here and get a full refund. You see?"

"But I didn't go," Quail said. "I won't have gone, no matter what proofs you provide me with." He took a deep, unsteady breath. "And I never was a secret agent with Interplan." It seemed impossible to him that Rekal, Incorporated's extra-factual memory implant would do its job—despite what he had heard people say.

"Mr. Quail," McClane said patiently. "As you explained in your letter to us, you have no chance, no possibility in the slightest, of ever actually getting to Mars; you can't afford it, and what is much more important, you could never qualify as an undercover agent for Interplan or anybody else. This is the only way you can achieve your, ahem, lifelong dream; am I not correct, sir? You can't be this; you can't actually do this." He chuckled. "But you can *have been* and *have done*. We see to that. And our fee is reasonable; no hidden charges." He smiled encouragingly.

"Is an extra-factual memory that convincing?" Quail asked.

"More than the real thing, sir. Had you really gone to Mars as an Interplan agent, you would by now have forgotten a great deal; our analysis of true-mem systems—authentic recollections of major events in a person's life—shows that a variety of details are very quickly lost to the person. Forever. Part of the package we offer you is such deep implantation of recall that nothing is forgotten. The packet which is fed to you while you're comatose is the creation of trained experts, men who have spent years on Mars; in every case we verify details down to the last iota. And you've picked a rather easy extra-factual system; had you picked Pluto or wanted to be Emperor of the Inner Planet Alliance we'd have much more difficulty . . . and the charges would be considerably greater."

Reaching into his coat for his wallet, Quail said, "Okay. It's been my life-long ambition and I can see I'll never really do it. So I guess I'll have to settle for this."

"Don't think of it that way," McClane said severely. "You're not accepting second-best. The actual memory, with all its vagueness, omissions and ellipses, not to say distortions—that's second-best." He accepted the money and pressed a button on his desk. "All right, Mr. Quail," he said, as the door of his office opened and two burly men swiftly entered. "You're on your way to Mars as a secret agent." He rose, came over to shake Quail's nervous, moist hand. "Or rather, you have been on your way. This afternoon at four-thirty you will, um, arrive back here on Terra; a cab will leave you off at your conapt and as I say you will never remember seeing me or coming here; you won't, in fact, even remember having heard of our existence."

His mouth dry with nervousness, Quail followed the two technicians from the office; what happened next depended on them.

Will I actually believe I've been on Mars? he wondered. That I managed to fulfill my lifetime ambition? He had a strange, lingering intuition that something would go wrong. But just what—he did not know.

He would have to wait to find out.

The intercom on McClane's desk, which connected him with the work-area of the firm, buzzed and a voice said, "Mr. Quail is under sedation now, sir. Do you want to supervise this one, or shall we go ahead?"

"It's routine," McClane observed. "You may go ahead, Lowe; I don't think you'll run into any trouble." Programming an artificial memory of a trip to another planet—with or without the added fillip of being a secret agent—showed up on the firm's work-schedule with monotonous regularity. In one month, he calculated wryly, we must do twenty of these . . . ersatz interplanetary travel has become our bread and butter.

"Whatever you say, Mr. McClane," Lowe's voice came, and thereupon the intercom shut off.

Going to the vault section in the chamber behind his office, McClane searched about for a Three packet—trip to Mars—and a Sixty-two packet: secret Interplan spy. Finding the two packets, he returned with them to his desk, seated himself comfortably, poured out the contents —merchandise which would be planted in Quail's conapt while the lab technicians busied themselves installing the false memory.

A one-poscred sneaky-pete side arm, McClane reflected; that's the largest item. Sets us back financially the most. Then a pellet-sized transmitter, which could be swallowed if the agent were caught. Code book that astonishingly resembled the real thing . . . the firm's models were highly accurate: based, whenever possible, on actual U.S. military issue. Odd bits which made no intrinsic sense but which would be woven into the warp and woof of Quail's imaginary trip, would coincide with his memory: half an ancient silver fifty cent piece, several quotations from John Donne's sermons written incorrectly, each on a separate piece of transparent tissue-thin paper, several match folders from bars on Mars, a stainless steel spoon engraved PROPERTY OF DOME-MARS NATIONAL KIBBUZIM, a wire tapping coil which—

The intercom buzzed. "Mr. McClane, I'm sorry to bother you but something rather ominous has come up. Maybe it would be better if you were in here after all. Quail is already under sedation; he reacted well to the narkidrine; he's completely unconscious and receptive. But—"

"I'll be in." Sensing trouble, McClane left his office; a moment later he emerged in the work area.

On a hygienic bed lay Douglas Quail, breathing slowly and regularly, his eyes virtually shut; he seemed dimly—but only dimly—aware of the two technicians and now McClane himself.

"There's no space to insert false memory-patterns?" McClane felt irritation. "Merely drop out two work weeks; he's employed as a clerk at the West Coast Emigration Bureau, which is a government agency, so he undoubtedly has or had two weeks vacation within the last year. That ought to do it." Petty details annoyed him. And always would.

"Our problem," Lowe said sharply, "is something quite different." He bent over the bed, said to Quail, "Tell Mr. McClane what you told us." To McClane he said, "Listen closely."

The gray-green eyes of the man lying supine in the bed focussed on McClane's face. The eyes, he observed uneasily, had become hard; they had a polished, inorganic quality, like semi-precious tumbled stones. He was not sure that he liked what he saw; the brilliance was too cold. "What do you want now?" Quail said harshly. "You've broken my cover. Get out of here before I take you all apart." He studied McClane. "Especially you," he continued. "You're in charge of this counter-operation."

Lowe said, "How long were you on Mars?"

"One month," Quail said gratingly.

"And your purpose there?" Lowe demanded.

The meager lips twisted; Quail eyed him and did not speak. At last, drawling the words out so that they dripped with hostility, he said, "Agent for Interplan. As I already told you. Don't you record everything that's said? Play your vid-aud tape back for your boss and leave me alone." He shut his eyes, then; the hard brilliance ceased. McClane felt, instantly, a rushing splurge of relief.

Lowe said quietly, "This is a tough man, Mr. McClane."

"He won't be," McClane said, "After we arrange for him to lose his memory-chain again. He'll be as meek as before." To Quail he said, "So *this* is why you wanted to go to Mars so terribly badly."

Without opening his eyes Quail said, "I never wanted to go to Mars. I was assigned it—they handed it to me and there I was: stuck. Oh yeah, I admit I was curious about it; who wouldn't be?" Again he opened his eyes and surveyed the three of them, McClane in particular. "Quite a truth drug you've got here; it brought up things I had absolutely no memory of." He pondered. "I wonder about Kirsten," he said, half to himself. "Could she be in on it? An Interplan contact keeping an eye on me . . . to be certain I didn't regain my memory? No wonder she's been so derisive about my wanting to go there." Faintly, he smiled; the smile—one of understanding—disappeared almost at once.

McClane said, "Please believe me, Mr. Quail; we stumbled onto this entirely by accident. In the work we do—"

"I believe you," Quail said. He seemed tired, now; the drug was continuing to pull him under, deeper and deeper. "Where did I say I'd been?" he murmured. "Mars? Hard to remember—I know I'd like to see it; so would everybody else. But me—" His voice trailed off. "Just a clerk, a nothing clerk."

Straightening up, Lowe said to his superior, "He wants a false memory implanted that corresponds to a trip he actually took. And a false reason which is the real reason. He's telling the truth; he's a long way down in the narkidrine. The trip is very vivid in his mind—at least under sedation. But apparently he doesn't recall it otherwise. Someone, probably at a government military-sciences lab, erased his conscious memories; all he knew was that going to Mars meant something special to him, and so did being a secret agent. They couldn't erase that; it's not a memory but a desire, undoubtedly the same one that motivated him to volunteer for the assignment in the first place."

The other technician, Keeler, said to McClane, "What do we do? Graft a false memory-pattern over the real memory? There's no telling what the results would be; he might remember some of the genuine trip, and the confusion might bring on a psychotic interlude. He'd have to hold two opposite premises in his mind simultaneously: that he went to

Mars and that he didn't. That he's a genuine agent for Interplan and he's not, that it's spurious. I think we ought to revive him without any false memory implantation and send him out of here; this is hot."

"Agreed," McClane said. A thought came to him. "Can you predict what he'll remember when he comes out of sedation?"

"Impossible to tell," Lowe said. "He probably will have some dim, diffuse memory of his actual trip, now. And he'd probably be in grave doubt as to its validity; he'd probably decide our programming slipped a gear-tooth. And he'd remember coming here; that wouldn't be erased —unless you want it erased."

"The less we mess with this man," McClane said, "the better I like it. This is nothing for us to fool around with; we've been foolish enough to —or unlucky enough to—uncover a genuine Interplan spy who has a cover so perfect that up to now even he didn't know what he was—or rather is." The sooner they washed their hands of the man calling himself Douglas Quail the better.

"Are you going to plant packets Three and Sixty-two in his conapt?" Lowe said.

"No," McClane said. "And we're going to return half his fee."

"Half! Why half?"

McClane said lamely, "It seems to be a good compromise."

As the cab carried him back to his conapt at the residential end of Chicago, Douglas Quail said to himself, It's sure good to be back on Terra.

Already the month-long period on Mars had begun to waver in his memory; he had only an image of profound gaping craters, an ever-present ancient erosion of hills, of vitality, of motion itself. A world of dust where little happened, where a good part of the day was spent checking and rechecking one's portable oxygen source. And then the life forms, the unassuming and modest gray-brown cacti and maw-worms.

As a matter of fact he had brought back several moribund examples of Martian fauna; he had smuggled them through customs. After all, they posed no menace; they couldn't survive in Earth's heavy atmosphere.

Reaching into his coat pocket he rummaged for the container of Martian maw-worms—

And found an envelope instead.

Lifting it out he discovered, to his perplexity, that it contained five hundred and seventy poscreds, in cred bills of low denomination.

Where'd I get this? he asked himself. Didn't I spend every 'cred I had on my trip?

With the money came a slip of paper marked: *one-half fee ret'd. By McClane.* And then the date. Today's date.

"Recall," he said aloud.

"Recall what, sir or madam?" the robot driver of the cab inquired respectfully.

"Do you have a phone book?" Quail demanded.

"Certainly, sir or madam." A slot opened; from it slid a microtape phone book for Cook County.

"It's spelled oddly," Quail said as he leafed through the pages of the yellow section. He felt fear, then; abiding fear. "Here it is," he said. "Take me there, to Rekal, Incorporated. I've changed my mind; I don't want to go home."

"Yes sir, or madam, as the case may be," the driver said. A moment later the cab was zipping back in the opposite direction.

"May I make use of your phone?" he asked.

"Be my guest," the robot driver said. And presented a shiny new emperor 3-D color phone to him.

He dialed his own conapt. And after a pause found himself confronted by a miniature but chillingly realistic image of Kirsten on the small screen. "I've been to Mars," he said to her.

"You're drunk." Her lips writhed scornfully. "Or worse."

" 'S god's truth."

"When?" she demanded.

"I don't know." He felt confused. "A simulated trip, I think. By means of one of those artificial or extra-factual or whatever it is memory places. It didn't take."

Kirsten said witheringly, "You *are* drunk." And broke the connection at her end. He hung up, then, feeling his face flush. Always the same tone, he said hotly to himself. Always the retort, as if she knows everything and I know nothing. What a marriage. Keerist, he thought dismally.

A moment later the cab stopped at the curb before a modern, very attractive little pink building, over which a shifting, poly-chromatic neon sign read: REKAL, INCORPORATED.

The receptionist, chic and bare from the waist up, started in surprise, then gained masterful control of herself. "Oh hello Mr. Quail," she said nervously. "H-how are you? Did you forget something?"

"The rest of my fee back," he said.

More composed now the receptionist said, "Fee? I think you are mistaken, Mr. Quail. You were here discussing the feasibility of an extra-factual trip for you, but—" She shrugged her smooth pale shoulders. "As I understand it, no trip was taken."

Quail said, "I remember everything, miss. My letter to Rekal, Incorporated, which started this whole business off. I remember my arrival here, my visit with Mr. McClane. Then the two lab technicians taking me in tow and administering a drug to put me out." No wonder the firm had returned half his fee. The false memory of his "trip to Mars" hadn't taken—at least not entirely, not as he had been assured.

"Mr. Quail," the girl said, "although you are a minor clerk you are a good-looking man and it spoils your features to become angry. If it would make you feel any better, I might, ahem, let you take me out . . ."

He felt furious, then. "I remember you," he said savagely. "For instance the fact that your breasts are sprayed blue; that stuck in my mind. And I remember Mr. McClane's promise that if I remembered my visit to Rekal, Incorporated I'd receive my money back in full. Where is Mr. McClane?"

After a delay—probably as long as they could manage—he found himself once more seated facing the imposing walnut desk, exactly as he had been an hour or so earlier in the day.

"Some technique you have," Quail said sardonically. His disappointment—and resentment—were enormous, by now. "My so-called 'memory' of a trip to Mars as an undercover agent for Interplan is hazy and vague and shot full of contradictions. And I clearly remember my dealings here with you people. I ought to take this to the Better Business Bureau." He was burning angry, at this point; his sense of being cheated had overwhelmed him, had destroyed his customary aversion to participating in a public squabble.

Looking morose, as well as cautious, McClane said, "We capitulate, Quail. We'll refund the balance of your fee. I fully concede the fact that we did absolutely nothing for you." His tone was resigned.

Quail said accusingly, "You didn't even provide me with the various artifacts that you claimed would 'prove' to me I had been on Mars. All that song-and-dance you went into—it hasn't materialized into a damn thing. Not even a ticket stub. Nor postcards. Nor passport. Nor proof of immunization shots. Nor—"

"Listen, Quail," McClane said. "Suppose I told you—" He broke off. "Let it go." He pressed a button on his intercom. "Shirley, will you disburse five hundred and seventy more 'creds in the form of a cashier's check made out to Douglas Quail? Thank you." He released the button, then glared at Quail.

Presently the check appeared; the receptionist placed it before McClane and once more vanished out of sight, leaving the two men alone, still facing each other across the surface of the massive walnut desk.

"Let me give you a word of advice," McClane said as he signed the check and passed it over. "Don't discuss your, ahem, recent trip to Mars with anyone."

"What trip?"

"Well, that's the thing." Doggedly, McClane said, "The trip you partially remember. Act as if you don't remember; pretend it never took place. Don't ask me why; just take my advice: it'll be better for all of us." He had begun to perspire. Freely. "Now, Mr. Quail, I have other business, other clients to see." He rose, showed Quail to the door.

Quail said, as he opened the door, "A firm that turns out such bad work shouldn't have any clients at all." He shut the door behind him.

On the way home in the cab Quail pondered the wording of his letter of complaint to the Better Business Bureau, Terra Division. As soon as he could get to his typewriter he'd get started; it was clearly his duty to warn other people away from Rekal, Incorporated.

When he got back to his conapt he seated himself before his Hermes Rocket portable, opened the drawers and rummaged for carbon paper —and noticed a small, familiar box. A box which he had carefully filled on Mars with Martian fauna and later smuggled through customs.

Opening the box he saw, to his disbelief, six dead maw-worms and several varieties of the unicellular life on which the Martian worms fed. The protozoa were dried-up, dusty, but he recognized them; it had taken him an entire day picking among the vast dark alien boulders to find them. A wonderful, illuminated journey of discovery.

But I didn't go to Mars, he realized.

Yet on the other hand—

Kirsten appeared at the doorway to the room, an armload of pale brown groceries gripped. "Why are you home in the middle of the day?" Her voice, in an eternity of sameness, was accusing.

"Did I go to Mars?" he asked her. "You would know."

"No, of course you didn't go to Mars; *you* would know that, I would think. Aren't you always bleating about going?"

He said, "By God, I think I went." After a pause he added, "And simultaneously I think I didn't go."

"Make up your mind."

"How can I?" He gestured. "I have both memory-tracks grafted inside my head; one is real and one isn't but I can't tell which is which. Why can't I rely on you? They haven't tinkered with you." She could do this much for him at least—even if she never did anything else.

Kirsten said in a level, controlled voice, "Doug, if you don't pull yourself together, we're through. I'm going to leave you."

"I'm in trouble." His voice came out husky and coarse. And shaking. "Probably I'm heading into a psychotic episode; I hope not, but—maybe that's it. It would explain everything, anyhow."

Setting down the bag of groceries, Kirsten stalked to the closet. "I was not kidding," she said to him quietly. She brought out a coat, got it on, walked back to the door of the conapt. "I'll phone you one of these days soon," she said tonelessly. "This is goodbye, Doug. I hope you pull out of this eventually; I really pray you do. For your sake."

"Wait," he said desperately. "Just tell me and make it absolute; I did go or I didn't—tell me which one." But they may have altered your memory-track also, he realized.

The door closed. His wife had left. Finally!

A voice behind him said, "Well, that's that. Now put up your hands, Quail. And also please turn around and face this way."

He turned, instinctively, without raising his hands.

The man who faced him wore the plum uniform of the Interplan Police Agency, and his gun appeared to be UN issue. And, for some odd reason, he seemed familiar to Quail; familiar in a blurred, distorted fashion which he could not pin down. So, jerkily, he raised his hands.

"You remember," the policeman said, "your trip to Mars. We know all your actions today and all your thoughts—in particular your very important thoughts on the trip home from Rekal, Incorporated." He explained, "We have a telep-transmitter wired within your skull; it keeps us constantly informed."

A telepathic transmitter; use of a living plasma that had been discovered on Luna. He shuddered with self-aversion. The thing lived inside him, within his own brain, feeding, listening, feeding. But the Interplan police used them; that had come out even in the homeopapes. So this was probably true, dismal as it was.

"Why me?" Quail said huskily. What had he done—or thought? And what did this have to do with Rekal, Incorporated.

"Fundamentally" the Interplan cop said, "this has nothing to do with Rekal; it's between you and us." He tapped his right ear. "I'm still picking up your mentational processes by way of your cephalic transmitter." In the man's ear Quail saw a small white-plastic plug. "So I have to warn you: anything you think may be held against you." He smiled. "Not that it matters now; you've already thought and spoken yourself into oblivion. What's annoying is the fact that under narkidrine at Rekal, Incorporated you told them, their technicians and the owner, Mr. McClane, about your trip; where you went, for whom, some of what you did. They're very frightened. They wish they had never laid eyes on you." He added reflectively, "They're right."

Quail said, "I never made any trip. It's a false memory-chain improperly planted in me by McClane's technicians." But then he thought of the box, in his desk drawer, containing the Martian life forms. And the trouble and hardship he had had gathering them. The memory seemed real. And the box of life forms; that certainly was real. Unless McClane had planted it. Perhaps this was one of the "proofs" which McClane had talked glibly about.

The memory of my trip to Mars, he thought, doesn't convince me—but unfortunately it has convinced the Interplan Police Agency. They think I really went to Mars and they think I at least partially realize it.

"We not only know you went to Mars," the Interplan cop agreed, in answer to his thoughts, "but we know that you now remember enough to be difficult for us. And there's no use expunging your conscious memory of all this, because if we do you'll simply show up at Rekal, Incorporated again and start over. And we can't do anything about McClane and his operation because we have no jurisdiction over anyone except our own people. Anyhow, McClane hasn't committed any crime." He eyed Quail. "Nor, technically, have you. You didn't go to Rekal, Incorporated with the idea of regaining your memory; you went, as we realize, for the usual reason people go there—a love by plain, dull people for adventure." He added, "Unfortunately you're not plain, not dull, and you've already had too much excitement; the last thing in the universe you needed was a course from Rekal, Incorporated. Nothing could have been more lethal for you or for us. And, for that matter, for McClane."

Quail said, "Why is it 'difficult' for you if I remember my trip—my alleged trip—and what I did there?"

"Because," the Interplan harness bull said, "what you did is not in accord with our great white all-protecting father public image. You did, for us, what we never do. As you'll presently remember—thanks to narkidrine. That box of dead worms and algae has been sitting in your desk drawer for six months, ever since you got back. And at no time have you shown the slightest curiosity about it. We didn't even know you had it until you remembered it on your way home from Rekal; then we came here on the double to look for it." He added, unnecessarily, "Without any luck; there wasn't enough time."

A second Interplan cop joined the first one; the two briefly conferred. Meanwhile, Quail thought rapidly. He did remember more, now; the cop had been right about narkidrine. They—Interplan—probably used it themselves. Probably? He knew darn well they did; he had seen them putting a prisoner on it. Where would *that* be? Somewhere on Terra? More likely Luna, he decided, viewing the image rising from his highly defective—but rapidly less so—memory.

And he remembered something else. Their reason for sending him to Mars; the job he had done.

No wonder they had expunged his memory.

"Oh god," the first of the two Interplan cops said, breaking off his conversation with his companion. Obviously, he had picked up Quail's thoughts. "Well, this is a far worse problem, now; as bad as it can get." He walked toward Quail, again covering him with his gun. "We've got to kill you," he said. "And right away."

Nervously, his fellow officer said, "Why right away? Can't we simply cart him off to Interplan New York and let them—"

"*He* knows why it has to be right away," the first cop said; he too looked nervous, now, but Quail realized that it was for an entirely different reason. His memory had been brought back almost entirely, now. And he fully understood the officer's tension.

"On Mars," Quail said hoarsely, "I killed a man. After getting past fifteen bodyguards. Some armed with sneaky-pete guns, the way you are." He had been trained, by Interplan, over a five year period to be an assassin. A professional killer. He knew ways to take out armed adversaries . . . such as these two officers; and the one with the ear-receiver knew it, too.

If he moved swiftly enough—

The gun fired. But he had already moved to one side, and at the same time he chopped down the gun-carrying officer. In an instant he had possession of the gun and was covering the other, confused, officer.

"Picked my thoughts up," Quail said, panting for breath. "He knew what I was going to do, but I did it anyhow."

Half sitting up, the injured officer grated, "He won't use that gun on you, Sam; I pick that up, too. He knows he's finished, and he knows we know it, too. Come on, Quail." Laboriously, grunting with pain, he got shakily to his feet. He held out his hand. "The gun," he said to Quail. "You can't use it, and if you turn it over to me I'll guarantee not to kill you; you'll be given a hearing, and someone higher up in Interplan will decide, not me. Maybe they can erase your memory once more; I don't know. But you know the thing I was going to kill you for; I couldn't keep you from remembering it. So my reason for wanting to kill you is in a sense past."

Quail, clutching the gun, bolted from the conapt, sprinted for the elevator. If you follow me, he thought, I'll kill you. So don't. He jabbed at the elevator button and, a moment later, the doors slid back.

The police hadn't followed him. Obviously they had picked up his terse, tense thoughts and had decided not to take the chance.

With him inside the elevator descended. He had gotten away—for a time. But what next? Where could he go?

The elevator reached the ground floor; a moment later Quail had joined the mob of peds hurrying along the runnels. His head ached and he felt sick. But at least he had evaded death; they had come very close to shooting him on the spot, back in his own conapt.

And they probably will again, he decided. When they find me. And with this transmitter inside me, that won't take too long.

Ironically, he had gotten exactly what he had asked Rekal, Incorporated for. Adventure, peril, Interplan police at work, a secret and dangerous trip to Mars in which his life was at stake—everything he had wanted as a false memory.

The advantages of it being a memory—and nothing more—could now be appreciated.

On a park bench, alone, he sat dully watching a flock of perts: a semi-bird imported from Mars' two moons, capable of soaring flight, even against Earth's huge gravity.

Maybe I can find my way back to Mars, he pondered. But then what? It would be worse on Mars; the political organization whose leader he had assassinated would spot him the moment he stepped from the ship; he would have Interplan and *them* after him, there.

Can you hear me thinking? he wondered. Easy avenue to paranoia; sitting here alone he felt them tuning in on him, monitoring, recording, discussing . . . he shivered, rose to his feet, walked aimlessly, his hands deep in his pockets. No matter where I go, he realized. You'll always be with me. As long as I have this device inside my head.

I'll make a deal with you, he thought to himself—and to them. Can't you imprint a false-memory template on me again, as you did before, that I lived an average, routine life, never went to Mars? Never saw an Interplan uniform up close and never handled a gun?

A voice inside his brain answered, "As has been carefully explained to you: that would not be enough."

Astonished, he halted.

"We formerly communicated with you in this manner," the voice continued. "When you were operating in the field, on Mars. It's been months since we've done it; we assumed, in fact, that we'd never have to do so again. Where are you?"

"Walking," Quail said, "to my death." By your officers' guns, he added as an afterthought. "How can you be sure it wouldn't be enough?" he demanded. "Don't the Rekal techniques work?"

"As we said. If you're given a set of standard, average memories you get—restless. You'd inevitably seek out Rekal or one of its competitors again. We can't go through this a second time."

"Suppose," Quail said, "once my authentic memories have been cancelled, something more vital than standard memories are implanted. Something which would act to satisfy my craving," he said. "That's been proved; that's probably why you initially hired me. But you ought to be able to come up with something else—something equal. I was the richest man on Terra but I finally gave all my money to educational foundations. Or I was a famous deep-space explorer. Anything of that sort; wouldn't one of those do?"

Silence.

"Try it," he said desperately. "Get some of your top-notch military psychiatrists; explore my mind. Find out what my most expansive day-dream is." He tried to think. "Women," he said. "Thousands of them, like Don Juan had. An interplanetary playboy—a mistress in every city on Earth, Luna and Mars. Only I gave that up, out of exhaustion. Please," he begged. "Try it."

"You'd voluntarily surrender, then?" the voice inside his head asked. "If we agreed to arrange such a solution? *If* it's possible?"

After an interval of hesitation he said, "Yes." I'll take the risk, he said to himself. That you don't simply kill me.

"You make the first move," the voice said presently. "Turn yourself over to us. And we'll investigate that line of possibility. If we can't do it, however, if your authentic memories begin to crop up again as they've done at this time, then—" There was silence and then the voice finished, "We'll have to destroy you. As you must understand. Well, Quail, you still want to try?"

"Yes," he said. Because the alternative was death now—and for certain. At least this way he had a chance, slim as it was.

"You present yourself at our main barracks in New York," the voice of the Interplan cop resumed. "At 580 Fifth Avenue, floor twelve. Once you've surrendered yourself we'll have our psychiatrists begin on you; we'll have personality-profile tests made. We'll attempt to determine your absolute, ultimate fantasy wish—and then we'll bring you back to Rekal, Incorporated, here; get them in on it, fulfilling that wish in vicarious surrogate retrospection. And—good luck. We do owe you something; you acted as a capable instrument for us." The voice lacked malice; if anything, they—the organization—felt sympathy toward him.

"Thanks," Quail said. And began searching for a robot cab.

"Mr. Quail," the stern-faced, elderly Interplan psychiatrist said, "you possess a most interesting wish-fulfillment dream fantasy. Probably nothing such as you consciously entertain or suppose. This is commonly the way; I hope it won't upset you too much to hear about it."

The senior ranking Interplan officer present said briskly, "He better not be too much upset to hear about it, not if he expects not to get shot."

"Unlike the fantasy of wanting to be an Interplan undercover agent," the psychiatrist continued, "which, being relatively speaking a product of maturity, had a certain plausibility to it, this production is a grotesque dream of your childhood; it is no wonder you fail to recall it. Your fantasy is this: you are nine years old, walking alone down a rustic lane. An unfamiliar variety of space vessel from another star system lands directly in front of you. No one on Earth but you, Mr. Quail, sees it. The creatures within are very small and helpless, somewhat on the order of field mice, although they are attempting to invade Earth; tens of thousands of other such ships will soon be on their way, when this advance party gives the go-ahead signal."

"And I suppose I stop them," Quail said, experiencing a mixture of amusement and disgust. "Single-handed I wipe them out. Probably by stepping on them with my foot."

"No," the psychiatrist said patiently. "You halt the invasion, but not by destroying them. Instead, you show them kindness and mercy, even though by telepathy—their mode of communication—you know why they have come. They have never seen such humane traits exhibited by any sentient organism, and to show their appreciation they make a covenant with you."

Quail said, "They won't invade Earth as long as I'm alive."

"Exactly." To the Interplan officer the psychiatrist said, "You can see it does fit his personality, despite his feigned scorn."

"So by merely existing," Quail said, feeling a growing pleasure, "by simply being alive, I keep Earth safe from alien rule. I'm in effect, then, the most important person on Terra. Without lifting a finger."

"Yes indeed, sir," the psychiatrist said. "And this is bedrock in your psyche; this is a life-long childhood fantasy. Which, without depth and drug therapy, you never would have recalled. But it has always existed in you; it went underneath, but never ceased."

To McClane, who sat intently listening, the senior police official said, "Can you implant an extra-factual memory pattern that extreme in him?"

"We get handed every possible type of wish-fantasy there is," McClane said. "Frankly, I've heard a lot worse than this. Certainly we can handle it. Twenty-four hours from now he won't just *wish* he'd saved Earth; he'll devoutly believe it really happened."

The senior police official said, "You can start the job, then. In preparation we've already once again erased the memory in him of his trip to Mars."

Quail said, "What trip to Mars?"

No one answered him, so, reluctantly, he shelved the question. And anyhow a police vehicle had now put in its appearance; he, McClane and the senior police officer crowded into it, and presently they were on their way to Chicago and Rekal, Incorporated.

"You had better make no errors this time," the police officer said to heavy-set, nervous-looking McClane.

"I can't see what could go wrong," McClane mumbled, perspiring. "This has nothing to do with Mars or Interplan. Single-handedly stopping an invasion of Earth from another star-system." He shook his head at that. "Wow, what a kid dreams up. And by pious virtue, too; not by force. It's sort of quaint." He dabbed at his forehead with a large linen pocket handkerchief.

Nobody said anything.

"In fact," McClane said, "it's touching."

"But arrogant," the police official said starkly. "Inasmuch as when he dies the invasion will resume. No wonder he doesn't recall it; it's the most grandiose fantasy I ever ran across." He eyed Quail with disapproval. "And to think we put this man on our payroll."

When they reached Rekal, Incorporated the receptionist, Shirley, met them breathlessly in the outer office. "Welcome back, Mr. Quail," she fluttered, her melon-shaped breasts—today painted an incandescent orange—bobbing with agitation. "I'm sorry everything worked out so badly before; I'm sure this time it'll go better."

Still repeatedly dabbing at his shiny forehead with his neatly-folded Irish linen handkerchief, McClane said, "It better." Moving with rapidity he rounded up Lowe and Keeler, escorted them and Douglas Quail to the work area, and then, with Shirley and the senior police officer, returned to his familiar office. To wait.

"Do we have a packet made up for this, Mr. McClane?" Shirley asked, bumping against him in her agitation, then coloring modestly.

"I think we do." He tried to recall; then gave up and consulted the formal chart. "A combination," he decided aloud, "of packets Eighty-one, Twenty, and Six." From the vault section of the chamber behind his desk he fished out the appropriate packets, carried them to his desk for inspection. "From Eighty-one," he explained, "a magic healing rod given him—the client in question, this time Mr. Quail—by the race of beings from another system. A token of their gratitude."

"Does it work?" the police officer asked curiously.

"It did once," McClane explained. "But he, ahem, you see, used it up years ago, healing right and left. Now it's only a memento. But he remembers it working spectacularly." He chuckled, then opened packet Twenty. "Document from the UN Secretary General thanking him for saving Earth; this isn't precisely appropriate, because part of Quail's fantasy is that no one knows of the invasion except himself, but for the sake of verisimilitude we'll throw it in." He inspected packet Six, then. What came from this? He couldn't recall; frowning, he dug into the plastic bag as Shirley and the Interplan police officer watched intently.

"Writing," Shirley said. "In a funny language."

"This tells who they were," McClane said, "and where they came from. Including a detailed star map logging their flight here and the system of origin. Of course it's in *their* script, so he can't read it. But he remembers them reading it to him in his own tongue." He placed the three artifacts in the center of the desk. "These should be taken to Quail's conapt," he said to the police officer. "So that when he gets home he'll find them. And it'll confirm his fantasy. SOP—standard operating procedure." He chuckled apprehensively, wondering how matters were going with Lowe and Keeler.

The intercom buzzed. "Mr. McClane, I'm sorry to bother you." It was Lowe's voice; he froze as he recognized it, froze and became mute. "But something's come up. Maybe it would be better if you came in here and supervised. Like before, Quail reacted well to the narkidrine; he's unconscious, relaxed and receptive. But—"

McClane sprinted for the work area.

On a hygienic bed Douglas Quail lay breathing slowly and regularly, eyes half-shut, dimly conscious of those around him.

"We started interrogating him," Lowe said, white-faced. "To find out exactly when to place the fantasy-memory of him single-handedly having saved Earth. And strangely enough—"

"They told me not to tell," Douglas Quail mumbled in a dull drug-saturated voice. "That was the agreement. I wasn't even supposed to remember. But how could I forget an event like that?"

I guess it would be hard, McClane reflected. But you did—until now.

"They even gave me a scroll," Quail mumbled, "of gratitude. I have it hidden in my conapt; I'll show it to you."

To the Interplan officer who had followed after him, McClane said, "Well, I offer the suggestion that you better not kill him. If you do they'll return."

"They also gave me a magic invisible destroying rod," Quail mumbled, eyes totally shut, now. "That's how I killed that man on Mars you sent me to take out. It's in my drawer along with the box of Martian maw-worms and dried-up plant life."

Wordlessly, the Interplan officer turned and stalked from the work area.

I might as well put those packets of proof-artifacts away, McClane said to himself resignedly. He walked, step by step, back to his office. Including the citation from the UN Secretary General. After all—

The real one probably would not be long in coming.

Selectra Six-Ten
Avram Davidson

His Honor the Ed., F&SF
Dear Ed:
Well, whilst sorry that you didn't feel BELINDA
BEESWAX didn't exactly and immediately leap up and
wrap her warm, white (or, in this case, <u>cold</u>) arms
around you, so to speak, nevertheless I am bound to
admit that your suggestions for its revision don't
altogether seem difficult or unreasonable. Though,
mind you, it is against my moral principles to admit
this to any editor. Even you. However. This once.
I'll do, I think I shd be able to do the rewrites
quite soonly, and whip them off to you with the
speed of light. At least, the speed of whatever dim
light it is which filters through the window of our
local Post Office and its 87,000 friendly branches
throughout the country.

AVRAM DAVIDSON, *this field's most distinctive writer of short fiction,
was editor of F&SF for several years in the early 1960s, and he taught
me a lot about appreciating fiction. After I succeeded him as editor, he
sent me a story that I loved, but I asked for some changes on it before
taking it on. He made the changes and returned the story to his agent,
who promptly sold it to another market. Avram sent me this story instead; it appeared in the October 1970 issue.*

By the way, excuse absence of mrag, or even marger
Oh you would would you. Take that. And THAT.
AND THSTHATHAT. har har, he laughed harshly. The
lack of m a r g i n s. There. I have just gotten a
new tripewriter; viz an Selectra Six-Ten, with
Automated Carriage
Return
Return
Return
hahahaHA! I can't resist it, just impress the tab
and without sweat or indeed evidence of
labor of any swort, or sort, whatsoever,
ZING.
RETURN! You will excsuse me, won't you? There I
knew you would. A wild lad, Master Edward, I sez
to the Gaffer, I sez, but lor blesse zur its just
hanimal sperrits, at art h's a good lad, I sez.
WELL. Enough of this lollygagging ansd skylarking
Ferman. I am a WORKING WROTER and so to business.
Although, mind ewe, with this Device it seems more
like play. It hums and clicks and buzzes whilst
I am congor even cog cog cog got it now? gooood.
cogitating. very helpful to thought. Soothing. So.
WHERE we was. Yus. BELINDA BEESWAX. Soonly. I
haven't forgotten that advance I got six years ago
when ny wife had the grout. Anxious to please.
(Tugs forelock. Exit, pursued by a
Your Seruant to Command,
Avram

Eddy dear;
I mean, of course, Mr. Ferman Sir. Or is it now
Squire Ferman, with you off in the moors and crags
of Cornwall Connecticut. Sounds very Jamaica Inn,
Daphne Du Maurieresque. I can see you on wild and
stormy nights, muffled to your purple ears in your
cloak and shawl, going out on the rocky headlands
with False Lights to decoy the Fall River Line

vessels, or even the Late After-Theater Special of
the New York, New Haven, and Hartburn, onto
the Rocks. And the angry rocks they gored her
sides/Like the horns of an angry bull. Zounds they
don't indite Poerty like that anymore. I mean,
I don't have to tell you, ethn ethic pride, all
very well, enthic? e t h n i c, there, THAT wasn't
hard, was it deary? Noooo. Now you can ahve a piece
of treacle. Where was I. I mean, my grandfather
was a was a, well, acttually, no, he WAS n 't a Big
Rabbi In The Old Country, he drove a laundry wagon
in Yonkers, N.Y., but what Imeantosayis: "Over the
rocks and the foaming brine/They burned the wreck
of the Palatine "--can ALAN GUINZBURG write poetry
like that? No. Fair is fair.
Zippetty-ping. Kerriage Return. Automatic. Whheee!
After all Ed I have known you a very long time,
that time your old girl friend, the one you hired to
read Manuscripts, you remember? Nuf sed. And I know
you have only my own welfare at heart. Right? Right.
So you wouldn't be angry when I explain that Igot
the idea, whilst triping on my new tripewriter, that
if I carried out your nifty keen suggestions for
the rewrite of my BELINDA BEESWAX story, that would
drolly enough convert it into a Crime Story, as well
as F and SF. Just for the fun of it, then, I
couldn't resist sharyimg or even s h a r i n g, my
amusement at this droll conceit with Santiago
Ap Popkin, the editor over at QUENTIN QUEELEY's
MYSTERY MUSEUM. But evidentially I wasn't as clear
in my explanations as I should have been. Fingers
just ran away with themselves, laughing and
giggling over their shoulders (well, knuckles. be
pedantic), down the pike. ANYhow, Caligula Fitz-
Bumpkin somehow misunderstood. He is not, I mean we
must simply Face these things, and Seneca Mac Zipnick
is just NOT/ very bright. He, do you know what
simpleton did? this will hand yez a real alugh,*Ed:

Guy sent a check. Thought I was offering the story
to him. Boob. A doltish fellowe, Constantine O'Kaplan.
But, well, Ed, put yourself in my position. Could I
embarass the boy? Bring a blush to those downy
cheeks? Nohohohoho.
Well Ed it's just one of those things that we have
to face as we go through life: and the fact that
QQMM happens to pay four or is it five times what
F&SF pays, has got simply nothing to do with it.
Avile canard, and that's that.
However, I have not forgotten that advance
the time I was in Debtors Prison. And I will,
I will, promise you now NOW, I''l sit down at my
merry chuckling Selectra Six-Ten, and write
you a real sockadaol sok?dolager of a Science
Fiction story. VISCIOUS TERRESTRIAL BIPED
xxxxxxxxxxxxxxxXXXXXXXXXX ZZZZZZZzzzznnngfhfghhhBZZZ
blurtle blep ha ha, well, perhaps not quite
along those lines. Zo. So
"Forgiven"?
Thine ever so
Avram

Dear Ed:
Well, you mehk me sheahme, mahn, the way you have
forgiven me for that peculiar contretemps anent
BELINDA BEESWAX's going to the QUENTIN QUEELEY's
MYSTERY MUSEUM people instead. That yuck, Gerardo A
Klutskas. Anyway, I have really been sticking to
my last, tappetty-tapp. "Tap". ZWWWWEEPPP! Cling.
It's a veritable psychodrama of Semi-Outer Space.
XXXXXXXXXnnnnnggggg llullrp prurp plup ZZZZBBGGGgnn
INTELLIGENT NONCHITINOUS BIPED ATTEND ATTEND ATTEND
ATTEND haha it's always fun and games with this new
Selectra Six-Ten, clicketty-cluch, hmble-hmble-
hmble-hmble. Just you should drip by you the mouth,

---

*or "laugh", as some have it.--Ibid.

so enclosed is a couple pp of the first draft.
draught. drocht Spell it can't, not for sour owl
stools, but leave us remember the circumstances
under which it grew to maturity. More to be piddled
than centered. You like, huh? Huh? Huh . Thass whut
I thought. XXXxxZZZZzzzzxxxxngngngn clurkle cluhnkle
NOCHITINOUS BIFRU BIFURCATE ATTEND ATTEND ATTEND.
Agreat line, hey? Arrests you with its like
remorseless sweep, doesn't it? Well well,
back to the saline cavern
Love and kisses,
Avram

Dear ED:
See, I knew you would enjoy LOADSTAR EXPRESS.
Even the first draft gripped you like ursus
somethingorothera, didn't it? Yes. True, it was
rather rough. Amorphous, as you might say. But I
was going to take care of that anyway. Yesyes I
had that rough spot, pp 3-to-4 well in mind.
I admit that I hsdn't a hadn't exactly planned to do
it the way you tentatively suggest. But. Since you
do. It would be as well that way as any other.
Blush, chuckle. Not exactly what one would formerly
have considered for the pp of a family, or even
a Family Magazine. Tempura o mores, what? However.
WHY N T? XXXXXxxxx====ZZZZZzzzz bgbgbgbngngngn
bluggabluggablugga TATATA TA TA AT ATT AT ATTEND
ATTEND ATTEND TERRESTRIOUS BIFURCATE NONCHERIDER-
MATIC XXXNN FASCIST AGGRESSIVE BIPED goddam Must
quit reading alla them student Undrground Wellhung
Classified Revolt Papers. To work work WORK toil
"With fingers weary and worn, with eyelids heavy and
red/ Awoman sat in unwomanly rags, mumbling a crust
of bread." Can Laurence Ferlinghetti write lines
like that? Can Richard Gumbeiner? It is to laugh.
Anon, sir, anon. We Never Forget . Advances
advanced to us in our hour od Need, earned eternal

gratichude. clicketty-clunck.
Industrously, <u>Avram</u>

Dear Edward:
WowWowWOW! WOW-WOW/WOWW'. !gotcha at alst)) Ignore.
Confused by Joy. BUNNYBOY. B U N N Y B O Y, hippetty
goddam <u>HOP</u>, B*U*N*N*N*Y*B*O*Y* M*A*G*A*Z*I*N*E*.
You got that? Educational & Literary Compendium?
With the big tzitzkas? Tha-hats the one. <u>Bunnyboy</u>
Magazine has bumped a burse of bold, gumped a
gurse of XXXXXXX xHa xHa xHa bgnbgn of gold,
dumped a purse of gold in my lap. I kid y ou not.
NOT NOT. "Not." He adumbrated hilarriously.
EXPLOITIVE DIOXIDIFEROUS BIPEDS ah cummon now,
cumMON. Shhest, I hardly know what to say, and this
Selectra Six-Ten, elecrtified wit and terror, never
but <u>never</u> a case of The DULL LINE LABOURS, AND
THE WHEEL TURNS SLOW, goes faster than my MIND, my
mind is BLOWN, out through both ears, walls all
plastered with brain tissue.
Carriage return. When in doubt. Carstairs Macanley,
formerly of <u>Midland Review</u>, to which I sold,
years ago--but you don't want to hear about that,
anyway he is now and has been for some time past
Fiction Editor of <u>Bunnyboy</u> . So whilst making with
the clicketty-clack and addressing the MS of
LOADSTAR EXPRESS, I H happened to be thinking of
him, and just for kicks, you know, Ed,I mean, YOU.
Know <u>me</u>. Ed. Just abig, overgrown kid. So just for
k.i.c.k.s., I absentmindedly addressed it to him.
Laughed like a son of a gun' when I found out what
I'd done. And had already stamped the manila!
"Well . . ." (I figured) "I'll send it to good old
Ed at F&SF soons as Carstairs Macanley returns it.
Just to let him see what <u>I</u>'m doing these days.
Ed, you have never wished me nothing but good, Ed,
from the very first day we met, Ed, and I know that
the last thing on your pure, sweet mind, i would be

that I return the money to Bunyboy, and, besides, I
am almost 100% sure it's already in type: and we
could hardly expect them to yank it. You're a pro
yourself, Ed. But don't think for aminute, Eddy,
that I've got abig head and/or have forgotten that
advance you so, well, tenderly is really the only--
And, Ed, any time you're out on the West Coast,
just any time at all, night or day, give me a ring,
and we'll go out for dinner somewhere. "A Hot bird
and a cold bottle", eh Ed? Hows that b grabg bgrarg
XXXxx TREACHEROUS BgN BgN bGN TERCH XXXXXzzZZZ bgn
bgn bgn TREACHEROUS AMBULATORY TERRESTRIAL AGGRES-
SIVE BIPED ATTEND ATTNEDNA Attn bgna bgn cluck.
Please excuse my high spirits, my head is just
buzzing and clicking right now, Inever SAW such a
C*E*C*K in my L I F E L I F E in my life. Hey, Ed,
I could offer to rewrite the story for Bunnyboy
leaving out the parts you suggested, but I don't
think it would be right to deprive you of the
pleasure of seiing them in print. Wait for the
story. I"ll do you something else sometime.
Right now I'm going out and buy the biggest can of
typewriter cleaning fluid anybody ever saw WE
EXSALIVATE ON YOUR PROFFERED BRIBES EXPLOITIVE
TERCHEOROSE TERRESTRIAL BIPED AGGRESSIVE NONCHERO-
DERMATOID BIPED LANDING YOUR PLANETARY-RAPING PROBE
MODULEWS ON THE SACRED CHITIN OF OUR MOTHER-
WORLD FASCISTICLY TERMED "MOOM" XXXZZZZBGN BGN BGN
BGN BGN BGN IGNORING OUR JUST LONG-REPRESSED PLEAS
FOR YOUR ATTEND ATTE ND ATTEnD OHmigod
ed oh ed my god i i oh
e
d
e
d
o
bgna bgna bgna bgna bgna bgna bgna bgna bgna bgna
bpur bpur bpur bpur bpur bpur bpur bpur bpur BURP

Dance Music
for a Gone Planet
Sonya Dorman

Snow fills the treadmarks where
the General's tank foundered.
A prime Minister stretches
his neck from the wall,
eyes leaking glass.
Tissue thin,
paper of roses peels,
quilts open into blizzards
while we crank up the dark machine
and dance until the parquet shrieks.
The excavators smile
with iron teeth and eat the bricks;
we put another record on.
One day our sons will rummage
in this dump and rig
a new dance hall.

Problems of Creativeness

Thomas M. Disch

THERE WAS A DULL ACHE, a kind of hollowness, in the general area of his liver, the seat of the intelligence according to the *Psychology* of Aristotle—a feeling that there was someone inside his chest blowing up a balloon, or that the balloon was his body. Sometimes he could ignore it, but sometimes he could not ignore it. It was like a swollen gum that he must incessantly probe with his tongue or finger. Perhaps it was filled with pus. It was like being sick, but it was different too. His legs ached from sitting.

Professor Offengeld was telling them about Dante. Dante was born in 1265. *1265,* he wrote in his notebook.

He might have felt the same way even if it weren't for Milly's coldness, but that made it worse. Milly was his girl, and they were in love, but for the last three nights she had been putting him off, telling him he should study or some other dumb excuse.

Professor Offengeld made a joke, and the other students in the auditorium laughed. Birdie ostentatiously stretched his legs out into the aisle and yawned.

"PROBLEMS OF CREATIVENESS" *was published in the April 1967 issue. It went on, in somewhat metamorphosed form, to become "The Death of Socrates" in Thomas Disch's novel entitled* 334. *Mr. Disch has been a regular contributor to F&SF since 1964. His best-known novels include* Camp Concentration *and, most recently,* On Wings of Song.

"The hell that Dante describes is the hell that each of us holds inside his own, most secret soul," Offengeld said solemnly.

Shit, he thought to himself. It's all a pile of shit. He wrote *Shit* in his notebook, then made the letters look three dimensional and shaded their sides carefully.

Offengeld was telling them about Florence now, and about the Popes and things. "What is simony?" Offengeld asked.

He was listening, but it didn't make any sense. Actually he wasn't listening. He was trying to draw Milly's face in his notebook, but he couldn't draw very well. Except skulls. He could draw very convincing skulls. Maybe he should have gone to art school. He turned Milly's face into a skull with long blond hair. He felt sick.

He felt sick to his stomach. Maybe it was the Synthamon bar he had had in place of a hot lunch. He didn't eat a balanced diet. That was a mistake. For over two years he had been eating in cafeterias and sleeping in dorms. Ever since high school graduation in fact. It was a hell of a way to live. He needed a home life, regularity. He needed to get laid. When he married Milly they were going to have twin beds. They'd have a two-room apartment all their own, and one room would just have beds in it. Nothing but two beds. He imagined Milly in her spiffy little hostess uniform, and then he began undressing her in his imagination. He closed his eyes. First he took off her jacket with the Pan-Am monogram over the right breast. Then he popped open the snap at her waist and unzipped the zipper. He slid the skirt down over the smooth Antron slip. The slip was the old-fashioned kind with lace along the hem. Her blouse was the old-fashioned kind with buttons. It was hard to imagine unbuttoning all those buttons. He lost interest.

The carnal were in the first circle, because their sin was least. Francesca de Rimini. Cleopatra. Elizabeth Taylor. The class laughed at Offengeld's little joke. They all knew Elizabeth Taylor from the junior year course in the History of Cinema.

Rimini was a town in Italy.

What the hell was he supposed to care about this kind of crap? Who *cares* when Dante was born? Maybe he was *never* born. What difference did it make to *him*, to Birdie Ludd?

None.

Why didn't he come right out and ask Offengeld a question like that? Lay it on the line. Put it to him straight. Cut out the crap.

One good reason was because Offengeld wasn't there. What seemed to be Offengeld was in fact a flux of photons inside a large synthetic crystal. The real flesh-and-blood Offengeld had died two years ago. During his lifetime Offengeld had been considered the world's leading Dantean, which was why the National Educational Council was still using his tapes.

It was ridiculous: Dante, Florence, the Simoniac Popes. This wasn't the goddamn Middle Ages. This was the goddamn 21st Century, and he was Birdie Ludd, and he was in love, and he was lonely, and he was unemployed, and there wasn't a thing he could do, not a goddamn thing, or a single place to turn in the whole goddamn stinking country.

The hollow feeling inside his chest swelled, and he tried to think about the buttons on Milly's imaginary blouse and the warm, familiar flesh beneath. He did feel sick. He ripped the sheet with the skull on it out of his notebook, not without a guilty glance at the sign that hung above the stage of the auditorium: PAPER IS VALUABLE. DON'T WASTE IT. He folded it in half and tore it neatly down the seam. He repeated this process until the pieces were too small to tear any further, then he put them in his shirt pocket.

The girl sitting beside him was giving him a dirty look for wasting paper. Like most homely girls, she was a militant Conservationist, but she kept a good notebook, and Birdie was counting on her to get him through the Finals. One way or another. So he smiled at her. He had a real nice smile. Everybody was always pointing out what a nice smile he had. His only real problem was his nose, which was short.

Professor Offengeld said: "And now we will have a short comprehension test. Please close your notebooks and put them under your seats." Then he faded away, and the auditorium lights came on. A taped voice automatically boomed out: *No talking please!* Four old Negro monitors began distributing the little answer sheets to the five hundred students in the auditorium.

The lights dimmed, and the first Multiple Choice appeared on the screen:

1. Dante Alighieri was born in (a) 1300 (b) 1265 (c) 1625 (d) Date unknown.

As far as Birdie was concerned the date was unknown. The dog in the seat beside him was covering up her answers. So, when was Dante born? He'd written the date in his notebook, but he didn't remember now. He looked back at the four choices, but the second question was on the screen already. He scratched a mark in the (c) space and then erased it, feeling an obscure sense of unluckiness in the choice, but finally he checked that space anyhow. When he looked up the fourth question was on the screen.

The answers he had to choose from were all wop names he'd never heard of. The goddamn test didn't make any sense. Disgusted, he marked (c) for every question and carried his test paper to the monitor at the front of the room. The monitor told him he couldn't leave the room till the test was over. He sat in the dark and tried to think of Milly. Something was all wrong, but he didn't know what. The bell rang. Everyone breathed a sigh of relief.

334 East 11th Street was one of twenty identical buildings built in the early 1980's under the Federal Government's first MODICUM program. Each building was 21 stories high (one floor for shops, the rest for apartments); each floor was swastika-shaped; each of the arms of the swastikas opened onto four 3-room apartments (for couples with children) and six 2-room apartments (for childless couples). Thus each building was able to accommodate 2,240 occupants without overcrowding. The entire development, occupying an area of less than six city blocks, housed a population of 44,800. It had been an incredible accomplishment for its time.

SHADDUP, someone, a man, was yelling into the airshaft of 334 East 11th Street. WHY CAN'T YOU ALL SHADDUP? It was half past seven, and the man had been yelling into the airshaft for forty-five minutes already, ever since returning from his day's work (three hours' bussing dishes at a cafeteria). It was difficult to tell whom precisely he was yelling at. In one apartment a woman was yelling at a man, WHADAYA MEAN, TWENTY DOLLARS? And the man would yell back, TWENTY DOLLARS, THAT'S WHAT I MEAN! Numerous babies made noises of dissatisfaction, and older children made louder noises as they played guerrilla warfare in the corridors. Birdie, sitting on the steps of the stairwell, could see, on the floor below, a thirteen-year-old Negro girl dancing in place in front of a dresser mirror, singing along with the transistor radio that she pressed into the shallow declivity of her pubescent breasts. I CAN'T TELL YOU HOW *MUCH* I LOVE HIM, the radio sang at full volume. It was not a song that Birdie Ludd greatly admired, though it *was* Number Three in the Nation, and that meant something. She had a pretty little ass, and Birdie thought she was going to shake the tinselly fringes right off her street shorts. He tried to open the narrow window that looked from the stairwell out into the airshaft, but it was stuck tight. His hands came away covered with soot. He cursed mildly. I CAN'T HEAR MYSELF THINK, the man yelled into the airshaft.

Hearing someone coming up the steps, Birdie sat back down and pretended to read his schoolbook. He thought it might be Milly (whoever it was was wearing heels), and a lump began to form in his throat. If it were Milly, what would he say to her?

It wasn't Milly. It was just some old lady lugging a bag of groceries. She stopped at the landing below him, leaning against the handrail for support, sighed, and set down her grocery bag. She stuck a pink stick of Oraline between her flaccid lips, and after a few seconds it got to her and she smiled at Birdie. Birdie scowled down at the bad reproduction of David's *Death of Socrates* in his text.

"Studying?" the old woman asked.

"Yeah, that's what I'm doing all right. I'm studying."

"That's good." She took the tranquilizer out of her mouth, holding it like a cigarette between her index and middle fingers. Her smile broadened, as though she were elaborating some joke, honing it to a fine edge.

"It's good for a young man to study," she said at last, almost chuckling.

The tune on the radio changed to the new Ford commercial. It was one of Birdie's favorite commercials, and he wished the old bag would shut up so he could hear it.

"You can't get anywheres these days without studying."

Birdie made no reply. The old woman took a different tack. "These stairs," she said.

Birdie looked up from his book, peeved. "What about them?"

"What about them! The elevators have been out of commission for three weeks. That's what about them—three weeks!"

"So?"

"So, why don't they fix the elevators? But you just try to call up the MODICUM office and get an answer to a question like that and see what happens. Nothing—that's what happens!"

He wanted to tell her to can it. She was spoiling the commercial. Besides, she talked like she'd spent all her life in a private building instead of some crummy MODICUM slum. It had probably been years, not weeks, since the elevators in this building had been working.

With a look of disgust, he slid over to one side of the step so the old lady could get past him. She walked up three steps till her face was just level with his. She smelled of beer and Synthamon and old age. He hated old people. He hated their wrinkled faces and the touch of their cold dry flesh. It was because there were so many *old* people that Birdie Ludd couldn't get married to the girl he loved and have a baby. It was a goddamned shame.

"What are you studying about?"

Birdie glanced down at the painting. He read the caption, which he had not read before. "That's Socrates," he said, remembering dimly something his Art History teacher had said about Socrates. "It's a painting," he explained, "a Greek painting."

"You going to be an artist? Or what?"

"What," Birdie replied curtly.

"You're Milly Holt's steady boy, aren't you?" He didn't reply. "You waiting for Milly tonight?"

"Is there any law against waiting for someone?"

The old lady laughed right in his face. Then she made her way from step to step up to the next landing. Birdie tried not to turn around to look after her, but he couldn't help himself. They looked into each other's eyes, and she laughed again. Finally he had to ask her what she was laughing about. "Is there a law against laughing?" she asked right back. Her laughing grew harsher and turned into a hacking cough, like in a Health Education movie about the dangers of smoking. He wondered if maybe she was an addict. Birdie knew lots of men who used tobacco, but somehow it seemed disgusting in a woman.

Several floors below there was the sound of glass shattering. Birdie looked down the abyss of the stairwell. He could see a hand moving up the railing. Maybe it was Milly's hand. The fingers were slim, as Milly's fingers would be, and the nails seemed to be painted gold. In the dim light of the stairwell, at this distance, it was difficult to tell. A sudden ache of unbelieving hope made him forget the woman's laughter, the stench of garbage, the screaming. The stairwell became a scene of romance, like a show on television.

People had always told him Milly was pretty enough to be an actress. He wouldn't have been so bad-looking himself, if it weren't for his nose. He imagined how she would cry out "Birdie!" when she saw him waiting for her, how they would kiss, how she would take him into her mother's apartment . . .

At the eleventh or twelfth floor the hand left the railing and did not reappear. It hadn't been Milly after all.

He looked at his guaranteed Timex watch. It was eight o'clock. He could afford to wait two more hours for Milly. Then he would have to take the subway back to his dorm, an hour's ride. If he hadn't been put on probation because of his grades, he would have waited all night long.

He sat down to study Art History. He stared at the picture of Socrates in the bad light. With one hand he was holding a big cup; with the other he was giving somebody the finger. He didn't seem to be dying at all. His Midterm in Art History was going to be tomorrow afternoon at two o'clock. He really had to study. He stared at the picture more intently. Why did people paint pictures anyhow? He stared until his eyes hurt.

Somewhere a baby was crying. SHADDUP, WHY DON'T YA SHADDUP? ARE YA CRAZY OR SOMETHIN? A gang of kids impersonating Burmese nationals ran down the stairs, and a minute later another gang (U.S. guerrillas) ran down after them, screaming obscenities.

Staring at the picture in the bad light, he began to cry. He was certain, though he would not yet admit it in words, that Milly was cheating on him. He loved Milly so much; she was so beautiful. The last time he had seen her she'd called him stupid. "You're so stupid," she said, "you make me sick." But she was so beautiful.

A tear fell into Socrates' cup and was absorbed by the cheap paper of the text. The radio started to play a new commercial. Gradually he got hold of himself again. He had to buckle down and study, goddamnit!

Who in hell was Socrates?

Birdie Ludd's father was a fat man with a small chin and a short nose like Birdie's. Since his wife's death he'd lived by himself in a MODICUM dorm for elderly gentlemen, where Birdie visited him once a month. They never had anything to talk about, but the MODICUM people insisted that families should stick together. Family life was the single greatest cohesive force in any society. They'd meet in the Visitor's Room, and if either of them had gotten letters from Birdie's brothers or sisters they'd talk about that, and then they might watch some television (especially if there was baseball, for Mr. Ludd was a Yankee fan), and then right before he left, Birdie's father would hit him for five or ten dollars, since the allowance he got from MODICUM wasn't enough to keep him supplied with Thorazine. Birdie, of course, never had anything to spare.

Whenever Birdie visited his father, he was reminded of Mr. Mack. Mr. Mack had been Birdie's guidance counsellor in senior year at P.S.

125, and as such he had played a much more central role in Birdie's life than his father had. He was a balding, middle-aged man with a belly as big as Mr. Ludd's and a Jewish-type nose. Birdie had always had the feeling that the counsellor was toying with him, that his professional blandness was a disguise for an unbounded contempt, that all his good advice was a snare. The pity was that Birdie could not, in his very nature, help but be caught up in it. It was Mr. Mack's game and had to be played by his rules.

Actually Mr. Mack had felt a certain cool sympathy for Birdie Ludd. Of the various students who'd failed their REGENTS, Birdie was certainly the most attractive. He never became violent or rude in interviews, and he always seemed to want so hard to *try.* "In fact," Mr. Mack had told his wife in confidence one evening (she was an educational counsellor herself), "I think this is a splendid example of the basic inequity of the system. Because that boy is *basically* decent."

"Oh *you,*" she'd replied. "Basically, you're just an old softie."

And, in fact, Birdie's case was not that exceptional. Congress had passed the Revised Genetic Testing Act (or REGENTS, as they were known popularly) in 2011, seven years before Birdie turned eighteen and had to take them. By that time the agitation and protests were over, and the system seemed to be running smoothly. Population figures had held steady since 2014.

By contrast, the first Genetic Testing Act (of 1998) had altogether failed its hoped for effect. This act had merely specified that such obvious genetic undesirables as diabetics, the criminally insane, and morons were not to be allowed the privilege of reproducing their kind. They were also denied suffrage. The act of 1998 had met virtually no opposition, and it had been easy to implement, since by that time civic contraception techniques were practiced everywhere but in the most benightedly rural areas. The chief, though unstated, purpose of the Act of 1998 had been to pave the way for the REGENTS system.

The REGENTS were tripartite: there was the familiar Stanford-Binet intelligence test (short form); the Skinner-Waxman Test for Creative Potential (which consisted in large part of picking the punch lines for jokes on a multiple choice test); and the O'Ryan-Army physical performance and metabolism test. Candidates failed if they received scores that fell below one standard deviation in two of the three tests. Birdie Ludd had been nervous on the day of his REGENTS (it was Friday the 13th, for Christ's sake!), and right in the middle of the Skinner-Waxman a sparrow flew into the auditorium and made a hell of a racket so that Birdie couldn't concentrate. He hadn't been at all surprised to find that he'd failed the I.Q. test and the Skinner-Waxman. On the physical Birdie got a score of 100 (the modal point, or peak, of the normal curve), which made him feel pretty proud.

Birdie didn't really believe in failure, not as a permanent condition. He had failed third grade, but had that kept him from graduating high school? The important thing to remember, as Mr. Mack had pointed out to Birdie and the 107 other failed candidates at a special assembly, was that failure was just a point-of-view. A positive point-of-view and self-confidence would solve most problems. Birdie had really believed him then, and he'd signed up to be retested at the big downtown office of the Health, Education, and Welfare Agency. This time he really crammed. He bought *How You Can Add 20 Points to Your I.Q.* by L. C. Wedgewood, Ph.D. (who appeared on the bookjacket in an old-fashioned suit with lapels and buttons) and *Your REGENTS Exams,* prepared by the National Educational Council. The latter book had a dozen sample tests, and Birdie worked all the easy problems in each test (the only part that really counted, the book explained, were the first thirty questions; the last thirty were strictly for the junior geniuses). By the day of the retesting, Birdie had a positive point-of-view and lots of self-confidence.

But the tests were all wrong. They weren't at all what he'd studied up on. For the I.Q. part of the test he sat in a stuffy cubicle with some old lady with a black dress and repeated telephone numbers after her, forward and backward. With the Area Code! Then she showed him different pictures, and he had to tell her what was wrong with them. Usually nothing was wrong. It went on like that for over an hour.

The creativity test was even weirder. They gave him a pair of pliers and took him into an empty room. Two pieces of string were hanging down from the ceiling. Birdie was supposed to tie the two strings together.

It was impossible. If you held the very end of one string in one hand, it was still too short, by a couple feet, to reach the other string. Even if you held the tip of the string in the pliers, it was too short. He tried it a dozen times, and it never worked. He was about ready to scream when he left that room. There were three more crazy problems like that, but he hardly even tried to solve them. It was impossible.

Afterwards somebody told him he should have tied the pliers to the end of the string and set it swinging like a pendulum. Then he could have gone over and got the string, come back with it, and *caught* the string that was swinging like a pendulum. But then why had they given him *pliers!*

That bit with the pliers really made him angry. But what could he do about it? Nothing. Who could he complain to? Nobody. He complained to Mr. Mack, who promised to do everything in his power to help Birdie be reclassified. The important thing to remember was that failure was just a negative attitude. Birdie had to think positively and learn to help himself. Mr. Mack suggested that Birdie go to college.

At that time college had been the last thing Birdie Ludd had in mind for himself. He wanted to *relax* after the strain of P.S. 125. Birdie wasn't the college *type*. He wasn't anybody's fool, but on the other hand he didn't pretend to be some goddamn brain. Mr. Mack had pointed out that 73% of all high school graduates went on to college and that three-quarters of all college freshmen went on to take their degrees.

Birdie's reply had been, "Yeah, but . . ." He couldn't say what he was thinking; that Mack himself was just another goddamn brain and that of course *he* couldn't understand the way Birdie felt about college.

"You must remember, Birdie, that this is more now than a question of your educational goals. If you'd received high enough scores on the REGENTS you could drop out of school right now and get married and sign up for a MODICUM salary. Assuming that you had no more ambition than that . . ."

After a glum and weighty silence, Mr. Mack switched from scolding to cajoling: "You do want to get married don't you?"

"Yeah, but . . ."

"And have children?"

"Yeah, of course, but . . ."

"Then it seems to *me* that college is your best bet, Birdie. You've taken your REGENTS and failed. You've taken the reclassification tests and gotten *lower* scores there than on the REGENTS. There are only three possibilities open after that. Either you perform an exceptional service for the country or the national economy, which is hardly something one can count on doing. Or else you demonstrate physical, intellectual, or creative abilities markedly above the level shown in the REGENTS test or tests you failed, which again poses certain problems. Or *else* you get a B.A. That certainly seems to be the easiest way, Birdie. Perhaps the only way."

"I suppose you're right."

Mr. Mack smiled a smile of greasy satisfaction and adjusted his massive stomach above his too-tight belt. Birdie wondered spitefully what sort of score Mack would have got on the O'Ryan-Army fitness test. Probably not 100.

"Now as far as money goes," Mack went on, opening Birdie's career file, "you won't have to be concerned over that. As long as you keep a C average, you can get a New York State Loan, at the very least. I assume your parents will be unable to help out?"

Birdie nodded. Mr. Mack handed him the loan application form.

"A college education is the right of every United States citizen, Birdie. But if we fail to exercise our rights, we have only ourselves to blame. There's no excuse today for not going to college."

So Birdie Ludd, lacking an excuse, had gone to college. From the very first, he had felt as though it were all a trap. A puzzle with a trick solution, and everyone had been shown the trick except Birdie. A labyrinth that others could enter and depart from at will, but whenever Birdie tried to get out, no matter which way he turned, it always led him back to the same dead end.

But what choice did he have? He was in love.

On the morning of the day of his Art History test Birdie lay in bed in the empty dorm, drowsing and thinking of his truelove. He couldn't quite sleep, but he didn't want to get up yet either. His body was bursting with untapped energies, it overflowed with the wine of youth, but those energies could not be spent brushing his teeth and going down to breakfast. Come to think of it, it was too late for breakfast. He was happy right here.

Sunlight spilled in through the south window. A breeze rustled the curtain. Birdie laughed from a sense of his own fullness. He turned over onto his left side and looked out the window at a perfect blue rectangle of sky. Beautiful. It was March, but it seemed more like April or May. It was going to be a wonderful day. He could feel it in his bones.

The way the breeze blew the curtain made him think of last summer, the lake breeze in Milly's hair. They had gone away for a weekend to Lake Hopatcong in New Jersey. They found a grassy spot not far from the shore but screened from the view of bathers by a windbreak of trees, and there they had made love almost the entire afternoon. Afterwards they just lay side by side, their heads reclining in the prickly grass, looking into each other's eyes. Milly's eyes were hazel flecked with gold. His were the blue of a cloudless sky. Wisps of her hair, soft and unmanageable after the morning swim, blew across her face. Birdie thought she was the most beautiful girl in the world. When he told her that she just smiled. Her lips had been so soft. She had not said one cruel thing.

He remembered kissing her. Her lips. He closed his eyes, to remember better.

"I love you so much, Birdie, so terribly *much*." She had said that to him. And he loved her too. More than anything in the world. Didn't she know that? Had she forgotten?

"I'll do anything for you," he said aloud in the empty dorm.

She smiled. She whispered into his ear, and he could feel her lips against his earlobe. "Just one thing, Birdie. I only ask one thing. You know what that is."

"I know, I know." He tried to twist his head around to silence her with a kiss, but she held it firmly between her two hands.

"Get reclassified." It sounded almost cruel, but then she had let him go, and when he looked into her golden eyes again he could see no cruelty, only love.

"I want to have a baby, darling. Yours and mine. I want us to be married and have our own apartment and a baby. I'm sick of living with my mother. I want to be your wife. I'm sick of my job. I only want what every woman wants. Birdie, please."

"I'm trying. Aren't I trying? I'm going to school. Next year I'll be a junior. The year after that I'll be a senior. Then I'll have my degree. And then I'll be reclassified. We'll get married the same day." He looked at her with his wounded-puppydog look, which usually stopped all her arguments.

The clock on the wall of the dorm said it was 11:07. *This will be my lucky day,* Birdie promised himself. He threw himself out of bed and did ten pushups on the linoleum floor, which somehow never seemed to get dirty, though Birdie had never seen anyone cleaning it. Birdie couldn't push himself up from the last pushup, so he just rested there on the floor, his lips pressed against the cool linoleum.

He got up and sat on the edge of the unmade bed, watching the white curtain blow in the wind. He thought of Milly, his own dear beautiful lovely Milly. He wanted to marry her *now*. No matter what his genetic classification was. If she really loved him, that shouldn't make any difference. But he knew he was doing the right thing by waiting. He knew that haste was foolish. He knew, certainly, that Milly would have it no other way. Immediately after he'd failed the reclassification test, he had tried to persuade her to take a refertility pill that he had bought on the black market for twenty dollars. The pill counteracted the contraceptive agent in the city water.

"Are you crazy?" she shouted at him. "Are you off your rocker?"

"I just want a baby, that's all. Goddamnit, if they won't let us have a baby legal, then we'll have a baby our own way."

"And what do you think will happen if *I* have an illegal pregnancy?"

Birdie remained stolidly silent. He *hadn't* thought, he didn't, he wouldn't.

"They'll give me a therapeutic abortion and I'll have a black mark against my record for the rest of my life as a sex offender. My God, Birdie, sometimes you can be positively dumb!"

"We could go to Mexico . . ."

"And what would we do there? Die? Or commit suicide? Haven't you read any newspapers in the last ten years?"

"Well, other women have done it. I've read stories in the papers *this* year. There was a protest. Civil rights and stuff."

"And what happened then? All those babies were put in federal orphanages, and the parents were put in prison. *And* sterilized. God, Birdie, you really didn't know that, did you?"

"Yeah, I knew that, but . . ."

"But what, stupid?"

"I just thought—"

"You *didn't* think. That's your problem. You never think. I have to do the thinking for both of us. It's a good thing I've got more brains than I need."

"Uh-huh," he said mockingly, smiling his special movie-star smile. She could never resist that smile. She shrugged her shoulders and, laughing, kissed him. She couldn't stay angry with Birdie ten minutes at a time. He'd make her laugh and forget everything but how much she loved him. In that way Milly was like his mother. In that way Birdie was like her son.

11:35. The Art History test was at two o'clock. He'd already missed a ten o'clock class in Consumer Skills. Tough.

He went to the bathroom to brush his teeth and shave. The Muzak started when he opened the door. It played WHAM-O, WHAM-O,

WHY AM I SO HAPPY? Birdie could have asked himself the same question.

Back in the dorm he tried to telephone Milly at work, but there was only one phone on each Pan-Am second-class jet, and it was busy all through the flight. He left a message for her to call him, knowing perfectly well she wouldn't.

He decided to wear his white sweater with white Levis and white sneakers. He brushed whitening agent into his hair. He looked at himself in front of the bathroom mirror. He smiled. The Muzak started to play his favorite Ford commercial. Alone in the empty space before the urinals he danced with himself, singing the words of the commercial.

It was only a fifteen minute subway ride to Battery Park. He bought a bag of peanuts to feed to the pigeons in the aviary. When they were all gone, he walked along the rows of benches where the old people came to sit every day to look out at the sea and wait to die. But Birdie didn't feel the same hatred for old people this morning that he had felt last night. Lined up in rows, in the full glare of the afternoon sun, they seemed remote. They did not pose any threat.

The breeze coming in off the harbor smelled of salt, oil, and decay, but it wasn't a bad smell at all. It was sort of invigorating. Maybe if Birdie had lived centuries ago, he might have been a sailor. He ate two large bars of Synthamon and drank a container of Fun.

The sky was full of jets. Milly could have been on any one of them. A week ago, only a week ago, she'd told him, "I'll love you forever and a day. There'll never be anyone but you for me."

Birdie felt just great. Absolutely.

An old man in an old-fashioned suit with lapels shuffled along the walk, holding on to the sea-railing. His face was covered with a funny white beard, thick and curly, although his head was as bare as a police helmet. He asked Birdie for a quarter. He spoke with a strange accent, neither Spanish nor French. He reminded Birdie of something.

Birdie wrinkled his nose. "Sorry. I'm on the dole myself." Which was not, strictly speaking, true.

The bearded man gave him the finger, and then Birdie remembered who the old man looked like. Socrates!

He glanced down at his wrist, but he'd forgotten to wear his watch. He spun around. The gigantic advertising clock on the facade of the First National Citibank said it was fifteen after two. That wasn't possible. Birdie asked two of the old people on the benches if that was the right time. Their watches agreed.

There wasn't any use trying to get to the test. Without quite knowing why, Birdie Ludd smiled to himself.

He breathed a sigh of relief and sat down to watch the ocean.

"The basic point I'm trying to make, Birdie, if you'll let me finish, is that there are people more qualified than I to advise you. It's been three years since I've seen your file. I've no idea of the progress you've made, the goals you're striving for. Certainly there's a psychologist at the college. . . ."

Birdie squirmed in the plastic shell of his seat, and the look of accusation in his guileless blue eyes communicated so successfully to the counsellor that he began to squirm slightly himself. Birdie had always had the power to make Mr. Mack feel in the wrong.

". . . . and there are other students waiting to see me, Birdie. You managed to pick my busiest time of day." He gestured pathetically at the tiny foyer outside his office where a fourth student had just taken a seat to wait his three o'clock appointment.

"Well, if you don't *want* to help me, I guess I can go."

"Whether I want to or not, what can *I* possibly do? I still fail to see the reason you missed those tests. You were holding down a good C-average. If you'd just kept plugging away . . ." Mr. Mack smiled weakly. He was about to launch into a set-piece on the value of a positive attitude, but decided on second thought that Birdie would require a tougher approach. "If reclassification means as much to you as you say, then you should be willing to work for it, to make sacrifices."

"I *said* it was a mistake, didn't I? Is it my fault they won't let me take make-ups?"

"Two weeks, Birdie! Two weeks without going to a single class, without even calling in to the dorm. Where were you? And all those midterms! Really, it does look as though you were *trying* to be expelled."

"I said I'm *sorry!*"

"You prove nothing by becoming angry with me, Birdie Ludd. There's nothing I can do about it any more—nothing." Mr. Mack pushed his chair back from the desk, preparing to rise.

"But . . . before, when I failed my reclassification test, you talked about other ways to get reclassified besides college. What were they?"

"Exceptional service. You might want to try that."

"What's it mean?"

"In practical terms, for you, it would mean joining the Army and performing an action in combat of extraordinary heroism. And living to tell about it."

"A guerrilla?" Birdie laughed nervously. "Not this boy, not Birdie Ludd. Who ever heard of a guerrilla getting reclassified?"

"Admittedly, it's unusual. That's why I recommended college initially."

"The *third* way, what was that?"

"A demonstration of markedly superior abilities." Mr. Mack smiled, not without a certain irony. "Abilities that wouldn't be shown on the tests."

"How would I do that?"

"You must file intention with the Health, Education, and Welfare Agency three months in advance of the date of demonstration."

"But what is the demonstration? What do I do?"

"It's entirely up to you. Some people submit paintings, others might play a piece of music. The majority, I suppose, give a sample of their writing. As a matter of fact, I think there's a book published of stories and essays and such that have all achieved their purpose. Gotten their authors reclassified, that is. The great majority don't, of course. Those who make it are usually nonconformist types to begin with, the kind that are always bucking the system. I wouldn't advise—"

"Where can I get that book?"

"At the library, I suppose. But—"

"Will they let anyone try?"

"Yes. Once."

Birdie jumped out of his seat so quickly that for an unconsidered moment Mr. Mack feared the boy was going to strike him. But he was only holding his hand out to be shaken. "Thanks, Mr. Mack, thanks a lot. I knew *you'd* still find a way to help me. Thanks."

The Health, Education, and Welfare people were more helpful than he could have hoped. They arranged for him to receive a federal stipend of $500 to help him through the three month "developmental period." They gave him a metal ID tab for his own desk at the Nassau branch of the National Library. They recommended several bona fide literary advisors, at various hourly consultation rates. They even gave him a free copy of the book Mr. Mack had told him about. *By Their Bootstraps* had an introduction by Lucille Mortimer Randolphe-Clapp, the architect of the REGENTS system, which Birdie found very encouraging, though he didn't understand all of it too clearly.

Birdie didn't think much of the first essay in the book, "The Bottom of the Heap, an Account of a Lousy Modicum Childhood." It was written by 19-year-old Jack Ch——. Birdie could have written the same thing himself; there wasn't a single thing in it that he didn't know without being told. And even Birdie could see that the language was vulgar and ungrammatical. Next was a story that didn't have any point, and then a poem that didn't make any sense. Birdie read through the whole book in one day, something he had never done before, and he did find a few things he liked: there was a crazy story about a boy who'd dropped out of high school to work in an alligator preserve, and an eminently sensible essay on the difficulties of budgeting a MODICUM income. The best piece of the lot was called "The Consolations of Philosophy," which was written by a girl who was both blind and crippled! Aside from the textbook for his ethics course, Birdie had never read philosophy, and he thought it might be a good idea, during the three month developmental period, to try some. Maybe it would give him an idea for something to write about of his own.

For the next three or four days, however, Birdie spent all his time just trying to find a room. He'd have to keep his expenses to a bare minimum if he was going to get along those three months on only $500. Eventually he found a room in a privately-owned building in Brooklyn that must have been built a century ago or longer. The room cost $30 a week, which was a real bargain spacewise, since it measured fully ten feet square. It contained a bed, an armchair, two floor lamps, a wooden table and chair, a rickety cardboard chest-of-drawers, and a rug made of genuine wool. He had his own private bathroom. His first night there he just walked around barefoot on the woolen rug with the radio turned up full volume. Twice he went down to the phone booth in the lobby in order to call up Milly and maybe invite her over for a little housewarming party, but then he would have had to explain why he wasn't living at the dorm, and (for she certainly must be wondering) why he hadn't called her since the day of the Art History test. The second time he came down to the lobby he got into a conversation with a girl who was waiting for a phone call. She said her name was Fran. She wore a tight dress of peekaboo plastic, but on her body it wasn't especially provocative since she was too scrawny. It was fun to talk to her though, because she wasn't stuck up like most girls. She lived right across the hall from Birdie, so it was the most natural thing in the world that he should go into her room for a carton of beer. Before they'd killed it, he'd told her his entire situation. Even about Milly. Fran started crying.

It turned out that she'd failed the REGENTS herself—all three parts.
Birdie was just starting to make out with her when her phone call came
and she had to leave.

Next morning Birdie made his first visit (ever) to the National Library. The Nassau branch was housed in an old glass building a little to
the west of the central Wall Street area. Each floor was a honeycomb of
auditing and microviewing booths, except for 28, the topmost floor,
which was given over to the electronic equipment that connected this
branch with the midtown Morgan Library and, by relays, with the Library of Congress, the British Museum Library, and the Osterreichische
National-bibliothek in Vienna. A page, who couldn't have been much
older than Birdie, showed him how to use the dial-and-punch system in
his booth. A researcher could call up almost any book in the world or
listen to any tape without needing to employ more than a twelve-figure
call-code. When the page was gone, Birdie stared down glumly at the
blank viewing screen. The only thing he could think of was the satisfaction it would give him to smash in the screen with his fist.

After a good hot-lunch Birdie felt better. He recalled Socrates and the
blind girl's essay on "The Consolations of Philosophy." So he put out a
call for all the books on Socrates at senior high school level and began
reading them at random.

At eleven o'clock that night Birdie finished reading the chapter in
Plato's *Republic* that contains the famous Parable of the Cave. He left
the library in a daze and wandered hours-long in the brilliantly illuminated Wall Street area. Even after midnight it was teeming with
workers. Birdie watched them with amazement. Were any of them
aware of the great truths that had transfigured Birdie's being that night?
Or were they, like the poor prisoners of the cave, turned to the rock-
face, watching shadows and never suspecting the existence of the sun?

There was so much *beauty* in the world that Birdie had not so much
as dreamt of! Beauty was more than a patch of blue sky or the curve of
Milly's breasts. It penetrated everywhere. The city itself, hitherto that
cruel machine whose special function it had been to thwart Birdie's
natural desires, seemed now to glow from within, like a diamond struck
by the light. Every passer-by's face was rife with ineffable significances.

Birdie remembered the vote of the Athenian Senate to put Socrates to
death. For corrupting the youth! He hated the Athenian Senate, but it
was a different sort of hate from the kind he was used to. He hated
Athens for *a reason*. Justice!

Beauty, truth, justice. Love, too. Somewhere, Birdie realized, there was an explanation for everything! A meaning. *It all made sense.*

Emotions passed over him faster than he could take account of them. One moment, looking at his face reflected in a dark shopwindow, he wanted to laugh aloud. The next, remembering Fran sprawled out on her shabby bed in a cheap plastic dress, he wanted to cry. For he realized now, as he had not on the night before, that Fran was a prostitute, and that she could never hope to be anything else. While Birdie might hope for anything, anything at all in the (now suddenly so much wider) world.

He found himself alone in Battery Park. It was darker there, less busy. He stood alone beside the sea-railing and looked down at the dark waves lapping at the concrete shore. Red signal lights blinked on and off as they proceeded across the night sky to and from the Central Park airport. And even this scene, though it chilled him in ways that he could not explain, he found exhilarating, in ways that he could not explain.

There was a *principle* involved in all this. It was important for Birdie to communicate this principle to the other people who didn't know of it, but he could not, quite, put his finger on just what principle it was. In his newly-awakened soul he fought a battle to try to bring it to words, but each time, just as he thought he had it, it eluded him. Finally, towards dawn, he went home, temporarily defeated.

Just as he went in the door of his own room, a guerrilla, wearing the opaque and featureless mask of his calling (with the ID number stenciled on the brow), came out of Fran's room. Birdie felt a brief impulse of hatred for him, followed by a wave of compassion and tenderness for the unfortunate girl. But he did not have the time, that night, to try and help her; he had his own problems.

He slept unsoundly and woke at eleven o'clock from a dream that stopped just short of being a nightmare. He had been in a room in which two ropes hung down from a raftered ceiling. He had stood between the ropes, trying to grasp them, but just as he thought he had one in his grasp, it would swing away wildly, like a berserk pendulum.

He knew what the dream meant. The ropes were a test of his *creativeness*. That was the principle he had sought so desperately the night before. Creativeness was the key to everything. If he could only learn about it, analyze it, he would be able to solve his problems.

The idea was still hazy in his mind, but he knew he was on the right track. He had some cultured eggs and a cup of coffee for breakfast and went straight to his booth at the library to study. Though he had a slight fever, he seemed to feel better than he had ever felt in his whole life. He was free. Or was it something else? One thing he was sure of: nothing in the past was worth shit. But the future was radiant with promise.

He didn't begin work on his essay until the very last week of the developmental period. There was so *much* that he had had to learn first. Literature, painting, philosophy, everything he had never understood before. There were still many things, he realized, that he couldn't understand, but now he firmly believed that eventually he would. Because he *wanted* to.

When he did begin working on his essay, he found it a more difficult task than he had anticipated. He paid ten dollars for an hour's consultation with a licensed literary advisor, who advised him to cut it. He was trying to cram in too many things. Lucille Mortimer Randolphe-Clapp had given more or less the same advice in *By Their Bootstraps*. She said that the best essays were often no more than 200 words long. Birdie wondered if future editions of *By Their Bootstraps* would contain his essay.

He went through four complete drafts before he was satisfied. Then he read it aloud to Fran. She said it made her want to cry. He did one more draft of it on June 8th, which was his 21st birthday, just for good luck, and then he sent it off to the Health, Education, and Welfare Agency.

This is the essay Birdie Ludd submitted:

PROBLEMS OF CREATIVENESS

By Berthold Anthony Ludd

"The conditions of beauty are three:
wholeness, harmony, and radiance."
Aristotle.

From ancient times to today we have learned that there is more than one criteria by which the critic analyzes the products of Creativeness. Can we know which of these measures to use. Shall we deal directly with the subject? Or "by indirection find direction out."

We are all familiar with the great drama of Wolfgang Amadeus Goethe—"The Faust." It is not possible to deny it the undisputed literary pinnacle, a "Masterpiece." Yet what motivation can have drawn him to describe "heaven" and "hell" in this strange way? Who is Faust if not ourselves. Does this not show a genuine need to achieve communication? Our only answer can be "Yes!"

Thus once more we are led to the problem of Creativeness. All beauty has three conditions 1, The subject shall be of literary format. 2, All parts are contained within the whole. And 3, the meaning is radiantly clear. True creativeness is only present when it can be observed in the work of art. This too is the philosophy of Aristotle.

The criteria of Creativeness is not alone sought in the domain of "literature." Does not the scientist, the prophet, the painter offer his own criteria of judgement toward the same general purpose? Which road shall we choose, in this event?

Another criteria of Creativeness was made by Socrates, so cruelly put to death by his own people, and I quote: "To know nothing is the first condition of all knowledge." From the wisdom of Socrates may we not draw our own conclusions concerning these problems? Creativeness is the ability to see relationships where none exist.

The machine that did the preliminary grading gave Berthold Anthony Ludd a score of 12 and fed the paper into the Automatic Reject file, where the essay was photostated and routed to the OUTMAIL room. The OUTMAIL sorter clipped Birdie's essay to a letter explaining the causes which made reclassification impossible at this time and advised him of his right to seek reclassification again 365 days from the day on which his essay had been notarized.

Birdie was waiting in the lobby when the mail came. He was so eager to open the envelope that he tore his essay in two getting it out. The same afternoon, without even bothering to get drunk, Birdie enlisted in the U. S. Marines to go defend democracy in Burma.

Immediately after his swearing-in, the sergeant came forward and slipped the black mask with his ID number stenciled on the brow over Birdie's sullen face. His number was USMC100-7011-D07. He was a guerrilla now.

The Quest for Saint Aquin

Anthony Boucher

THE BISHOP OF ROME, the head of the Holy, Catholic and Apostolic Church, the Vicar of Christ on Earth—in short, the Pope—brushed a cockroach from the filth-encrusted wooden table, took another sip of the raw red wine, and resumed his discourse.

"In some respects, Thomas," he smiled, "we are stronger now than when we flourished in the liberty and exaltation for which we still pray after Mass. We know, as they knew in the Catacombs, that those who are of our flock are indeed truly of it; that they belong to Holy Mother the Church because they believe in the brotherhood of man under the fatherhood of God—not because they can further their political aspirations, their social ambitions, their business contacts."

" 'Not of the will of flesh, nor of the will of man, but of God . . .' " Thomas quoted softly from St. John.

The Pope nodded. "We are, in a way, born again in Christ; but there are still too few of us—too few even if we include those other handfuls who are not of our faith, but still acknowledge God through the teachings of Luther or Lao-tse, Gautama Buddha or Joseph Smith. Too many men still go to their deaths hearing no gospel preached to them

WILLIAM ANTHONY PARKER WHITE, *also known as Anthony Boucher, was (along with J. Francis McComas) the founding editor of F&SF, and the man who conceived the idea and set the tone of the magazine. He was a leading writer, editor and critic in both the sf and mystery fields until his death in 1968. "The Quest for Saint Aquin" (an SFWA Hall of Fame story) appeared in the January 1959 issue.*

but the cynical self-worship of the Technarchy. And that is why, Thomas, you must go forth on your quest."

"But Your Holiness," Thomas protested, "if God's word and God's love will not convert them, what can saints and miracles do?"

"I seem to recall," murmured the Pope, "that God's own Son once made a similar protest. But human nature, however illogical it may seem, is part of His design, and we must cater to it. If signs and wonders can lead souls to God, then by all means let us find the signs and wonders. And what can be better for the purpose than this legendary Aquin? Come now, Thomas; be not too scrupulously exact in copying the doubts of your namesake, but prepare for your journey."

The Pope lifted the skin that covered the doorway and passed into the next room, with Thomas frowning at his heels. It was past legal hours and the main room of the tavern was empty. The swarthy innkeeper roused from his doze to drop to his knees and kiss the ring on the hand which the Pope extended to him. He rose crossing himself and at the same time glancing furtively about as though a Loyalty Checker might have seen him. Silently he indicated another door in the back, and the two priests passed through.

Toward the west the surf purred in an oddly gentle way at the edges of the fishing village. Toward the south the stars were sharp and bright; toward the north they dimmed a little in the persistent radiation of what had once been San Francisco.

"Your steed is here," the Pope said, with something like laughter in his voice.

"Steed?"

"We may be as poor and as persecuted as the primitive church, but we can occasionally gain greater advantages from our tyrants. I have secured for you a robass—gift of a leading Technarch who, like Nicodemus, does good by stealth—a secret convert, and converted indeed by that very Aquin whom you seek."

It looked harmlessly like a woodpile sheltered against possible rain. Thomas pulled off the skins and contemplated the sleek functional lines of the robass. Smiling, he stowed his minimal gear into its panniers and climbed into the foam saddle. The starlight was bright enough so that he could check the necessary coordinates on his map and feed the data into the electronic controls.

Meanwhile there was a murmur of Latin in the still night air, and the Pope's hand moved over Thomas in the immemorial symbol. Then he extended that hand, first for the kiss on the ring, and then again for the handclasp of a man to a friend he may never see again.

Thomas looked back once more as the robass moved off. The Pope was wisely removing his ring and slipping it into the hollow heel of his shoe.

Thomas looked hastily up at the sky. On that altar at least the candles still burnt openly to the glory of God.

Thomas had never ridden a robass before, but he was inclined, within their patent limitations, to trust the works of the Technarchy. After several miles had proved that the coordinates were duly registered, he put up the foam backrest, said his evening office (from memory; the possession of a breviary meant the death sentence), and went to sleep.

They were skirting the devastated area to the east of the Bay when he awoke. The foam seat and back had given him his best sleep in years; and it was with difficulty that he smothered an envy of the Technarchs and their creature comforts.

He said his morning office, breakfasted lightly, and took his first opportunity to inspect the robass in full light. He admired the fast-plodding, articulated legs, so necessary since roads had degenerated to, at best, trails in all save metropolitan areas; the side wheels that could be lowered into action if surface conditions permitted; and above all the smooth black mound that housed the electronic brain—the brain that stored commands and data concerning ultimate objectives and made its own decisions on how to fulfill those commands in view of those data; the brain that made this thing neither a beast, like the ass his Saviour had ridden, nor a machine, like the jeep of his many-times-great-grandfather, but a robot . . . a robass.

"Well," said a voice, "what do you think of the ride."

Thomas looked about him. The area on this fringe of desolation was as devoid of people as it was of vegetation.

"Well," the voice repeated unemotionally. "Are not priests taught to answer when spoken to politely."

There was no querying inflection to the question. No inflection at all —each syllable was at the same dead level. It sounded strange, mechani . . .

Thomas stared at the black mound of brain. "Are you talking to me?" he asked the robass.

"Ha ha," the voice said in lieu of laughter. "Surprised, are you not."

"Somewhat," Thomas confessed. "I thought the only robots who could talk were in library information service and such."

"I am a new model. Designed-to-provide-conversation-to-entertain-the-way-worn-traveler," the robass said slurring the words together as though that phrase of promotional copy was released all at once by one of his simplest binary synapses.

"Well," said Thomas simply. "One keeps learning new marvels."

"I am no marvel. I am a very simple robot. You do not know much about robots do you."

"I will admit that I have never studied the subject closely. I'll confess to being a little shocked at the whole robotic concept. It seems almost as though man were arrogating to himself the powers of—" Thomas stopped abruptly.

"Do not fear," the voice droned on. "You may speak freely. All data concerning your vocation and mission have been fed into me. That was necessary otherwise I might inadvertently betray you."

Thomas smiled. "You know," he said, "this might be rather pleasant —having one other being that one can talk to without fear of betrayal, aside from one's confessor."

"Being," the robass repeated. "Are you not in danger of lapsing into heretical thoughts."

"To be sure, it *is* a little difficult to know how to think of you—one who can talk and think but has no soul."

"Are you sure of that."

"Of course I— Do you mind very much," Thomas asked, "if we stop talking for a little while? I should like to meditate and adjust myself to the situation."

"I do not mind. I never mind. I only obey. Which is to say that I *do* mind. This is very confusing language which has been fed into me."

"If we are together long," said Thomas, "I shall try teaching you Latin. I think you might like that better. And now let me meditate."

The robass was automatically veering further east to escape the permanent source of radiation which had been the first cyclotron. Thomas fingered his coat. The combination of ten small buttons and one large made for a peculiar fashion; but it was much safer than carrying a rosary, and fortunately the Loyalty Checkers had not yet realized the fashion's functional purpose.

The Glorious Mysteries seemed appropriate to the possible glorious outcome of his venture; but his meditations were unable to stay fixedly on the Mysteries. As he murmured his *Aves* he was thinking:

If the prophet Balaam conversed with his ass, surely, I may converse with my robass. Balaam has always puzzled me. He was not an Israelite; he was a man of Moab, which worshiped Baal and was warring against Israel; and yet he was a prophet of the Lord. He blessed the Israelites when he was commanded to curse them; and for his reward he was slain by the Israelites when they triumphed over Moab. The whole story has no shape, no moral; it is as though it was there to say that there are portions of the Divine Plan which we will never understand . . .

He was nodding in the foam seat when the robass halted abruptly, rapidly adjusting itself to exterior data not previously fed into its calculations. Thomas blinked up to see a giant of a man glaring down at him.

"Inhabited area a mile ahead," the man barked. "If you're going there, show your access pass. If you ain't, steer off the road and stay off."

Thomas noted that they were indeed on what might roughly be called a road, and that the robass had lowered its side wheels and retracted its legs. "We—" he began, then changed it to "I'm not going there. Just on toward the mountains. We—I'll steer around."

The giant grunted and was about to turn when a voice shouted from the crude shelter at the roadside. "Hey Joe! Remember about robasses!"

Joe turned back. "Yeah, tha's right. Been a rumor about some robass got into the hands of Christians." He spat on the dusty road. "Guess I better see an ownership certificate."

To his other doubts Thomas now added certain uncharitable suspicions as to the motives of the Pope's anonymous Nicodemus, who had not provided him with any such certificate. But he made a pretense of searching for it, first touching his right hand to his forehead as if in thought, then fumbling low on his chest, then reaching his hand first to his left shoulder, then to his right.

The guard's eyes remained blank as he watched this furtive version of the sign of the cross. Then he looked down. Thomas followed his gaze to the dust of the road, where the guard's hulking right foot had drawn the two curved lines which a child uses for its sketch of a fish—and which the Christians in the catacombs had employed as a punning symbol of their faith. His boot scuffed out the fish as he called to his unseen mate, " 's OK, Fred!" and added, "Get going, mister."

The robass waited until they were out of earshot before it observed, "Pretty smart. You will make a secret agent yet."

"How did you see what happened?" Thomas asked. "You don't have any eyes."

"Modified psi factor. Much more efficient."

"Then . . ." Thomas hesitated. "Does that mean you can read my thoughts?"

"Only a very little. Do not let it worry you. What I can read does not interest me it is such nonsense."

"Thank you," said Thomas.

"To believe in God. Bah." (It was the first time Thomas had ever heard that word pronounced just as it is written.) "I have a perfectly constructed logical mind that cannot commit such errors."

"I have a friend," Thomas smiled, "who is infallible too. But only on occasions and then only because God is with him."

"No human being is infallible."

"Then imperfection," asked Thomas, suddenly feeling a little of the spirit of the aged Jesuit who had taught him philosophy, "has been able to create perfection?"

"Do not quibble," said the robass. "That is no more absurd than your own belief that God who is perfection created man who is imperfection."

Thomas wished that his old teacher were here to answer that one. At the same time he took some comfort in the fact that, retort and all, the robass had still not answered his own objection. "I am not sure," he said, "that this comes under the head of conversation - to - entertain - the - way - weary - traveler. Let us suspend debate while you tell me what, if anything, robots do believe."

"What we have been fed."

"But your minds work on that; surely they must evolve ideas of their own?"

"Sometimes they do and if they are fed imperfect data they may evolve very strange ideas. I have heard of one robot on an isolated space station who worshiped a God of robots and would not believe that any man had created him."

"I suppose," Thomas mused, "he argued that he had hardly been created in our image. I am glad that we—at least they, the Technarchs —have wisely made only usuform robots like you, each shaped for his function, and never tried to reproduce man himself."

"It would not be logical," said the robass. "Man is an all-purpose machine but not well designed for any one purpose. And yet I have heard that once . . ."

The voice stopped abruptly in midsentence.

So even robots have their dreams, Thomas thought. That once there existed a super-robot in the image of his creator Man. From that thought could be developed a whole robotic theology . . .

Suddenly Thomas realized that he had dozed again and again been waked by an abrupt stop. He looked around. They were at the foot of a mountain—presumably the mountain on his map, long ago named for the Devil but now perhaps sanctified beyond measure—and there was no one else anywhere in sight.

"All right," the robass said. "By now I show plenty of dust and wear and tear and I can show you how to adjust my mileage recorder. You can have supper and a good night's sleep and we can go back."

Thomas gasped. "But my mission is to find Aquin. I can sleep while you go on. You don't need any sort of rest or anything, do you?" he added considerately.

"Of course not. But what is your mission."

"To find Aquin," Thomas repeated patiently. "I don't know what details have been—what is it you say?—fed into you. But reports have reached His Holiness of an extremely saintly man who lived many years ago in this area—"

"I know I know I know," said the robass. "His logic was such that everyone who heard him was converted to the Church and do not I wish that I had been there to put in a word or two and since he died his secret tomb has become a place of pilgrimage and many are the miracles that are wrought there above all the greatest sign of sanctity that his body has been preserved incorruptible and in these times you need signs and wonders for the people."

Thomas frowned. It all sounded hideously irreverent and contrived when stated in that deadly inhuman monotone. When His Holiness had spoken of Aquin, one thought of the glory of a man of God upon earth —the eloquence of St. John Chrysostom, the cogency of St. Thomas Aquinas, the poetry of St. John of the Cross . . . and above all that physical miracle vouchsafed to few even of the saints, the supernatural preservation of the flesh . . . "for Thou shalt not suffer Thy holy one to see corruption . . ."

But the robass spoke, and one thought of cheap showmanship hunting for a Cardiff Giant to pull in the mobs . . .

The robass spoke again. "Your mission is not to find Aquin. It is to report that you have found him. Then your occasionally infallible friend can with a reasonably clear conscience canonize him and proclaim a new miracle and many will be the converts and greatly will the faith of the flock be strengthened. And in these days of difficult travel who will go on pilgrimages and find out that there is no more Aquin than there is God."

"Faith cannot be based on a lie," said Thomas.

"No," said the robass. "I do not mean no period. I mean no question mark with an ironical inflection. This speech problem must surely have been conquered in that one perfect . . ."

Again he stopped in midsentence. But before Thomas could speak he had resumed, "Does it matter what small untruth leads people into the Church if once they are in they will believe what you think to be the great truths. The report is all that is needed not the discovery. Comfortable though I am you are already tired of traveling very tired you have many small muscular aches from sustaining an unaccustomed position and with the best intentions I am bound to jolt a little a jolting which will get worse as we ascend the mountain and I am forced to adjust my legs disproportionately to each other but proportionately to the slope. You will find the remainder of this trip twice as uncomfortable as what has gone before. The fact that you do not seek to interrupt me indicates that you do not disagree do you. You know that the only sensible thing is to sleep here on the ground for a change and start back in the morning or even stay here two days resting to make a more plausible lapse of time. Then you can make your report and—"

Somewhere in the recess of his somnolent mind Thomas uttered the names, "Jesus, Mary, and Joseph!" Gradually through these recesses began to filter a realization that an absolutely uninflected monotone is admirably adapted to hypnotic purposes.

"*Retro me, Satanas!*" Thomas exclaimed aloud, then added, "Up the mountain. That is an order and you must obey."

"I obey," said the robass. "But what did you say before that."

"I beg your pardon," said Thomas. "I must start teaching you Latin."

The little mountain village was too small to be considered an inhabited area worthy of guard-control and passes; but it did possess an inn of sorts.

As Thomas dismounted from the robass, he began fully to realize the accuracy of those remarks about small muscular aches, but he tried to show his discomfort as little as possible. He was in no mood to give the modified psi factor the chance of registering the thought, "I told you so."

The waitress at the inn was obviously a Martian-American hybrid. The highly developed Martian chest expansion and the highly developed American breasts made a spectacular combination. Her smile was all that a stranger could, and conceivably a trifle more than he should ask; and she was eagerly ready, not only with prompt service of passable food, but with full details of what little information there was to offer about the mountain settlement.

But she showed no reaction at all when Thomas offhandedly arranged two knives in what might have been an X.

As he stretched his legs after breakfast, Thomas thought of her chest and breasts—purely, of course, as a symbol of the extraordinary nature of her origin. What a sign of the divine care for His creatures that these two races, separated for countless eons, should prove fertile to each other!

And yet there remained the fact that the offspring, such as this girl, were sterile to both races—a fact that had proved both convenient and profitable to certain unspeakable interplanetary entrepreneurs. And what did that fact teach us as to the Divine Plan?

Hastily Thomas reminded himself that he had not yet said his morning office.

It was close to evening when Thomas returned to the robass stationed before the inn. Even though he had expected nothing in one day, he was still unreasonably disappointed. Miracles should move faster.

He knew these backwater villages, where those drifted who were either useless to or resentful of the Technarchy. The technically high civilization of the Technarchic Empire, on all three planets, existed only in scattered metropolitan centers near major blasting ports. Elsewhere, aside from the areas of total devastation, the drifters, the morons, the malcontents had subsided into a crude existence a thousand years old, in hamlets which might go a year without even seeing a Loyalty Checker—though by some mysterious grapevine (and Thomas began to think again about modified psi factors) any unexpected technological advance in one of these hamlets would bring Checkers by the swarm.

He had talked with stupid men, he had talked with lazy men, he had talked with clever and angry men. But he had not talked with any man who responded to his unobtrusive signs, any man to whom he would dare ask a question containing the name of Aquin.

"Any luck," said the robass, and added "question mark."

"I wonder if you ought to talk to me in public," said Thomas a little irritably. "I doubt if these villagers know about talking robots."

"It is time that they learned then. But if it embarrasses you you may order me to stop."

"I'm tired," said Thomas. "Tired beyond embarrassment. And to answer your question mark, no. No luck at all. Exclamation point."

"We will go back tonight then," said the robass.

"I hope you meant that with a question mark. The answer," said Thomas hesitantly, "is no. I think we ought to stay overnight anyway. People always gather at the inn of an evening. There's a chance of picking up something."

"Ha, ha," said the robass.

"That is a laugh?" Thomas inquired.

"I wished to express the fact that I had recognized the humor in your pun."

"My pun?"

"I was thinking the same thing myself. The waitress is by humanoid standards very attractive, well worth picking up."

"Now look. You know I meant nothing of the kind. You know that I'm a—" He broke off. It was hardly wise to utter the word *priest* aloud.

"And you know very well that the celibacy of the clergy is a matter of discipline and not of doctrine. Under your own Pope priests of other rites such as the Byzantine and the Anglican are free of vows of celibacy. And even within the Roman rite to which you belong there have been eras in history when that vow was not taken seriously even on the highest levels of the priesthood. You are tired you need refreshment both in body and in spirit you need comfort and warmth. For is it not written in the book of the prophet Isaiah Rejoice for joy with her that ye may be satisfied with the breasts of her consolation and is it—"

"Hell!" Thomas exploded suddenly. "Stop it before you begin quoting the Song of Solomon. Which is strictly an allegory concerning the love of Christ for His Church, or so they kept telling me in seminary."

"You see how fragile and human you are," said the robass. "I a robot have caused you to swear."

"Distinguo," said Thomas smugly. "I said *Hell,* which is certainly not

taking the name of *my* Lord in vain." He walked into the inn feeling momentarily satisfied with himself . . . and markedly puzzled as to the extent and variety of data that seemed to have been "fed into" the robass.

Never afterward was Thomas able to reconstruct that evening in absolute clarity.

It was undoubtedly because he was irritated—with the robass, with his mission, and with himself—that he drank at all of the crude local wine. It was undoubtedly because he was so physically exhausted that it affected him so promptly and unexpectedly.

He had flashes of memory. A moment of spilling a glass over himself and thinking, "How fortunate that clerical garments are forbidden so that no one can recognize the disgrace of a man of the cloth!" A moment of listening to a bawdy set of verses of *A Space-suit Built for Two,* and another moment of his interrupting the singing with a sonorous declamation of passages from the *Song of Songs* in Latin.

He was never sure whether one remembered moment was real or imaginary. He could taste a warm mouth and feel the tingling of his fingers at the touch of Martian-American flesh; but he was never certain whether this was true memory or part of the Ashtaroth-begotten dream that had begun to ride him.

Nor was he ever certain which of his symbols, or to whom, was so blatantly and clumsily executed as to bring forth a gleeful shout of "God-damned Christian dog!" He did remember marveling that those who most resolutely disbelieved in God still needed Him to blaspheme by. And then the torment began.

He never knew whether or not a mouth had touched his lips, but there was no question that many solid fists had found them. He never knew whether his fingers had touched breasts, but they had certainly been trampled by heavy heels. He remembered a face that laughed aloud while its owner swung the chair that broke two ribs. He remembered another face with red wine dripping over it from an upheld bottle, and he remembered the gleam of the candlelight on the bottle as it swung down.

The next he remembered was the ditch and the morning and the cold. It was particularly cold because all of his clothes were gone, along with much of his skin. He could not move. He could only lie there and look.

He saw them walk by, the ones he had spoken with yesterday, the ones who had been friendly. He saw them glance at him and turn their eyes quickly away. He saw the waitress pass by. She did not even glance; she knew what was in the ditch.

The robass was nowhere in sight. He tried to project his thoughts, tried desperately to hope in the psi factor.

A man whom Thomas had not seen before was coming along fingering the buttons of his coat. There were ten small buttons and one large one, and the man's lips were moving silently.

This man looked into the ditch. He paused a moment and looked around him. There was a shout of loud laughter somewhere in the near distance.

The Christian hastily walked on down the pathway, devoutly saying his button-rosary.

Thomas closed his eyes.

He opened them on a small neat room. They moved from the rough wooden walls to the rough but clean and warm blankets that covered him. Then they moved to the lean dark face that was smiling over him.

"You feel better now?" a deep voice asked. "I know. You want to say 'Where am I?' and you think it will sound foolish. You are at the inn. It is the only good room."

"I can't afford—" Thomas started to say. Then he remembered that he could afford literally nothing. Even his few emergency credits had vanished when he was stripped.

"It's all right. For the time being, I'm paying," said the deep voice. "You feel like maybe a little food?"

"Perhaps a little herring," said Thomas . . . and was asleep within the next minute.

When he next awoke there was a cup of hot coffee beside him. The real thing, too, he promptly discovered. Then the deep voice said apologetically, "Sandwiches. It is all they have in the inn today."

Only on the second sandwich did Thomas pause long enough to notice that it was smoked swamphog, one of his favorite meats. He ate the second with greater leisure, and was reaching for a third when the dark man said, "Maybe that is enough for now. The rest later."

Thomas gestured at the plate. "Won't you have one?"

"No thank you. They are all swamphog."

Confused thoughts went through Thomas' mind. The Venusian swamphog is a ruminant. Its hoofs are not cloven. He tried to remember what he had once known of Mosaic dietary law. Someplace in Leviticus, wasn't it?

The dark man followed his thoughts. *"Treff,"* he said.

"I beg your pardon?"

"Not kosher."

Thomas frowned. "You admit to me that you're an Orthodox Jew? How can you trust me? How do you know I'm not a Checker?"

"Believe me, I trust you. You were very sick when I brought you here. I sent everybody away because I did not trust them to hear things you said . . . Father," he added lightly.

Thomas struggled with words. "I . . . I didn't deserve you. I was drunk and disgraced myself and my office. And when I was lying there in the ditch I didn't even think to pray. I put my trust in . . . God help me in the modified psi factor of a robass!"

"And He did help you," the Jew reminded him. "Or He allowed me to."

"And they all walked by," Thomas groaned. "Even one that was saying his rosary. He went right on by. And then you come along—the good Samaritan."

"Believe me," said the Jew wryly, "if there is one thing I'm not, it's a Samaritan. Now go to sleep again. I will try to find your robass . . . and the other thing."

He had left the room before Thomas could ask him what he meant.

Later that day the Jew—Abraham, his name was—reported that the robass was safely sheltered from the weather behind the inn. Apparently it had been wise enough not to startle him by engaging in conversation.

It was not until the next day that he reported on "the other thing."

"Believe me, Father," he said gently, "after nursing you there's little I don't know about who you are and why you're here. Now there are some Christians here I know, and they know me. We trust each other. Jews may still be hated; but no longer, God be praised, by worshipers of the same Lord. So I explained about you. One of them," he added with a smile, "turned very red."

"God has forgiven him," said Thomas. "There were people near— the same people who attacked me. Could he be expected to risk his life for mine?"

"I seem to recall that that is precisely what your Messiah did expect. But who's being particular? Now that they know who you are, they want to help you. See: they gave me this map for you. The trail is steep and tricky; it's good you have the robass. They ask just one favor of you: When you come back will you hear their confession and say Mass? There's a cave near here where it's safe."

"Of course. These friends of yours, they've told you about Aquin?"

The Jew hesitated a long time before he said slowly, "Yes . . ."

"And . . . ?"

"Believe me, my friend, I don't know. So it seems a miracle. It helps to keep their faith alive. My own faith . . . *nu,* it's lived for a long time on miracles three thousand years old and more. Perhaps if I had heard Aquin himself . . ."

"You don't mind," Thomas asked, "if I pray for you, in my faith?"

Abraham grinned. "Pray in good health, Father."

The not-quite-healed ribs ached agonizingly as he climbed into the foam saddle. The robass stood patiently while he fed in the coordinates from the map. Not until they were well away from the village did it speak.

"Anyway," it said, "now you're safe for good."

"What do you mean?"

"As soon as we get down from the mountain you deliberately look up a Checker. You turn in the Jew. From then on you are down in the books as a faithful servant of the Technarchy and you have not harmed a hair of the head of one of your own flock."

Thomas snorted. "You're slipping, Satan. That one doesn't even remotely tempt me. It's inconceivable."

"I did best did not I with the breasts. Your God has said it the spirit indeed is willing but the flesh is weak."

"And right now," said Thomas, "the flesh is too weak for even fleshly temptations. Save your breath . . . or whatever it is you use."

They climbed the mountain in silence. The trail indicated by the co-ordinates was a winding and confused one, obviously designed deliberately to baffle any possible Checkers.

Suddenly Thomas roused himself from his button-rosary (on a coat lent by the Christian who had passed by) with a startled "Hey!" as the robass plunged directly into a heavy thicket of bushes.

"Coordinates say so," the robass stated tersely.

For a moment Thomas felt like the man in the nursery rhyme who fell into a bramble bush and scratched out both his eyes. Then the bushes were gone, and they were plodding along a damp narrow passageway through solid stone, in which even the robass seemed to have some difficulty with his footing.

Then they were in a rocky chamber some four meters high and ten in diameter, and there on a sort of crude stone catafalque lay the uncorrupted body of a man.

Thomas slipped from the foam saddle, groaning as his ribs stabbed him, sank to his knees, and offered up a wordless hymn of gratitude. He smiled at the robass and hoped the psi factor could detect the elements of pity and triumph in that smile.

Then a frown of doubt crossed his face as he approached the body. "In canonization proceedings in the old time," he said, as much to himself as to the robass, "they used to have what they called a devil's advocate, whose duty it was to throw every possible doubt on the evidence."

"You would be well cast in such a role Thomas," said the robass.

"If I were," Thomas muttered, "I'd wonder about caves. Some of them have peculiar properties of preserving bodies by a sort of mummification . . ."

The robass had clumped close to the catafalque. "This body is not mummified," he said. "Do not worry."

"Can the psi factor tell you that much?" Thomas smiled.

"No," said the robass. "But I will show you why Aquin could never be mummified."

He raised his articulated foreleg and brought its hoof down hard on the hand of the body . . . Thomas cried out with horror at the sacrilege —then stared hard at the crushed hand.

There was no blood, no ichor of embalming, no bruised flesh. Nothing but a shredded skin and beneath it an intricate mass of plastic tubes and metal wires.

The silence was long. Finally the robass said, "It was well that you should know. Only you of course."

"And all the time," Thomas gasped, "my sought-for saint was only your dream . . . the one perfect robot in man's form."

"His maker died and his secrets were lost," the robass said. "No matter we will find them again."

"All for nothing. For less than nothing. The 'miracle' was wrought by the Technarchy."

"When Aquin died," the robass went on, "and put died in quotation marks it was because he suffered some mechanical defects and did not dare have himself repaired because that would reveal his nature. This is for you only to know. Your report of course will be that you found the body of Aquin it was unimpaired and indeed incorruptible. That is the truth and nothing but the truth if it is not the whole truth who is to

KC

care. Let your infallible friend use the report and you will not find him ungrateful I assure you."

"Holy Spirit, give me grace and wisdom," Thomas muttered.

"Your mission has been successful. We will return now the Church will grow and your God will gain many more worshipers to hymn His praise into His nonexistent ears."

"Damn you!" Thomas exclaimed. "And that would be indeed a curse if you had a soul to damn."

"You are certain that I have not," said the robass. "Question mark."

"I know what you are. You are in very truth the devil, prowling about the world seeking the destruction of men. You are the business that prowls in the dark. You are a purely functional robot constructed and fed to tempt me, and the tape of your data is the tape of Screwtape."

"Not to tempt you," said the robass. "Not to destroy you. To guide and save you. Our best calculators indicate a probability of 51.5 per cent that within twenty years you will be the next Pope. If I can teach you wisdom and practicality in your actions the probability can rise as high as 97.2 or very nearly to certainty. Do not you wish to see the Church governed as you know you can govern it. If you report failure on this mission you will be out of favor with your friend who is as even you admit fallible at most times. You will lose the advantages of position and contact that can lead you to the cardinal's red hat even though you may never wear it under the Technarchy and from there to—"

"Stop!" Thomas' face was alight and his eyes aglow with something the psi factor had never detected there before. "It's all the other way round, don't you see? *This* is the triumph! *This* is the perfect ending to the quest!"

The articulated foreleg brushed the injured hand. "This question mark."

"This is *your* dream. This is *your* perfection. And what came of this perfection? This perfect logical brain—this all-purpose brain, not functionally specialized like yours—knew that it was made by man, and its reason forced it to believe that man was made by God. And it saw that its duty lay to man its maker, and beyond him to his Maker, God. Its duty was to convict man, to augment the glory of God. And it converted by the pure force of its perfect brain!

"Now I understand the name Aquin," he went on to himself. "We've known of Thomas Aquinas, the Angelic Doctor, the perfect reasoner of the church. His writings are lost, but surely somewhere in the world we can find a copy. We can train our young men to develop his reasoning still further. We have trusted too long in faith alone; this is not an age of faith. We must call reason into our service—and Aquin has shown us that perfect reason can lead only to God!"

"Then it is all the more necessary that you increase the probabilities of becoming Pope to carry out this program. Get in the foam saddle we will go back and on the way I will teach you little things that will be useful in making certain—"

"No," said Thomas. "I am not so strong as St. Paul, who could glory in his imperfections and rejoice that he had been given an imp of Satan to buffet him. No; I will rather pray with the Saviour, 'Lead us not into temptation.' I know myself a little. I am weak and full of uncertainties and you are very clever. Go. I'll find my way back alone."

"You are a sick man. Your ribs are broken and they ache. You can never make the trip by yourself you need my help. If you wish you can order me to be silent. It is most necessary to the Church that you get back safely to the Pope with your report you cannot put yourself before the Church."

"Go!" Thomas cried. "Go back to Nicodemus . . . or Judas! That is an order. Obey!"

"You do not think do you that I was really conditioned to obey your orders. I will wait in the village. If you get that far you will rejoice at the sight of me."

The legs of the robass clumped off down the stone passageway. As their sound died away, Thomas fell to his knees beside the body of that which he could hardly help thinking of as St. Aquin the Robot.

His ribs hurt more excruciatingly than ever. The trip alone would be a terrible one . . .

His prayers arose, as the text has it, like clouds of incense, and as shapeless as those clouds. But through all his thoughts ran the cry of the father of the epileptic in Caesarea Philippi:

I believe, O Lord; help thou mine unbelief!